# GATEKEEPER
## Rayne Auster

Dreamspinner Press

Published by
Dreamspinner Press
4760 Preston Road
Suite 244-149
Frisco, TX 75034
http://www.dreamspinnerpress.com/

Gatekeeper

Cover Art by Anne Cain    annecain.art@gmail.com
Cover Design by Mara McKennen

ISBN: 978-1-61581-280-6

Printed in the United States of America
First Edition
March, 2010

eBook edition available
eBook ISBN: 978-1-61581-281-3

Dedicated to:

Mariete V., Gesie M.,
Andrea M., Sharleen C., and Risuru.
Thank you for picking me up each time
I fell in my efforts to get a novel published.

# GATEKEEPER

## BOOK ONE

# BONDING

Legends, fables, and myths: tales filled with mystery, wonder, and a touch of the impossible. Tales rooted in times long gone by, begun from mere fact, but as is usual with the retelling of tales, gaining life of their own with each embellishment made. As with all life, they grow and change, impacted by the times in which they exist, the times that define the interpretation of these tales. Yet one constant remains… hidden within their depths is a thread of truth, a lesson to be learned.

Time: the greatest ally and yet, at the same time, the greatest enemy of legends. Time adds mystery, intrigue, hides facts, and fuels the human curiosity, fuels the desire for knowledge of truth. Yet at the same time it is capable of obscuring the truth to such a degree that often facts are nigh impossible to separate from fiction. Such is the case with the legends of the Gatekeepers.

"WHY must I bond?" Amber eyes flashing in discontent, Kaji shifted as the tailor made some last-minute adjustments to his rather opulent outfit, glaring at a dark-haired man in the doorway.

"Milord." Karl's smile did little to ease Kaji's temper. "We have already been through this. It's tradition and law."

Kaji's eyes flashed once more, but he remained silent, knowing there was no arguing with tradition and law. However, he couldn't seem to shake the feeling that something was wrong. When the tailor stepped aside, Kaji heaved a sigh of relief, only to wince when the hairdresser got hold of him instead.

Resisting the urge to shift again, Kaji waited patiently as a thin golden band was placed onto his head. The hairdresser then proceeded to braid his long hair into an intricate pattern around it. He hated how restricted this style made him feel but knew that if he argued, the response he'd receive would be that it was tradition. This was a difficult point to dispute, as tradition ruled Duiem and its people. And so, as demanded by tradition, Kaji stepped out of the temple dressed in various shades of gold, bronze, and copper, the colors shimmering and blending together, creating the illusion of a brilliant coastal sunset, further complemented by the sun shining off of Kaji's bright red hair.

Stepping into the bonding circle, he glanced up to meet the gaze of his intended, intricately dressed in flowing robes that complemented his own despite the fact that they were colored white, silver, and pale pearly blue. The girl was breathtaking, deep violet eyes contrasting with her dark auburn curls, a rather nicely curved figure, and the grace that clearly marked her as noble.

Saya was the daughter of Kiyou Jai, the head of the Kiyou clan and head priest of the Taiyou order. Still, Kaji could not shake the feeling that something was gravely wrong. He knew his mate was to be of the Kiyou clan and that no other was near him in age, yet something nagged him. Some instinct in the back of his mind was dead convinced that something, he knew not what, was wrong.

A priest dressed in various shades of red and orange stepped onto the platform situated just outside of the bonding circle and began the ceremony. The circle itself was set into the ground, intricately done up with interwoven strands of silver and gold, a long-forgotten symbol for both unity and contrast. After the traditional blessings had been spoken, silence fell upon the watching crowd as the priest held out the ceremonial dagger, it too, a marriage of silver and gold, the two metals intertwined in a dance of life and death as the sun glinted off the blade.

ANIOL shivered as he was dragged through the crowd, his bound wrists burning in pain as the rope cut into his skin, his hands slick with the blood that seeped out of the wounds the rope burn left upon his slender wrists. He stumbled when his captor impatiently tugged upon the rope tied to a collar around his neck that clearly marked him as a slave.

The strange surroundings, the strange people, and the unfamiliar clamor of voices was rushing in on him, making him feel claustrophobic, causing fear to well up and lodge itself in his throat. He clenched his eyes shut in a desperate attempt to separate himself from what was threatening to drive him past the boundaries of uncertainty and into the territory of downright terror. Sadly, his action only complicated his situation as he tripped and tumbled to the ground, landing painfully on his side, hissing to keep from crying out at the sharp pain that coursed through his hip.

He winced when a large hand slapped him across the head and cursed him for falling and delaying their progress. That same hand then dug into his arm and dragged him up and forward as his unknown captor began to once more lead him toward an unknown destination.

Just as Aniol was about to give up all hope, something unexpected happened. Something soft and warm brushed over his wrists where they were tied behind his back, followed by a flash of silver, and then he was free, the rope falling away from his wrists and slipping away from the collar he still wore. He stared in shock as his captor felt the change in tension and turned, realizing something had gone wrong. The man's face turned red with rage, and he began shoving his way through the crowd toward Aniol. It was then that Aniol spotted a slim figure smiling at him, one with pale blue-silver hair and violet eyes winking at him, just before smoothly cutting the purse away from the his captor's belt. Purse in hand, the mysterious figure melted into the crowd before disappearing entirely.

The sound of steel being drawn shocked Aniol out if his stupor. He suddenly realized that his captor was drawing his sword and was but a breath away from being close enough to use it. Aniol shot into movement just as the man lifted his sword and swung it down, disregarding the crowd around them. Screams broke out, fear cutting into the earlier atmosphere of joviality and spreading like wildfire. Aniol's movement was enough to spare him his life but not enough for him to escape unscathed as cold steel bit into the tender flesh of his right arm, cutting it like a knife through butter and leaving a gaping wound stretching from his wrist to his elbow.

Ducking when the man raised the blade once more, Aniol clutched his arm to his chest and ran headlong into the confused and fearful people, using the fear and confusion to his advantage as he weaved a pattern through the crowd. Blindly staring at the ground, he wasn't really watching where he was going.

With only thoughts of escape in his mind, what transpired next came as a horrific surprise. Unaccustomed to his surroundings, he misjudged his next step. The sudden transition of shoving through a crowd to having no people to push disoriented him and caused him to lose his balance.

He fell forward into a circle surprisingly and strangely clear of people. Glancing up, he met the shocked, violet eyes of a beautiful girl moments before she stumbled back from him, fear evident upon her face.

He had but a moment to register her features before his momentum drove him into someone else, causing him to reach out with both arms in a desperate attempt to prevent himself from once more landing on the hard ground. He winced as sharp pain flared in his hip, a new wound added to those he already possessed.

Shocked, horrified gasps filled the air as his gaze traveled up to meet wide amber eyes. A silver and gold blade fell from limp fingertips, clattering unnoticed to the ground, rolling toward the edge of the circle as the amber gaze shifted to the left. Aniol followed after, looking at their intertwined arms, his right arm clinging to the stranger's left. His eyes widened when he noticed a wound similar to his own upon the stranger's left arm, their blood intermingling.

The fallen blade slid to a halt at the edge of the silver and gold circle, two tiny drops of blood falling off of it into tiny breaks in the circle's metalwork, breaks long ago forgotten, thus sealing it and making it complete.

# Bondmate

Prophecy: that which is meant to guide us through the course of our lives, defining the path we are meant to travel in order to bring about some great change.

Yet one thing always seems to get in the way: free will. Nothing can take away the free will granted to all man, the will to choose which path one will travel. The free will that seeks to interfere with prophecy is not only that of the one the prophecy seeks to guide but also that of those who surround the one.

Until fulfilled, each first born heir of royalty in the land of Duiem is born with a prophecy meant to guide the land toward peace and salvation, guiding him toward repentance for a sin committed a long time ago. Only part of this prophecy is revealed upon the child's birth, a vital part that if fulfilled will strengthen the firstborn's will of mind, body, and soul. If not fulfilled, it will weaken his desire to fight, break the prophecy, and subsequently pass the responsibility for change onto the next descendant.

What is the prophecy itself? Whom one shall wed. It is not a concrete command, but a mere guide in where one's partner is to be found. Prophecies that have come before include: a thief, one of the Meriel family, a gypsy, and a wanderer, yet the most noble of all be the one for one named Conflagration. He is to wed one of royal blood.

KAJI swallowed in shock as the sheer impact of what had just occurred registered. He tightened his grip when the young man who had inadvertently stumbled upon and ruined the bonding ceremony tried to pull away, though Kaji knew it was already too late. There was no turning back. The priest, automatically reaching out to interfere with what was happening, froze in mid-motion at Kaji's words.

"Continue," Kaji ordered. His voice was calm and sure, hiding the chaos, confusion, and panic warring for attention deep within him. A loud gasp of shock rippled through the guests, followed by surprised and rather affronted whispers. Kaji ignored it all, knowing there was nothing anyone—neither he, the priest, nor they—could do. Continuing was the only option they had left open to them. The remainder of the ceremony was just a show. The true bond had already been sealed.

The priest continued, his tone filled with resignation, the same resignation that now dwelled within Kaji's heart. Kaji watched the young man before him, carefully taking note of his features. He wanted to know everything about the one he was now bonded to. The first thing he noticed was the rather small body, a body that seemed to have seen much abuse. Then he noticed the wounds. The gash on the young man's right arm was bleeding profusely, far more than what would have been required by the ceremony. Added to that, the young man now had a wound in his hip.

Kaji frowned when he realized it was a wound he himself had given the boy. True, it had been accidental, but that didn't change the fact that the wound was there and obviously not helping the slim figure before him.

Apprehension coursed through him with the realization that the stranger he had just bonded to was not faring well, and he began to fear that the young man would not live should his wounds remain untreated for much longer. Kaji didn't know why, but this bothered him, a gut-wrenching fear of losing the young man overtaking him. He blamed the bond, but whether it was the bond influencing his feelings or not, he knew that he had to keep his little mate alive.

Suddenly restless, Kaji looked up at the priest, desperate for the last words of the rite to be uttered. Then the circle in which Kaji and the stranger stood flared, the light lost within the afternoon glare, remaining unnoticed by all. The blade that lay at the edge of the circle was now clean, spotless, as if no blood had ever marred its surface.

Kaji scooped the young man up into his arms and marched through the crowd, knowing it would part for him. He glared at anyone who moved just a fraction too slowly. His boots made a decisive sound upon the ground, his golden clothes now marred with blood red billowing around him in his haste as he headed straight for the infirmary. His breath quickened in panic and his rather haughty aristocratic pace became more of an uncontrolled run when he realized the young man had become a dead weight in his arms, passing out from rather obvious loss of blood.

ANIOL blinked, trying to shake off his disorientation as he woke. Colors swam and danced before him, drifting back toward their respective places, slowly defining what he was in fact seeing. He sat up slowly, lethargy dragging at his body, making the smallest movement a rather strenuous undertaking. His gaze snapped to the right when a rather outraged hiss came from that direction.

"You should not be moving," a rich, stern voice reprimanded him. Someone rather forcefully pushed him back down. Aniol blinked in confusion, trying to make sense of what was happening to him. It was then that the person beside him came into focus, bright red hair framing a face defined by strong features. Aniol reached out, unthinking, wanting to make sure that the hair was real, only to flinch back in uncertainty.

The stranger's gaze focused upon Aniol, making him feel like prey beneath the gaze of a predator. He was mesmerized in that moment when death was sure and escape was futile.

"Who are you?" The rich voice demanded. The stranger before him was obviously accustomed to being obeyed. There was no uncertainly his tone, only surety that he would be obeyed. And obeyed he was.

Aniol bit his lip, pausing but a moment before responding, his voice soft and timid from years of disuse. "Aniol."

"Aniol? No family name?" The redhead raised a disbelieving eyebrow.

Aniol shook his head, wanting to drop his eyes but unable to do so, firmly caught in the redhead's amber gaze.

"Whose slave are you?" The redhead barked.

Aniol jerked at the tone, blinking in confusion. "Slave?"

The redhead gestured to the collar Aniol wore. "Slave," he repeated.

Aniol finally managed to tear his gaze from the redheaded stranger and looked down in his lap at his hands, marred by marks of bondage, the rope burns peering out from beneath his bandaged arm. He traced the marks lightly, swallowing before speaking. "I was taken…by some men… about three weeks ago."

"Taken? From your home?"

Aniol shook his head. "No. I was…." He paused, considering his words carefully. "Lost," he finished.

"Lost? What were you before you became… lost?" It was apparent the redhead was suspicious. He wasn't buying Aniol's lie, but he was going along with it.

Aniol licked his lips, trying to figure out the answer to that question before shaking his head in defeat. "I don't really know." He whispered the response, true and honest. His entire life lacked definition, lacked learning, and lacked all that most took for granted. What he recalled was cold, loneliness, and rough demands for visions and predictions of the future… none of which he could grant.

"Look at me."

Aniol was compelled by that voice, but not because of its tone, nor because of its orders, but because of something far more subtle. He sensed a slim strand of uncertainly and pleading in that tone, and that was what drew him to obey.

"How did you get here?" The redhead whispered the question, perhaps fearing the answer.

Aniol licked his lips once more, feeling thirsty and weary. As if reading his mind, the redhead grabbed a glass from the bedside table and reached beneath Aniol to lift his head. "Shh," the redhead comforted softly when Aniol winced. "I'm not going to hurt you." Aniol swallowed, relaxing slowly, for some reason trusting the words. He allowed the redhead to help him and sipped carefully from the glass. The cool liquid soothed his dry throat, giving him new energy to use in order to deal with the other discomforts that still plagued him.

He nodded when he had drunk enough, and the redhead carefully lowered him back down again, treating Aniol with more affection than he had received in his entire life. Once settled, as comfortable as he was likely to be, Aniol licked his lips once more and spoke in his usual slow and careful manner, attempting to answer the question he had been presented with. "I was attacked... by some men." He swallowed nervously, clenching his eyes closed in remembered terror. "They took me to a place I did not know... and left me to... die." He paused, gathering himself. "Then I was found, tied up... and brought to a city... a city where the men intended to sell me. Someone cut my ropes.... The man who had me was furious. He tried to kill me... so I ran and then...." His eyes snapped open in sudden realization. "I bumped into you." He whispered in shock, feeling himself go suddenly pale. "I ruined something."

The redhead gave him a wry smile before running a hand through his hair. "'Ruined' would not be the best way to describe it, I think." The redhead's tone was dry. "Maybe more along the lines of disrupted and changed, creating an alternate future," he stated in resignation.

Aniol licked his lips nervously. He desperately wanted to ask about what he had disrupted, yet fear held him back. Fear of knowledge. Many would consider him a fool to fear something as intangible as knowledge, but experience had taught him that knowledge could be a two-edged, dangerous blade.

"I am Kaji," the redhead said, introducing himself. "Kaji Taiyouko." He paused, obviously waiting for Aniol to react. He frowned when he didn't receive the response he'd expected and then continued to speak. "I'm your bondmate."

# SILVER

Legends speak of a land rich in silver, of white-tipped blue mountain ranges, torrents of water, and white tears falling from the sky. They speak of a time when trade and wealth were shared freely between Duiem and the Land of Silver, the people living in peace, harmony, splendor and equality. Among the legends concerning the Land of Silver, there is one that mentions a sacred union, a union that if shattered shall bring about chaos and disaster. Another legend speaks of how this union was betrayed.

ANIOL stared at Kaji in shock, unsure if he had heard correctly. Had Kaji just called him his bondmate? He frowned in confusion as he struggled to sit up, wanting to be at eye level with Kaji, seeking some way to confirm the truth of those words. His frown turned into a scowl when Kaji moved forward to either assist or hinder him. Aniol didn't know which because he slapped Kaji's hands away before the other man was even able to touch him. "What do you mean bondmate?" he demanded roughly, voice still weak but containing a hard undertone. He was breathing heavily, panting from both agitation and the exertion of his movements.

Amber eyes watched him for a moment, narrowed in suspicion. Kaji seemed to take in every detail before speaking in a slow, calm voice. "You disrupted a bonding ceremony by bonding yourself to me at a key point," Kaji stated, watching Aniol like a hawk, reading the young man's reactions. "All of the conditions have been met."

"Bonded to you? Conditions?" Aniol was verging on hysteria.

Kaji pointed at the bandage on Aniol's right arm before raising his own left one. Without speaking a word, he calmly rolled his sleeve down to reveal a long cut on his inner arm, traveling from his wrist to about halfway to his elbow. He then reached out and took Aniol's right arm, not giving him time to flinch away. He turned Aniol's arm so that his inner arm faced up.

"Yours is here," he stated simply, tracing a diagonal line across the bandage, stopping mere inches from Aniol's elbow. "It's messy, too long, and too deep, but all of that is irrelevant to the bonding. You mixed your blood with mine, left arm to right," he stated, looking up to meet Aniol's wide eyes. "You are Taè."

Aniol blinked the word completely unfamiliar to him. "Taè?"

Kaji remained silent for a moment, watching Aniol closely before giving Aniol the most wicked smile the young man had ever seen—and Aniol had seen some really wicked ones. He'd been approached by some really sick and sadistic people during his twenty-three years of life, by people who all wanted to find a way to use him for their own gain. They usually approached him with a smile in an attempt to win his trust, but Aniol had long ago given up on trusting anyone. As wicked as Kaji's smile was, though, Aniol realized there was no malice in it; it was filled with pure mischief. "The girl," Kaji explained, still smiling.

"I'm not a girl!" Aniol protested, pulling his arm away from Kaji and holding it to his chest, doing his best to glare at the redhead before him.

Kaji's smile softened as he watched Aniol carefully. He cocked his head to the side as something caught his attention. "Did you know that your eyes change color with your emotions?"

Aniol shifted back at the words, adding a pout to his glare. He had not known that, seeing as he didn't know the color of his own eyes to begin with. Having this stranger before him know more about his eyes than he knew did not sit well with him. It made him feel rather inadequate and strangely sad.

"They are a very interesting color to begin with, but as your moods shift, so do the colors in your eyes. They have a misty quality about them, and it's almost as if the mist in them is alive, shifting and changing as rapidly as your moods." Kaji settled back into his seat, giving Aniol some space.

Aniol watched him for a moment, desperately trying to figure him out. He wanted to know what Kaji was thinking. He absently chewed his lip, momentarily distracted by the look Kaji was giving him and the feelings that look stirred within him. He didn't understand the mixture of apprehension and excitement. Aniol's frown returned when he realized he'd been sidetracked by Kaji's comment. "I am not a girl," he repeated.

"I never said you were a girl." Kaji lifted a hand to silence the protest he could see forming on Aniol's lips. "I said you were Taè. The role of Taè in a union is normally taken by the girl or the partner that will be representing the girl for all intents and legal purposes. One of the impacts of that is that you take on my family name. But seeing as you don't appear to have a family name, that shouldn't be too much of a problem. The cut on your right arm marks you as Taè. Mine"—he gestured to his own arm—"being on the left marks me as Govà: male, or head of family. I need to get new bonding bracelets made, but I don't know what to put on them in representation of your family."

"Bonding bracelets?" Aniol asked in confusion.

Kaji's brow furrowed. "Yes, bonding bracelets. A pair or bracelets is worn by bonded couples so that they may be identified as such. Each pair is unique, created by merging the family insignias of both partners in order to create a new symbol. They hide most of the scar made by bonding and represent to all that the wearer is bonded, identifying whom they are bonded to as well. Anyone with a scar not wearing a bonding bracelet is widowed." Kaji paused, looking for a delicate way to phrase his next words. "Why are you unaware of this? Surely some time during the course of your life you would have witnessed or at least heard about a bonding?"

Aniol winced, dropping his gaze hastily in an attempt to hide the reaction. He took a moment to compose himself before looking up once more. "I don't get out much."

Kaji frowned at the words, concern visibly flickering through him. He tilted his head to the side in contemplation before speaking, leaving his questions unasked for the moment. "Three things are needed for a bonding to be complete: the cuts on the arm, the intermingling of blood, and the circle. We've already discussed the first. One partner receives a cut on the right arm, the other on the left for the reason I have already explained. The intermingling of blood is a dual process. The blood mixes on the blade used to create the cuts and is then mixed again by pressing the pair's arms together. It is thus that two separate individuals become one. Technically, the cut on your arm was done with a different blade, but your blood was mixed with mine on the ceremonial blade I was using in the bonding ceremony when I cut you with it." Kaji pointed at Aniol's side. "The third is the circle. The two bonding need to be standing together within a complete circle. This symbolizes the lifelong commitment they have to one another. No other should be in the circle with them as it may disrupt the bonding and make it unstable." Kaji gave Aniol a wry smile. "You pushed Saya out when you stumbled into the circle, so we were the only two in the circle at the time of the actual bonding. Thereafter it is usually customary to exchange bonding bracelets. This is not necessary as the bracelets are more a social symbol and not involved in the actual bonding ceremony itself. The bracelets are embossed with a symbol that uniquely identifies a bonded couple. I had bracelets made for Saya and me, but they are rather obviously inappropriate now. I will have new ones made as soon as I can figure out what to put on them." Kaji fell silent, watching Aniol for a reaction.

Aniol licked his lips, shifting uncertainly. "I don't know anything about my family," he admitted softly.

Kaji sighed, running an absent hand through his hair, further mussing the already messy red hair. "I guess it's a dilemma that requires some careful consideration, then. You should get some sleep." Kaji reached forward to gently push Aniol back down onto the bed, tugging white sheets up after Aniol was once more lying down. "We will speak further of this once you've had your rest."

Aniol blinked at him, trying to keep his eyes open but failing as exhaustion took over once more. "I don't want to sleep," he murmured tiredly.

Kaji smiled, his entire countenance softening at the sheer audacity of the rather contrary comment Aniol had made. He reached out to brush a stray strand of silver-blue hair out of Aniol's face. "I'm sure you don't," he stated just as softly, waiting for Aniol to drift off before standing up and leaving the infirmary.

Kaji paced back and forth, mind racing as he tried to deal with everything that had happened. The disruption of his bonding ceremony had not only been unexpected but had also ruined the prophecy. This worried him, but not nearly as much as misty grey-blue eyes that haunted him wherever he went. His new mate was an enigma, a mystery that begged for some kind of resolution. He had no idea where the young man had come from, who his family was, or how to deal with him. He'd seen the fear on Aniol's face, the fear that caused the mist in his eyes to coil as if preparing to strike out in defense. Yet Kaji couldn't understand it. He wanted to know what caused that odd mist.

He fisted his hands, contemplating actually doing something constructive in an attempt to distract himself and turn his thoughts away from his newly acquired mate. Growling deep in his throat, Kaji resumed his pacing, knowing it was futile. The same questions he'd had since first seeing the young man still went round and round in his head, unanswered and sadly joined by even more questions as a result of his efforts to resolve the original set. What had Aniol gone through? What brought him here? What was he, Kaji, supposed to do next?

Deciding that his pacing was not actually accomplishing anything, Kaji turned and strode out the room, his steps quick and sure. He headed straight toward the object of his distraction, walked into the infirmary and picked his mate up in one easy movement before he turned to leave. One glare silenced the doctor who was about to protest.

Kaji glanced down at the slim, too-light figure cradled in his arms. Aniol was still asleep and absolutely enthralling. The young man had long strands of the softest hair, shades of blue and silver mingling and shifting, changing as the young man's hair moved. His skin, what little of it that was not covered in yellow, purple, and blue bruises, was burned ragged by sun he was obviously unaccustomed to, the dark red looking rather painful. Aniol had long lashes that rested against his cheeks in his sleep, hiding his most striking feature: his rather strange eyes. Those eyes were unusual, a deep, clear blue tinted by shades of grey and made stranger by the light mist that seemed to travel through them.

Kaji walked straight into his own quarters and bent down to place Aniol onto black sheets decorated with red embroidery. As he leaned over, something slid from beneath Aniol's clothes and struck Kaji's knee as it slipped to the ground. Kaji's turned toward the object in curiosity. Unable to locate it with a cursory glance, he settled Aniol before releasing the young man and shifting away to search for the fallen object. What he found caused him to gasp in disbelief. Lying on his rich red carpet was a silver chain with a tiny teardrop pendant. The pendant was made of moonstone.

# ELONGING

Promises: fragile words of hope, hard to keep, easy to break, the impact far greater than one can ever imagine. The thing about promises is that not all of them are explicitly stated. Some are implied, formed by situation. All hurt when broken and betrayed.

Betrayal: There is little that cuts deeper than being betrayed, the breaking of trust a hard lesson to learn.

Gatekeepers: those able to see, to open, and to maintain harmony. Those who were meant to be protected were promised such, only to be betrayed by the very ones that were meant to protect them: their Wardens.

KAJI hurried as he strode down the hallway, wanting to get through his duties as soon as possible so that he could return to his quarters and check on Aniol. The young man had developed a fever that night when the cut on his arm became infected. The blade that had been used to cut him had not been very clean.

Kaji was concerned. True, he didn't know Aniol as of yet but the young man was his mate, bonded to him, and bonding was a lifetime commitment. Kaji wanted to make the best of it. Besides, prophecy aside, this was not all that much different than if he had been bonded to Saya. He didn't actually know the girl, either, as she had been tracked down for him by the council that sought to ensure that every effort possible was made in order to fulfill the prophecy passed down in his family for generations. As demanded by tradition, his bonding ceremony had been on the day he legally became of age. Only his partner had been rather... unexpected.

"Kaji!"

Kaji paused. He turned to face the culprit who dared interrupt him when he was in a hurry, scowling and tapping his foot in agitation. "Yuan." Kaji inclined his head in greeting, glaring at Yuan though he knew he would be ignored.

Yuan, as usual, was completely oblivious to Kaji's displeasure, and he grinned at Kaji as he paused beside the redhead. "I hear that was some really interesting bonding ceremony you had there." Kaji raised his eyebrows in question. "I heard you bonded to a slave." Kaji remained silent, hoping that Yuan would take the hint and leave him alone, thus allowing him to do what he needed to do. Yuan, however, did not take hints rather well, even blatant ones that all but screamed at him. "Is he a pleasure slave?" he teased lightly.

The words had barely passed Yuan's lips when he found himself up against the wall, Kaji's hands fisted in his clothes and raising him high enough that his feet no longer touched the ground. "Don't you dare speak of my mate in that manner!" Kaji said, the threat of further violence radiating off his body.

Yuan blinked in shock, raising his hands in defeat, remaining silent until Kaji released him. "Seriously," Yuan said, his tone soft in an attempt to be soothing. "I'm sorry to hear that your prophesied union has been ruined."

Kaji watched him for a long moment, still tense and ready to strike at the slightest provocation before shrugging. "It matters not." He turned away from the blond before him and resumed his earlier stride. "What's done is done."

Yuan hurried after him, having to half-run simply in order to keep up. He was really curious about Kaji's mate. "So what have you been able to find out so far?" Yuan asked. "Know who he belongs to? How he escaped? What he was doing running around bleeding in the city?"

"He's not a slave," Kaji stated bluntly, still walking forward, not even turning to face Yuan as he spoke.

"Not a slave?" Yuan questioned in confusion. "What do you mean not a slave? I heard he wears the collar of one."

"He does." Kaji stopped abruptly. Yuan's momentum carried him a few steps past Kaji before he stopped and turned back to face him. Kaji continued when he had his attention once more. "Swear that you will not reveal what I am about to show you to anyone," Kaji demanded.

Yuan watched him in silence, then nodded in agreement. "I swear." Kaji reached into a pocket, pulled something out, and raised his hand in demonstration, showing Yuan what he held. Yuan's breath caught in his throat in shock. "Is that...?"

"Silver." Kaji stated confirming Yuan's suspicions. "What's more...." He opened his palm, allowing the rest of the chain to drop down, handing from his fingertips. "Moonstone. Pure and unmarred moonstone."

Yuan gaped in disbelief. That amount of silver could buy a title and a considerable amount of land. Silver was extremely rare in Duiem. No mines for the metal existed. What little silver Duiem possessed circulated as it passed from one owner to the next. Moonstone was even rarer. Unmarred moonstone, unheard of. "Who...?" Yuan started to ask, unable to voice the rest of the question due to shock.

"I don't know," Kaji responded, knowing exactly what Yuan wanted to ask, before turning and walking away. Yuan was too stunned to follow.

A SOLITARY figure crosses a white, desolate room lit by a tiny window that admits but a shimmer of light, the only light the room ever sees. The light reflects off of the white floor and walls, bathing the tiny room in a misty, almost otherworldly glow. The pale light reveals a barren room barely filled with the basic necessities of living: one tiny bed, covered in white sheets, and a white sketchpad upon the bed, a black charcoal drawing marring its surface, almost seeming to mock the white purity of the room.

The room darkens when the solitary figure pauses by the tiny window, the light redirected from the floor to settle around the figure creating a dark silhouette of a small, slim boy. A thin hand reaches out to touch the edge of the window; the boy looks out in sorrow and longing.

A loud, violent bang shatters the reverie enveloping the room, causing the slight figure to tense and turn in terror. Only the movement is never completed, red marring the overwhelming white that defines the room as the small figure crumples to the floor, his vision filled with the deepest black.

It is some time before the young man begins to wake, misty eyes opening only to snap shut at the pain that flares through his head. Sharp spikes flare through his skull, the light and movement only aggravating his wound. His brow furrows in concentration as he tries sift through his foggy memories in an attempt to figure out what had occurred, only to be met by pain and darkness. Failure to determine what placed him into his current state leads the young man's focus to shift toward trying to determine what his current state is.

The first thing to register is the subtle heat of the sun upon his skin, an unfamiliar sensation, the whisper of which he only knew from standing before his tiny window each day. The subtle heat is soon wiped away by the chill in the air, the cold wind cutting into him. The second thing he registers is the sound of hooves and a swaying motion. Confused and uncertain, the young man tries to open his eyes once more, taking it more slowly this time until his gaze is met with various shades of dusty brown and dirty white, shifting and ever-changing as he moves.

The creature grinds to a halt; rough hands reach out to grab him and pull him down onto the coarse, cold ground. The young man hisses softly as he falls, rough ground cutting into delicate skin, marring it, just as his white room had been marred, stained by red and sin.

Misty eyes grow wild with terror as the attacker drags the small figure toward the unknown. Fear colors the young man's perceptions, clouding his judgment. Events register as jagged shards of pain and panic. His arms, shoulders, and wrists burn, sprained and torn in his attempts to fight his bonds. Cold steel bites into his ankle, the sound of the closing clip sealing his fate forever, and then… his entire world is turned upside-down.

Gone is the painful grip, replaced by something far worse: the cold of imminent death. Water rushes in on the young man's senses, the amount of which he has never even imagined, let alone comprehended or seen. It rushes in to claim his life. Cold steel persistently drags him under, sparing him no hope for redemption. Inexperience and lack of knowledge drag the young man toward death when he gasps in shock, swallowing water as he goes under.

Despite his fear, he does not give up, fighting the water as it steals his life, and when he can fight no longer he gives himself up to encroaching darkness inevitably rushing in. Moments before being claimed, a stray thought drifts through his clouded mind, and he wonders why death seems to come so peacefully, gentle warmth cradling him as it draws him into its arms.

ANIOL woke to find himself alone. He sat up, black sheets sliding off his warm skin and pooling at his waist. He frowned down at the sheets, wondering where he was. The last time he woke he'd been surrounded by white sheets, lying on a small single bed. Now he was in a huge bed the size of which he'd never imagined, let alone seen. The bed was decorated in black and red.

He peered to the side, noting the deep red carpet before looking up in order to take in his surroundings. The bed had four wooden posts with a frame at the top from which transparent red curtains hung. To the right there was a large desk and padded chair; to the left there was another table with two seats around it, and at the foot of the bed there was a huge dresser. All of the furniture in the room was made of intricately carved dark wood.

Aniol slipped sideways out of bed, smiling when his feet sank into the dark carpet. He hissed as he stood up fully, a sudden rush of dizziness nearly flooring him. He took a moment to gather himself, breath coming in short pants as waves of heat rushed through him. Once the room stopped spinning, he took a few steps forward, pausing for a moment to orient himself. A small object on the bedside table caught his attention. He turned to face it and immediately wished he hadn't. He felt the heat drain from him, the fact defying the sunburn he had. Lying upon the bedside table was a small reddish brown purse, marked with beige embroidery.

Aniol reached out toward it, hand trembling violently. His breath caught in the back of his throat as he opened it carefully to look inside. Suspicion confirmed, the purse fell from his suddenly limp fingers and crashed to the floor, scattering coins and more notably a small angel-shaped pendant made of silver and gold to the floor. Aniol had seen his captor handle the pendant beside a camp fire, bragging about how he'd acquired it.

Aniol didn't know what the purse was doing there, but fear urged him to run and hide before he was found and accused of being a thief. His breath quickened in panic, and he turned, desperately searching for a door. The movement only served to make him dizzy again, so he forced himself to stop. Closing his eyes, he took a moment to regroup before opening them once more and searching the room at a more measured pace. Upon spotting the door, he headed toward it as fast as his protesting body would allow, opening it just a sliver to peer out.

Finding the corridor empty, he darted into it, randomly choosing a direction. He lost his way several times in his attempt to flee, stumbling into areas he had already visited a few times before finally finding himself at the front gate. It hadn't been too difficult to hide in the shadows whenever he saw someone walking toward him. The front gate, however, posed a little more of a challenge, as there were two guards standing beside it, until he noticed a few servants leaving via a side route. He followed the servants and walked right past the stationed guard. The guard didn't even spare him a second glance, his ragged, torn clothes serving in his favor.

Finally free, he slipped into a dark alleyway, leaning against the wall in exhaustion. Energy drained, he slipped to the ground, curling in on himself. He shivered, shaking not from cold, but from the heat that was burning him up from the inside out.

PURE, uncontrolled rage coursed through Kaji, threatening to take over his ability to reason. He stared down at the huddled figure before him, the cool night air biting into his skin. Reaching down, he grabbed Aniol's left wrist, hauled the small figure up without so much as a word, and headed back toward the entrance to the alley. Slipping out, he turned and continued to walk, dragging the silent figure behind him, Kaji's fury about to make him crack at any moment.

The rest of the journey was uncomfortable as Kaji's anger drove him relentlessly forward despite the fact that Aniol stumbled awkwardly behind him. Kaji sent the two guards heated glares as he walked past, angry that they had somehow allowed this to happen in the first place. Dragging Aniol to his room, Kaji used his foot to slam the door behind him before shoving Aniol before him, the momentum of the movement causing Aniol to fall onto the bed, wide-eyed and pale.

"What the hell did you think you were doing?" The bubbling fury finally exploded out of Kaji. "How dare you do this to me? I spent all day searching for you! I was worried sick!" Kaji yelled at the top of his voice, venting his rage, not even pausing to give Aniol any time to respond. "Do you have any idea what it did to me? Any idea at all?"

Needing to breathe, Kaji stopped yelling, using the reprieve to look at Aniol, who lay upon his bed, staring up at him in silence. His bondmate's mouth was agape in shock. For some reason, the reaction irritated Kaji, grating on his nerves and aggravating him even further. It seemed Aniol didn't understand why he was so upset. He stalked over to the bed and crawled up onto it so that he loomed over Aniol. He glared down at his mate, amber gaze locked with wide, deep blue-gray eyes stained dark with Aniol's shock. Kaji was surprised when the misty color in Aniol's eyes swirled into motion, moving across the irises with a life of its own, but he ignored the oddity. He was no stranger to the concept of magic and had a more pressing matter to focus on.

"Let me put this into simpler terms," Kaji said, his tone suddenly soft but no less angry for it. "Terms you might actually understand. You are mine. You belong to me." The next sentence was spoken slowly, possessive aggression coloring each and every word. "Don't. Ever. Try. To. Run. Away. From. Me. Again." That said, Kaji bent down to seal Aniol's open mouth with his lips, kissing the young man aggressively, exploring every inch of his mate's mouth, withdrawing only when he drew a whimper from Aniol.

# GRIEF

It's rather amazing, the manner in which legends are told. Each event is described in detail. Analogies are given in order to impact upon the listener, to emphasize what has occurred, the mistakes that have been made, and the lessons which are to be learned.

The last legend of the Gatekeepers is a classic example of this storytelling approach. It tells of a world torn asunder, wailing its grief into the night, bleeding to death from mortal wounds. This analogy is used to describe a single act of betrayal and its impact upon Duiem and its people.

SILENCE permeated the room, the sound of rustling pages the only disturbance in the air. Kaji was seated on the bed, leaning against the headboard, legs stretched out before him and crossed at the ankles. He also had a pile of paperwork in his lap. Aniol was curled up against Kaji's right side, fast asleep, a white cloth upon his forehead.

The drama of the previous evening had settled down rather quickly after the kiss. Kaji had gotten off of Aniol and stormed out, slamming the door as he left, but not before posting a guard at the door. He had threatened the guard with death should Aniol manage to slip out again. When Kaji had finally calmed down, he returned to find Aniol curled in on himself, fast asleep and still feverish. He had then gone to fetch some cold water and a cloth which he promptly placed onto Aniol's forehead. Weary from the long tiring day, Kaji had then shifted Aniol so that the young man was in his bed beneath the blankets and slipped in beside him, drifting off into a fitful sleep filled with worry.

Having had a restless night, Kaji had risen with the morning sun, glancing out for a moment before he got dressed and settled himself on the bed with paperwork that he needed to get done. He'd stared at papers for an hour before glancing at Aniol, noting the rather pained expression on the young man's face. That was when he reached out and brought the young man closer, allowing Aniol to curl into him. Thus he found himself in his current state, absently flicking through papers and occasionally changing the cloth on Aniol's forehead in an attempt to control the fever.

Paper rustled once more as Kaji turned a page and began to read another document. He frowned, rereading as something caught his attention. This was followed by hectic movement as he began to page through the various documents, seeking confirmation of what he saw. Minutes later the rustling stopped. Kaji looked up, scowling, lost deep in thought. It would appear that the country was far worse off than he'd been led to believe. He didn't usually read the documents that were presented to him requiring his signature for two main reasons. For one, he trusted his advisors, though he did so wrongfully, if the contents of the documents were to be believed. The second reason was that until now, he'd been too young to legally rule; his signature was a mere formality to get him used to the procedures of ruling. That had changed on his bonding day, the day he'd turned twenty-five.

If not for Aniol, he wouldn't have read these documents, either. The only reason he was reading them in the first place was because Aniol was ill, and Kaji didn't want to leave the boy's side. The simplest way to actually perform any of his duties from his quarters was to deal with the documents that required his signature. Seeing as he intended to stay here all day and that this granted him a bit of extra time, he had decided to read while he waited for Aniol to wake.

His scowl deepened as his rage increased. Kaji did not like being played for a fool. He hated being deceived, but most of all, he hated being used. The papers thumped down onto the bed beside him, rage carrying Kaji half off the bed before his movement was interrupted by a small whimper from Aniol. Kaji had intended to storm out the room, find his advisors, and get into a screaming match combined with maybe some blood, maybe some pain, and maybe some death. Not his own, of course. Aniol's whimper, however, halted those plans and prompted Kaji to reach out in concern.

The moment he touched Aniol he winced, engulfed by a bright white light. The light faded as quickly as it appeared, overwhelming Kaji with the scene it revealed. He saw a huge thundering river, the sheer volume of which rushed out of control and threatened to take the embankment with it, overrunning its boundaries and flooding into land covered in white. The cold was unbelievable, like nothing he'd ever felt, biting into his flesh and causing him to shudder and his teeth to chatter.

Before he managed to fully take in the scene, it shattered. Splinters of color faded with dizzying speed, creating the illusion of bright light before transporting him to another place entirely. Realizing that he could see faint outlines, Kaji narrowed his eyes, carefully taking in his surroundings. He found himself in a bare white room, the cold not as bad, but a chill still managed to sink into his bones. He registered a small single bed with ragged white sheets upon it before turning to see the rest of the room. A gasp of shock escaped him. He could see a dark, dirty brown mark staining the wall and floor beside the window, adding a touch of morbid color to the scene, for it was dried blood. Kaji would know the sight anywhere.

He tensed, head shooting up when he heard voices echoing through empty space. Kaji began to panic. He had no idea where he was, but it appeared that he would soon be discovered, and something, he did not know what, told him that it wouldn't be a good thing. He spun, desperately searching for somewhere to hide, seeking a way to escape the small barren room, only there was nowhere to hide, nowhere to run. The room held but one small bed and a torn, abused sketchpad upon the floor, and it had a single exit. Unfortunately the voices were coming from the direction of the exit.

Kaji stared at the door, now able to hear and make out what was being said.

"I keep telling you, there is nothing here." The door creaked open as the man finished speaking. Kaji's breath hitched in his throat as he stood frozen in place, staring into violet and blue eyes. Two men stood at the door, looking straight at him.

The blue-eyed man spoke, guiding the second man into the room. "It looks like someone broke in, killed him, and ran." Kaji winced as they approached him, waiting for them to challenge him. He frowned when they ignored him and walked toward him almost as if he wasn't there. "As you can see, it was quite violent. We already disposed of the body."

"But what I don't understand is why anyone would do such a thing." The purple-eyed man spoke, swinging his hand toward the scene at the window and toward Kaji's chest. Kaji flinched, moving back, but he hadn't moved nearly fast enough. He closed his eyes, waiting for the blow... a blow that never came as the other man's hand passed right through him.

Kaji's eyes snapped open in shock. The realization of what had occurred was an even heavier blow than the physical one would have been. A chill—one not due to the cold air—ran through him, settling in his lower body, filling him with dark fear.

"I can think of a few reasons." The blue-eyed man responded smoothly. "He was feared and hated. He was a demon."

"He was not a demon!" The purple-eyed man said through clenched teeth.

The blue-eyed man raised his arms in an effort to placate the other. "All right, he was not a demon. However, I'm sorry to say that is what he was known as."

"What do you mean 'what he was known as'?" the purple-eyed man demanded. "No one was supposed to have known of his existence."

"Well, you see...."

Kaji had forgotten his fear and was now leaning closer, avidly listening to the exchange between the two men when suddenly their voices began to fade. "No, no, no, not yet," Kaji muttered to no avail. White light encompassed him once more, and when next it faded, he found himself back in his own quarters, his hand upon Aniol's burning hot forehead.

Kaji had little time to contemplate what had just happened as other more urgent matters consumed him. Aniol was far too hot, his fever having rather obviously gone out of control. Pushing the strange vision he'd just had into the back of his mind, Kaji bent down and picked Aniol up in one smooth motion, turning and running out the room, sheets, the edges stuck between Aniol and himself, trailing upon the ground.

Kaji kicked the door to the infirmary open, calling out for help. His desperate plea was followed by a flurry of activity, a rush of movement, and events that if he'd been asked later to describe he would've been unable to piece together, his mind to ravaged by worry.

The next thing Kaji knew he was in the corridor outside the infirmary pacing back and forth, threatening to wear a permanent mark into the stone upon which he walked. He tensed at every sound, whirling toward the infirmary door, hoping for some kind of news, preferably good.

After what seemed to be an eternity, the infirmary door creaked open, and Kaji rushed over toward it, questioning the healer before she had even managed to step out. "And? How is he? Can I see him?"

The healer remained silent for a moment, watching Kaji carefully before responding. "We need to talk," she said softly.

Kaji paled, his usually sharp eyes losing their focus as he began to tremble violently. "No," he whispered. "No, we don't need to talk. What I need is to see him. He's going to be okay!"

The healer reached out and placed a hand lightly on Kaji's shoulder, turning him and leading him toward a bench situated besides the infirmary door. She pushed him down, seating herself besides Kaji before speaking. "The infection has spread. It's too late. The medication we're giving him isn't working. I'm sorry; there's nothing more we can do. It's up to him now."

"No," Kaji repeated, shaking his head, silent tears pouring down his face. He knew he shouldn't be this affected by someone he barely knew, but he was. It was tearing him apart, and the pain of it was worse than having a blade shoved into his chest and twisted around. "He's not going to die!" Kaji yelled, the exclamation followed by loud sobs of grief.

# EW HOPE

Prophecy. The prophecy of redemption is an intricate piece meant for the royal family of the sun. Duiem committed the sin, and so it should be Duiem that atones for it. It's a rather simple prophecy, at least upon the surface, as one never realizes the complexity of the contracts that truly bind.

Each generation shall receive the opportunity to atone for the sins committed against the Gatekeepers.

The means by which to do so seemed simple enough: find and bond with the one meant for you and together restore harmony. The only catch is that sun must bond with moon. A momentous task, considering the Gatekeepers are dead, considering the links between sun and moon are torn asunder. That is why the council was formed. Their sole purpose is to find the destined one of the moon.

Only a few descendants of the moon still reside in the land of the sun, dying out as generations go by, the destined union prophesied less likely with each new royal heir. Descendants are marked by their eyes and hair. Pale eyes and hair of blue, purple, grey, silver, or white, identifiers that mark the soul as one of Careil. In order to assist the royal family in finding the destined one, a clue is given. The clue meant for one named Conflagration was: one of royal blood.

But sometimes the shadows in men's hearts seek to prevent that which is meant to be. They seek to obscure the truth through deception and kill all who hold true knowledge. Blood was spilled upon the day of Flame's birth, truth hidden by lie. The clue was changed to: one from the Kiyou clan. So it was that Conflagration was betrothed to Saya, who had eyes of violet.

KAJI was standing, arms crossed over his chest and foot tapping with pent-up energy. The tension in the air was thick and palpable, swirling in the air between Kaji and the object of his displeasure. An uncomfortable silence  complicated the situation even further. Kaji cleared his throat as he searched for something to say. "What did you think you were doing? Threatening to die on me?" he demanded roughly, his glare intensifying.

Misty blue-grey eyes blinked up at him in confusion. "Um…." Aniol stated, unable to find a coherent response to Kaji's demanding questions, the questions not making much sense to him.

Kaji continued to glare, the tapping of his foot increasing in speed as he allowed the silence to grow once more. "Just for the record," he snapped in an effort to protect himself, "I did not cry."

Aniol jerked back, blinking at Kaji once more. Aniol was seated up in bed, white sheets pooled at his waist as he stared up at Kaji, who appeared to be fuming mad. Aniol didn't exactly understand why, nor know what he'd done this time. He'd woken a few minutes earlier feeling better than he had in days. He'd tried to sit up, only to realize he had a weight upon his chest. Looking down, he had spotted bright red hair. Realizing Kaji was sleeping, seated beside the bed he lay in, head resting on him, Aniol had watched the redhead for a few moments before the discomfort in his body had demanded he move. Aniol shifted, pushing at the redhead, only to have Kaji jump up with a yell of panic. That was when Kaji had noticed he was awake and started yelling at him.

Aniol frowned in confusion at Kaji's words and the implication in them. "O… kay," he said uncertainly, unsure as to how Kaji wanted him to respond.

Kaji's shoulders slumped, all the anger suddenly draining out, leaving as quickly as it had come. Kaji ran his hands through his hair before pulling them down over his face. He was weary and rather worn. He sank back down into the seat he had leapt out of in his anger. "How do you feel?" he asked softly, reaching out to touch Aniol's forehead, glaring at him when Aniol flinched away.

Aniol blinked in surprise. Kaji's touch was soft and gentle upon his skin, tracing his features as if seeking to confirm that he was all right. Kaji's hand then moved to his bandaged arm, carefully beginning to unwind the material. Aniol watched him in silence. The light touch upon his arm was a pleasant sensation that made him want to cry in gratitude at the consideration he was being shown. He bit his lip to prevent himself from doing so.

Aniol flinched at the unexpected rush of cool air upon his skin, looking down at his own arm and the healing wound there. He glanced up once more when Kaji ran a finger lightly over the forming scar. "It looks much better now." Kaji said softly, the relief in his voice apparent.

An unfamiliar sensation coursed through Aniol's body at the touch: a pleasant warmth that was faintly ticklish. He wanted more of the touch and everything that it meant. He wanted to be important to someone, to anyone.

"It should be fine now. It just needs to be kept clean." Kaji turned away momentarily, reaching beside the bed to pick up a cloth. He dipped the cloth into a cool gel and then lightly brushed it over the wound, catching Aniol's hand in his left when Aniol tried to flinch away once more. The gel was even cooler than the air had been. "It's all right. I won't hurt you." Placing the cloth back down, he moved some objects around on the table, found what he sought, and turned back toward Aniol. He gave Aniol a small reassuring smile and reached for Aniol's arm once more, placing clean bandages upon the wound, his touch as gentle as ever.

Aniol continued to watch in silence, wanting to protest when Kaji released him but not daring to. He frowned in confusion when Kaji leant forward to brush some damp, sticky strands of hair out of his face, tucking them behind Aniol's ears. "You seriously need a bath." Kaji stated with a light chuckle.

"Why are you doing this?" Aniol whispered, his voice hoarse.

Kaji frowned taking Aniol's wounded right hand into his own, his thumb brushing soothing circles over Aniol's skin. "What do you mean, why?" Kaji inquired. "You are my mate."

Aniol didn't understand how that made a difference. "What does that have to do with anything?"

An expression of horrified shock flickered over Kaji's face before vanishing as he spoke. "It has everything to do with it." Kaji's voice was rough, and his left hand clutched Aniol's right rather tightly, causing pain to flare through Aniol's arm. Aniol ignored the pain. "It means we are

bonded. You belong to me and I belong to you. This is a bond for life."
Kaji held up their intertwined arms, the arms marked by the wounds.
"Blood to blood. It's for life. It's a promise to care for and protect one
another. It has everything to do with it."

Aniol stared at him, very confused, but deep down, he was pleased.
Kaji's words made him feel things he had never felt before. He jerked in
shock once more, the motion seeming to be becoming an integral part of
him when he felt another soft brush against his forehead, this time the
touch not a hand but lips as Kaji dropped a light kiss upon his forehead,
almost as if to emphasize his words. "But you don't know me," Aniol
whispered.

Kaji withdrew, shaking his head. "It matters not. I don't know Saya
either, and she was supposed to be my bondmate. Now my bondmate is
you." His grip on Aniol's hand finally loosened, and now his fingers were
once more playing with Aniol's hand. "The bonding binds us together. If
we were not compatible, we would not be bound fully. We would only
have the physical marks upon our skin and would not be able to sense each
other on any other level." He gave Aniol a small smile. "I can feel the
deeper bond, though. I can feel you in the back of my mind." Kaji cocked
his head to the side, watching Aniol before taking a shot in the dark. "Just
as you can feel me."

Aniol wondered if it were true. He closed his eyes to check,
searching his own mind, a mind he was weary of and often shied away
from, his visions and dreams residing in a dark corner. He frowned when
he realized Kaji was right. He could feel that he was no longer alone. A
bright golden circle surrounded him, encompassing all of him, both the
lighter side and the dark. He opened his eyes in surprise, staring at Kaji,
the mist in his eyes swirling with unknown, undefined emotion.

Kaji smiled, Aniol's expression confirming his suspicions. "Now,
let's get you out of here." Kaji held out his hand, hoping Aniol would take
it. He wanted Aniol's trust but wanted Aniol to choose to give it. "It's not
like they can help you here anyway." He knew that this was probably not a
good idea, but he wanted Aniol beside him. Just the previous day, he'd
been weeping in grief, convinced Aniol would die, and now here he was
sitting beside the boy who was awake and cool to the touch, almost as if
he'd never been sick to begin with. Kaji neither understood nor knew what
had happened, but he wasn't about to question it.

He sighed in relief when Aniol reached out timidly and took his hand, allowing himself to slip out of bed. Kaji moved forward and scooped Aniol up into his arms when Aniol wobbled, unstable upon his feet. Kaji raised his eyebrows in challenge when the young man in his arms scowled at him.

"I'm not an invalid." Aniol protested, pouting. "What?" he questioned when Kaji only raised his eyebrows further.

Kaji shook his head, heading toward the exit to the infirmary. "Nothing," he replied, a bounce in his step. Kaji was on cloud nine and all was right with the world. All concern, thoughts of death, and the impact of certain papers he had read were far from his thoughts as he sought to celebrate the day and the new hope he had been given.

# DECEPTION

Deception: A poison far worse than any other, striking from places unforeseen, striking when least expected. It was this poison that led to the betrayal of the Gatekeepers. One man, a royal son, had a silver tongue and a remarkable talent for using it, a talent to deceive. He spread a word here, a whisper there, and encouraged the rumors and lies to grow, leading to deliberate deception.

His deception played on flaws inherent in man's heart: greed, distrust, anger, uncertainty, and lust for power. The deceiver was a talented musician, expertly playing on all these weaknesses, on coincidence, and on threads of discontent with the skills of a master. He lay in wait until his prey was most vulnerable, most susceptible to believing in shadows that did not exist, the prey already set up by chance and rumor to be blinded by the shadows within their own hearts.

And so it was he convinced the Wardens that their Gatekeepers were about to betray them, about to take power, thus granting riches to the Land of Silver, leaving Duiem to die. So, instead of being the betrayed, the Wardens became the betrayers, striking first in what they believed to be defense. The few Wardens who did not succumb to the twisted lies were dubbed traitors and killed along with their Gatekeepers by those they once called their comrades.

ANIOL and Kaji were once more stuck in a staring match of sorts, Aniol actually taking part this time, returning the glare he received. "I am not a child," he protested, animosity thick in his tone.

Kaji's lips set in a stubborn frown. "You're not getting out of that bed," he repeated firmly. "You're still recovering. I nearly lost you. There's no way I'm allowing it to happen again."

"You don't have me to begin with," Aniol snapped in return, all but bristling as he fought with the redhead who seemed to have taken over his life. "You can't lose what you don't have."

"Like hell I don't have you." Kaji leaned in from where he was seated beside Aniol on the bed, now very much in Aniol's personal space, his breath mingling with Aniol's. He smirked when Aniol's breathing quickened. Kaji knew exactly what was happening. "We are bonded." Kaji spoke slowly, knowing his warm breath touched Aniol's lips. His smirk grew wider when Aniol tensed, licking his lips.

"I...." Aniol licked his lips once more, Kaji's exhale upon them doing strange things to him. A rush of heat ran through him for a moment, convincing him that he was feverish once more, only... it was different, different in a way Aniol could neither understand nor explain. It was making him nervous, tying his stomach up in knots, and making him want to draw both away and toward Kaji at the same time. The conflicting emotions were driving him mad, confusing him, and keeping him in place in indecision. "I had no"—he licked his lips again trying to rid himself of the emotions Kaji was stirring—"say in that."

"Neither... did... I," Kaji whispered in return before leaning in to capture Aniol's lips, kissing the young man aggressively, giving Aniol little choice in the matter as he invaded the young man's mouth with his tongue. Sweet... Aniol was sweet, wet, and warm, a flavor and sensation Kaji was fast becoming addicted to. He wanted more and searched deeper, running his tongue along Aniol's teeth before aggressively meeting his tongue.

Aniol gasped in shock when Kaji took possession of his mouth, the sound lost somewhere within Kaji's mouth. The heat running through him rushed down, pooling in his stomach and his hips, making his skin hypersensitive, hungry and desperate for touch as he subconsciously drew closer to Kaji. His eyes drifted closed when Kaji drew him into the kiss, demanding a response and getting one, reluctant at first but growing in hunger and eagerness as Aniol's confidence grew.

Kaji soon had Aniol whimpering and tugging at his hair, not

knowing what he was asking him for. Releasing Aniol's mouth, Kaji nipped at the young man's bottom lip before moving toward the edge of his little mate's jaw, leaving bites along the way. Aniol shivered in his arms, hands fisting in Kaji's hair. He panted heavily, his head thrown back in complete submission.

Kaji lapped at Aniol's jaw, soothing one of his bites before changing direction, moving his kisses along the jaw toward Aniol's ear. Reaching the bottom of it he licked the lobe before nipping at the skin just behind it, skin that turned out to be a rather sensitive spot on Aniol. Aniol gasped, arching into Kaji, electricity running though his body with such intensity that it scared him, causing him to panic, his earlier whimpers of pleasure now whimpers of fear as Aniol fought to get away, his arms shoving Kaji with enough strength to let him know that his affections were no longer wanted.

Kaji withdrew, panting just as heavily as Aniol was, amber eyes seeking out misty blue-grey, noting that they were wide and filled with traces of left over lust, confusion, and fear. He gathered Aniol close, running his fingers soothingly through his long, silver-blue hair in an attempt to calm him. Aniol confused him. His reactions were naïve and terror-filled, yet at the same time longing. Aniol seemed to hunger for touch and affection, and certainly he reacted favorably and eagerly to intimacy, almost as if he'd never been touched and wanted to draw the sensation out for as long as possible. But then in contradiction, he would flinch away, giving Kaji the impression that Aniol feared him, shivering like a beaten child reprimanded for doing something wrong.

Kaji realized that maybe the two reactions were not so contrary after all. Maybe Aniol was not used to affection and like any other wanted it, yet because he was unaccustomed to it, maybe he feared it. Kaji's gaze flickered down to the shivering form in his arms, contemplating the implications of his realization. How had Aniol been brought up? Without affection?

The sheer rage that shot through him at the thought shocked even Kaji, his breath hissing out in his attempt to control his desire to beat the living daylights out of whoever had done this to Aniol.

KAJI won the argument. He slipped out of his quarters the moment Aniol fell asleep and went in search of his advisor. He paused before an oak door, contemplating knocking before disregarding that idea and storming right in. His rather dramatic entrance was met by his advisor's calm, dark brown eyes meeting his own anger-filled amber. Karl bowed low, ignoring the obvious anger radiating off of Kaji. "How may I help you, my liege?"

Kaji's eyes narrowed even further, the usual respectful address suddenly sounding like a mockery of him now that he knew what his advisor had been doing behind his back. "You can help me by explaining this." He tossed a bunch of papers onto the advisor's desk, the pages sliding across it, halting mere millimeters before the edge of the desk. "Why do I not know anything about this? I don't recall authorizing mobilization of troops into that area. It's not our land."

Karl remained calm. "The dispute started a long time ago, my liege, before your coming of age and bonding ceremony. I was responsible for running this country in your stead. Something had to be done. The Saikin are a violent race, causing much disruption among the people."

Karl's smooth response grated on Kaji's nerves. "The Saikin are dying, attacked on all sides by our people for their water," he snapped through gritted teeth, shifting the papers to find the one he sought. "Here is a petition asking for assistance and intervention. A petition I never saw and knew nothing about. A petition that was denied. How do you explain that?"

Karl raised his eyebrows in surprise, the action too smooth to be anything but rehearsed. Kaji recalled seeing the motion many times over the years. "I, too, knew nothing about this, my liege," he stated, shrugging and raising his hands in what Kaji now perceived to be false innocence.

"Really?" Kaji raised an eyebrow in challenge, sliding the copy of the document to the side to reveal a second copy of the same document. "This one happens to have your signature on it."

Karl suddenly reassessed his opinion of the young man before him. "It's forged," he replied calmly, watching Kaji. He knew Kaji didn't believe him but also knew that he didn't need to believe him as there was nothing Kaji could do about it. Kaji couldn't relieve him of his office without the council's support, and technically, even if the signature was not forged, Karl had done nothing wrong because he had the power to deny the petition before Kaji came of age.

Kaji fought to contain the boiling rage within him as Karl, the man he had trusted all of his life, the man who was supposed to protect him, brushed him off. The rage peaked when Karl gave him a small sly smile, seeming to taunt him with his lack of power to do anything. He was now suspicious of Karl's doings but knew he didn't have enough evidence to do anything about it. In essence, his hands were tied by bureaucracy.

"I'm not signing this," Kaji snarled. "Our people are dying well enough without the aid of the army to assist them!"

"The Saikin are not our people," Karl stated. "They are a rebel force existing solely to fight against your rule, my liege."

"They've done nothing wrong," Kaji retorted. "All they want is to be left alone in land that is legally theirs."

"They stole that land from the crown."

"That land was 'given' to them," Kaji ground out.

Karl shrugged nonchalantly, dismissing the argument. "That is only hearsay. There is no record of that, my liege. Our people need that land; it's one of the few places where water remains. We need it to survive."

"By 'stealing' it?" Kaji demanded. "By killing them? Do we not have enough death already, what with a war between us and the Ruel, a war no one can remember the reason for any longer? I will not condone such death, Saikin, either in Ruel or Taiyou!"

"So we should die instead?" Karl inquired monotonously. "When there is water available? We should simply let out people die of thirst?"

"No!" Kaji snapped. "We negotiate!"

"We'd get killed before we're even close enough to shout."

"You don't know that," Kaji insisted. "Have you even tried?"

"We didn't need to try. Do you know how many soldiers we've already lost to their spears? I can present the report to you, my liege, if you so wish."

"That's because we are 'attacking' them!" Kaji yelled, fighting his frustration.

"No more than they are attacking us," Karl stated smoothly.

Kaji ground his teeth together, knowing there was no point in continuing this discussion. Karl had a smooth argument for everything. Kaji turned and stormed back out, slamming the door as he left. If Karl thought that this was over, he was sorely mistaken. Kaji did not intend to drop this. He intended to do something about it even if it killed him.

# DI-HYDROGEN OXIDE

A long time ago, harmony existed between the lands of silver and gold, the two sharing strengths and weaknesses and in essence supporting each other. The Land of Gold provided earth and fire, while the Land of Silver provided water and air, the four elements flowing between the two so that balance may be obtained.

Gatekeepers are essential to achieve the fragile balance, responsible for maintaining the flow of elements between the lands. This is accomplished through the careful guardianship of the gates, fragile portals linking two worlds that are in essence but two halves of the same whole. In order to accomplish this, each Gatekeeper is given the ability see that which is revealed to no other, thus luring the Gatekeeper's mind away from reality. So it is that the Gatekeeper cannot protect himself, and thus requires a Warden, who represents the other half of his balance of power.

A balance of trust and duty existed between the Gatekeepers and their Wardens. One could not exist or function without the other. Two souls were bound in a single purpose for life, but perhaps trust, purpose, and duty were not enough. Perhaps one needed more. Perhaps one needed... love.

ANIOL blinked in confusion when Kaji stormed into the room, swept him off the bed, and placed him on his feet. "Come on." Kaji turned to his dresser and pulled out some random clothes. These he tossed at Aniol before turning the small young man and guiding him to the bathroom.

The black tiles were cold in contrast to the warmth of the carpet, pulling a hiss of surprise from Aniol. Kaji shook his head, smiling at him before pointing at an enormous bath filled to the brim with water, water that due to their current crisis was cleansed and circulated. "Get yourself clean and dressed. I'll be back in half an hour." That said, Kaji slipped out, leaving behind a baffled young man.

Aniol frowned, trying to figure out what Kaji wanted him to do. He stared at the large pool of water Kaji had pointed to, fear and reluctance deeply rooted within him. He glanced down at the clothes in his arms in confusion, wondering why Kaji would give him such fine material to use as a cloth to bathe himself with. He let the material drop, the frown deepening when he realized he held a long emerald green robe. Okay... no cloth, no bowl, and no white bar of soap. Aniol was completely lost. The only familiar thing in the bathroom was the water, but the sheer quantity of it gave him pause, remembered terror causing him to shake in fear.

He swallowed, knowing he couldn't ignore Kaji's command to get himself clean. He carefully folded the emerald robe, placing it upon the tiles before warily approaching the water, almost as if expecting it to bite him. Once there, he glanced around for something to use as a cloth. Finding nothing in the vicinity, he took off his own torn and ragged clothes and knelt down beside the water. He warily rinsed out the clothes, his motions slow and cautious, his fear of the water working against him. Once the cloth was clean enough he began to wash himself with it, dipping it into the water before running it over his skin. He was half done when Kaji walked in once more calling out. "Aniol? Are you all right?"

Aniol leaped up in horror, holding his soaked clothes in front of him, a meager cover as Kaji watched him in confusion. Kaji noted how small and vulnerable Aniol looked standing at the edge of the bath with his wet clothes clutched in his hands.

"What are you doing?" Kaji inquired in confusion.

Aniol scowled at Kaji, the clothes in his hand held in a death grip. "Bathing," he said before adding a confused frown to his scowl. "You asked me to."

Kaji raised his eyebrows at that, taking careful note of Aniol's position, the wet clothes he wore, and the young man's emotional state. "How?" he asked, still baffled.

Aniol bit his lip, his grip on the clothes he held tightening. He dropped his gaze before speaking. "I didn't want to use the nice robe you gave me… so I'm using this." He moved the ragged clothes he held just a fraction in indication not wanting to expose himself anymore than he already was. He completely missed Kaji's incredulous expression before a deep chuckle coming from Kaji's chest drew his gaze up once more.

Kaji shook his head. "That's not how I meant you to do it." He strode forward to gather Aniol into his arms, causing Aniol to gasp in surprise. He then walked forward, not caring that he himself was still fully clothed. He walked down the stairs into the rather deep bath, hissing in shock when Aniol began to panic and thrash around. "Hey!" He protested trying to hold onto Aniol. "You're going to fall! Aniol!" Kaji dropped Aniol's lower body hastily lowering him so he was standing on his own. "It's all right." He scowled at him. "See. It's not that deep."

Aniol trembled, blinking up at Kaji in surprise. "It's not pulling me under," he whispered in awe.

Kaji reached out to brush stray strands of hair out of Aniol's face. "No, it isn't. Told you it's not that deep. And there's a seat over there." He pointed to the left. "Feel up to giving it a try?" He held his hand out.

Aniol glanced in the direction Kaji had pointed to, seeming to draw in on himself, the cloth he clutched moving closer to his chest in a defensive motion. "Will you go first?" Aniol asked uncertainly.

Kaji allowed himself a small momentary frown of confusion before nodding. "Yes, I'll go first." He still held his hand out, patiently waiting for Aniol to take it. Mixed emotions coursed through him: frustration, confusion, anger, and pity. Something or someone had badly frightened Aniol, making him timid and wary, and Kaji was having a difficult time being patient. He longed for Aniol to open up, to trust him, and to release some of that strength he occasionally saw when the young man fought with him.

He kept his face passive as Aniol took his hand, giving the young man's hand a gentle squeeze before leading Aniol slowly through the water to the bench. Kaji sat down on it, his own clothes now soaked. He patted at the bench beside him. Aniol paused for a moment in uncertainty before sitting down beside Kaji with a shaky smile. Kaji beamed, Aniol's small gesture of trust worth the patience he had to suffer.

He reached into a cupboard situated behind him and returned with a small bath cloth. Reaching for a bottle, he poured some liquid onto it before reaching over to run the cloth over Aniol's shoulder and waited for a reaction. When Aniol remained silent, neither protesting nor flinching away, Kaji continued, running the cloth over Aniol's skin.

His breath began to deepen as he watched Aniol's eyes, captivated by their hue and the shifting shadows within them, captivated by the secrets they held. He licked his own lips, picking up Aniol's habit as he fought the urge to take an entirely different course of action. He lifted his little mate's long hair up, brushing the cloth over the young man's neck before moving it down his back. Aniol's eyes drifted closed, and Kaji had but a moment to regret the loss before they were replaced by something entirely different. Aniol turned in order to give Kaji better access to his back, his head falling forward, long hair pooling over his shoulders to drift lazily upon the water, giving Kaji a perfect view of his slim neck. Unable to resist, Kaji leaned forward and lapped at the juncture between Aniol's throat and neck. His mate gasped in surprise. Kaji continued his ministrations, the touch now more of a caress than an actual cleaning motion as he kissed the spot he'd lapped, sucking on it suddenly. He was inexplicably desperate to leave some kind of mark upon the pale flesh revealed to him.

Mark in place, Kaji released Aniol's skin, leaning back to once more resume his original task of cleaning Aniol's back. He watched Aniol's small frame move with each deep breath he took, proving that Aniol was just as affected by him as he was by Aniol.

Once done with Aniol's back, Kaji rinsed the cloth. He pulled, gently guiding the young man back to him. He stopped when he felt Aniol tense. "Tilt your head back," Kaji instructed softly. "I just want to wash your hair." Aniol relaxed and obeyed. Tugging Aniol back into his lap, Kaji immersed Aniol's hair in water. He brushed his fingers through the long pale strands now pooled in his lap, making sure all the hair was wet. He took a moment to enjoy the sensation before lifting Aniol up once more. He then proceeded to gently wash Aniol's hair, massaging the shampoo into his scalp. Aniol relaxed, letting his head fall back in pleasure, thus exposing himself further to Kaji.

Kaji struggled to control his breathing and arousal. The sight before him was positively erotic. He'd never imagined that taking a bath could be considered erotic, but it was oh so…. His fingers itched to do more than simply wash Aniol's hair, longed to wander over more of the slim body. A slim body he had yet to taste, to explore.

He resisted the urge, finishing with the long silver strands and tugging lightly at Aniol's shoulders, gently pulling the young man's head back into his lap to rinse the hair. He took great pleasure in the action, the strands touching his skin caressing him as he ran his fingers through the hair brought to life by the water.

Kaji took his time, lazily pulling his fingers through the silky strands, rinsing the soap out of it. He was fascinated by the lighter color revealed beneath the grime. It was only when Aniol gave a small gasp that he realized his fingers had wandered, moving to Aniol's chest. His bondmate's skin was as soft and smooth as the silky hair he'd been playing with a moment before. It was his fingers lightly brushing over a nipple that had caused the young man to hiss.

Kaji pulled back as if burnt, face turning bright red in embarrassment. He hadn't meant to do that. He sat Aniol up, hastily handing him the cloth he'd used earlier before standing. Water dripped off of his soaked clothes. Kaji gruffly cleared his throat, lust, embarrassment, concern, and self-incrimination coursing through him. "I'll let you finish," he said, speaking so fast that the words were almost garbled. Then he waded through the water as fast as his legs would carry him before jumping out of the bath and exiting the bathroom to deal with his wet clothes and one "other" pressing problem.

Aniol clutched the cloth, his ragged clothes forgotten and lost unnoticed sometime earlier. He stared after Kaji in confusion, having no clue what had happened.

# PROMISE

Bonding. No greater promise can be made between two people than that of bonding. Left to right, blood to blood, sealed within a circle. It is a tradition passed down since the dawn of time. Left and right signify opposites, and blood signifies balance and unity. A circle binds it all together, for infinity. There is no beginning and no end.

Balance is a fragile equality between opposing elements, each fighting against yet at the same time supporting the other in an age-old dance for dominance. It is a battle in which neither side is allowed to conquer the other, for from lack of balance chaos is borne.

ANIOL stared at Kaji, stumbling after the redhead as he was once more dragged around. He'd finished his bath and dressed in the emerald green robe, figuratively drowning in them. The garment was far too large for his slim build. Kaji had stared at him for a moment as he exited the bathroom before grabbing him by the wrist and leading him out of the room without so much as a word. They were now walking through what appeared to be a market, stalls lining the sides of the rather crowded streets. It was noisy and made Aniol nervous, bringing him to the borders of panic. He had to clench his teeth in order to keep from calling out.

He didn't understand Kaji. There were times when he could see the frustration and aggression radiating off of him, yet Kaji had not struck him, had yet to do anything more aggressive than completely possess his mouth. The thought brought a flush to Aniol's skin, embarrassment and other remembered emotions tinting his skin a pale pink.

Aniol didn't understand why Kaji continued to touch him. If Kaji was not playing with his hair or pulling him into his lap, he was curling up beside Aniol and dropping random kisses upon his skin. He did not know why Kaji would "want" to touch him let alone do so gently and with such care. Didn't Kaji know Aniol was tainted? A frown marred Aniol's forehead at the thought, apprehension filling his gut as he already anticipated and dreaded the moment Kaji found out and withdrew from him in disgust.

Aniol's frown was intercepted by a finger pressing into his forehead. "Don't do that," Kaji stated softly, poking him. "It mars your pretty face. You should be smiling, not frowning." Aniol blinked up at Kaji.

Kaji smiled and shook his head at the look on Aniol's face. It was a baffled look he was growing accustomed to seeing and a look he intended to keep there for a while; at least if Aniol was baffled he wasn't frowning or panicking. He fully intended to replace that confused look with a smile, but for now he would take what he could get and be grateful for it. He pointed at a small grey building. "We're here," he stated simply before guiding Aniol inside.

Aniol followed Kaji in silence, absently wondering where "here" was and why they'd come in the first place. He paused, momentarily surprised by the contents of the small building. Metalwork of all sorts lined various shelves, works ranging from weapons to decorative pieces and even to jewelry, all of which fascinated Aniol as he'd never seen anything of the sort. His mouth formed a small O as he opened it in wonder, eagerly taking everything in.

Kaji watched Aniol in fascination, the young man's wonder bringing a smile to his face. He reached forward and lightly tapped Aniol's jaw, teasing him about his open mouth before turning to the shopkeeper and speaking in a soft tone so that Aniol couldn't hear. He reached over the counter and retrieved a red velvet bag before turning and taking Aniol by the wrist once more. "Come on," he said, guiding Aniol around the counter and into the back, lifting Aniol and seating him on a workbench he found there.

A rather jovial plump old man approached them, his carrot-colored hair lined with grey. He smiled at Kaji, his eyes wrinkling at the corners. "So this is the little mate I've heard so much about," he said in greeting, tapping Kaji on the shoulder before turning to Aniol. "You are quite right, he is rather enchanting," Mika said, grinning as Aniol's eyes widened and shifted to Kaji before dropping to the ground, his cheeks tinted a faint pink.

Mika clapped his hands together. "Let me see what I can do." He reached out to Aniol. Aniol tensed in fear and moved away as large hands approached his throat, leaning back and nearly falling off of the workbench in the process. Mika halted his motion, looking to Kaji for assistance.

Kaji didn't notice Mika's look; he was too busy looking at Aniol in concern. He approached his little mate and placed a finger below his chin, turning his head and forcing Aniol to look at him. "Mika is not going to hurt you," he stated softly. "We want to remove that collar. It doesn't contain a clasp. I looked." He kept his finger beneath Aniol's chin, making sure he understood.

Aniol swallowed nervously before giving a small nod. Kaji released him but didn't step away as Mika reached forward once more. Aniol tensed as Mika's hands settled upon the collar, fiddling with the thin black band. It took all of his self control to remain in place, and he clenched his hands tightly in his lap, his hands turning a deathly white from the force of his grip.

Kaji took one of the hands, running his fingers soothingly over the wrist, over the mark he could feel through the bandage, the mark that bound them together. "And?" he inquired when Mika withdrew, feeling Aniol begin to relax now that Mika was no longer touching him. Kaji didn't know why, but the way Aniol seemed to trust him made him feel really warm and satisfied. He continued to play with Aniol's right hand and fingers now that Aniol had relaxed his grip.

"It has to be cut off," Mika stated, giving Kaji an apologetic look.

Kaji's brow furrowed in concern. Aniol looked terrified; his right hand now desperately clutched Kaji's left. Kaji's frown deepened when Aniol released his hand. Kaji watched as Aniol reached out toward him, hand trembling, only to blink in surprise at Aniol's next action.

Aniol swallowed nervously before poking at the frown on Kaji's brow. "You shouldn't do that. It mars your pretty face," he stated, quoting Kaji's earlier statement. Glancing at Mika, he nodded, accepting what they'd just been told. He knew they wanted what was best for him, and he knew Kaji wouldn't hurt him. He didn't know how he knew, but deep down inside his heart he knew. Only trust did not come easy to him.

Kaji stared at Aniol for a long moment, utterly shocked by Aniol's unexpected action. Reaching out, he grabbed Aniol's right hand with his left and nodded at Mika. Mika turned to pick up his tools and walked around the bench so that he stood behind Aniol. Aniol tensed, clenching his eyes tightly shut when Mika reached out to touch him. He dropped his head forward, knowing the gesture would make the work easier. Kaji reached out and brushed Aniol's long hair off the back of his neck and to the side, a part of him not wanting Mika or anyone else to touch what was his.

Once Mika was certain both were ready he began to work. Soon a clatter of metal falling to the ground broke the rather thick and tense silence that had descended upon the workshop. The collar fell to the ground, cut into two neat pieces. Mika dropped his tools and slipped out of the workroom, giving Kaji and Aniol some time alone together.

Kaji watched Aniol, watched his chest move along with deep, panicked breaths that he could tell Aniol was trying to hide from him. He reached out and tilted Aniol's face up, patiently waiting for the raging mist in Aniol's eyes to calm. He noticed Aniol's lip was swollen, chewed ragged in the young man's attempts to keep from losing control. He reached out, using a thumb to pull the lip out from beneath Aniol's teeth, tracing the lip lightly to soothe it. Kaji dropped his hand and reached for the red velvet bag he'd hooked onto his belt. He opened it, removing what it held before holding it out to Aniol, still remaining silent.

Aniol glanced down surprised to see what Kaji held. In his hands were two bracelets, the work intricate and beautiful. The bracelets were made of red-gold inset with a symbol that Aniol knew was meant to represent their bonding. In the center of each bracelet was a sun, made of the purest amber, partially eclipsed by a moon made of moonstone, representing a partial solar eclipse. Decorating the edges of each bracelet was a fine intricate design of interwoven yellow gold and silver in a fine balance. The bracelets were breathtaking in both their simplicity and splendor.

Aniol's breath hitched when Kaji placed them beside him, reaching for his right hand and undoing the bandage he still wore. Once done, Kaji dropped a soft kiss upon the healing wound and took up one of the bracelets, clipping it into place, the metal cool upon Aniol's heated skin, a contrast emphasizing the contrast of the sun and moon.

Kaji then pulled up his left sleeve and held out his wrist expectantly. When Aniol frowned in confusion, Kaji pointed at the second bracelet. Seeing the uncertainty on Aniol's face, Kaji reached out to place a finger upon his lips, stemming any protest before picking up the second bracelet and placing it into Aniol's hands, holding his left wrist out once more.

Aniol swallowed nervously, reaching out and positioning the bracelet before carefully and more than a little uncertainly clipping it closed, thus sealing the promise made the day they had bonded by blood.

Kaji beamed at him, reaching into a pocket and pulling out a small silver chain. A familiar teardrop pendant dangled off of it. "The chain was broken," he explained hastily. "I had it fixed." He reached over and fastened it around Aniol's neck.

Aniol touched the pendant in relief. He was shamed that he hadn't even noticed its disappearance but was extremely relieved to have it back, seeing it was the only possession he owned, the value of it entirely sentimental as he had no idea as to its true worth. "Thank you," he stated softly.

ANIOL stumbled again, breath hitching when someone jostled him. They were once more in the crowd, pushing their way through the people heading toward another unknown destination when Kaji paused, something catching his eye. He walked to the side, pulling Aniol along behind him before stopping beside a fruit stall. "Wait here a moment," Kaji ordered, disappearing into the crowd before Aniol even had a chance to respond.

Aniol reached out in panic, his face falling in dejection when Kaji disappeared. His entire frame shrank in on itself, and he dropped his gaze, backing into the shadows, away from the crowd. He stood there shivering, rubbing his hands along his arms, trying to rid himself of the goose bumps scattered over his skin. It was this withdrawal that was to be his downfall; a large hand covered his mouth while he was still distracted and dragged him into the shadows of the alleyway beside which he stood. Aniol didn't have the opportunity to cry out, and the crowd did not even notice the disappearance of one small boy.

Meanwhile Kaji stood beside a stall covered in fine, pale blue-white silk, a rare material found only in the distant mountains of Duiem. He fingered the material, smiling as he considered the design he wanted made from it, a design that would suit his little mate perfectly and would serve as his bonding gift to Aniol. He didn't want Aniol to see the material just yet, wanting to surprise him. He wanted to see Aniol's awe when he saw the gift, when he saw the way light played over the material, bringing out shades of silver, deep blue, and purple, the material seeming to have a life and mystery of its own.

Kaji jerked at a cold touch upon his shoulder, turning rapidly, a dagger hidden at his side already half drawn as instinct took over. He blinked in surprise when his gaze was met by eyes of deep purple. Standing before him was a lean, lithe boy, hair the exact same shade as Aniol's, dressed in ragged torn street clothes, feet bare. He pointed to the right, to the stall he had left Aniol beside, Kaji's gaze automatically following. "Someone has taken your mate." The boy's voice was soft, lilting, and musical, and he was gone before Kaji's gaze managed to return to him.

# BLOOD

The betrayal of the Gatekeepers did not go unnoticed, outrage running rampant among the people when the Gatekeepers were killed. Blessed yet cursed as keepers of secrets, a tribe of seers and prophets banded together, seeking retribution for the grave sin that had been committed by one from their own land. They sought to right the terrible wrong and hoped to help the Land of Gold atone for the sin it had committed against the Land of Silver.

Only... how do you bring the dead to life? Impossible... and so their protest could only be a vocal one. The people of the tribe cried out in grief and mourning and begged the king to take the life of the one who had started it all as atonement. The plea, however, fell upon deaf ears. The deceiver's lies had already clouded the king's heart, his lust for power corrupting his soul.

Rage consumed the tribe, anger at being left unheard, their warnings unheeded. This rage tainted them, drove them beyond reason, and forced them into action never before taken by the peaceful people. The rage drove them to the blade, propelled them to heated battle... pushed them to war. Joined by others similarly outraged, they attacked the kingdom and those responsible for the death of the Gatekeepers, attacked people they were once a part of and started the largest internal conflict in recorded history.

And so began the reign of blood.

ANIOL struggled with his captor. He twisted, uncaring of whether he hurt himself, fear and the desperate need to escape the only thoughts in his mind. Yet all his efforts came to nothing. The attacker was too strong and his grip too firm as he dragged Aniol farther into shadow and farther away from the crowd and the safety it suddenly represented. Moments earlier, that same crowd had threatened Aniol, the sheer mass of people overwhelming his senses, making him wish to be out of it, yet now he wished for nothing more than to be back in it, safely hidden from his attacker among the crowd of anonymous faces.

Aniol gasped when he was slammed against a wall, disbelief coursing through him as his terrified gaze was met with a very familiar face. It was his captor. Aniol's breathing quickened as he desperately tried to fight panic and the urge to pass out.

The man was livid, an angry scar now marring his right cheek. "And so the prodigal slave returns," he spat, a vein throbbing in his temple. "Nice to have you back, my sweet." He slammed the slim figure into the wall once more, using the action as emphasis. "Do you have any idea what you've already cost me?" He slapped Aniol. He reeked of alcohol, eyes glazed and red-rimmed with more than just rage. "Thief! Thief, whore, and bastard slave! I'll make you pay!" He pulled Aniol forward and slammed him even more violently into the wall, causing Aniol's head to snap and bounce off the hard bricks. His captor raised his arm to strike him once more.

Aniol whimpered, raising his right arm in defense. A stray beam of light reflected off the bracelet he wore, the symbol upon it clearly visibly for a moment, shining from within, almost as if the sun emblem made of amber had come to life. He closed his eyes, waiting for a blow that never landed. Aniol suddenly found himself free his captor's grip.

A blur of movement came from the top of the buildings to Aniol's right, and his captor was violently pulled off of him; there was a flash of silver, and then the situation was reversed. Aniol's captor found himself against the wall, staring into cold, hard, chocolate brown eyes. A sandy-haired stranger held a blade to his gut.

Aniol opened his eyes in time to see the stranger give Aniol's captor a rather cold smile, the kind of smile that sent shivers down your back. "That young man is not yours," he said in a tone that could almost be considered conversational if not for the cold threat it contained. "Did you not see the bonding circle upon his wrist? Did you not see the royal insignia upon that bonding circle?" The stranger watched as the Aniol's captor's eyes widened in realization. "What you have done can be considered treason against the crown," the stranger continued smoothly, his grin growing colder when Aniol's captor began to sweat. "And considering we are at war, I guess you know what the price of treason is, right?" He spoke the words cheerfully, too cheerfully for in his next motion; he buried his blade in the man's gut, smiling coldly as the warmth of the man's lifeblood ran over his hands.

That was when Aniol's captor overcame his initial shock, beginning to struggle. However, it was futile. The sandy-haired stranger was far stronger than he, holding him in place, unfazed by his struggles, the movement only serving to push the blade deeper. He held the man there, watching, waiting until the man's struggles ceased and the light faded from his eyes before withdrawing the blade and stepping back, casually wiping the blade clean with a handkerchief which he then proceeded to use to wipe the excess blood off his hands.

He turned to meet Aniol's horrified gaze, his smile softening and actually gaining some life, losing the cold edge it had when he was dealing with Aniol's captor. He inclined his head. "I'm Rogue. Pleased to meet you, mate of Kaji." He pointed at the bracelet. "I heard you were quite the mystery." He sent Aniol's dead captor a disgusted glance. "Come, let's get you back to Kaji. I'm sure he's rather frantic by now." Rogue turned to walk out of the alley, not offering Aniol his hand as he sensed the young man would be wary of the blood still upon it. He paused when Aniol did not follow. "Well? What are you waiting for?"

KAJI was indeed frantic, pushing his way through the crowd, blade drawn, desperately searching for pale blue-silver hair among the crowd of dark and red. He'd prefer to find hair that belonged to Aniol, but if he could find the young man who had warned him, maybe he'd be able to get enough information to actually find his mate. He stumbled when he reached the edge of the crowd, searching the darkness of yet another empty alley, anger and despondency rising.

He blamed himself entirely for this. It was he who had left Aniol alone, thus abandoning his mate and exposing him to possible danger. He raged against himself for it and desperately hoped that Aniol would live long enough for him to atone for his grave mistake. The sound of a pebble hitting the ground startled him, and he whirled, eagerly seeking only to find nothing. Unable to bear the panic any longer, he ran out, heading for the next possible empty alley, fearing that at any moment he would find a pale, still, battered form, or worse… nothing.

Kaji leaped back when he saw a flash of silver sail toward him, the dagger landing pined in the ground between his feet. "Reactions still as sharp as ever, I see." A dry voice drew his attention up.

Kaji's eyes shot up to meet familiar deep chocolate brown framed by sandy hair. "I don't have time for this, Rogue."

Rogue ignored him, throwing a dagger to the right when Kaji attempted to leave, effectively blocking Kaji's progress. "What? No time to greet an old friend? My, you have grown cold. Maybe you should've bonded to me after all."

"Rogue!" Kaji protested, dead panicked now. "I really don't have time for this! Someone's taken my mate. For all I know he could be dead."

Rogue smiled at Kaji. "Already lost him?" he asked, shaking his head. "My, my, you never were really good at keeping an eye on what's yours. Remember the time you lost that dagger." He pointed to the dagger Kaji currently clutched.

"*Rogue!*" Kaji pleaded in desperation. "Please… don't…."

The smile faded from Rogue's face, and he jumped down, landing softly. "Calm down. He's right over there." He pointed to where Aniol stood, arms wrapped around himself as he watched the confrontation between Rogue and Kaji.

"You bastard!" Kaji yelled. Dropping his blade, he punched Rogue in the stomach, Rogue doubling over from the sheer force of the blow. Not even giving Rogue a chance to react, Kaji turned and rushed over to Aniol, gathering the young man close and holding him. He buried Aniol's face against his shoulder, trying to soothe the terror he could feel radiating off of him. "Where did you find him?" he asked Rogue softly, once he was sure he could speak without losing control of himself.

Rogue winced, rubbing his stomach as he bent down to pick up Kaji's fallen blade. He absently reminded himself to remember Kaji had a mean left hook before teasing him in the future. "In an alleyway farther down. Some man was claiming it was nice to have him back. Was passing by when I noticed the bracelet." He gestured to the bracelet on Aniol's right wrist. "I recognized your symbol. Figured you wouldn't approve of having your mate beaten. Rather smart design by the way, having the sun done in amber. Sometime you'll have to explain the reason for the moon to me, though."

Kaji nodded, running a hand down Aniol's back. "You figured right." His tone was deadly cold as he asked, "Where is he?"

"Dead." Rogue knew Kaji well enough to realize, without having to ask, that Kaji was referring to Aniol's captor.

"Good." Kaji nodded in satisfaction. "I'll take care of the legal matters."

"Don't worry about it. I suggest you direct the excess energy toward looking after what's yours first." Rogue didn't even flinch when Kaji sent him a heated glare. Rogue knew Kaji was well aware of the point he was making.

Kaji nodded in acceptance of the reprimand he'd been given. "Thank you." He closed his eyes, taking a moment to bury his face into Aniol's hair, savoring the scent and the fact that he was still alive and well before glancing up at Rogue once more. "I missed you. I was starting to get worried."

Rogue grinned. "I'm not all that easy to get rid of. I'll continue to haunt you for years to come," he threatened playfully.

"You'd better," Kaji retorted. "Meet me tonight, the usual place. I need to talk to you." He relaxed when Rogue nodded, not realizing he'd tensed as he had awaited response. "Thank you." He picked his mate up and headed back into the crowd.

Rogue watched him leave, shaking his head in surprise, a small smile upon his lips. He didn't recall Kaji being that sentimental. In fact, the last time he'd seen him, Kaji had been vehemently fighting against having a mate, angry that he had to be bonded and "trapped into lifelong torment," as he so called it. It seemed as if the lifelong torment was treating Kaji well. Rogue chuckled lightly before slipping back into the shadows, already planning on teasing Kaji about it when they met later that night.

# Gatekeeper

Visions are strange entities with lives of their own. Their interpretation is, more often than not, left open to debate, their true meaning discovered only after the event which they are heralding has occurred. Predictions are the future foreseen, an unstable form of visions. The truth of a prediction can be changed in an instant, by a single action that ripples through the fabric of time.

Consequently, visions of the future simply contain possibilities, thousands upon thousands of threads influenced by differing circumstances, all of which will lead to specific outcomes. Action and consequence are predicted. If only the action chosen could be as easily predicted.

Sometimes a pattern emerges among the visions, a pattern that demonstrates the likelihood of a particular outcome over several others, a pattern that merges several threads, all of which ultimately lead to the same future. Destiny, one might call it. So it was with the visions predicting the Gatekeepers' end.

Since the Gatekeepers' end was foreseen, why is it that no one interfered, one might ask? The reason is because many paths lead to the same end. How is one to choose the right path to influence? How does one create the desired impact without risking further disaster? All it takes is a single mistake, one wrong move to alter time itself and to accidentally bring about that which one seeks to prevent, to bring it about sooner with more violence and with more death.

At least without interference, there was some hope that the Gatekeepers would survive. So all anyone could do was watch and wait for the chosen future to reveal itself.

KAJI was once again surrounded by white. This time however, he could see traces of blue and purple swirls coloring the marble room he found himself in. Velvet hangings of a dark blue hung upon the wall, displaying an insignia he'd never seen before. He could see the night sky and a full moon surrounded by tiny pinpoints of white stars. Kaji once again found himself in unfamiliar surroundings, confused, because this time there had been no bright flash of white light. This time the transition had been far more subtle. Black faded into the white, which had then shifted to form shapes and color.

He turned, seeking, eyes traveling over the rather opulent surroundings, over the black lamps shaped into intricate forms emitting a pale light that shimmered amongst the shadows they created. The light illuminated sculptures and paintings. Depictions of moonlit scenes lined the walls between the hangings, and carved pillars held up a large ceiling with what appeared to be the entire night sky painted upon it. Finally, a deep blue carpet led to what was obviously a throne.

That was when he saw it, a flash of familiar silver blue hair, a slight figure pacing in the distance. Aniol! The sight of his little mate spurred Kaji into motion. He headed toward the young man in the distance only to have his footsteps falter. Something was not right, and it wasn't the strange vision he appeared to be having.

Kaji stopped a few steps away from the pacing figure watching him. Now that he really looked, it was more than apparent that it wasn't Aniol. The young man was too tall, too firmly built, and possessed of a lean, predatory strength. Kaji couldn't fathom why he'd even for a moment mistaken the young man for Aniol. The way he moved was entirely wrong, like the predator he represented, each move smooth and calculated. The posture he carried was one used to being obeyed. The figure turned, and Kaji gasped in shock.

The young man had grey-blue eyes the exact same shade as Aniol's, only they lacked the mist that lived within Aniol's, the mist that drifted through his little mate's eyes with a life of its own, reflecting every emotion he had. These eyes were hard, weary, and tired, strain apparent within them, yet they remained less tragic, less hurt than Aniol's misty counterparts.

The young man looked straight at Kaji, almost as if he could see him. A slight frown marred his features, the similarity to Aniol's frown sending a deep chill down Kaji's spine. He didn't have the right. This stranger didn't have the right to have any resemblance to Aniol. None whatsoever!

Deep-seated bitterness coursed through Kaji at the thought. There was something about this young man that bothered him. No matter how hard he tried, he couldn't shake the gut feeling that there had been some kind of injustice done to Aniol, an injustice this young man before him was somehow involved in.

He frowned when the man began to walk toward him, taking deliberate steps. He paused just before him, his frown deepening further as he continued to stare intently at where Kaji stood. Kaji was horrified when the young man reached out to him. Just before the young man's fingers made contact, the scene shattered, breaking apart like splintered glass.

Kaji jerked up in bed, panting heavily. He glanced out the window, realizing it was really late—or early, depending on how one looked at it. Earlier that evening he'd been seated on the bed, waiting for Rogue, Aniol seated beside him. He'd glanced at Aniol's face, seeing the lifeless look upon it, and it had scared him. Aniol had looked hollow and empty, and the look had hurt Kaji to the core because he knew Aniol's experience earlier had been the cause of it. Not knowing what to say, he'd pulled the small young man into his arms and lain upon the bed, hoping Aniol would fall asleep. Only… it seemed he, too, had fallen asleep.

Kaji turned to stare at Aniol, the mist in his mate's eyes raging, coloring them a murky white, fading with each deep breath the young man took. Aniol was half sprawled over Kaji's lap, seated between his knees, a supporting hand laid upon his chest. It appeared that he'd still had Aniol in his arms when he'd woken, violently jerking up and probably waking Aniol as well. Which, if the pale tense look upon Aniol's face was anything to go by, was a good thing. It would appear that the vision, for Kaji was now certain that was what it was, had disturbed Aniol as much as it had disturbed him.

Kaji watched Aniol carefully, mind racing, trying to deal with the visions, Aniol, and their implications. Just who exactly was Aniol? Or more specifically, *what* was he? Kaji only realized he'd spoken the questions aloud when Aniol flinched, body tense, his skin, impossibly, by Kaji's reckoning, paling even further.

Kaji pulled back when Aniol shoved the hand he'd been resting on Kaji's chest forward, pushing Kaji away, with the same motion sliding himself back from Kaji. The action was hurried and carried him all the way to the edge of the bed. Aniol stared at Kaji with wide eyes. Tension in the room was thick, the only audible sound that of Aniol's deep, panicked breaths.

Kaji watched in silence, reprimanding himself and his half-awake state for voicing a question that obviously should've been kept to himself. But what was done could not be undone, so Kaji remained silent, watching Aniol, waiting for him to choose his course of action.

Aniol watched Kaji just as intently as Kaji watched him, fighting to bring his breathing back under control. Kaji's question had shocked him to the core. He didn't know why, seeing as he'd been expecting it. Only he desperately wished it had been asked later, much, much later. Aniol dropped his gaze, deep guilt within his heart making it difficult to meet Kaji's any longer. He felt as if he'd somehow deceived Kaji even though no lie had passed his lips. Yet wasn't he lying by omission?

Aniol played with the bonding bracelet upon his right wrist, using a finger to lightly trace the design upon it. The sun and… moon. A symbol that was meant to be only for the two of them… a promise to cherish and protect.

Aniol swallowed past a large lump in the back of his throat, trying to gather the courage to speak. "I'm a Seer," he whispered, his voice hoarse, biting his lip and using a sleeve of the white pajama he wore to wipe his eyes, desperately trying to fight the tears he could feel welling in the corners of them. He didn't want to cry, didn't want Kaji to see him cry, but was losing the battle miserably.

Kaji frowned in confusion. Aniol's declaration made sense, yet didn't. He shook his head. It wasn't quite right. Yes, he saw that Aniol believed he was a seer, but somehow Kaji couldn't believe it. Too many things, things he knew about seers, did not add up. "No, you're not," he stated with certainty. He had absolutely no idea why he was so sure, but he just knew that Aniol wasn't a Seer. "Seers have white eyes."

Aniol looked up at Kaji, still wiping away stray tears that simply refused to remain unshed. He stared at Kaji for a moment before speaking, his lip trembling, causing his voice to waver. "I was told I have a stain of white in my eyes," he whispered. "The taint of a demon, but even as a demon, there's something wrong with me." Aniol paused to take a deep breath and nip at his own lips before continuing to speak. "My visions of the future don't make any sense. They never come true."

Kaji shook his head once more. "I don't know what you are, but I do know this: you are not a Seer," Kaji said with unwavering certainty. "You do have white in your eyes, but it's not pure white; it resembles mist that dulls the bright, contrasting colors in your eyes as it moves, but they are not completely white. They are distinctly a mixture of blue and grey. Furthermore, Seers are completely blind, and as for the visions...." Kaji paused, uncertain as how to continue, he himself not knowing the nature of the visions he'd seen through Aniol. "I don't know what they are," he admitted, "but they appear to be from another place. My throne room is not decorated in shades of blue, and no part of Duiem that I know of uses an insignia that represents the night sky, stars, and moon."

Kaji frowned, something nagging him from the back of his mind, a bedtime story, a legend he'd heard long ago. "And the only place I've heard such an insignia mentioned," he continued slowly, frowning in concentration, "is in a bedtime story my mother used to tell me before she died. It was a really old story, a legend." Kaji's frown deepened as he retrieved memories long ago forgotten, hidden in the depths of his mind. "It was one of the legends about... the... Gate...keepers," he finished slowly on a hoarse whisper. He stared at Aniol in shock, going as pale as Aniol, the implication of his words suddenly hitting him like a ton of bricks, leaving him breathless.

"Gatekeeper," Kaji whispered again in realization. Aniol was a Gatekeeper. He suited the description perfectly. Visions of another place, eyes alive with pale mist, the intense fever during the first vision Kaji had experienced, the miraculous healing, the slim, almost magical appearance, the color of his hair, his eyes; everything, all of it suddenly made sense. But Kaji was finding it difficult to believe, even in the face of all the overwhelming evidence, for Gatekeepers were only a legend, a story, and even if they had existed, they were all dead.

# REVELATION

Often what appears to be is not what is at all. Often what we think we know is but an illusion, hiding all that we do not. Prophecy is not as set in stone as one might think. As with all things, there is room for error and room for change, which is why a prophecy is never fully revealed to those it impacts.

The return of the Gatekeepers is hoped for, longed for. For with that will come the return of harmony, yet... only if the right choices are made, the right actions taken. Choices and actions which should not be influenced, as one should never interfere with free will.

"WELL, this is an interesting development." Rogue slipped into the room via the window, stepping lightly onto the carpeted floor. His gaze was sharply focused upon Aniol. Inside, he was kicking himself. He should've realized sooner, should've known Aniol could be nothing but a Gatekeeper, the mist in his eyes all but advertising the fact to anyone who bothered to look closer and take note of it. Unfortunately, Gatekeepers had been dead for so long that few still believed they had ever existed, and all the details, such as the mist within a Gatekeeper's gaze, had been lost along the way. Only a chosen few were privy to the knowledge. Rogue and Kaji were among them.

Aniol returned Rogue's stare, disconcerted by the intensity with which he was being scrutinized by both Kaji and Rogue. Kaji was staring at him in disbelief, and Rogue appeared to be trying to memorize every hair upon his head. He slumped, trying to make himself as small as possible. Confusion and anxiety ran through him. He had absolutely no idea what Kaji was going on about. He had no idea what a Gatekeeper was and why it would make Kaji and Rogue look at him in such a manner. Frankly, if the looks were anything to go by, he didn't really want to know.

Finally Rogue broke his own stare, glancing at Kaji. "Are you his Warden?" he asked bluntly.

The question shook Kaji out of his stupor, and he turned to Rogue in surprise. "Of course not! I didn't even know he was a Gatekeeper until a moment ago!"

Rogue nodded. "Fine. Then you have a new bodyguard, or at least he"—he inclined his head at Aniol—"does. No arguments. We can't have the only Gatekeeper to appear in centuries killed because of some suspicious idiot running around with a cause, and until he finds his Warden, he's going to need protection. Come to think of it, if history is to be believed, he might even need protection 'from' his Warden. I pray it's not the case, for if history repeats itself, we have no hope of ever restoring the balance that was lost."

"Hold on a minute!" Kaji protested. "Do you mean to say the legends actually contain some truth?"

Rogue raised an eyebrow at Kaji, without words clearly asking, *Who the hell do you think you're kidding?* "You're bonded to a Gatekeeper and still have doubt?"

"I've seen nothing to prove that he's a Gatekeeper!" Kaji protested. "Just because he has the right coloring, the right eyes, and sees visions of another world doesn't mean he can actually open the gate to it!"

"Visions of another world?" Rogue inquired carefully.

"Yes," Kaji retorted. "Visions of another world. There was an insignia on deep blue cloth: moon and stars." Rogue glanced at Aniol's bonding bracelet.

Aniol watched the scene in shock. He suddenly realized why Kaji had made reference to the insignia in the room he'd dreamed about that night. Kaji had somehow seen what he had, seen the vision, the room, the throne, the wall hangings, and… the young man.

"You saw this insignia?" Rogue asked carefully, glancing at Aniol and noting the shock on his face. There was no longer any doubt: Aniol *was* a Gatekeeper, and Kaji…. Rogue shook his head, overwhelmed by everything that was being revealed. He turned back to Kaji, waiting for a response.

"Yes, I did." Kaji declared. "There were hangings inside what could only be a great marble throne room. They looked like our hangings except that they were deep blue and silver instead of red and gold, and imprinted upon them was an image of the moon and stars, as I've said, instead of the sun." Kaji said no more, not mentioning the young man in the throne room. He didn't know why, but it seemed wrong to mention him and his resemblance to Aniol.

Rogue nodded. "So why did you want to see me?" he asked, deliberately changing the subject. He watched Aniol out of the corner of his eye.

Kaji, for his part hadn't noticed the shock upon Aniol's face, trying to give himself time to deal with the enormity of the revelations that had just been made. "I want some information."

Rogue nodded. "Sure. You know the drill."

"The usual fee?" Kaji inquired.

"Depends on the information you require," Rogue responded.

"I want to know what Karl has been up to." When Rogue raised his eyebrows in question, Kaji continued. "I found a document stating that he wants to deploy a greater part of our arms to fight the Saikin. Apparently the drought has reached a crisis, and he wants to take over the land to get to their water. I think there's more to it than that."

Rogue's face remained emotionless. None of this news to him. He'd known about this for a while already. "Information on Karl will be expensive," he stated flatly. "What do you want the information for?"

Kaji met Rogue's gaze with his own. "I'm sick of war, Rogue. Both the ancient one with the Ruel and the new one with the Saikin." His features hardened in anger. "To make matters worse I knew nothing about the Saikin war until a few days ago. I despise being used. It's pointless to keep killing our people when there are few enough of us already. Why must we keep fighting our own, shedding our own blood, wounding this country even further?"

Rogue watched Kaji for a moment. "Your lack of knowledge and

Karl's actions are your own fault," he pointed out. "All these years you let him do as he pleased without question."

Kaji pursed his lips, checking his anger. It wasn't directed at Rogue; it was directed at himself. "I realize that, Rogue," he admitted. "I should've paid more attention to what Karl was doing with the power my father granted him, but you have to admit, there was nothing I could have done until my coming of age, which wasn't all that long ago."

Rogue nodded in agreement, once more glancing at Aniol. The young man appeared to have calmed down and leaned against the headboard, a pillow in his arms as he watched their conversation in silence. There were hidden depths to that boy, Rogue realized. Hidden depths and a sharp mind, if the look in Aniol's eyes was anything to go by. He turned back to Kaji. "At least you might have been prepared. Tell you what. You bring peace, and I'll waive the fee. I'll return tomorrow with what information I have. Tonight, talk to your Gatekeeper. Tomorrow morning, I suggest you go to the library and find a small brown book, unlabeled, situated in the right block, third shelf from the top, second book from the edge. You might also want to start packing." With that, Rogue was gone, the faint movement of the curtain at the window the only sign that he'd ever been there.

Kaji turned to Aniol, watching the young man closely. Aniol was clutching a pillow, and surprisingly, he spoke first. "Are you going to leave me?" he asked softly.

Kaji's gaped, truly shocked at the question. "Leave you? Of course not. Why would I do that?"

"Because I am tainted," Aniol stated simply. He was unnaturally calm.

Kaji scowled, suddenly angry. He was angry at the person who had told Aniol such a blatant lie and angry at Aniol for accepting it. "You are not tainted!" Kaji said, perhaps a little too forcefully as his anger overcame his common sense.

Aniol didn't even flinch, the anger a more recognizable emotion to him. It was a reaction that made more sense than the acceptance Kaji had been showing thus far. "You were supposed to bond with someone else," he said.

"Saya?" Kaji inquired. "I already told you. I didn't know her either, and I happen to know she's love with someone else."

"Then why would you bond with her?" Aniol asked, confused by the concept. He knew he was naïve about the ways of the world, having been exposed to so little of them, but the impression he'd gotten was that bonds were treasured and mates were meant to care for one another.

"Prophecy," Kaji explained. "The land is dying. We have seen little rain over the past number of centuries, and it's believed that it's a punishment for killing all the Gatekeepers." Kaji gave Aniol a pointed look. Aniol ignored it, not wanting to ask what a Gatekeeper was, still not sure if he wanted to know. "It's said that if Duiem atones for the sin committed by the Wardens so long ago, balance will return to the lands of silver and gold. No one knows quite how this atonement is supposed to be accomplished, but one thing they do know is that there's a prophecy that guides the way."

Kaji paused, grabbed his own pillow, and dumped it into his lap. "Not much of the prophecy is revealed. All that's known is that the first step toward fulfilling it is to bond sun and moon together. Sun refers to people from Duiem and moon refers to people from the Land of Silver, I guess. I never really believed this land existed not until...." Kaji let the rest of the sentence hang before continuing. "Anyway, this prophecy is solely for the royal family of Duiem, and even then, it's only for the eldest son, the one that will inherit the throne. Each generation, the person required to fulfill the prophecy changes, and so with each firstborn son, a new prophecy is given. It provides a clue that is meant to help the person find the one they are meant to bond with. If the heir finds the person they are destined to bond with, he has a better chance of fulfilling the original prophecy. One thing remains constant, though: the person that's bonded must have what is known as the blood of the moon running through their veins. The way to recognize someone like that is by their hair or eyes: pale grey, silver, blue, or purple hair, or eyes of the same colors."

Kaji remained silent for a moment, allowing his words to sink in. "My prophecy, revealed upon my birth, stated that I should bond to one from the Kiyou clan. Saya is the only person that fit the criteria, the only one in the clan with eyes that reveal inheritance from the moon. Violet. Neither she nor I wanted the bonding, but in order to save our people, we were both willing to do it. She's the daughter of the head of our religion.

She'll find a good mate. In some circles, she has higher standing than I."

"So I ruined your chances of fulfilling the prophecy," Aniol stated, horrified.

Kaji shook his head. "Perhaps, perhaps not. The prophecy that predicts the partner I should've bonded to predicts the *most likely* manner in which to fulfill the original prophecy, not the *only* manner. Everything happens for a reason, and neither you nor I had any control over the events that occurred on the day of our bonding. Perhaps, and I hate to say it, having never been much of a believer before now"—Kaji pulled a face—"perhaps there's a greater purpose in play here."

# PLAY ME FOR A FOOL

The art of deception is both intricate and deadly. In order to be successful, the deceiver needs to be able to twist perception and encourage trust. So it is that the mere existence of trust does not ensure that things are well.

The relationship between Gatekeepers and their Wardens was a fragile balance of trust, a fragile balance that was tipped by deception. The Gatekeepers blindly trusted their protectors, never questioning the wisdom of that trust. They believed unfailingly that their Wardens would not, *could* not betray them. Gatekeepers and Wardens had been partners for centuries, their bond tried and tested by time itself.

Yet times change. Men's hearts change, and that which tempts them bides it time, becoming more powerful as hearts weaken. And so one becomes blinded by the very trust that is meant to strengthen, foolishly forgetting to test and establish a trust that is true. Such foolishness can get one killed. It is such foolishness that killed the Gatekeepers.

DUST was thick in the air, filling the area with the musty scent of a room long forgotten and abandoned. A tall figure slipped into the darkness. The lamp he held illuminated an old library, chasing away the shadows that had consumed it moments earlier. The light, however, couldn't chase away the years of neglect or the marks lack of care had left within the room.

Kaji glanced to the right, counting in his head before reaching out to pull down a tiny book from one of the bookshelves lining the walls, its brown cover ragged, the binding unmarked. If he hadn't known it was there, he would've missed it, as the book was slim and plain, hidden among huge elaborate volumes and covered with dust. The old library had been sealed a long time ago and a decree had been issued forbidding anyone entry for reasons unknown. Kaji suspected the reason was hidden within the small, rather inconsequential-looking volume he held.

He slipped back out of the abandoned library, heading toward the room he was supposed to perform most of his duties in. The room, even though used on a regular basis, was as abandoned as the library, its original purpose long neglected, shadowed by lies and deceit. Kaji sat down at his desk, brushing the dust off of the small book he held before opening it. He frowned at the words that met his gaze. It contained the prophecy that spoke of Duiem's betrayal and the need for atonement. Kaji eagerly leafed through the book, hoping desperately it would reveal more, telling him how he could fulfill the prophecy even though he hadn't bonded with his destined mate. He was disappointed. The book held but the barest reference to the original prophecy before shifting focus to the prophecies that had been given to each firstborn son in the Taiyouko family.

Kaji frowned in confusion. Why did Rogue want him to read this? He knew his own prophecy, knew it was doomed as he'd been accidentally bonded to Aniol instead of Saya. Kaji paged rapidly through the book, looking for another section only to be disappointed. No, there wasn't more to the book. The book was simply a record of the prophecies given to each firstborn son of the royal family. Kaji was about to page back to the beginning so he could read the book in chronological order when something caught his eye. The last record, the one meant for him, read: "Conflagration: one of royal blood."

Kaji's breath escaped in a hiss. That couldn't be right. He was supposed to bond with one of the Kiyou clan. That was what he'd been told all his life. One from the noble clan that guides the country's faith. It was true that the Kiyou clan was highly regarded, in some circles even having a higher standing than that of royalty, but one thing was certain: one from the Kiyou clan was not one of royal blood. By law it was forbidden for anyone in the royal family to wed one from the family that governed the church. That restriction was set in place for good reason—so that order might be kept, so that matters of governance could be kept separate from matters of the faith. That law had been waived when Kaji received his prophecy so he might bond with one from the Kiyou clan.

Kaji's heart raced in fear and anger. Karl's deception was far greater than he'd anticipated, and he feared what Karl planned. A move to merge the royal line with that which led the faith couldn't be mere coincidence. As to his prophecy: one of royal blood? It seemed he was doomed to fail before he'd begun. Neither Saya nor Aniol fulfilled the true criteria of a prophecy that had been hidden from him. Kaji glanced up, for the first time in his life truly believing in another hand at work, for if he had bonded with Saya, he would've created the forbidden bond between faith and politics and the possible repercussions of that would be…. A chill ran down Kaji's spine, his mind dancing away from the thought in horror.

Kaji glanced back down at the slim volume before closing it with care. He opened a drawer and slipped it into a hidden compartment he'd discovered in his desk, a desk that had once belonged to his father. Sliding both the compartment and drawer closed, Kaji stood, turned, and walked out with purpose in his stride.

ANIOL woke to find himself alone. Panic coursed through him for a moment. Closing his eyes, he forced himself to take deep breaths in order to calm down. Kaji had said he wouldn't leave him, had taken him into his arms last night and soothed the panic Aniol had managed to hide beneath unnatural calm.

He'd been terrified of what Rogue and Kaji had said, terrified that Kaji was going to abandon him, but Kaji's reaction to the question had been rather vehement. Kaji didn't consider him to be tainted. Aniol still found that difficult to believe, but it was true. He'd seen the truth of it reflected in Kaji's eyes.

Aniol didn't want him to leave, didn't want to be alone. He'd been alone for all of his life, and now that he'd been shown affection, he hungered deeply for it. Thus it was that he slipped out of bed and padded out of the room in search of Kaji, his bare feet barely making a sound.

KAJI groaned, dropping his head into his arms, despondency heavy in his heart. He'd gone to see Karl, demanding that Karl allow him to see the various papers that were being handled by him and those under him, demanding that Karl let him run his kingdom. He had been rather surprised at Karl's lack of argument. Karl readily accepted his demands and told him he'd have the papers ready in an hour.

Kaji had been rather pleased with himself, convinced he'd taken a step in the right direction. He was certain things were going to pick up, that he would be able to start correcting his neglect. Then he'd walked into his office to find a desk piled high with papers, the pages overflowing onto the floor and filling half the room. Even worse, the papers had no order; they were random pages simply scattered about. It was so bad that pages belonging to the same document were not even together. It seemed that Karl knew him too well, Kaji realized.

Karl's approach was effectively killing two birds with one stone. Karl was keeping Kaji both distracted and placated by giving him the rather unmanageable load of paperwork, knowing Kaji didn't have the patience to go through and sort all of it, and he was right. The sheer load of paperwork was a daunting task that had Kaji both stressed and depressed, and he had slumped in his chair, head in his arms, desperately wondering how he was to tackle this.

"I am such a fool." Kaji stated forlornly. Despite the fact that he was momentarily lost in despair, he still managed to sense Aniol's presence the moment his mate arrived, looking up to meet Aniol's misty gaze. "Through my foolish neglect, I've given up control and now...." He ran his gaze over the paperwork. "Now I don't know how to take it back again." He faced Aniol one more, looking utterly dejected.

Aniol remained silent, not knowing what to say, not knowing how to comfort Kaji and desperately wishing he could. He padded into the room with his usual grace, bare feet silent upon the carpet. He paused beside the desk watching Kaji for a moment before picking up a page and handing it to Kaji silently, his meaning clear.

Kaji stared at the page before turning back to Aniol. He gave him a wry smile. "The documents are not sorted," he pointed out dejectedly. "In fact, entire pieces of documents appear to be missing." Kaji ran a tense hand through his red hair, frustration radiating off of him.

"Then sort," Aniol said softly. He knew it wasn't what Kaji *wanted* to hear. But it was what he *needed* to hear. Kaji was too honorable to just let this slide. Not doing what was right would bother the redhead more than the frustration of sorting the documents did. Kaji just needed a little push, a little support, and belief in his abilities.

"How?" Kaji inquired in frustration. "How do I sort all of this?" Kaji gestured at the room.

"One page at a time." A voice from the doorway caused both Aniol and Kaji to turn. Standing there was a man, sun reflecting off of his hair, giving it a bright yellow shine. Yuan stepped into the office, inclining his head at Aniol before bowing low to Kaji. He stood, watching Kaji. "If I may be blunt?"

Kaji rolled his eyes. "Cut the crap, Yuan. You've never needed my permission to be blunt before; why would you require it now?" he asked, Yuan's antics momentarily distracting him from his depression.

"True," Yuan retorted with a smile. "Mainly because you never really listen to what I say."

Kaji's eyes widened at that. He hadn't realized that Yuan knew he never really paid much attention when he spoke. Yuan tended to chatter, going off on tangents more often than not, and that bored Kaji out of his mind. Kaji nodded, for once in his life taking the hyperactive blond seriously. "All right, point to you." He waited for Yuan to speak.

Yuan pulled a face, all of a sudden not sure if he really wanted Kaji's undivided attention for what he wanted to say. "You got yourself into this," he stated, pointing to the papers in the room, then raising his hands defensively to forestall any protest from Kaji. "Through no fault of your own, true, but you trusted too much. You took too much for granted. You let too much slip from your hands and from your sight, and now that you have realized it, you need to rectify it."

"You knew," Kaji said, shocked. "Am I the only one that didn't know? Why didn't you tell me?" Bitterness coursed through him, leaving an ugly taste in his mouth.

Yuan watched Kaji for a moment before shaking his head. "No, I also didn't know, but since your bonding, there have been whispers in the palace. Whispers and rumors fueled by discontent and strife. People are restless, bitter that you didn't bond with your prophesied mate," he added hastily knowing Kaji would blame himself.

"It would've been worse if I had bonded with Saya," Kaji said, glancing at Aniol, his heart wrenching at the guilt he saw flicker over the young man's features. He wanted to rush over and comfort him but knew that Aniol didn't want him to know. So he pretended not to see.

Yuan raised his eyebrows in surprise. "Why?"

Kaji reached into the desk and pulled out the slim volume he'd been reading. He silently held it out to Yuan. "Read the last entry," he said when Yuan took the book.

Yuan paged through the book, reaching the last entry and reading it. Suddenly he was still, motionless, a state entirely unnatural for him. Yuan slowly raised his head.

"It would seem Karl's deception was far greater than I could've ever imagined possible," Kaji said bitterly. "One of royal blood, not one of the Kiyou clan."

Yuan went pale. "If you had bonded with her…."

"I would have broken taboo," Kaji finished the sentence, glancing at Aniol, reassuring himself that his little mate understood the impact of the words. He hoped it would soothe the guilt Aniol felt. Aniol looked confused, the mist in his eyes swirling as he contemplated the words. Kaji turned back toward Yuan, intending to speak to Aniol about it later, in private.

Yuan clutched the thin volume as his mind raced. He straightened, filled with strength and determination Kaji didn't realize he possessed. "Right," Yuan stated decisively, his tone cold and hard with anger. "Our plan of action is as follows: we take back the power that's been taken from you, by force if necessary." And for a moment, Yuan even managed to scare Kaji.

# HANDLE WITH CARE

The slaughter of the Gatekeepers led to the reign of blood, and with it chaos. The chaos grew, gaining momentum with each new incident, each new death until even nature itself joined in the fray. Waves of scorching heat swept through the Land of Gold, ravaging and laying to waste all that stood within its path. Rivers and lakes dried up, poisoned by the hatred that had infected its people. The land, once green with life, became dry, parched with thirst, and soaked red with blood. Chaos fueled more chaos, wound upon wound, over and over again—and bloodshed became a way of life.

KAJI sighed, rubbing his hands over his eyes in exhaustion. It had already been an overwhelmingly long day, and it didn't look like it was going to be over any time soon. He, Yuan, and Aniol had been busy sorting through the large stack of papers the entire day and had even taken their meals in Kaji's office. It was now horribly late, and Kaji was exhausted. He didn't recall ever doing so much work in one day. He felt as if he'd done more reading in this single day than he had in his entire life.

He and Yuan had had many heated debates over some of the documents, scrutinizing the contents as they sorted. Reading all these documents out of order was confusing, but they appeared to be making progress, and Kaji was beginning to get an idea as to what was happening. Karl ruled with an iron fist. Several pleas for assistance had been denied, and small villages had been destroyed, their inhabitants either killed or imprisoned for what was recorded to be rebellion. Kaji suspected the rebellion had never happened. Furthermore, the prices of trading and goods had been increased, and taxes had been raised. He was surprised he hadn't been assassinated by his own people yet.

Kaji clutched the bridge of his nose with two fingers, trying to fight the headache he could feel pounding deep in his skull. It was a slow dull thud that intensified as he breathed. He clenched his eyes shut when a particularly acute wave of pain coursed through him, his breath hitching before growing shallow as he tried to control the pain and nausea that went along with it.

"Are you all right?" Yuan inquired softly, his soft words drawing Aniol's attention. Aniol was seated in a corner of the room, surrounded by neat piles of paper. Yuan stood beside Kaji's desk clutching a few pages which he'd been in the process of scrutinizing before noticing the pain upon Kaji's face.

Kaji pulled a face, glancing at Aniol who remained silent, simply sitting and watching him, concern swirling within the misty depth of his eyes. "I'm just tired." He rubbed his forehead, trying to rid himself of the pain but to no avail.

"Migraine, huh?" Yuan inquired, not about to have his concern pushed aside by Kaji's stubborn pride. With things as they were, they couldn't afford to have Kaji wear himself down. That would please Karl to no end, and Yuan suspected that was exactly what the advisor was trying to accomplish by giving Kaji all this paperwork. "You should go lie down. We can finish this tomorrow."

Kaji shook his head, jaw set in a stubborn line. "I can't quit now. I have to get this done." He reached over to pick up another page.

Yuan forcefully slammed the pages down onto the desk. "You've neglected this for years, Kaji," he snapped. "There's no way in hell you are going to fix it in one night. Bed." He pointed at the door. "Now."

Kaji stared at Yuan, jaw slack in disbelief. He couldn't believe Yuan was speaking him in that manner. "You shall not speak to me in that manner," he said, practically bristling. "I am your King."

Yuan was not about to be intimidated by Kaji. He didn't even bother to acknowledge Kaji's rank as he continued to speak. "Either you get yourself up off of that damned seat and get yourself to bed, or I'm going to haul your ass there and sit on you to keep you there."

Anger flashed through Kaji. He didn't like to be spoken to in that manner and certainly not by someone he'd always seen as rather frivolous, weak even. "I'd like to see you try."

Kaji truly didn't expect Yuan to take him up on his challenge and consequently was utterly shocked when the blond stalked over and slung Kaji over his shoulder before he even had time to register what was happening. Then, without so much as a word, Yuan stalked out of Kaji's office, carrying him with ease.

Kaji began to struggle as Yuan exited the room, outraged by how he was being treated, only to groan and slump over when another intense wave of pain pounded its way through his skull. He silently vowed to never underestimate Yuan again, as it seemed the young man had more strength in his wiry body than Kaji had initially suspected.

Kaji raised his head at the soft tap of bare feet upon stone. He didn't know how he'd managed to pick up on the sound of those footsteps, as Aniol barely made a sound when he moved, but Kaji could sense his mate's movements in an instant. There was just something about Aniol's presence that drew him. He held Aniol's concerned gaze for but an instant before groaning, relaxing once more.

Yuan marched straight into Kaji's room and dropped Kaji onto the bed before promptly sitting down on top of him. Kaji blinked in surprise before scowling up at Yuan, displeasure radiating off of him. "What the hell do you think you are doing?" he demanded.

"What I promised I'd do," Yuan retorted. "I gave you a choice. You chose this. You only have yourself to blame."

"Get the hell off of me," Kaji ground out from between gritted teeth.

Yuan gave him a sly smile. "Make me," he challenged.

The instant Kaji moved, intending to struggle, Yuan leaned to the side, grabbed Aniol's wrist, and pulled him forward. A mere moment later, Aniol was sprawled over Kaji's chest. Sheer surprise and shock froze Kaji in place, Aniol keeping him there. Yuan slid off of Kaji and headed for the door. "Now go to sleep. I'm ordering the guard at your door not to let you take a single step out of this room until eight o'clock. That should give you about five hours of sleep, as it is now already three in the morning." That said, he slipped out, closing the door with a soft click.

Kaji blinked up at Aniol, returning the rather baffled look he was on the receiving end of, neither young man knowing how to proceed. "Um…." Kaji started, cursing himself the moment he did so. What kind of eloquent response was that? It may not have been much, but it was enough to spur Aniol into motion. He scrambled away, turning bright red.

Kaji grabbed his wrist without thinking, halting Aniol's retreat in mid-motion. Aniol stared at Kaji, waiting for him to speak, straddling his thighs. Kaji groaned as he felt other emotions begin to stir within him, Aniol's proximity and rather suggestive position sending his thoughts straight into the gutter. It was a gutter he'd love to explore with zeal. Only his desire was interrupted by hundreds of men trying to drill their way out of his skull, eliciting another groan from him, this one entirely from pain.

Aniol shifted, climbing over him and crawling to his side. He reached out to him, hand pausing a few centimeters from Kaji's skin, the mist in his eyes swirling violently as he fought with himself. He wanted to help, wanted to soothe away the pain, but fear of touch caused him to hesitate in uncertainty.

Kaji sighed in relief, eyes drifting closed in pleasure when Aniol's fingertips brushed across his forehead. He was amazed at what a simple touch from his little mate could achieve, the tension melting away taking some of the pain with it. Kaji slowed his breath as he allowed himself to relax into Aniol's touch, his touch butterfly soft.

"Could you…?" Kaji paused in uncertainty, keeping his eyes closed. He didn't want to see the tension and fear that might cross Aniol's face with his request. "Could you, um, tell me a little about yourself?" he asked, wincing when he felt Aniol tense. His eyes snapped open, amber gaze searching Aniol's misty one. "I know you say you don't know much, but could you tell me what you do know? What you remember?" Kaji fought to keep the pleading from his tone. He was desperate, eager to know more about the young man who consumed him so.

Aniol watched him, fingers unmoving upon Kaji's forehead. Kaji waited as Aniol fought an inner battle, considering what to say. Aniol's tongue darted out to lick his lips, momentarily distracting Kaji before he spoke. "There's not all that much to tell." His fingers resumed their motion upon Kaji's forehead. "I never had any friends… or lovers. I'm not much of a people person, I guess." His tone was wry, almost as if he were laughing at some private joke, mocking himself. "As I said… I didn't get out all that much, not before I came here. I don't know my parents. I don't remember them. I have no idea what happened to them. Maybe they died; maybe they didn't want me." Aniol spoke casually, almost as if he were speaking about someone else, yet Kaji still couldn't miss the deep pain Aniol was trying to hide. "I like to read and draw a little, but other than that, I don't do much else. I'm not good at anything else. Not even taking care of myself," Aniol finished miserably, his insecurity now laid bare.

Kaji remained silent, contemplating Aniol's words. They'd been simple, containing neither embellishment nor elaboration. It was a rather lonely way to describe one's life. He wondered what it was that Aniol was hiding from him. He was desperate to ask but also knew that now was not the time. He got the impression that what little he'd been told was a lot when it came to Aniol. "Thank you," he said, allowing his eyes to drift closed once more, simply savoring Aniol's gentle touch that gently pulled him toward oblivion, fingers brushing away the pain, a soothing distraction from the questions that still remained unanswered: about Karl, his kingdom, his next actions, and most importantly of all, Aniol.

# BETRAYAL

Betrayal is difficult to bear, more so when one realizes one has been tricked into becoming the betrayer. The bitter taste of betrayal was the last pain experienced by the Gatekeepers as they died, killed by those they had given unconditional trust to, killed by their protectors. But none experienced the bitterness as much as the Wardens who discovered the lie and realized the great sin they themselves had committed. They possessed but a brief moment of sanity before being driven over the edge by grief and self-hatred: and so it was that the blood of the Gatekeepers was joined by that of their Wardens, those driven past endurance by grief, unable to live with the sin they had committed.

ANIOL'S fingers danced across his flesh, their soothing touch now more sensual than before. Warm candlelight danced over pale naked skin, tantalizing him, the dance of light and shadow slowly revealing the secrets of his mate's naked form. Giving in to temptation, Kaji ran his hands over Aniol's naked flesh, marveling at the contrast of his tan skin against the white of Aniol's.

Aniol arched into his touch and released a soft mewl of pleasure. The sheer want and submission in the movement sent desire right through Kaji, appealing to his dominant, possessive streak. Growling deep in his throat, he reached up to bury his fingers in Aniol's silver hair, the blue hue within in it reminding him of the mysteries of night. Tugging softly, he pulled Aniol to him and claimed his lips in a slow, soft, sensual kiss.

Fearing a more a more aggressive approach would scare Aniol, he kept his touch light and gently coaxed Aniol into reciprocating. Each kiss was more painstaking than the one that came before, a rush of heat pooling in his groin, every nerve in his body on fire. Having his mate in his arms, pressed tightly against his naked skin, was sinful pleasure of the most intense degree. Each movement woke a hunger within him, gently urging him onward as his kisses became more possessive, completely invading the sweet heat of Aniol's mouth.

Unable to resist, Kaji slid his hands from Aniol's hair and down onto his heated, naked flesh. The skin was soft as silk and slick with sweat, a faint flush of arousal now coloring it a pale pink. Tearing his lips from Aniol's, Kaji bent down to capture a pink nipple, biting it to bring it to peak. The action tore a cry of pleasure from Aniol's lips, and the sound was music to Kaji's ears. Aniol arched further into Kaji's touch, and his thigh rubbed against Kaji's penis. All the blood rushed from Kaji's head to his groin, filling him with heat that beat in rhythm to the longing in his blood, with the desire to lay claim to his mate wiping all thoughts of possibly stopping from his mind.

Moving his hand further down, he traced the entrance into Aniol's ass with his forefinger. Aniol quivered with the touch, tensing when Kaji's finger got too close. "Shh," Kaji whispered, gently rubbing the globes of Aniol's ass. "I won't hurt you." He lapped at Aniol's nipple, gently soothing the flesh before moving on to the other one. Sucking the pink flesh into his mouth, he slipped a finger into Aniol's ass, all but groaning at the tight heat.

Aniol's breath escaped in on a whisper, the sound but a small affirmation of discomfort, but Kaji ignored it, gently thrusting his finger in and out, getting Aniol used to the invasion. The moment Aniol's muscles began relax, Kaji pulled his finger out. Reaching for a vial of oil, he trickled the slick liquid onto Aniol's skin. Discarding the vial, he thrust his finger back in. He gently resumed the friction and pushed a second finger in, scissoring them to stretch Aniol for him. Abandoning the second nipple, Kaji licked and nipped his way back up Aniol's chest, over his throat and back to his lips, claiming them just in time to swallow Aniol's pained whimper as he added a third finger.

Moving his free hand up, he brushed his fingers through Aniol's hair in an attempt to soothe him while he searched for Aniol's prostate with his invading fingers. The tension in Aniol's body was working against him, but he persisted, smiling when he finally brushed against something spongy deep within Aniol's body. Aniol let out another cry, his face no longer marred by tension. His whimpers of pain changed to pants of pleasure, his body slowly relaxing beneath the onslaught of Kaji's fingers deep within him.

Satisfied that Aniol was as relaxed as he ever would be, Kaji slipped his fingers from Aniol's body. He shifted Aniol onto his knees and parted his legs, exposing him. Lining himself up with Aniol's ass, he then thrust in, groaning deeply at the sensation of tight, slick heat, encompassing his painfully hard, throbbing length. Burying himself balls-deep, he paused, forcing himself to slow lest he lose control.

The seconds seemed like hours, and the minutes seemed like an eternity, each moment stretched out with him balanced on the edge of pleasure, the pain of it a mind-bending contradiction. Shifting, he began to move, quickly losing himself to the rhythm of thrusting deep into his mate, thus claiming what was rightfully his.

The sheer heated pleasure of the act took possession of his blood, driving him ever higher, ever closer to climax, and just as he was about to reach it… the dream shattered, slipping from his grasp. Fantasy fought with reality, pulling him into a half-awake state, and his exhausted mind tried to make sense of it all. Disappointment coursed through him with the realization that it had all been a dream. Too tired to protest the torment of his mind and body, he slipped back into slumber with the knowledge that even though his little mate remained unclaimed, he still remained by Kaji's side, bonded to him for life.


KAJI woke slowly, drifting gently out of one of the most restful slumbers he'd had in a long time, with something niggling him in the back of his mind. Something was missing. It was this realization that pulled him roughly out of his pleasant doze, tearing the remnants of his more-than-pleasant dream from his mind. He leaped out of bed, too groggy to register anything except for the fact that Aniol was missing. He hastily scanned the room and then ran into the bathroom. Finding it empty, he turned around and ran to his bedroom door, pulling it violently open and running out without a moment's pause. He didn't get very far, for he ran straight into someone.

Kaji stumbled back, the momentum of the collision threatening to throw him off balance. Barely saving himself from falling, Kaji glanced up, his panicked amber gaze meeting deep brown. Kaji gaped at Yuan, a flood of anger shooting through him, accompanied by a deep sense of betrayal. Cradled in Yuan's arms was Aniol, the small young man held close to Yuan's chest.

Kaji wanted to scream, wanted to start punching, but most of all he itched to snatch Aniol out of Yuan's arms, but he resisted temptation. It would appear that Aniol and Yuan had been up to something behind his back, and Kaji really didn't know what to do about it.

Yuan, for his part, saw the rage burning deep within Kaji. Kaji's face was too expressive for Yuan to miss it, not after having known Kaji for most of his life. He followed Kaji's gaze to his own arms, horrified as he realized what Kaji must be thinking. He shook his head, holding his arms and Aniol's sleeping form out to Kaji. "I found him in your study," he said hastily. "He was asleep on the floor. The guard you assigned to follow him around says he was in there all night. He was up all night. Apparently he fell asleep just before I got there. I was looking for you. There's nothing going on between us, I swear."

Kaji glanced to the side, spotting the guard he'd assigned to Aniol. Seeing the man give a small nod of confirmation, he turned back to Yuan and reached out to take Aniol's slim form, relief crashing down on him. He flushed, suddenly ashamed of his own thoughts and overreaction.

He turned without a word and walked back into the room, cradling Aniol in his arms. He bent down and placed Aniol gently onto the bed before turning to Yuan, who still stood in the doorway. "I'll meet you in my office in ten minutes," he said softly, to which Yuan nodded, closing the door and slipping away.

Ten minutes later Kaji walked into his office only to have his jaw drop open in shock. The room was lined with neat piles of paper along the wall, each pile perfectly aligned, each stack meticulously neat. The chaos of the previous day's paperwork was now perfectly organized.

Kaji walked to a random pile, staring in disbelief as he began to flick through it. "It's all sorted," Yuan said. "The documents are reassembled and placed into piles according to the topics they're related to. I've already checked several of these piles. There doesn't appear to be any error. Some of the documents, such as these"—Yuan walked to a pile and dug out some documents, handing them to Kaji—"I wouldn't have placed together. I would've never linked the mining reports with the reports concerning takeovers of these regions due to supposed village rebellions. The mining reports appear inconsequential but when paired together with these takeovers…." Yuan left the rest unsaid, meeting Kaji's shocked gaze.

"He did all this in one night?" Kaji whispered in awe.

"Actually I think he did all this in one day and night. We did kind of leave him to his own devices. I didn't really think he'd be able to sort documents of this nature," Yuan admitted.

"So he spent the whole day, ignored by us, sitting in a corner, sorting my documents according to topic?"

Yuan gave Kaji a cheeky smile. "It would appear so." The playful smile faded and he was serious once more. "Who exactly is he?" he asked. "That pendant you found aside, there's no way he's a commoner, let alone a slave."

Kaji watched Yuan for a minute, wandering how much he should tell him before shrugging. "I don't really know," he stated simply. "Aniol says he never knew his parents. He doesn't even know his last name, so we can't even search for his family line using the records."

Yuan shook his head in disbelief. "But surely someone would've reported him missing?"

Kaji shook his head. "There have been no reports of anyone matching Aniol's description missing. I looked."

Yuan frowned in contemplation, absently paging through the documents before him. "But surely he's had some form of education. Maybe someone within the guild of scholars would remember him. I mean, his features are certainly unique enough."

"You know, I never thought of that," Kaji admitted, surprised. "But then again…." He pointed at the papers. "I had no idea he was capable of this."

Yuan nodded, handing Kaji some papers. "Shall we then?" He raised an eyebrow when Kaji groaned. "We can't let all his efforts be wasted, now can we?"

KAJI was once more on the losing side of a confrontation with Karl. "What are you trying to say, sire?" Karl challenged smoothly. "Are you trying to say that the head councilman is a traitor, selling our secrets to the enemy?"

Kaji gritted his teeth, trying to resist the urge to just kill the man before him and have done with it. "No," he snapped. "I'm merely questioning some of the paperwork you've given me. I find it strange that what would appear to be some kind of secret communication about selling state secrets would be causally stored among them."

"Really?" Karl raised an eyebrow at that. "I certainly saw no such documentation."

Kaji's desperately tried to control his temper in an attempt to approach this rationally and as a ruler should, but Karl's smooth, practiced responses were driving Kaji insane. "Of course you didn't. Because you planted them there."

"Why ever would I plant such documents?" Karl questioned.

"I don't know," Kaji snarled in response, knowing he'd long ago lost his battle for composure but not really caring. "You're up to something, and I want to know what it is!"

"Up to something, sire?" Karl raised an eyebrow. "Certainly you are delusional. I have never harmed a hair on your head. In fact, I've done nothing but protect and assist you these past thirteen years."

"Nothing but deceive and use me, you mean!" Kaji snapped back.

"If you have been deceived, sire, it is certainly through no fault of my own," Karl responded smoothly, causing the hair on Kaji's neck to rise. That response held a hidden barb that Kaji did not miss. Defeated, Kaji turned and stormed out the room, slamming the door as he left.


THE next morning things took a turn for worse. Kaji was woken by the loud sound of his door slamming open and guards storming into his quarters. Aniol, who'd been sleeping curled up against his back, sat up at the sound as well, eyes filled with confusion, bringing the mist in his eyes to life.

"What's the meaning of this?" Kaji demanded, shielding Aniol with his body, trying to take stock of the situation. "Hey!" he cried out as he was grabbed by two of the guards, fighting them blindly when they pulled him away from Aniol, whom he was desperately trying to protect.

The guards didn't speak as they twisted his arms behind his back while another guard grabbed Aniol, shoving the young man violently against the bedpost before clipping shackles over the boy's thin wrists.

"Cease and desist!" Kaji yelled, confusion fueling the rage hot within his veins. "That's an order!" Kaji was ignored; the guard who held Aniol dragged the young man back and away from him. Kaji snarled, animalistic rage getting the better of him as he fought to get away. He'd promised to protect Aniol, and he'd be damned if he didn't give his all to keep that promise. "I order you to release him! Now!" Kaji ordered voice cold with anger. "Release him or I'll have you all killed." Kaji hissed in pain when one of the guards who held him captive twisted his arm into an unnatural position.

"See." A familiar voice cut into Kaji's rage, drawing his attention to the door. Karl stood in the doorway accompanied by a tall man with streaks of grey in his dark hair. Karl had brought one of the Kiyou Jai, the head of the Kiyou clan, and that could only mean one thing: Karl wanted the church to declare him unfit to rule. "You see." Karl continued to speak. "He's no longer fit to rule. The poor boy has lost his mind."

Kaji's was struck by a sudden realization. He knew exactly what Karl was trying to do. "Like hell I have! This is a setup. You're setting me up! You can't do this!" He struggled, now trying to get to Karl, not Aniol, but it was to no avail. The guard's grip was too strong, and the men who held him had him effectively pinned.

Karl gave him a look filled with false pity, all obviously a show for the other men in the room. Kaji's eyes widened in fear and horror, his struggles ceasing, body limp within his captor's grip. "No," he whispered. "No, this isn't happening." He desperately searched out the Jai's gaze, trying to plead for assistance. He desperately hoped the man accompanying Karl did not believe Karl's lies, for if the man believed, then all was lost, for he was the head of the faith and the only man in the country who could declare Kaji unfit to rule.

"Poor, poor boy." Karl continued shaking his head. "It's all the fault of that demon boy whose blood tainted our king." Karl pointed at Aniol. Kaji watched in horror as Karl approached the guard who was restraining Aniol with far more force than necessary, for Aniol did not fight. He simply stood there staring at Kaji, the mist in his eyes coiling as if it were about to attack. "It's because of his blood running in our king's veins that our king has taken leave of his senses, throwing around wild accusations against me, against the council, and against the church. The demon is obviously controlling him, obviously wants to throw this land into even more turmoil and destroy us all."

Kaji shook his head in disbelief, whispering no over and over again, unable to believe that this was real. He tensed when Karl grabbed Aniol's hair, pulling it, exposing Aniol's vulnerable throat. He wanted to leap at Karl, to rip the man's throat out, but he knew there was nothing he could do, nothing except watch in horror as the scene unfolded, a living nightmare come to life from his deepest and darkest fears and imaginings. Kaji clenched his hands at the pain he could see on Aniol's face.

"Just look at his eyes." Karl spoke smoothly, confidently. "What human possesses eyes such as these?"

"No!" Kaji cried out. "No! He's not a demon!" He struggled once more, wanting only to be by Aniol's side, not caring what they did to him, wanting only to protect the slim young man he'd grown attached to. Defeat crushed him when Kiyou Jai gave him a look filled with pity, and in that instant, Kaji knew all was lost. The last words he comprehended before he began to scream were words he never wished to hear again. Words that should've never been used in the first place, not in reference to Aniol. "Take him to the dungeon."

# ESCAPE AND DEATH

Sacrifice. It's a necessity of war, for no battle has been won without the loss of life. Though it is a tragic event, it has great power and can offer a great life lesson. Ponder this: how can one ever know the true meaning of joy, happiness, and pleasure without ever having experienced despair, sadness, and pain? How can one truly appreciate the value of life without experiencing loss? One cannot—and lack of such understanding leads to complacency, disregard, and petty concern.

Perhaps that is what the Gatekeepers were: a sacrifice to remind people who had grown complacent and ungrateful that peace, stability, and trust are gifts that should never be taken for granted. Perhaps the sacrifice of the Gatekeepers was meant to teach a lesson, to open eyes, to enlighten minds, and to tear people out of their complacent lifestyles. Only... what happens when the sacrifice is too great?

"MY, MY, you have been busy." Rogue's dry comment instantly drew Kaji's desperate gaze toward him. "You have to give me the name of your decorator. I need to make a note to avoid him." Rogue continued stepping lightly into the room, doing his best to avoid the mess Kaji had made of his quarters. Furniture had been overturned, papers scattered, and clothing and bedding tossed upon the floor. Unable to take out his rage on those that were doing this to him, Kaji had taken it out upon the room he now found himself imprisoned in. Karl had ordered him locked in his own suite, thus creating a gilded cage with no escape.

"Where the hell have you been?" Kaji demanded, too tense and fearful to even consider his words. "You're late. You were supposed to have returned days ago."

Rogue watched him for a moment before shrugging, seating himself upon Kaji's bed. "What can I say? I run on my own schedule."

"Your own schedule?" Kaji retorted. "Own schedule? If you'd come when you promised, maybe this could've been prevented."

Rogue glanced up meeting Kaji's stare dead on. "Something came up," he said. "Security got rather tight here, and I had to find another way in. Done interrogating me yet?" He raised an eyebrow in challenge, waiting for Kaji to respond.

Kaji deflated and sank to sit beside Rogue. "This is all my fault," he stated forlornly, burying his face into his hands. "I never saw this coming, never expected him to try such a thing." He shook his head, glancing up to meet Rogue's rather intense gaze. "How on earth did he manage to convince Jai that I've lost my sanity?"

Rogue raised an eyebrow in surprise before pointing to the room. "Your room looks like this, and you can still ask that question?" he retorted before shaking his head. "No, your temper had little to do with it; though it certainly didn't help convince him you were sane. Karl has some documents with your signature on them. These documents detail how you hired a rather unethical scribe to forge Karl's and Jai's signatures on some political documents, supposedly with the intent to set them up."

"I did no such thing!" Kaji protested horrified. "It was Karl I was accusing, not the head councilman! Not Jai! I saw no such documents!"

Rogue shrugged. "Be that as it may, these documents do in actual fact exist, and they do in actual fact bear your signature."

"I signed no such thing!" Kaji insisted angrily. He knew it was unreasonable to direct the anger at Rogue. Rogue wasn't accusing him, he was merely stating fact, but Kaji couldn't stop himself, bitter self-recrimination finding no other release.

Rogue watched him in silence, giving Kaji a little time to recover from the outburst before speaking carefully. "Kaji, please don't overreact, but you might've actually signed those." Rogue raised his hands seeing the anger and indignation cross Kaji's features. "Let me finish. You signed a lot of papers before you came of age, and I know you didn't read all that many of them. It's possible and highly probable that Karl was planning this for a long time already, and he got you to sign those papers ages ago, maybe even years ago."

Kaji gaped at Rogue. He felt like the biggest fool, angry and bitter, filled with regret, and the thing he regretted the most was getting Aniol involved. "Rogue, I have a favor to ask of you… please. I have nothing with which to pay you, but please, please save Aniol," Kaji pleaded, not above begging when it came to this request.

He paled when Rogue shook his head. "Don't beg. It doesn't become you. Why don't you order me to? You're far better suited to giving orders than you are to begging." Rogue stared straight at Kaji in silent challenge.

Kaji looked away, guilt and self-hatred within him making him unable to meet Rogue's stare. He shook his head in denial. "I don't think so," he stated, tonelessly. "I'm no ruler, Rogue. I'm nothing but a fool that has led his country to its destruction."

Rogue remained silent, watching, waiting before speaking when it became apparent that Kaji was going to say no more on the matter. "You made a mistake, granted, but you're certainly no fool. Naïve maybe, too trusting, definitely, but not a fool. Nothing you say will convince me of that. Are you just going let Karl win? I thought better of you. You never gave me the impression of being a quitter. You've always been pigheaded, stubborn, and tenacious, all of these qualities that are invaluable to a ruler if used correctly, if balanced with wisdom, patience, and mercy. Regardless of what anyone may do or say, you're this country's king. Now stop wallowing in self-pity, get your ass off of that bed, and damn well start acting like it."

Kaji stared at Rogue in disbelief. He wasn't surprised at the tone, as Rogue had always been rather blunt, but he was more than a little shocked at the content. Considering the circumstances under which they'd met, his words were rather surprising. He never thought he'd hear Rogue of all people telling him he was fit to rule. "Um… Rogue—" Kaji started to speak, trying to point out the massive contradiction when he was interrupted.

"That was years ago," Rogue snapped. "Don't bring it up again. It has no bearing on what's happening now."

"But—"

"No. That is past, this is present, and I honestly believe you would make a good king if given the chance."

Kaji stared at Rogue, unable to relate everything he knew about Rogue to the words he now uttered. "Um," he stalled hesitantly, still looking for something to say. Rogue only raised an eyebrow in question, egging Kaji on with his silence alone. Kaji's eyes narrowed at the smirk he could see hiding on Rogue's lips, his depression suddenly replaced with new resolve, Kaji's usual stubborn spirit waking once more. "Very well," he said decisively. "I order you to get me out of here and take me to Aniol."

The hidden smirk escaped, spreading over Rogue's features. "Now that's more like it, but I can only follow the first half of that order." He held out his hand. "Let's get out of here."

"But—" Kaji protested.

"I said you should order me." Rogue retorted. "I never said I would obey. You should know better by now. Now let's get out of here while we still have time. I didn't scale your wall, setting pins in it for naught." That said, Rogue gave Kaji no more time to protest, grabbing him by the wrist before striding toward the window. He leaped up, pulling Kaji along with him. "Don't scream," he ordered as he jumped, still holding Kaji's wrist.

*TAP, tap, tap... plonk.* Drop by drop, water dripped down onto a cold, hard floor, the sound echoing with sinister finality, seeming to ring the death knell, one small last breath at a time. Death hung thick in the air, its very essence soaked into stone, tainting it, soiling it, forever to be cold, lifeless, and abandoned.

Yet fear, dread, and horror came not from the blood-soaked stone but from the shadows of life that still dwelt there. Prisoners were but empty husks with dull, lifeless eyes, souls already dead, bodies decaying with each breath as they moaned, gasped, and rasped, merely waiting for the end.

Damp, gelid air filled with death and disease, darkness, and the cries of the dying hid a man whose very existence seemed a contradiction to the atmosphere, his silver-blue hair giving off a faint light, mist coiling within pale eyes, desperate for release... only the young man did not comprehend, did not understand what needed to be done, and so he remained imprisoned, hanging off a wall, cold iron biting into his pale, sensitive skin.

Aniol shifted, trying to escape the pain and discomfort, blood trickling from several open wounds, each inflicted by terror. He could almost smell it as the guards beat him, their fear driving them toward brutality in a desperate bid to gain control over him. The violence was a paradox in and of itself as the guards had each used it to prove they didn't fear him, yet it was their very fear of him and the unknown that drove them to do it.

Aniol slumped once more, too short to reach the ground and use that as leverage in his efforts to ease the deep pain throbbing throughout his body, pain he no longer knew the origins of as his battered, abused body had not been free of it since he had arrived here. In fact, it had only increased and then grown numb, distant at times as cold seeped into his skin, tendrils of death reaching out toward him as it hungered to add his soul to the many it had already claimed within this dark hole of depravation.

*Tap, tap, tap... plonk. Drip, drip, drip.* It was an endless cycle, never ceasing, never giving rest, working on nerves fraught raw with pain, fear, and despair, threatening to drive his very mind into the realms of insanity or death. He had no other means of coping with the torment, the sickly air, the death, misery, terror, horror, screams, and touch.

*Touch.* The cold touch of those reaching out, pulling him toward their depravity, their soulless forms hungry for the life force that still remained within him, drawn to it like moth to flame. *Touch.* The rough touch of the guards, each trying to outdo the other, trying to prove their courage and their strength with how violent they can be. *Touch...* the cold touch of stone, cold air seeping into every cell, stealing heat, stealing life, and taking his very breath along with it. *Touch...* a warm touch brushed against the cold shackles holding Aniol's in place. Since his eyes were closed in weariness and pain, the warm touch was unexpected, its very unfamiliar nature seeming to hold promise of nightmares to come. A loud scream cut through the thick, rancid air like a knife, filled with terror and hysteria as he slipped toward the edge of insanity.

# Sanctuary

The chaos following the death of the Gatekeepers was completely unexpected, the sheer magnitude unimagined. No one had realized how fragile the balance between the Land of Silver and the Land of Gold was nor how important the Gatekeepers really were. And so the rebellion of the elements and land and the destructive force of the tipped scales came as a rather unpleasant shock. A wakeup call. Yet realization came too late, paid for in blood, paid for over and over again as centuries went by.

The high price gave birth to despair, and with despair came resolve to set things right regardless of how long it took, regardless of the price that still remained to be paid in atonement for their sin. The price of doing nothing was far greater. It was this resolve that brought forth the prophecy, and the prophecy brought forth the council, a council whose sole purpose it was to seek and find a way to fulfill the prophecy, to atone and to restore balance.

The passage of time becomes the enemy, as original purpose is forgotten, fading into the mists of memory with each generation that goes by until all that's left is tradition, tradition with lack of understanding, lacking the drive and lacking the purpose to truly do what is required.

"DON'T scream? *Don't scream?* What kind of warning was that?" Kaji protested, his heart still beating wildly with terror. A moment ago he'd been convinced that he was going to die as he fell from the third floor, but he should've known Rogue had something up his sleeve. Yet, even if he'd known what Rogue had planned, he wouldn't have been able to avoid the fear that shot through him along with the conviction that he was going to die. He would never have believed that thin cord, only parts of it glimmering in the moonlight, could hold him, let alone the combined weight of both of them.

Kaji had no idea how Rogue had managed to rig what seemed to be a complicated series of ropes and hooks unseen, and frankly he knew better than to ask. The trip to the ground had been rather rapid, not giving Kaji much time to register exactly what was happening. All he recalled was biting his lip in order to keep from crying out in fear while he clutched Rogue's wrist as they seemed to sail through the air. The moment their feet had touched the ground he'd begun his rant, whispering instead of yelling as he knew they were not out of danger yet.

Rogue raised an eyebrow at his question, eyes darting around, always on the alert for danger. "It worked, didn't it?" he whispered in return. "You didn't scream and didn't back out."

Kaji frowned at the words, knowing Rogue had a point but not liking the fact very much. He didn't like being thought a coward and most certainly didn't like being thrown into situations without so much as a heads up. "You didn't give me a chance to. You didn't give me enough time to react let alone scream or back out."

For a moment, Rogue's gaze flickered to him, a faint smirk upon his lips. "That was the point." His attention snapped to the right. Rogue moved with the speed of a striking cobra, quickly ducking into an alleyway, pushing Kaji against the wall and holding a finger to his own lips in signal for silence. His tension carried over to Kaji, who stilled and listened, trying to sense what Rogue sensed.

Heavy footsteps could be heard upon the cobblestones, footsteps of several people heading in the same direction, all in rhythm, right, left, right, each perfectly synchronized with the others. It was a rhythm, a beat so ingrained into the soldiers that it went unnoticed by them, but it was this beat that betrayed their location, announcing it to everyone in the city. Rogue spun, grabbing Kaji by the wrist and heading deeper into the maze of alleyways, deeper into the shadows, twisting and turning, taking seemingly random turns and all the while muttering under his breath. "Where is he? He's late. What is taking him so long?"

Kaji frowned at Rogue in confusion, absently wondering what

Rogue was going on about as he ran. He had long ago lost his way among the maze of alleyways Rogue was running through, one alley looking like another, dark, cluttered, narrow, and abandoned.

Rogue suddenly paused once more, pushing Kaji back into a crack, a narrow space Kaji had not seen, a space barely big enough for his slim form. Rogue casually leaned against him, shielding him, lighting a makeshift cigarette and taking a drag. Tendrils of smoke drifted into the air, a glimmer of red at the tip of the cigarette in bright contrast against the backdrop of black.

Soft footsteps and the rattle of a loose pebbles clattering over the ground gave away the intruder's position. This was followed by rustling of cloth, soft breath, and the distinctive scrape of metal being drawn. A guard peered around the corner, sword in hand, taking in the lone figure leaning against the wall, lazily smoking.

Rogue glanced up, raising his eyebrows in feigned surprise, cigarette hanging limply from a mouth slightly agape and seemingly frozen in shock. The guard took one look at him before turning and leaving, not even walking into the alleyway, not even suspecting Rogue was not alone.

Rogue promptly dropped the cigarette, crushed it beneath a boot, and muttered darkly about how much he hated the damned sticks. He turned, grabbed Kaji's wrist, and dragged him from his hiding place, heading to the entrance of the alleyway that the guard had just abandoned.

Peering around the corner, Rogue carefully noted the guard's progress, waiting for an opportunity to run past without being noticed. When the guard stepped into an alley further down the road, Rogue ran across the street, dragging Kaji along without warning. Once on the other side, he slipped into yet another alley before halting their progress in yet another dark corner. Rogue then proceeded to tap his foot in impatience, muttering darkly in dissatisfaction. He was reprimanding someone for being late while threatening to skin them and make them pay for their audacity. Kaji didn't want to point out that Rogue was not exactly the most punctual person he knew.

ABOUT half an hour later, Rogue sighed in relief, all the tension draining from his body. He slipped into yet another alley, pausing beside a shadow that was just a touch deeper than those surrounding it. A surprised breath escaping Kaji when he realized what he saw. Standing in the alley was a tall figure dressed in black with pitch black hair and eyes so dark his very pupils blended into them. Draped upon his back was a familiar if now battered pale form with pale hair shrouded by dark cloth. "You're late," Rogue said softly.

"Says the one who runs on his own schedule," Anei retorted, glancing at Kaji. He stepped back when Kaji tried to reach out toward the burden he carried, shifting to adjust the weight upon his back. "He passed out," he explained. "As light as he is, it's still difficult dodging guards while carrying a dead weight."

"But you do it so nicely," Rogue whispered, placing a restraining arm upon Kaji's shoulder, letting Kaji know he shouldn't interfere yet. "You've had plenty of practice, after all."

Anei rolled his eyes. "Now there's the pot calling the kettle black. Let's get out of here. The guards are still about, and if we linger it won't be long before we're discovered." Rogue nodded in agreement. Kaji looked back at Aniol's limp, pale form, as they moved away, longing to have the Aniol in his arms instead, distrustful of someone he'd never seen, let alone met.

Rogue once more led him through the alleyways, seeming to weave a rather obscure path through them, first turning right, then left, then right again, all the while trailed by a shadow bearing a small burden upon his back. Kaji blinked when instead of turning into yet another alley, Rogue turned into a doorway, rapped three times on the door, paused, and then rapped three times more.

The sound of metal locks sliding open preceded the door creaking as it was opened a mere crack, and a pale face peered out. Upon recognizing Rogue the occupant opened the door, hastening them in before just as quickly closing it once more, metal locks clicking back into place. A rather chubby man led them through a tavern, taking them up the servant's stairs all the way to the attic. Once the party had entered, the door dropped closed, and the man was gone, leaving the four alone once more.

Anei walked to one of the two beds within the rather small attic, gently maneuvering Aniol around and placing him down. Kaji was at Aniol's side even before he was done. "Remind me to never take you up on your offer for a challenge again," Anei said as he stretched. "That was a little more challenging than I expected. I mean, the palace dungeons, Rogue?"

"You did say you could get anything out of anywhere, Anei. Maybe you should think twice before making such broad statements next time," Rogue said.

Anei shook his head, brushing stray strands of hair out of his face. "I got him out, did I not?"

"Granted," Rogue agreed, glancing at Kaji, who'd taken off the dark cloth that had been draped over Aniol in order to hide his rather distinctive features and was now running his hands over the slim form, seeking and taking note of injuries.

"So what now?" Anei asked, bringing Rogue's attention back to him. "Their absence has already been noticed. How are you going to smuggle two people with such distinctive features out of the city? Two people that all the guards are already on the lookout for?"

"With difficulty," Rogue said, meeting Anei's gaze. "Could you do me a favor? Spread the word that we need an escape route. Send out some spies and gather information on Karl's actions and on the level of security in the city. Find out who could possibly help us and who could possibly hinder us. Use your information network to get what information you can, and I'll use mine. We meet again tomorrow evening, early, and compare notes, and then we plan."

"Such a simple request. You must be losing your edge, Rogue," Anei said, grinning and ducking when Rogue tossed a dagger at him, the blade burying itself deep into the wooden wall behind Anei. "Yes, definitely lost your edge," Anei said cheekily before giving Rogue a serious look. He nodded once, sealing the deal and slipping soundlessly out of the room, his movements as subtle as the shadows he resembled and was named after.

# MASTER OF SHADOWS

Efforts to fulfill prophecy can bring the strangest people together, binding them in single purpose, of single mind and heart, for prophecy looks not to profession, life, and skill, but looks to men's hearts. An individual's life is defined by circumstance, for one cannot take advantage of opportunities that do not arise within one's lifetime. Yet, if one's heart and will are strong enough, even circumstance can be overcome and opportunity can be created.

It is those who are strong of heart that are sought out by prophecy, for prophecy can only be fulfilled by breaking circumstance, escaping what one *is* in order to reach for what one is meant *to be*.

Consequently, the effort required to fulfill a prophecy is monumental, requiring that one be willing to go against circumstance, to fight till one's last breath, to fight in the face of disbelief, ridicule, and tribulation in order to accomplish that which must be done, paying the price for another.

KAJI glanced up the moment Anei left, fear thick in his throat. "He's hurt," he stated softly, his voice laced with a sliver of uncertainty. He felt rather helpless. He wanted Aniol to be all right but knew such was not the case.

Rogue nodded, walking to the bed. He waved his hand, indicating Kaji should move, and once Kaji had done so, he seated himself beside Aniol's pale form. He began to gently run his hands over Aniol's body, looking for broken bones. Finding none, he pointed at his backpack beside the second bed. "Could you please fetch that for me?" he asked softly, wanting to give Kaji something to do as the redhead was now shifting restlessly upon the bed, his movements agitated.

Kaji slipped off the bed, relieved to be distracted, if even for a moment. If there was one thing that Kaji hated, it was feeling useless, and nothing in his limited experience had ever made him feel more helpless than knowing that Aniol was hurt and he didn't know how to help. He picked up the black bag and carried it to Rogue, dropping it at his feet. "Who was that?" he asked as Rogue began to rummage in the bag. He was trying to distract his mind from the morbid paths it wished to follow, dark thoughts of pain, torture and death.

"Who? Anei?" Rogue asked, voice muffled by the fabric of his bag. He sat up, a small white cloth bag in his hands. Reaching in, Rogue pulled out some herbs, bandages, and a cloth. "I need hot water." he ordered absently, changing the topic, his attention dedicated to the task at hand. "Go to the kitchen and ask Simol for a bowl of hot water. Simol is the gentleman that's hiding us. Take the servant's stairs and make sure you're not seen. Officially speaking, we're not here. He doesn't know us and has never even seen anyone remotely resembling us."

Kaji nodded, reluctantly heading to the door in the floor. He knew that Rogue knew more about treating wounds than he himself would ever know, yet he couldn't bring himself to willingly leave Aniol behind. "I won't hurt him," Rogue said softly, sensing Kaji's uncertainty and correctly guessing the reason for it. "It shouldn't take all that long to get the hot water. Simol likes his tea and usually keeps water heated so that he may readily and easily prepare it at any time."

"I know," Kaji said in response to Rogue's first statement. "It's just that… it's my fault he's hurt to begin with. It's yet another mistake I have to add to a list already far too long, and I don't want him to wake and find me gone. I noticed he tends to shy away from people." He paused biting his lip as he considered his next words. "He seems to be getting used to me. He's beginning to, or at least he was—" Kaji had to pause again. He took a few deep wavering breaths, trying to regain control of himself and his voice once more. "He was beginning to trust me. I'm not sure if he'll still let me touch him, but I do know…." Once again he paused, wondering if he should make this admission. "I know he'll be upset if he wakes up alone and finds you touching him."

Rogue nodded in understanding. "Want me to go?" he asked.

Kaji watched him for a moment, seriously considering Rogue's words. He knew Aniol might be calmer if he was there when the young man woke, but at the same time he knew he wouldn't be all that good in dealing with the young man's injuries. Indecision flickered through him as he considered both options before him before shaking his head, decision made. "I'll be right back." He slipped out of the attic in search of Simol.

IT WAS with great relief that Kaji slipped back into the room. He cradled a bowl of heated water in his hands and walked carefully over to Rogue's side, taking great care not to spill it. Rogue nodded at the small table beside the bed, silently asking Kaji to place the bowl upon it. "If I didn't know it was here, there's no way I would've found this door," Kaji said softly, placing the bowl down with a dull thud.

"That's the beauty of this place," Rogue commented, dipping the cloth he held into the water and proceeding to wash the blood off of pale skin, his touch as gentle and unobtrusive as he could make it. He didn't want to frighten Aniol should he wake.

"Dare I ask who is usually hidden here?" Kaji asked. He pointed at the room and its contents. It was rather obvious the room was used on a regular basis, and considering the manner in which the entrance to it was concealed it was obvious what this room was used for. No normal person would fully furnish a room and then conceal the entrance to it if they had nothing to hide.

"Sometimes it's better not to know," Rogue said, relieved that Kaji seemed to have calmed down enough to attempt a normal conversation. He brushed at stray strand of Aniol's hair behind his ear so that he could wipe the blood off his pale cheek. "All you need to know is that we're receiving sanctuary when we need it."

Kaji nodded, accepting the rebuff for what it was. He guessed it was only fair that he not question any further. Rogue, Simol, and Anei had taken enough risks already without him asking them to take more. Perhaps they may—and knowing Rogue, did—have a few illegal pastimes on the side, but their intent in assisting him had been made clear, and considering his position, Kaji had no right to look a gift horse in the mouth.

He remained silent, contemplating Rogue's words, watching carefully as Rogue tended to Aniol before returning to his earlier question. "So, who is he? Anei?"

Rogue raised an eyebrow, his hand on Aniol's forehead, pausing for a moment before resuming his task. "He that walks in shadow," he responded simply.

Kaji's forehead creased in confusion. "That's rather vague. Can't you be more specific?"

"Can the desert wind cease its dance?" Rogue responded, placing the now red cloth beside the bowl of water and reaching for some herbs.

Kaji scowled at him. "It was a simple question."

"That received a simple answer."

"A vague one!" Kaji said, a trace of anger, tension, and impatience once more in his tone.

"Yet, a true one." Rogue paused his ministrations once more, glancing up to meet Kaji's rather heated amber glare. "Calm down a little and consider it for a moment."

Kaji scowled, but he followed Rogue's instruction, thinking carefully upon his words. Walking in shadow… shadows… walking… shadow, darkness, shade… Shade! "He's Shade?"

Rogue remained still, letting the tension build, before giving a single nod. "Shade is one of several names he bears."

"Master of shadows and head of the thieves' guild," Kaji whispered in awe, overwhelmed by the impact of the realization. "Why would he help me?" he demanded.

"Martial law is bad for business," Rogue deadpanned. "The number of guards patrolling the street has increased, and as is usual with this sort of patrol, they're doing as they please. They are taking advantage of their orders to track you down by any means possible and are harassing the residents, targeting innocent and guilty alike. As a result, paranoia and fear run rampant among the people. People are locking themselves away in their homes, not sleeping all that well, and jumping at every shadow, be it real or imagined."

Kaji raised an eyebrow in surprise. "And so the head of the thieves' guild is willing to help me. I thought we were on opposite sides."

Rogue shrugged. "You escape, you fight, you bring back peace, and business goes up. What does it matter which side you're on? It's a win-win situation for both sides. If you don't win...." Rogue paused for dramatic emphasis. "Risk is a part of business. This is purely a business decision."

"What if I'm not willing to fight? What if I simply give up and let Karl do as he pleases?" Kaji challenged.

"Then you won't be here." Rogue stated bluntly, turning to Aniol once more, proceeding to bandage the worst of the wounds. "It's mostly cuts and bruises with only a few gashes in danger of being infected." He smoothly changed the subject. "No broken bones, though he will definitely be uncomfortable with moving for the next couple of days. Also, the shackles have rubbed his left wrist raw; the bonding bracelet protected his right. At least they didn't re-open the wound there."

Kaji nodded, accepting the change in topic. He sat down beside Rogue, waiting for Rogue to finish. "What do you get out of it?" he asked, watching Rogue carefully.

Rogue didn't even flinch. He was unsurprised. He'd been expecting the question. "Hopefully... peace." He tied the last bandage into place. He then traced it gently with his fingertips, checking to make sure it was tight enough to actually stem the blood flow but loose enough not to restrict it entirely. Satisfied, he withdrew, allowing Kaji to slide forward and take his place.

Kaji remained silent, knowing that was the only answer he was going to receive. He reached out and grabbed Rogue's hand when Rogue moved to turn away. "Thank you," he said simply, locking his gaze with Rogue's, knowing there were no words to truly express his gratitude for all that Rogue had done that night.

# Warmth

Duty, respect, trust, honor, loyalty, morality, and honesty. These are the cornerstones that bound the Gatekeepers and Wardens together, the bonds that wove a link between two souls. Any or all of which could be present, any of which could be taken for granted.

The initial bond between a Warden and his Gatekeeper is based on an unnatural desire to protect, a desire so strong that it often overrides reason and common sense. Once a Gatekeeper and his Warden are bonded this desire fades, meant to be replaced by more real emotion, more honest desires, by a truly unique relationship.

It was thought that it would be enough to simply bring the Gatekeeper and his Warden together, to instill in them the duty, the importance of upholding balance, and to expect them to live together in the very balance they are meant to uphold. High expectations indeed… two strangers linked by fate, each supposed to resist tension and friction, working together in harmony based on little more than the knowledge that they are meant to be together. Time, however, proved that duty, responsibility, and mere knowledge were not enough.

THERE was a whisper of warm breath upon Aniol's skin, the touch senseless to a mind lost in darkness, to one lost in remembered fear and pain. He expected the trickle of breath to disappear yet it didn't fade, seeming to strengthen as his mind drifted toward consciousness. It seemed so… real, so tangible, it made him want to weep for hunger of it.

It had to be all a dream. For comfort, warmth, and care were things never granted to one such as him. Oh, but what a dream…. Aniol could feel it, taste it, sense it with all senses but one… his sight. He held his eyes shut, giving himself time to savor the heat and the relief it brought. Aniol kept his eyes shut for fear of shattering the illusion, for fear of being torn from the dream and pulled back into harsh reality.

The dream remained, wrapping Aniol in its arms as if to lure him into its spell, and so misty eyes drifted open slowly. Aniol's breath caught in the back of his throat as he waited for the dream to shatter, only to release it when it did not. Relief settled upon him. The cold was gone. The pain of a body held in an unnatural position was gone. All of it, the gelid air, the scent of death, the cries of madness, all of it was gone.

Aniol could still feel pain, a reminder of wounds inflicted upon him by fear, malice, and cold disinterest. It was the cold disinterest that scared him the most. The indifference shown by the man assigned to torture him, to make him scream for no reason except to inflict pain, thus punishing Aniol for that which he had no control over, his own existence. It scared him that his tormentor could so easily inflict pain without care and remain unaffected by it.

Aniol looked around in surprise. He was in a small room, the faint flicker of a candle illuminating it and giving life to Kaji's red hair. Kaji was asleep beside him, one arm resting on his stomach, warm breath brushing against his neck. Aniol reached out, running the fingers of his right hand through the silky softness of Kaji's hair, watching the way the light played over Kaji's features, softening them, the dance of light and shadow adding a touch of mystery. He withdrew his hand when Kaji sighed, shifting, settling deeper into the realms of sleep.

Reaching for the hand on his stomach, Aniol gently shifted it off, pausing for a moment before slipping out of the bed he shared with Kaji. Aniol traced out the contours of the room, his sharp mind taking in every nuance. He liked it; it was warm and alive. He reached out to trace the patterns on the wooden wall, awed by how the swirls, though random when taken in isolation, were ultimately part of a greater pattern, a greater purpose. The wall was warm to the touch and full of life, unlike the white walls he was more accustomed to, which were empty, lifeless, and cold.

Running his fingers along the wall, Aniol took a few careful steps forward, eyes following the path his fingers took. His forward progress was halted when he bumped into a warm, hard surface. Taking a step back, Aniol glanced up to see eyes dark as night and just as deep and mysterious. He swallowed in fear, taking another step back before jerking to a halt once more when the stranger smiled, cocking his head to the side. Aniol realized that upon closer inspection the eyes were not black, but deep, dark brown, their depths hiding swirls of life similar to those upon the wood.

Apprehension filled Aniol when the stranger reached out to brush gentle fingers through his hair. Aniol breathed a sigh of relief when the stranger dropped his hand and blinked in surprise when a rich warm voice broke the silence. "It's beautiful. Such an unusual color. Just like your eyes. Who exactly are you?" The stranger's words were softly spoken, to keep from disturbing Kaji.

Shaking his head in response, Aniol tensed and backed away another step. He rubbed his hands over his arms, trying to still the goose bumps the question had given him. "I don't know," he whispered miserably, confusion stirring the mist in his eyes to life.

Anei watched him, dark gaze instantly drawn to the swirling mist in Aniol's eyes and the fear he could see in them. He shook his head. "I'm not here to hurt you," he stated. "I'm simply passing through, and you intrigue me. Unsolved puzzles always intrigue me. Call it a quirk of my trade."

"Um… what do you do?" Aniol licked his lips, not sure if it was the right thing to ask.

"Procure and trade in goods," Anei responded, obviously amused by some hidden joke that Aniol did not understand.

Aniol frowned in confusion, the response not really making sense to him. "How do unsolved puzzles come into the picture?" He couldn't help but ask, as his own mind did not like unsolved puzzles either.

Anei's lips twitched, the corner of his lips now noticeably smiling. "I deal in rare, sometimes unobtainable goods. Goods that possess a history often forgotten by those that possess them."

"Goods that possess a history?"

Anei nodded, brushing a finger over Aniol's bonding bracelet. "Yes, goods that possess a history, purpose, and significance: goods that tell a story. Such goods are more valuable than silver and moonstone, for they possess a value that cannot be measured. Should they be made of silver and moonstone… so much the better."

Aniol blinked, suspecting there was more to what Anei was telling him. He licked his lips again; his gaze flicked to Kaji's sleeping form, the play of light on Kaji's red hair fascinating him as much as his own pale hair seemed to fascinate the stranger before him. He turned back, intending to at least ask for the stranger's name when one of the panels in the floor began to rise. Aniol backed away in surprise, stopping only when his back encountered an obstacle, a wall preventing further progress. Surprise turned to confusion and confusion to relief when he realized it was a door in the floor.

Rogue paused half way in. "I see you're awake," he said before continuing into the room, gaze flickering toward its other occupants. "You're rather early, Anei. I believe we agreed to meet tomorrow evening?"

"What can I say, I was curious about the goods I was requested to procure." Anei shrugged.

Aniol blinked in confusion, absently wondering at Anei's choice of words. He wasn't at all sure he liked the picture his mind was painting. It would explain Anei's strange sense of humor, though.

Rogue looked at Aniol before turning back to Anei. "He's off limits," Rogue said, shocking Aniol with his bluntness.

"I know that," Anei retorted. "What I want to know is what's so special about him. Why did we go to such great lengths to save him as well?"

"Kaji is rather attached to him," Rogue explained, obviously not about to say more than that as he busied himself with packing bags. Although Rogue made a big show of ignoring Anei, the tension in his body revealed that he was on edge.

A slight shift in the atmosphere spurred Aniol into movement. He turned, pale hair streaming out behind him at the speed of the movement, stray strands drifting past his face with momentum before settling upon his shoulders once more when he stopped, misty gaze locked with amber. He frowned in confusion when Kaji did not move. Kaji's stillness left him mystified, fearful even. It was unnatural and didn't suit Kaji's usual vibrant personality.

Aniol took a wary step toward Kaji, wanting to reach out in order to comfort his bondmate. For some unexplainable reason, he wanted Kaji's vibrant energy back. He wanted to see the life in Kaji's eyes, the stubborn set of his chin and the determined set of his shoulders, all of these which seemed to have been stolen by some unknown force that could make even the stubborn redhead question himself.

Aniol paused, his ingrained aversion to touch and lack of experience when it came to dealing with people fighting with his sudden desire to comfort the one who made him see the world in a different light. It was the latter desire that won in the end, Aniol's hesitant footsteps gaining more confidence as he approached Kaji, all the while silently watched by those amber eyes. Aniol sat down beside him, leaning into Kaji, touching him by the merest fraction of a shoulder upon shoulder, afraid that more would be unwelcome. Only it wasn't at all unwelcome. A warm arm wrapped around Aniol, drawing him closer into the embrace until he was once more surrounded by the warmth that had woken him so gently.

# DISCOVERY

Not all the tales speak of that which led to the betrayal of the Gatekeepers. Some merely describe how life was lived when harmony still existed between the Land of Silver and the Land of Gold. These tales speak of peace and prosperity. They speak of development, knowledge, wisdom, and a land truly blessed. These tales speak of water falling from the sky, cool wind upon skin, of soft blue light to illuminate the depths of night and of rainbows dancing across the sky.

If one were inclined to lose oneself to the tale, one would hear the soft whisper of sweet melodic laughter and feel the peace and serenity that once governed ordinary living. Extending one's imagination would lead to a land teeming with life and elegance, people blessed by the sun living together in harmony with those blessed by the moon.

Hidden within these tales lies an important clue to salvation. If one pays close enough attention, one will realize that within them lies the secret to finding a Gatekeeper. A Gatekeeper will be recognized by the mark he bears: living mist within pale moon child's eyes. Sadly, few still know the tales, and those who do have forgotten that within them lies truth.

KAJI heaved an inner sigh of relief when Aniol willingly approached him, the slight touch from his mate warming him to the core. Aniol still trusted him. He wrapped his arms around Aniol's slim frame, pulling the young man into his lap, holding him. "Find out anything?" he inquired curiously, watching Rogue.

Rogue dropped the bag he held and turned to Anei, silently raising an eyebrow in question, rather obviously wanting Anei to answer the question. Anei raised his eyebrows in return, silently mocking Rogue before turning toward Kaji. "All the city entrances have been barricaded. No one is to enter or leave the city, by royal decree. Interesting that, how a royal decree was given in order to hunt down the only one actually qualified to give such a decree." Anei couldn't help but add the last, finding the fact to be rather ironic.

"I guess it would be because some people consider themselves to be royalty," Kaji said calmly, even though within him turmoil reigned. "So basically we can't get out?"

"I wouldn't quite say that," Anei said. "There are other alternatives that are still under investigation."

"Such as?" Kaji asked, mind racing, fear thick in his throat.

"The sewer system," Anei responded bluntly, trying to get a reaction out of Kaji, hoping to see the royal waver at having to use an escape route so obviously beneath his station. Anei didn't hold much fondness for those who considered themselves to be better than all the rest based on nothing more than a mere accident of birth. He was of the opinion that station and the respect it held should be earned, not based on something as fickle as bloodline, for bloodline did not define a person's character and certainly had little influence on true nobility. He had no time or respect for the haughty ways and airs of the old nobility and was surprised when Kaji didn't even flinch, simply nodding as he accepted Anei's response.

Kaji frowned, thoughts racing as he considered the option for a moment. "Won't work," he stated bluntly. "Karl would've thought of that."

Anei was just about to voice his skepticism, believing Kaji was using the logic to avoid the sewers, when he was interrupted by Rogue. "He's right," Rogue confirmed. "I checked a couple of the routes, and all have guards stationed at their exits. Getting in would be easy enough; it's getting out of the sewer system that will be a problem. Unless we can find an exit that they've missed, that is."

Anei frowned. He hadn't expected Kaji to be right. It seemed their king really was sharper than he gave him credit for. Anei nodded, glancing at Rogue. "Then I guess we start searching every route we know, and if we find none unguarded, start thinking of a way to get rid of the guards."

"No killing!" Kaji ordered, his tone demanding obedience. When Anei and Rogue stared at him, he continued to speak in explanation. "I don't want unnecessary bloodshed. We've wounded this land enough. Most of those men are only doing as they're told. It's those in command that we need to get to."

Rogue and Anei exchanged glances. Silent concerns were exchanged before Rogue spoke. "It may not be possible. We might need to kill in order to escape."

"Then make it possible," Kaji ordered, amber gaze flashing. He was not going to give up on this one, not when there were innocent lives at stake.

Anei's dark eyes searched Kaji's amber ones, seeming to reach deep into his soul, searching for something. What? Kaji couldn't even begin to guess at. Seeming to have found it, Anei nodded, bowing low. "As you wish," he said simply before slipping out the room.

Kaji turned to look at Rogue, engaging in a silent contest of wills, each fighting for what they believed in, each unwilling to give way... until it was finally broken by Rogue's nod that let Kaji know that although he made no promises, Rogue would try to do as he asked.

Certain that he'd done all he could for the moment, Kaji turned to Aniol, surprised to see misty eyes watching intently. "I'm sorry," Aniol said, the soft words breaking the silence between them.

Kaji frowned in confusion. "What for?"

Aniol licked his lips, his body filled with subtle tension. Kaji picked up on it only because he cradled the slim form within his arms, and it bothered him. Kaji was of the opinion that Aniol was far too secretive. His bondmate kept far too many fears to himself, and that attitude made Aniol wary of everything and everyone around him, Kaji included. Kaji hurt for him, wishing he could find a way to just wipe the slate upon which Aniol's past was written clean, thus starting over, hopefully to never expose Aniol to pain or to fear.

"None of this is your fault," Kaji continued in a soft tone, suspecting, based on what little he knew about him, that Aniol was blaming himself. "In fact, if not for you, I wouldn't have realized it was going on in the first place. I would've been fooled, and the country would be in turmoil anyway, only instead of Karl giving the orders it would be a blind king. I'd be responsible for it, just as I'm responsible for all that's already transpired while I allowed myself to be blinded. There's no way I would've been able to deal with all those documents without your assistance. I wouldn't have been able to link some of those if you hadn't placed them together. Even if I'd realized that I was being deceived, I would've remained ignorant of how broad the deception really was. So don't you dare apologize."

"But you've been declared insane, unfit to rule... because of me... because of my eyes... because of who I am," Aniol whispered, guilt heavy in his tone.

Kaji shook his head. "No. That is my own fault, not yours. Karl went to great lengths to set me up, and I was too blind to notice it before it was too late. He had all the documents ready and was just waiting for the right moment. If it hadn't been you, he would've found another reason to declare me insane. And with my temper...." Kaji gave Aniol a rueful glance, remembering Rogue's words from earlier that evening. "He wouldn't have had to look too hard, I guess. It's because of me that you got involved, that you were taken and...." Kaji paused tracing one of Aniol's bandages with his left hand. "I'm sorry." He shook his head when Aniol opened his mouth to protest. "Don't worry, we'll be fine," he said, wishing he could believe those words.


KAJI rubbed at his forehead as he walked down the stairs, trying to rid himself of the dull pain gathering there, the pain that was threatening to become a full-blown migraine if he wasn't careful. Each evening Rogue would slip out, look for an escape route, and gather information from Anei, trying to figure out what was happening in the city. Each evening the prognosis got worse. Fear in the city was growing each day. The despair people were starting to feel brought out the worst in them. Kaji had heard reports of beatings, false accusations and riots, people willing to accuse one another of harboring the fugitives because of fear, and paranoia. Tavern brawls and reports of drunkenness were escalating. Hatred was thick in the air. Distrust and suspicion were spreading like a disease, turning friend against friend, and petty crime upon the streets was on the increase. The crime, Kaji knew, had nothing to do with the thieves' guild, for Anei was extremely displeased with the situation.

Kaji winced when his headache flared. He had misjudged the last step, nearly tripping when he missed it, dropping down two stairs instead of one. The rather abrupt movement caused the pain in his head to flare in protest. Still wincing, he stepped into the kitchen without thinking, the throbbing pain in his forehead making him forget caution, forget to be wary, and so he neglected to first check if it was safe to enter. He glanced up and froze in place, horror filling through him. His amber gaze met Yuan's green-flecked brown, both pairs going wide in shock and recognition.

# Action, reaction

Action and consequence are inseparable; one is irrevocably linked to the other. Simple physics dictates that every action has an opposite but equal reaction. It is a rather simple chain of events one would think: Action equals reaction. It should be easy enough to predict and to control. Perform an action, and as a result, the reaction should be consistent and predictable.

If only life were that simple. If only action were the only contributing factor when predicting reaction. One forgets that although action and reaction are irrevocably linked, there are other factors that come into play, other forces that change the dynamics between the two and can lead to rather unexpected results.

So although every action has a reaction, sometimes the consequences can be far greater, far more damaging than initially anticipated, influencing even that which is not seen. Like a small pebble falling into a pond, rippling and disturbing the water far beyond its reach, its effect is present long after the initial impact. It is this that explains the impact the Gatekeepers' deaths had upon the land, an action so great that the ripples of it, the consequences, could still be felt centuries later.

"WHERE have you been?" Yuan demanded, approaching Kaji. He walked right past him, grabbing his arm as he did so. He led Kaji straight back into the stairwell, using the shadows to obscure their presence, and shoved him into a corner, glaring at him. "Do you have any idea how worried I've been? I've been looking all over for you. I thought they killed you and were using the excuse of your disappearance to barricade the city."

Kaji swallowed, trying to rid himself of the thick lump in his throat before speaking. "Yuan," he whispered, still trying to get over the shock of being found. "Are you alone? Were you followed? How did you find us?" Kaji fired the questions rapidly, not really caring that he wasn't giving Yuan time to respond.

Yuan glared at Kaji. "No, I wasn't followed. Yes, I'm alone." He bristled at the questions, still angry that Kaji had disappeared, causing him to worry. "You still haven't told me where you've been all this time. How you escaped and what you're doing here, of all places."

"Yuan, swear, on your life that you'll tell no one that you've seen me," Kaji demanded, ignoring Yuan's questions. "Swear on your life that you won't reveal our location."

"Who the hell do you think I am?" Yuan snapped in anger and indignation. "Of, course I won't tell anyone you're here, because I'm not leaving."

Kaji shook his head when he realized exactly what Yuan was implying. "No, Yuan. You can't come. Go home. You have a family to protect. I can't allow you to risk your life for me."

"I'm not exactly giving you a choice in the matter," Yuan retorted.

Kaji glared, suddenly standing tall, fully in command, a king in charge of his people. "Go home, Yuan. Go home and forget you saw me. That's an order." His tone was cold, fully expecting obedience without question.

Yuan returned the glare. "No." His response was simple, firm, stubborn.

"Are you disobeying a direct order?" Kaji growled, a hidden threat in his tone.

"I guess I am. Or then again, maybe not, seeing as you've been declared unfit to rule." Yuan spoke slowly, daring Kaji to do something about it.

Anger and desperation filled Kaji. This wasn't how he wanted things to play out. Yuan was his closest friend, and he wanted to protect him, not endanger him. He dropped his commanding posture, switching to pleading. "Please, Yuan, I'll never forgive myself if you get hurt."

"And I'll never forgive myself if I abandon you when you need me the most," Yuan said softly. "You are and always will be my liege. It's my given duty to protect you, but first and foremost, you'll always be my friend, and it's my privilege to be by your side in times of trouble."

"Don't do this, Yuan," Kaji pleaded, feeling the impact of his powerlessness and hating it with a passion. He wasn't used having his orders disobeyed, and it stung. This entire situation was of his own making, and it disturbed him that others were endangered because of it.

Yuan stubbornly crossed his arms over his chest. "So how did you escape?" he asked, ignoring Kaji's plea.

Kaji remained silent for a moment, watching Yuan, searching for weakness. Finding none, he sighed, absently rubbing as his forehead, the migraine that had been threatening now arrived. "Rogue and Anei got us out," he admitted.

"Rogue," Yuan exclaimed even before Kaji had managed to finish speaking, the name a curse word upon his lips. Yuan's entire posture was hostile, body tense and bristling defensively. "What is he doing getting involved?"

Kaji was not surprised by Yuan's animosity. He expected that reaction. "Yuan. He got me out. He got Anei to free Aniol from the dungeon, and now they're trying to get us out of the city. He's not out to hurt me."

"Not out to hurt you?" Yuan almost forgot to keep his voice down. "He tried to kill you, for crying out loud! How is that not trying to hurt you?" Yuan's tone was heated. If not for the situation they were in, he'd be yelling at the top of his lungs.

"That was a long time ago," Kaji said. "Leave it be."

"Leave it be? How can I leave it be? He would just as soon stab you as help you if it was to his advantage. What I don't understand is how you can trust him the way you do. What are you paying him?"

Kaji didn't like how Yuan questioned his judgment. "He's asked for nothing in return." His face was an expressionless mask. He was still and cold, creating emotional distance between him and Yuan, the only life within him was the fire within his amber gaze.

"He's an assassin for hire. He was hired to kill you. What part of that warrants the trust you give him?"

"He's yet to kill me," Kaji retorted.

"Oh, that makes so much sense," Yuan spat, sarcasm heavy in his tone. "Trust an assassin hired to kill you because he failed. He failed because you woke and dodged his blade, so instead of your heart, he got your shoulder. He failed because he didn't expect you to sleep armed, and he certainly didn't expect you to put up such a resistance after being stabbed. He failed because you wounded him so badly that he still carries the scar, I'll bet!"

"That was years ago," Kaji said. "Leave it be."

Yuan's eyes widened in sudden realization. "You're still with him!" He fought to keep his tone down. "Are you truly nothing but a fool?"

Kaji narrowed his eyes. "I guess you're right. I am but a fool who trusts too easily. A fool that has blindly led his country to its downfall and whose only option is to flee, praying that something may still be done to right the grievous harm I've committed. Yes, Yuan, you're right, I'm nothing but a fool, but I do know that Rogue isn't going to kill me. Not yet. He's had ample opportunity, and if he truly wanted me dead, he wouldn't have gone to so much trouble to get me out. He got Aniol out. He knows I have nothing but my life to use as payment, and if that's his price then so be it. Consider it punishment for my blind foolishness."

Yuan gaped at Kaji, shocked by his words and the truth he could sense in them. He closed his jaw, swallowing, gathering himself before nodding in acceptance, knowing that that he could not turn Kaji from the path the he'd chosen. He couldn't ease the burden of guilt the young king bore, a burden that weighed heavily upon Kaji's conscience. He could see determination to do what needed to be done and could do nothing but accept it and obey. He would stay by Kaji's side and hopefully be there to help pick up the pieces of a wounded soul when the time came. For better or worse, he intended to fight by Kaji's side.

Kaji watched Yuan nod, no longer putting up any resistance. He was uncertain enough as it was about the future and didn't want Yuan complicating it, making him question the only thread of stability that remained in his life. Kaji looked toward the kitchen. "I came down to fetch lunch," he said softly.

"I'll go fetch the tray." Yuan slipped back into the kitchen, retrieved a tray that lay upon the table, and followed Kaji up the servant's stairs.

Kaji and Yuan slipped into the attic to find Aniol and Rogue seated on Rogue's bed, scrutinizing a piece of paper. Aniol's long silver-blue hair was loose, pooling over his shoulder, creating a curtain that obscured his features from view. Rogue glanced up, immediately sensing that Kaji had not returned alone. His dark gaze met Yuan's, boring right into it, picking up on the animosity and immediately returning it.

"Mind introducing me to your friend?" Rogue asked carefully, tension and displeasure thick in his tone.

Kaji's gaze flickered between the two, sensing the standoff. He knew Rogue had picked up on Yuan's animosity and didn't appreciate it. Rogue hated people who made assumptions about him before meeting him, judging him before even bothering to get to know him. Kaji sent Yuan a look filled with displeasure. He thought they'd resolved this, but it would appear that while accepting his judgment, Yuan was certainly not going to like it. He heaved a deep sigh before speaking, tone rather curt. "Yuan, Rogue. Rogue, Yuan. He will be coming with us." When Rogue's eyes narrowed, he continued. "I've already tried to dissuade him. It would appear he's already made up his mind."

Rogue remained silent, evaluating the risk of trusting Yuan before nodding reluctantly. "I guess a spare pair of hands will come in handy. He'd better take care of himself and put that blade at his side to good use." With that, Rogue turned back to the paper he'd been scrutinizing before Yuan and Kaji had walked in. Yuan, for his part, was shocked, tray still in hand. He'd gone to a lot of effort to hide the blade, a cloak hanging loosely from his shoulders, and yet Rogue had picked up on it in mere seconds.

# PASS

Time has an interesting impact upon many things, upon life, upon custom, upon tradition, emotion, and upon legend. Regardless of what one may think, history always impacts the present, influences it. What came before defines what is, establishing rules, laws, and brotherhoods.

The death of the Gatekeepers resulted in legends and a prophecy, a prophecy that binds the royal family, even in the present. Each royal heir shall continue to be bound until the price for treachery has been paid, the sins atoned for, until balance is brought back to the Land of Gold.

Few realize the true impact of the prophecy. This impact is far greater than anyone could have ever foreseen, touching not only those of royal blood but reaching to even those hidden in shadow, guiding them, symbolism and moral codes based on legend, molding them for a purpose far greater than any they could see, generation by generation.

*Drip, drip, drip.* Cold sinking deep into bones, horror, panicked breaths, darkness, and remembered terror. A pale form tensed, misty eyes wide and alert, darting around the darkness in fear, seeking, searching, waiting for the darkness to engulf him, waiting for the pain, the terror, the screams, the madness, and the cold heartless touch....

Aniol's body jerked round at a soft touch upon his shoulder, waking suddenly. Kaji looked at him in concern. Aniol swallowed nervously, trying to shake off the remembered horrors that threatened to overwhelm him, all because of a single sound... drip, drip, drip, water falling drop by drop, its echo resounding through his body, bringing back memories better left buried. He forced himself to take deep breaths, pushing the memories back.

He wasn't in the dungeon anymore. He wasn't held captive and wasn't about to be tortured. He was free, or at least free of imprisonment, shackles, and pain. Nightmares, terror, uncertainty, and conflict were another matter entirely. They were in the sewers, Anei and Rogue leading, Yuan trailing. The darkness, the cold damp, and the sound of water had tugged Aniol into memories that still haunted him.

Kaji's touch on his shoulder was gentle, comforting, the heat spreading slowly, into his arm, his chest, and further down, the gentle warmth replacing the bone-chilling cold that fear and memory had instilled in him. The tension drained out of him, calmed his breath, and brought his mind back from the edge of madness. Kaji seemed to relax with him, the concerned, fearful look in his gaze replaced by relief. He ran his hand down Aniol's arm, tracing the contours beneath his fingertips, heat flowing from him into Aniol. The gentle touch traveled further down until his fingers grabbed hold of Aniol's, weaving and linking them together.

Aniol turned and continued on forward, tightly clutching Kaji's fingers. He used the warmth to keep the nightmares of all-too-real memories at bay. They weren't allowed to speak, not unless necessary, lest they be heard above ground. Anei and Rogue had managed to find a single, unguarded exit to the city. It was small and rather obscure, long ago forgotten and abandoned by society, the ancient sewer passages prone to cave-ins.

Aniol blinked in confusion when suddenly he walked right into Anei's back, hard warmth as immovable as any wall. The thief was tense, coiled like a predator ready to strike. His breath hitched when Kaji walked into him, Kaji's warmth enveloping him in a lover's embrace for but a moment before fading when Kaji stepped back, leaning round Aniol to search for the obstacle that had halted their progress.

Standing before Rogue was a slim young man dressed in ragged clothes. His feet were bare and his violet eyes were framed by pale silver-blue hair, the exact same shade as Aniol's. Aniol blinked, all eyes suddenly upon him. Rogue, Anei, Yuan, and Kaji were all obviously linking him to the boy, based on physical resemblance. He shook his head in denial, wanting nothing more than to run in order to rid himself of the scrutiny he was under. Only warm fingers clutching at his held him in place, a silent message of support and trust.

Everyone turned back to the violet-eyed stranger when the young man spoke, the calm voice barely seeming to reach their ears; yet, for some reason the words he spoke remained clear. "It's a trap. They wait for you beyond the stone quarry. They hide the guard in hopes of seeming weak, yet watch and wait, expecting you to fall."

Rogue blinked in shock, Anei's brow furrowed in thought, and they both cursed softly beneath their breaths. It made sense. They had wondered how this single exit seemed to have been missed but had not wanted to think too deeply upon it, desperation leading to blind hope. Finding this single exit had taken all of their resources. Karl seemed to have contacts everywhere. He even used petty criminals as informants, allowing them free reign of the city in exchange for the information they supplied. This free reign was extracting a heavy price from the thieves' guild. The usual business was difficult to conduct when others, not part of the guild, were given legal right to do as they pleased.

"What know you of this?" Anei demanded. Something about the stranger niggled his senses. There was something familiar about him. It was in the way he moved, spoke, and carried himself. He took in the slim form before him, noting two hidden daggers, rope, and bag, all discreetly hidden among the rags he wore, blending in with the young man's clothes. The clothes barely seemed to cover his slim form yet still managed to hide the tools he carried, tools of the trade. The pieces fell into place, and Anei wasn't sure he liked the conclusion he had to make. This young man had been well trained, and that could mean only one thing. "What gates doth ye pass through?" Anei whispered, speaking an age-old challenge used to identify those belonging to various guilds across the land, a challenge taken and adapted from the legends of the Gatekeepers.

"Gates of shadow and time," the young man responded easily, violet eyes locked with dark.

Anei shook his head in denial. He didn't know him. The young man didn't belong to his guild. He would know if he did. Yet the response had been instantaneous, smooth, clear, and precise. There was only one way to find out for sure. "And who be the keeper of the gates?" he asked, looking for identification, a pass phrase each thief was given, one shared among a thief and his superior, identifying the region which one was responsible for and the superior one reported to. Perhaps the guild had a new recruit he was unaware of.

The response he received was unexpected, causing him to pale. "He that shifts through time and space, a ghost, a whisper, a secret never told."

"Kiev," Anei whispered, a cold chill sinking deep into him. He watched as the violet-eyed youth turned to face Rogue, pointing to the right.

"Further down and toward the right, there's a crack in the wall. It's not very big and covered by a root of a tree. It leads to a passage, built long ago. The passage connects the palace to an escape into the desert. Most of it has long since caved in. None of the original entrances still remain, and the exit will need some work to clear, but enough of it remains for you to use as an escape, if you're willing to endure the tight space."

The shock on Anei's face unnerved Rogue. Something about the slim pale figure before them didn't quite strike him as right. The boy spoke true. His gut instinct told him so, but there was something off about him, something not quite natural, and Anei's reaction to the young man only served to confirm Rogue's suspicions. His gaze went to Kaji, who was leaning against Aniol, clinging to the young man's hand so tightly that both their hands were white. Both Aniol and Kaji were staring at the pale figure with recognition in their eyes. They knew this boy.

Rogue sent Kaji a questioning glance, silently asking for advice and confirmation. When Kaji gave a small nod, he turned back to the figure and nodded, nerves on edge when the figure turned and began to guide them down the passage, weaving through the sewers. His steps were sure and certain, as if he were walking within his own home, pale hand trailing along the right wall.

He paused before a large root that trailed down the wall. Reaching forward, he pulled crumbling concrete from the wall, filling the sewers with the dark dank scent of earth. He pointed at the dirt converging round the root. "The crack is hidden behind that dirt," he said.

Rogue wondered what the strange young man was waiting for. He reached out and tapped the dirt, clumps coming loose and falling to his feet. A particularly hard tap revealed a small hole where the dirt crumbled away, brittle and loose. He gave the dirt another hard tap, watching as it disintegrated before his eyes, falling away to reveal a slim hole leading to a crack in the wall, barely large enough for a person to slip through sideways.

He turned to meet the violet eyes filled with knowledge, certainty, and quiet power. It felt like they could reach into his soul and read him like a book. Disconcerted, he glanced sideways, meeting Anei's similarly shocked gaze, the thief just as off balance as he was. When he turned back, the young man was gone, as if he'd never been there to begin with.

Rogue licked lips suddenly dry, the chill from earlier returning with a vengeance as he asked, whispering hoarsely. "Anei... who exactly is Kiev?"

"Leader of the guild of shadows," Anei whispered, staring in shock at the crack before them, at an entrance the guild had not known about, situated within a long abandoned corridor beneath the city.

"Is that not you?" Rogue inquired in disbelief, unable to comprehend what had just occurred, the hair on the back of his neck rising, bristling, alive in warning.

"One of my predecessors. Rogue...." Anei paused making sure he had Rogue's attention. "Kiev is dead. That pass phrase is old and died along with Kiev... I'm the only person alive that should still know it. You see, each leader of the guild has a special pass phrase, and the only people he shares it with are his right- and left-hand men. When he dies, the leader of the guild changes and so does the pass phrase. I was Kiev's right hand man at the time of his death, and his left-hand man died not too long after Kiev did."

# DESERT SANDS

The Ruel used to be a tribe of peace. Those belonging to the tribe are meant to be keeper of secrets, seers, and peace makers.

The people in the Land of Gold are by nature strong, fierce, and fiery warriors. They are a temperamental race, the heat of the sun running deep within their veins. This heat threatens to overwhelm them and often colors their view with rage. They are a defensive, overprotective people easily driven to sword, to violence, and to war.

So it is that this heat needs to be controlled and soothed, cool logic balancing temper and rage, gentleness balancing strength. Such was the task allocated to the Ruel, a tribe charged with keeping peace. The Ruel were royal advisors meant to temper the heat within the Taiyouko blood, blood of those closest to the sun.

The Ruel became a tribe of bitterness. They are bitter with the knowledge that they let the heat of the sun drive Taiyouko into madness, into foolishness, and into sin, thus destroying balance and with it peace. Bitter, helpless, and disillusioned, the tribe allowed themselves to be caught within the very web of sin and betrayal they sought to avoid. And that is how a peaceful tribe turned to sword, to war, to blood, and to death, betraying those they failed to serve.

SCORCHING waves of heat shimmered in the distance as a small group of people made its way across the desert. The dry heat and lack of moisture played with their minds, taunting the wanderers with visions of vanishing water that remained forever just beyond their reach. Skin hungered for the cool relief it promised, aching at the denial. Lethargy and exhaustion drained physical strength, the will to fight adrift in a mind nearly insane, hidden within shadows of hallucination and fever heat.

Misty eyes drifted closed. A slim figure stumbled and fell, Aniol's mind adrift, lost in unbearable heat. Gentle hands caught him, setting him back upon weary feet, pulling his mind away from fever dreams and back to life, back to sanity and arid dry heat, never changing yet remaining not the same.

Aniol opened his eyes, silently meeting Kaji's concerned gaze. He licked his lips, trying to soothe the cracked, bleeding flesh. The cloak he wore, meant to protect his skin from the sun, weighed him down, trapping the heat. It got heavier with each step he took, draining what little energy he still had, and with it, his will to carry on. He was weary, body, mind, and spirit. The desert wore him down, allowing no escape from the harsh elements that surrounded him.

They'd been walking for five days now. Five days of searing heat and rough sand beating against them, tearing into their skin, relentlessly getting into eyes, mouth, and nose. Five days of intense sunlight blinding the eyes, blurring shapes, drawing tears the dehydrated bodies could not spare. Each day the waves of heat seemed to grow in intensity. As bad as the days were, the nights were no better, chill sinking deep into overheated skin, a kiss of death draining even the unnatural heat of burns.

Day and night—neither provided escape, the two extremes taunting Aniol, his body driven forward by sheer will alone, original purpose and goal forgotten. All that remained was his stubborn pride refusing to let him be weak and give up.

Kaji reached out, weakly taking Aniol's hand, lending him what little strength he still possessed. Aniol blinked, turning forward once more, placing one foot before the other, following Rogue's vague form. His throat was dry, screaming for water. They no longer had any, adding thirst to the list of discomfort and pain the desert inflicted upon them.

Then he could walk no further, knees buckling beneath him, stubborn pride no longer enough to keep his weary body moving. Aniol was lost in hallucination, and he fell to his knees, left hand reaching out to stop his fall, right still intertwined with Kaji's. The hot sand scorched and blistered his skin, but he didn't care. The sun seared his eyes as Kaji pulled at his right hand, desperate for him to stand. Kaji didn't register the lack of response, his own reactions driven by survival instinct, mind driven past logical thought.

A second touch joined Kaji's, gentle and certain, lifting Aniol's pale hand, now covered by raw, red blisters, off the burning sand. It lifted him onto broad shoulders, settling him, carrying him forward with hidden strength and iron-hard determination. Aniol let go, slipping into oblivion.

COOL moisture calmed fevered skin, soothed the sharp needles of pain, and called to a wandering mind, luring it back to consciousness. Misty eyes drifted open once again, meeting bright emerald green, the color of grass, trees, and life. Aniol flinched away from the strange girl. She frowned, emerald eyes framed by hair dark as night. She still clutched the damp cloth she'd been using to calm the fever in his skin. Aniol returned her frown, breath deep and shallow, panic still coursing through his veins. His mind raced, trying to figure out why he was no longer in the desert with Rogue, Yuan, and Kaji. He glanced around the room, desperately searching for someone familiar.

Fear drove him to his feet. The girl's resulting cry unheard, Aniol ran, fleeing the room, searching for red hair, heart pounding, uncertainty thick in his throat. He ignored Yuan's sleeping form in the room beside his and continued his search. He found Kaji next. Relief so deep he had to fight back a sob enveloped him. Kaji was resting in the cool room, breath slow and even, a damp cloth on his forehead.

Aniol walked into the room, footsteps light, controlling his deep breathing, slowing it as panic passed. He knelt beside Kaji's sleeping form, crawling forward, drawn to him, uncaring of the pain of his blistered skin.

He lay beside Kaji, shifting warily closer, fearful that the redhead would once more be taken from him. Aniol stilled, resting mere centimeters away from Kaji, watching his chest moving. He longed to breach the remaining space, but fear and uncertainty held him back, the instinct to remain distant ingrained into his very being by loneliness and neglect, bringing memories of pain and torture to the fore. Yet these memories were accompanied by softer ones. Memories of gentleness, comfort, strength, and care and memories of pleasure like nothing he'd ever experienced. He ached for that pleasure, wanting to savor the sweet taste of Kaji again. It was a hunger and sweet pain of an entirely different nature, all given to him by the redhead beside him, chipping away at his distrust, soothing his fear, and luring him into emotion he'd never had the courage to demand.

Timidly, he reached out, pale hand trembling in aftershock of intense fear followed by relief, followed by uncertainty and a rush of conflicting feelings and desires. He brushed his fingers through the silky red strands that were ruffled by their journey and damp with water. Aniol watched in wonder as the strands slipped through his fingers with liquid grace. He was filled with awe, unable to yet believe that he had the right to touch, caress, and savor human warmth.

Feeling an additional presence in the room, his gaze shot up, hand frozen in mid-motion, red strands of hair twisted between his fingers. Rogue was standing in the doorway, watching him. He slipped into the room carrying a bowl of water and a cloth. Kneeling beside the mat upon which both Kaji and Aniol now rested, he dipped a cloth into the water and reached out toward Aniol, pausing when the young man jerked away. Aniol winced, freezing in place when his fingers encountered resistance, for they were still tangled within Kaji's hair pulling on the strands. He turned to Kaji, fearing that he'd woken him.

"He's dehydrated. Suffering from heat stroke. So are you." Rogue reached forward as he spoke, taking advantage of Aniol's moment of distraction, using it to drop the damp cloth he held onto the young man's forehead. Picking up the cloth that rested on Kaji's forehead, he dipped it into the bowl of water, wringing out the excess before brushing it over Kaji's skin. "Lira will bring you some water to drink in a moment." Rogue spoke softly, keeping his gaze on Kaji, giving Aniol space to think. "You gave her quite a fright, running out like that. She was only trying to help. I guess it's my fault. I should've expected as much, known better than to separate you from Kaji, only I didn't expect you to wake so soon. I guess I wasn't thinking. He's fine, you know. The heat got to him, just as it did to you, Yuan, and…." He hesitated before adding, "me."

Rogue glanced up when a familiar girl slipped into the room. She watched Aniol in curiosity. Her movements were graceful and sensual, sexuality radiating off of her with every step. She handed Rogue a small cup along with a jug, her hand brushing over his, lingering a moment too long before she stepped back and left the room, her hips swaying seductively.

Rogue turned his attention back to Kaji and Aniol. He poured some water into the cup and held it out. Aniol gave him a wary glance, sitting up carefully. The damp cloth on his forehead fell into his lap. He reached toward the water, suddenly overwhelmingly thirsty, dry throat pleading for the moisture. "Easy," Rogue warned, not releasing the cup, lifting it toward Aniol's lips. He tilted it but a fraction, allowing water to trickle into Aniol's mouth. "Drink it slowly, just a little at a time."

Aniol's grabbed Rogue's hands, trying to get to the water, the slow pace Rogue was forcing onto him pulling a whimper of pain from his throat. His body craved the water, desperate to gulp down the life-giving liquid. Rogue pulled away; Aniol's meager strength was not even a challenge as he held the cup out of Aniol's reach.

"Drink it slowly, a little at a time," Rogue repeated. "If you don't, you'll only end up throwing it up, dehydrating yourself even further. Okay?" He waited for Aniol to nod before passing the cup to him.

Aniol cradled the cup, treating it as if what it held were more precious than moonstone, which to him, it was. He watched Rogue, asking for permission, trying to control the urge to simply ignore Rogue's words, consequences be damned. He took a careful sip, savoring the cool liquid as it flowed down his scorched throat, soothing the thorns lodged there and easing the discomfort. His hands trembled, turning white with the effort it took to resist gulping the liquid down. All too soon the cup was empty, the water gone.

Misty eyes opened once more, meeting chocolate brown, begging silently. "I'm still thirsty," he whispered hoarsely, a whimper of pleading in his tone.

Rogue reached out and retrieved the cup. "I know," he responded softly. "Lie down, rest a while, and when you next wake, when Kaji wakes, you can have more."

Aniol hated Rogue at that moment, hated to be denied, but logic won over emotion. Rogue had good reason to make him go slow. As much as his body protested, he allowed himself to lie down once more, shifting closer to Kaji, reaching toward him, fingers brushing over skin far too warm. He settled a hand on Kaji's arm, crossing the feared gap, touching to appease the second, far more primitive hunger that had nothing to do with his body's thirst for water. It refused to be truly satisfied, forever present deep within him, demanding that he touch, taste, savor, explore skin, heat, sweet scent, and pleasure. He longed for Kaji's touch, his gentleness, his kisses, and claiming of him. It was slowly wearing Aniol down, chipping at his fears, driving him to reach out, seeking relief, unaware of what he truly sought.

The heat on Kaji's skin drove the hunger back into a dark corner of his mind, concern taking precedence. He glanced up at Rogue, silently asking for reassurance. Rogue held his gaze for a moment before once more picking up the cloth he'd dropped when giving Aniol water. He dipped it into the water and moved to brush it over Kaji's skin, brushing it over Kaji's arm, over Aniol's hand, using the motion to drift up Aniol's arm toward his forehead, brushing it softly over Aniol's fevered skin.

Aniol watched him in silence, understanding the silent message, the silent reassurance, finally allowing his eyes to drift closed once more, savoring the cool light touch that moved from him, to Kaji and back again, soothing and healing them both. Aniol's breath calmed, deepened, mind drifting, losing track of Rogue's touch, drifting back toward oblivion and much-needed rest.

# COLD STEEL

The tale of the Ruel is a tragic one. It is a tale of people driven to desperate measures by despair, and it is a tale of helplessness and betrayal. Once the most peaceful nation in Duiem, it is now the most feared. Once the people used to be weavers of cloth, tales, and imagination, masters of dance. Now they are weavers of steel and masters of death, masters of a craft once unknown to them, masters of war.

ANIOL trailed the fingers of his left hand along the wooden posts lining the route they were taking as he followed after Kaji and Rogue. The discomfort, pain, thirst, and burning heat were but a vague distant memory. He'd been extremely relieved when Kaji had finally awakened, watching as Kaji fought a similar battle with his thirst. It had been extremely hard to drink a little at a time when their bodies wanted more, but it had been worth it, their thirst finally quenched with none of them worse for wear. Yuan had not been so fortunate. After waking with no one to supervise his wanderings, he had found a well of water and drank far too much, far too quickly. What followed had been a violent bout of vomiting. It was a mistake Yuan was still recovering from.

His mind drifted back to Anei, wondering how the thief was doing. Anei had not left the city. Just before they'd left, he'd felt a sliver of cold upon his shoulder. Turning, he was faced with violet eyes. The strange thief was not supposed to be there; he had left them by the tree root. The young man held out a familiar brown purse insistently. "Take it," his soft melodic voice insisted. Only Aniol seemed to hear it, the pale young man remaining unnoticed by Anei, Rogue, Kaji, and Yuan, who were busy saying their goodbyes. "He's dead. He no longer has a use for it."

Aniol traced a finger of his right hand over the purse within his pocket. He'd refused to take it, even in the face of the violet-eyed young man's insistence, yet had found it a day later. He had no idea when or how it had been slipped into his pocket but had no way to return it. So he held onto it, wondering about the violet-eyed stranger's insistence and his motives to help.

Aniol slid to a halt just behind Rogue and Kaji.

Rogue smiled, his eagerness apparent. He pointed at the visiting merchant they'd heard about, sitting in the distance peddling his wares, gloating over his gains. They'd heard the man had cheated a few of his customers, selling wares that were far below standard, fooling his customers with smooth words and vague promises and a no-return policy.

Rogue's face settled into a blank expression, none of his feelings revealed as he sauntered toward the merchant. Kaji shook his head, following in silence. Rogue paused before the man's goods, a large variety varying from perfumes and cloth to spices and even weapons. He walked over to the daggers displayed in a corner, trailing his fingers over a few of the blades, mentally evaluating each one and finding them lacking. He picked up one of the blades, a rather familiar mark catching his attention.

"I see you have fine taste," the merchant said smoothly, suddenly standing before Rogue, rubbing his hands in glee. "That is one of the finest blades made. Ruel craftsmanship as you can see."

Rogue raised an eyebrow, not even having to pretend to look surprised. "Ruel, you say?" He glanced down at the blade, shifting it, testing its balance. He eyed the mark carved upon the blade and saw a stylized arrow, symbolizing that all warriors possessed the same spirit of courage and strength within them. Beneath it, he could see Arwen, three rays signifying opposites and the balance between them. Together the two symbols were the mark of a Ruel craftsman, but he knew the blade was not made by the Ruel. A Ruel craftsman would rather give up his vocation than sell a blade of such inferior quality. The weight of the blade was completely wrong, the metal not tempered enough, and to make matters even worse, the balance was completely off.

He casually tossed the blade to his other hand, picking up two more off the table, each with the same design, each with the same flaws, blades obviously made by a novice. "Rather interesting," he commented, sending Kaji a glance, "but the thing is...." Rogue absently tossed the blade in his right hand up into the air, catching it as it came down. "We're not looking to buy blades. What we are, in actual fact, looking for is horses and supplies."

The merchant looked crestfallen for but a moment before shifting gears. "Of course," he said. "Supplies I can easily help you with. I have tents of the finest quality, bedrolls made from mountain bear pelt, soft and extremely rare. I also have several bags, water skins, flints, and other supplies you may need, all made by the best craftsmen in the land. Of course it's all rather pricey, but seeing as you have such a good eye, I'll give it all to you at a special price."

Rogue raised an eyebrow. "And the horses?"

"Unfortunately I don't have horses to sell," the merchant said.

"Really? I see three good ones in the pasture behind your stall. You mean to tell me you've brought them to the marketplace and they are not for sale?" He twirled the blade between his fingers, spinning it so fast it seemed to create a solid circle of steel in the very air before Rogue's fingertips.

The merchant nodded, sparing the spinning blade but a mere glance. "Those are my own personal horses. I used them to bring my stall here."

"A stall filled with the finest goods from across the land?" Rogue asked, eyeing the goods set up upon the various tables, all of them imitations, from what he could tell.

"But of course." The man's grin broadened only to fade, skin paling when the blade Rogue had been playing with sank into the wood beside him, missing his skin by a mere hair's breath, the wind caused by the movement actually ruffling his hair as the blade passed him by.

"I'm so sorry. Must've slipped," Rogue said, no remorse in his tone. He switched one of the two remaining blades he still held from his left hand to his right, lifting it before his eyes, squinting at it as he pretended to contemplate it. "There's something off about these blades, don't you think?" He tossed it high into the air, the blade spinning as it fell. He caught it by its tip, raising his eyebrows before calmly spinning it between his fingers as he had done with the blade that was now deeply embedded in the wood of the stall. "Seems rather off balance for a Ruel blade."

The merchant was silent, mesmerized by the movement of the blade that spun between Rogue's fingers. The merchant's fear was thick in the air and he nearly jumped out of his skin when Rogue spoke again. "In fact, it seems rather poorly made for a Ruel blade, don't you think?" He tossed the blade high up into the air, drew a blade from his belt, and showed it to the merchant while the other blade still spun in the air. "Looks nothing like this one, you know." He waved the gleaming blade before the merchant's face, Ruel mark clearly visible upon a gleaming blade, edge so sharp it seemed to shimmer and vanish in the sunlight.

Rogue reached behind his back with his left hand, still clutching one of the flawed daggers he'd picked up. He caught the dropping blade without even turning to see where it fell, caught it in mid-motion, now balancing the two flawed blades in his left hand, the gleaming Ruel blade he owned still clutched in his right. "Different color, not as sharp, and certainly not as well made." Rogue watched the sweat drip off of the merchant's face. "Now—" Rogue shifted, juggling all three blades, the bright silver of the true Ruel blade danced in the light, reflecting sunlight, the glare blinding, making the other two blades seem dull and lifeless. "—we were talking about horses."

The merchant swallowed, his attention caught by the dance of blades, following each blade as it arched through the air. He breathed heavily through his nose, desperately trying not to wet himself. "How many do you want?" he whispered hoarsely, trembling.

"All three," Rogue said calmly, juggling the blades ever faster, ever into more and more complicated patterns, eyes locked upon the merchant, not even glancing at the deadly silver in his hands.

Rogue grinned as he, Kaji, and Aniol walked away from the merchant. He'd just sealed what could be considered to be the perfect deal all around. Both he and the merchant were satisfied with the outcome. He walked away with three horses, two tents, four backpacks, three packs for the horses, four bedrolls, eight water skins, four blankets, and a purse still full of coin. The merchant walked away with his life. Perfect, all parties satisfied.

# Tension

Impact can be defined as a mere instant in time, one that brings about ripples of consequence. These ripples are both calmed and aggravated by various actions that seek to control the damage and aftershocks caused by the single of moment of impact. More often than not, the aftershocks can be far more devastating than the impact itself, waves plowing through all in their path, sheer momentum granting them unimaginable power.

The legends of the Gatekeepers describe an impact so great that its consequences are still felt centuries later. Yet these legends fail to speak of the consequences that rippled through time and changed the course of history itself, hurting those who had nothing to do with the death of the Gatekeepers.

Thus, the legends barely touch the surface of history and neglect to mention the many smaller tragedies that followed the Gatekeepers' death. Although far too many to imagine let alone count, these tragedies speak of the true impact the death of the Gatekeepers had and the price many had to pay for a mistake few had made.

Although these tales have been overshadowed and ignored, each is a small ripple in the fabric of time, tearing it apart bit by bit, as devastation continues to creep up on Land of the Sun. They are tales of pain, loss, innocence stolen, and sacrifice. Chaos continues to build, small tales, precious tales, true tales that simply wait for the time that they may be freely told.

ROGUE, Kaji, Aniol, and Yuan gathered around one of the bonfires currently scattered about the oasis settlement, the orange-, red-, and yellow-tinted light of the flames flickering, adding a hint of mystery to the scene. People were gathered together in order to feast and dance, all celebrating a festival long forgotten by the people of Kaji's city.

Kaji glanced over the faces gathered around the various fires, all smiling, relaxed, and happy. Excitement was thick in the air. He found it rather surprising that these people could be so carefree as they lived a hard life, living in a small oasis, their homes hidden from the sun in rock, completely surrounded by nothing but desert sands reaching as far as the eye could see and beyond.

Kaji's heart clenched painfully as sounds of laughter drifting into the night sky. These, too, were his people, people he did not know, living with customs he'd been completely ignorant of. Yet they remained innocent, untouched by his mistakes and Karl's cruelty. The laughter in the air pulled at his senses, the relaxed atmosphere such a contradiction to the fear, paranoia, and madness now taking over his beloved city.

Sadness radiated from him as he contemplated the freedom and the joy here, girls flirting lightly as they casually walked, their hips swaying seductively, men watching them, laughing, sharing tales around the fire, the smell of roasting meat in the air, children running, playing tag, completely innocent of the hardships of life. He wondered how long it could last, how much time remained before even this small desert settlement was touched and marred by war, death, and helpless despair.

A gentle hand upon his shoulder pulled his thoughts away from the downward spiral toward depression that they'd taken, pulling him away from thoughts of a dark future and into the bright present. He glanced up. Aniol silently held out a plate, piled high with food, to him. Kaji accepted the food gratefully, eager to try the rich assortment of meats and vegetables laid out upon it.

He scowled when he saw Aniol shake his head, refusing a plate obviously meant for him. Not about to let Aniol pass on food, Kaji reached over him for the plate Rogue was holding out. He retrieved the plate from the assassin and dropped it into Aniol's lap, his meaning rather clear. Eat or else. His mate ate far too little, and Kaji was no longer going to turn a blind eye to it. He raised an eyebrow in challenge when Aniol blinked at him in confusion. Reaching to Aniol's plate, he picked up a piece of meat, reached up, and shoved it between Aniol's parted lips, withdrawing his fingers when he was satisfied, and licked the stray juices off of them. He ignored the shocked expression on Aniol's face, turned to his own food, and began to eat, secretly watching Aniol from the corner of his eye. He felt a good deal of satisfaction when Aniol chewed and swallowed the food. He was all but over the moon when Aniol picked up more of the food of his own volition, eating slowly, carefully, his gaze continually flickering over toward Kaji.

Kaji picked up a roll, dipping it into some of the sauce on his plate before looking up and leaning around Aniol in order to attract Rogue's attention. "I have a question," he said, speaking just loudly enough to ensure that Rogue heard. "How much do you know about the Gatekeepers? Who they are, what they're capable of?"

Rogue tensed, looking at Aniol and then to the people gathered around the fires. He shook his head, speaking softly. "Not now. Not here," he said shortly. Kaji nodded in understanding and returned to his meal.

Yuan glanced at Kaji in curiosity. "Why are you asking about the Gatekeepers?" He frowned in confusion. "You know the legends. There can't be all that much truth in them. Not after so much time and embellishment. They all seem rather mythological, don't you think?"

Kaji raised his eyebrows in disbelief. "You believe in the prophecy," he pointed out.

"Parts of the prophecy," Yuan said. "I believe that we need balance, balance of temperament, law, faith, and life. I believe that people need the prophecy and the hope it gives to survive. I don't believe in magic or in mythological people that seem to be able to control our fate. Our fate is our own, and the death and destruction of Duiem is our own fault. I don't believe in Gatekeepers."

"You are both correct, yet at the same time entirely incorrect in your assumptions," Rogue interjected, pointedly not turning toward Yuan as he reprimanded him. "The Gatekeepers don't control your fate. No one but you can do that. You have free will that allows you to make decisions that influence what happens to you and those around you, thus determining your fate. Magic, however, does exist, only not in the sense you seem to understand it. There are things unseen, forces in play that you are unaware of. These forces influence one another, you and your ability to make decisions, for any decision made is based on current knowledge and current understanding. Gatekeepers are simply individuals that can see those forces, who understand them and the manner in which they influence the world around us. Thus they make decisions based on that sight and understanding, on knowledge you do not and never will possess."

An awkward silence settled upon them, filled with questions, confusion, and thick tension. Yuan, Aniol, and Kaji all expected Rogue to continue, but he didn't, having said all he intended to on the matter.

Aniol shifted. Getting up silently, he placed his plate, still full of food, upon the log he'd been seated on and walked away, conflicted and hurt by the exchange.

Rogue watched him leave, turning to face Kaji. Kaji was watching Aniol leave, completely oblivious to Rogue's scrutiny. "Go comfort your mate." Rogue spoke softly, his voice pulling Kaji's gaze to him. He gave Kaji a cheeky grin, thus dissolving the tension between them. "While you're at it, do something about the sexual tension between the two of you." Rogue's grin broadened at the look of shock upon Kaji's face. "Come on. It's so thick I could probably cut it with one of my daggers. We'll be here a few more days yet. There's nothing you can do about the situation in the city at the moment. You can, however, do something about this. You need to. He's desperate for your touch, your affection, and you are desperate for wanting him. You and he have been through a lot recently. You haven't had all that much time alone together, time to bond with your mate like you were supposed to. Go on take advantage of this time you've been given."

Kaji scowled at Rogue, shaking his head as he stood. Walking away from the fire without so much as a word, he slipped into the night, searching for a slim form and silver-blue hair. Rogue's words echoed through his mind, demanding to be heard. Rogue had hit the nail right on the head, confronted something he himself had been tiptoeing around for a while now, revealing desire he tried to keep hidden, even from himself. He had a desire and desperate need to know his slim, ethereal, and rather mysterious mate better. A desire to know him on a mental, emotional, spiritual, and physical level. He was drawn to Aniol with intensity he didn't understand.

Kaji's departure caused the remaining tension to thicken even further. Rogue met Yuan's glare rather calmly, raising his eyebrows as he waited for the blond to explode. When he did not, Rogue smirked at him, enjoying the fight for control he could see in Yuan's eyes. He had to admit, he gained a small measure of respect for Yuan when the blond didn't explode. He kept a hold of his temper, though animosity practically radiated from him. It reminded Rogue of a hissing cat, ready to leap at him, claws drawn. He was just about to give voice to his amusement when a sensual figure dropped into his lap.

He glanced up, meeting emerald green eyes and lips pouting seductively at him as a slim hand reached out to play with his hair. Lira shifted her body in Rogue's lap, running a bare foot down Rogue's calf, the bells wrapped around her ankle singing out softly into the night. She smiled at Yuan, triumph in her gaze when Rogue wrapped his arms around her, sparing a moment to ruffle her hair before losing himself in the fire once more.

# TOUCH

Love. What is its true meaning? When asked, every person will give his own definition, a definition uniquely theirs. Sacrifice. What is one willing to give up for the one they love, their heart, their soul, their other half? A tale, lost in the shrouds of time, speaks of a boy, a ruffian who would not be spared a second glance by anyone walking past him on the street. He is said to have had torn clothes, bare feet, and eyes haunted by all that he had seen. He was a young man whose existence was considered useless and without purpose.

The same tale speaks of a king with flaming eyes and flaming hair ruling the land with strength, targeted by shadows of death. He was a king of noble blood, power, and strength radiating off of his very being. A king who was meant to die. A king whose life would be irrevocably changed by the boy.

KAJI shivered, the cold wind biting into his flesh. He squinted, wind whipping his hair into his face, obscuring his sight. Stepping forward, he locked his gaze onto the slim figure before him, partially shrouded by shifting sands, silver-blue hair writhing in a frenzied dance, invisible fingers tugging and pulling on silky strands. He paused beside Aniol, clenching his teeth to keep them from chattering.

Aniol was still, frozen in place, seemingly unaffected by the wind and cold. If Kaji didn't know better, he'd have sworn Aniol was just an illusion, a ghost. His ethereal beauty surrounded by the night sky and the dancing sand was too strange to be real.

"I'm sorry about that," Kaji stated softly, watching the sands of the desert changing the patterns upon the dunes. The scene held a strange beauty. It was always sand and wind, yet never the same, shadows giving it an otherworldly quality. Kaji turned to face Aniol, seeing the young man give a violent shiver as if he'd just remembered that he still lived, still breathed, and still felt the elements upon his skin. Aniol wrapped his arms around himself, mirroring Kaji's pose.

"Yuan is a bit of an idiot sometimes," Kaji explained. "He doesn't think before he speaks. Rogue, on the other hand, has no patience for foolishness, and I get the feeling he classifies Yuan as foolish."

Aniol glanced at him, skin unusually pale, lips tinged in blue. The mist in his eyes swirled with life, a clear indication of inner turmoil. "Who am I?" His voice wavered, carried away by the wind.

"You are a Gatekeeper," Kaji said softly. "But first and foremost you are and always will be Aniol Taiyouko of Duiem... my mate."

Aniol blinked at Kaji, lips parted in shock, the cold forgotten. He hadn't expected that response or the certainty and confidence with which Kaji gave it. He hadn't expected to be given a last name. "Taiyouko?" he whispered in awe, questioning the declaration.

"It's my last name and now yours, as you are bonded to me. As my mate it's yours to bear." Kaji reached out to trace a finger over Aniol's blue-tinted lips, concerned at their color.

"But Yuan said the Gatekeepers don't exist," Aniol whispered, licking his lips, his tongue following the path Kaji's fingers had taken.

"They do exist," Kaji whispered in response. "You're living proof of that."

"How do you know?" Aniol frowned, withdrawing from Kaji, gaze once more drawn to the shifting sands he'd been mesmerized by earlier. "I don't have any special powers or abilities. I don't even have basic skills. I have nothing but confusing visions that make no sense, neither past nor present. They're disjointed. I'm nothing but a demon." Aniol paused, voice hitching, fighting back a desperate sob of pain. "I'm nothing but a replacement, a thief that's stolen someone else's place by your side."

Anger ripped through Kaji, raging in his blood, dulling his senses. The fevered emotion rid him of the chill, the wind unable to defeat the heat of his temper. He grabbed Aniol, turning the slim form with unintended violence, his anger taking control of his actions. The amber in his eyes seemed to glow with inner fire as he met Aniol's frightened expression. Aniol's eyes were nearly white with the mist that raged within them, hiding the true color of his eyes. "Look at me," Kaji demanded, angry at the distant look in Aniol's eyes and the withdrawal the swirling mist signified. "I will not let you run from this!"

The mist withdrew, retreating to reveal clear blue-grey eyes. Aniol's breath was shallow, his body tense, but his mind was for once clear and focused. "You're not a demon," Kaji insisted through gritted teeth. "Just because people are foolish, fearing something they do not understand, this doesn't place you in the wrong. Your birth is not a sin. Your existence is not a sin. Gatekeepers have been gone for so long that we no longer know who they truly were or what their abilities were. We no longer even know how to recognize one, having nothing but vague legends to go on. It's human nature to fear the unknown. People hold onto hope, desperate for the war and death to end, for the prophecy to be fulfilled, yet they no longer know what they are waiting for. I no longer know what we're waiting for!"

Kaji shook Aniol, infuriated by his self-deprecating words, wanting to shake them out of him. He paused his ranting for a moment, looking for a way to address the last of Aniol's concerns—the words that had hurt him the most. Aniol was not a replacement. He wanted Aniol, and his very soul was angry that Aniol would even question his affections or his place at Kaji's side.

Unable to find the words he was looking for, unable to express his fury or his hurt, he pulled Aniol into his arms and aggressively kissed him, shoving his tongue past Aniol's pale lips, not even giving Aniol time to protest. He ravaged Aniol's mouth, seeking to claim him, to mark him, to make him undeniably his.

Aniol froze in place, resisting Kaji, and remained unresponsive in the face of Kaji's heated invasion. Kaji growled deep in his throat, refusing to be defeated. He pulled Aniol so close that he could feel every contour of Aniol's body pressed firmly against his own, so close that even the cold wind could not rob them of the shared heat. The burning flames between them inevitably drew a response, a whimper from Aniol, who was overwhelmed by the possessive demand and hunger.

Aniol began to press closer to Kaji, hungry for more. Fire coursed through his veins, and tension built, begging for release. Slim hands reached up and fingers slid into red strands, taking them away from the wind, twisting the hair in his hands and tying Kaji to him. Aniol opened up to Kaji's invasion, desperate for more of the heated moisture, tongues dueling, a rough sensation and addiction to a flavor that belonged uniquely to Kaji.

Kaji's hands slid beneath the clothes Aniol wore, gently touching his skin, leaving a trail of fire in his wake, cradling Aniol's lower back while tracing absent lines along it. It wasn't what Aniol wanted, what he hungered for. Aniol whimpered when Kaji released his mouth to press kisses along his jaw, leaving behind fevered skin hungry for more. Aniol threw his head back, granting Kaji better access to the sensitive skin of his throat, wind catching his hair and whipping it around him, giving him an appearance that was wanton—an ethereal beauty ravished by seduction.

Whimpers turned into a gasp when Kaji reached his ear, biting it and then lapping at it with his tongue in order to soothe it, only to bite it again. Intense waves of pleasure with the pain, one sensation merging with the next, overwhelmed Aniol's senses.

Aniol's knees buckled, his mind no longer able to convince him to stand; the pleasure, the pain, and the hunger were all too intense. He would've fallen if not for Kaji's arms still around him.

Kaji reached beneath his buckling knees and lifted him smoothly, swinging him up into his arms and capturing Aniol's lips once more. The mist swirled lazily in Aniol's lust-filled eyes, now a deep blue, tinted with violet. Kaji drew Aniol's tongue into his mouth, sucking hard on it until he drew a deep wanton moan from the man in his arms. Kaji withdrew, smirking.

Turning, he walked toward their temporary home, cradling Aniol's slim form in his arms, his weight easy to bear. He easily climbed the stairs carved into stone, shifting Aniol when he turned the corner and walked straight into the rooms hidden in the rock. He walked into his room, surprised to see a fire already lit, the room warm, orange flames flickering cheerfully, his bed already prepared. Kaji spared it but a moment's thought before deciding to puzzle it out later, and he dropped Aniol onto the skins laid out on his bed.

An amber gaze traced over Aniol's form, hungrily taking in every detail like the faint pink flush upon pale skin and hooded eyes that strangely reminded him of a moonlit night sky. Unable to hold himself back any longer, he crawled over Aniol's small frame.

A slow smiled formed on his lips as he watched the young man beneath him, completely at his mercy, his for the taking. He dropped his thighs onto Aniol, grinding their hips together, mesmerized as Aniol gasped in surprise and a moan escaped his moist lips.

Kaji reclaimed Aniol's lips, swallowing Aniol's gasps of pleasure as he ground their bodies together, frenzied heat driving him forward and desperation for release clouding his mind. Delightful friction sent increasingly higher waves of lust through him. He ground his hips against Aniol's, ever harder, ever faster, not hissing when Aniol met him thrust for thrust and increased the force by arching his body, utterly consumed by the heat of the moment. Little whimpers and moans escaped his parted lips, turning Kaji on even more.

Pleasure mixed with desperation, and they lost themselves in an ancient rhythm as old as time, mindlessly increasing speed and force, blindly seeking release. Kaji thrust his tongue into Aniol's mouth, growling in animal lust, claiming Aniol all for his own as he matched the rhythm of his hips with his tongue. He swallowed the loud cry that escaped Aniol as the young man came, violent tremors running through Aniol as he tensed and arched into Kaji in release with a force that pushed Kaji over the edge along with him. Kaji gave a few last jerks as he joined his mate in ecstasy.

It was only later, when lust released its hold and bodies began to cool, Kaji's frame heavy upon Aniol's, that Kaji realized they were both still fully dressed.

# KEEPER OF MEMORIES

The Keeper of Memories is assigned but one task, one purpose in life: keep the memories of the past and of the present. Hold onto the memories off all those who came before and visions of important events, for each contains vital threads of knowledge, and knowledge is power. Find the worthy, guide them, yet at the same time keep them in the dark, never revealing that which need not be revealed, that which can influence certain fates, certain threads, never revealing anything until the time is right. Know the truth, watch over the lies. Wait days, months, years, centuries; wait for time. And when your time is up, pass the burden onto another.

SERENITY. There was no other word that could describe what Kaji felt when he looked down at his mate's sleeping form. Aniol's features were relaxed, for once not haunted by nightmares and strange visions. It was the most restful Kaji had ever seen him; his long pale eyelashes rested upon pale skin. His moist lips were parted, still bearing traces of his kisses.

Kaji reached out, tracing the skin lightly with a fingertip, watching as Aniol subconsciously shifted into his touch as if by natural instinct. He brushed a few pale strands out of Aniol's face, convinced that he would forever be fascinated by their shade. Unable to resist the urge, Kaji leant down to kiss Aniol's pale skin, savoring the saltiness mixed with a sweetness, a flavor uniquely belonging to Aniol. He traced the sensitive skin beneath Aniol's chin with a finger as he lapped at the skin lazily, absently wanting to finish what they'd started the night before. He was already addicted to Aniol, to the softness of his skin, the saltiness of his sweat, the heat and the sweet moans, and the cries of pleasure that escaped those sweet lips.

He longed to recapture the pleasure, to heighten it and take full advantage of it in order to ravish Aniol. After coming down from the high the previous evening, Kaji had been mortified by the realization that he'd completely lost control. He hadn't intended to go so far, yet at the same time he had intended to go much further, the two desires conflicting with one another.

Aniol had fallen asleep, breaths deep, relaxed and calm, the light of the flames in the fireplace creating shifting shadows upon his pale skin. Kaji had stripped them both of the soiled clothes, cleaning Aniol with a bowl of water and cloth he found beside the bed. He had spared a few moments to watch Aniol, hungrily taking in every detail, longing to touch, taste, and memorize, to possess, and most of all to mark. Yet he resisted the urge, not wanting to violate the innocence Aniol radiated, belying the act they had performed, the torment he had endured, and the neglect he'd obviously suffered. Kaji had dressed them both in clean clothes, knowing that once the flames in the fireplace died out, the night chill would slowly creep into the room. Curling up beside Aniol and drawing him close, Kaji had then fallen asleep.

Now he wanted more. He wanted Aniol again, hungering for the heat and longing to slide his skin over Aniol's, direct touch with no cloth in the way. Kaji smiled, lips curling against Aniol's skin, when his kisses drew a moan. Aniol arched into him, seeking more contact even though he was obviously still asleep.

Kaji drew away from Aniol, leaving some space between them while he dropped featherlight kisses onto pale flesh, occasionally teasing Aniol's skin with his tongue and his teeth, wanting to see how far he could take this before Aniol woke. A hungry whine escaped Aniol's parted lips, his body arching higher, seeking contact that remained elusive, seeking Kaji's heat. Aniol's fingers clenched into sheets, going white with tension, and he turned his face toward Kaji's lips, his own hungrily seeking.

Aniol opened his eyes, misty gaze meeting lust-filled amber, and reached out, twisting his fingers through Kaji's long hair, tugging at the strands in an attempt to pull Kaji closer. He wanted more of Kaji's lips and tongue upon his skin.

Kaji didn't allow Aniol control, instead drawing back and depriving him of touch entirely. He reached out and pushed Aniol back down when the young man tried to lift himself up to follow. Kaji smiled at the pleading whimper that escaped Aniol's throat. Intending to give just a touch, to tease and then withdraw, he bent down and captured Aniol's lips with his own, thrusting his tongue into the welcome heat. Only his plan was thwarted by heated moisture, by a flavor he was fast getting addicted to, by hungry whimpers, and most of all by Aniol's eager tongue meeting his halfway, thrusting against his, wet slick heat against wet slick heat that made Kaji hunger a different type of wet heat, a different way of thrusting. Just the thought of it made him hard, his body jerking against Aniol's giving him the friction he'd sought so hungrily only moment before. Lost in the sheer sensation, throbbing heat coursing through his veins, Kaji reached for Aniol's clothes, slipping his hands beneath them, suddenly desperate to rid them of the barrier. He longed to have his skin directly in contact with Aniol's, rubbing against it, touching the heat and silky softness. He released a loud moan for want of it, a moan that was interrupted by a shocked gasp.

Kaji froze mid-motion, right hand resting on Aniol's stomach, lips still firmly pressed against his mate's. He stared, meeting Aniol's eyes, terror and embarrassment clear in them. He reluctantly withdrew, looking up to see Lira standing in the doorway, bright red with mortification. It was mirrored by the flush of Aniol's skin as he sat up and attempted to straighten his clothes, shifting to hide behind Kaji. Kaji raised a questioning eyebrow at her, refusing to fix his own ruffled clothes and hair.

"Um...." Lira shifted, looking rather uncomfortable. "Rogue asked me to fetch you," she said in a rush before slipping out the room as fast as her feet could carry her.

Kaji sighed in dejection, running a tired hand through his red hair. Lira had killed the mood, just when he had Aniol where he wanted him. He growled deep in his throat, glaring at the empty doorway before turning to Aniol. Faced with a fearful expression, he reached out and brushed his hands over Aniol's face, brushing stray ruffled strands out of the young man's eyes, gently reassuring him the only way he knew how. Kaji leaned forward and dropped a soft kiss onto Aniol's forehead before standing to leave. "I'd better go see what Rogue wants."

"NOT. One. Word," Kaji said in warning when Rogue raised an eyebrow at him, obviously eyeing his rather ruffled appearance.

"I thought sex was supposed to make you more docile," Rogue said, not all that interested in self-preservation. "I told you to deal with the sexual tension, not gather more. It's rather defeatist, don't you think?"

Kaji growled deep in his throat, fighting his own frustration. He clenching his teeth, resisting the urge to say something he may later regret. "What do you want?" he snapped.

Rogue noted the coiled tension in Kaji's body and shook his head. It felt like his efforts had gone to waste. He'd stoked the fire, laid out the bed in Kaji's room, burnt incense, placed a bowl and cloth conveniently beside the bed, and even laced their drinking water with aphrodisiac. He couldn't figure out where he'd gone wrong. "You need to pack. We're leaving today."

"Pack what?" Kaji asked bitterly, remembering the circumstances under which he'd fled his city, leaving all he owned behind. "Wait a minute!" he exclaimed in sudden realization, the impact of Rogue's words finally registering. The assassin's words were contrary to what Rogue had uttered the night before. "You said we were going to be here a few more days."

Rogue shrugged, giving Kaji one of his infamous blank looks. "I lied."

Kaji snorted, fighting the urge to reach out and throttle the sandy-haired assassin for toying with him like that, for lying, for pushing him toward carnal desires, but most of all for interrupting him just when he was about to get what he hungered for the most. He closed his eyes, forcing himself to take a deep breaths calming himself enough to speak in a tone only mildly less aggressive than before. "Come to think of it, where exactly are we going?" He ground out between clenched teeth. "And if you dodge the question or ask me how much the answer is worth to me or try to deviate from the topic, I just might kill you. I have a right to know," Kaji added, threat deadly serious.

Rogue hid a smile. Kaji actually had a backbone hidden beneath all that temper and naivety. He ran an eye over Kaji's entire form, allowing the silence to build as he took note of a few details he'd missed earlier. He raised an eyebrow in surprise, noting the ruffled clothing, the mussed hair and Kaji's kiss-swollen lips. That would explain Kaji's bad temper. Once again he hid a smile as he thought of the expression on Lira's face. It would also explain her rather hasty departure. "We're going to see the Keeper of Memories."

"Keeper of Memories?" Kaji asked, losing hold of his anger and frustration in favor of confusion.

Rogue smiled, a secret-knowing tilt to his lips. "In order to restore balance as prophesied, you will need more information. You need to know more about Gatekeepers and Wardens. You need to gather knowledge of what happened, what is happening, and what could possibly happen in the future. The Keeper of Memories can offer you most of that. If he deems you worthy, that is."

# ROGUE

Legends are spread throughout the Lands of Gold and Silver, small parts of a much larger tale told over and over again, changing as generations pass, obscuring fact and hiding knowledge that was once common. Only a privileged few still possess any real knowledge, hints of truth obscured by time and tradition. Only a few know what to seek, how to see, and what truly was. Only the Ruel possess true knowledge, untainted by time. Only the Ruel still see the path that leads to the door of redemption, waiting, seeking, and hoping for the key that will one day open the lock upon it.

KAJI narrowed his eyes, trying to avoid the glare of the sun as much as possible. They were once more in the desert, nothing but arid sand stretching as far as the eye could see, whipped into motion by desert winds, whispering secrets in a language no human mind could comprehend.

Kaji leaned forward, shielding the small form in his lap. Aniol sat in front of him, obviously inexperienced when it came to riding. "These are desert horses," Kaji said, voice muffled by the cloth covering his mouth to protect it from the coarse sand. He held the reins of his black beast in his left hand, his right resting on Aniol's thigh, in order to catch his mate should the young man slip and fall. "They can go for long distances without water. Also they walk rather well on desert sand. Their hooves are large. They cover a large area and make it easier for weight to be distributed upon the sand, making it easier to walk," Kaji said softly, lazily tracing patterns upon Aniol's thigh with his fingertips, trying to distract him so he could relax into the motion of the beast they rode upon. "They are rather resilient beasts. They can walk for days without rest if they have to, though it's not always a good idea."

Kaji smiled when Aniol leaned his head back against his chest to peer up at him, his misty gaze obscured by his lashes as Aniol, too, had his eyes narrowed, trying to keep the wind and sand out of them. "Days?" he asked in disbelief.

Kaji nodded, still smiling. "Yes, days. We won't be able to keep up with them, though. We would fall off long before they'd tire of walking. They are nomadic creatures, which makes it rather difficult to capture and tame them. I mean, how do you track down a single beast in a desert spanning hundreds of miles?"

Aniol's brow furrowed in confusion. "The desert is that big? But I thought deserts were not all that common."

Kaji frowned, jerking back in surprise. "Not that common? Whoever told you that? Half of Duiem is desert, if not more. The rest is either wasteland or mountains covered in stone. We used to have a better climate, centuries ago, but we've had so little rain that everything has died. Even our water supply is gone."

Aniol shrugged, dropping his gaze. "I read it in books. I guess misconception is not all that difficult when you don't get out that much." His tone was laced with deep-seated bitterness.

"Books are not all bad," Kaji stated softly, wrapping the arm that had been resting on Aniol's thigh around his waist and drawing him closer. "Maybe you're a little naïve about the real world, but you'll learn." Kaji allowed silence to settle between them once more, the steady rocking motion of the horse lulling him. He turned to the right when Yuan reined his horse in beside him.

"Must we follow him?" Yuan inquired, lip curled in disgust, glaring heatedly at Rogue, who rode before them, guiding them through the desert. "I have no idea how you can trust him. He's up to something. He's going to get us killed, I swear."

"You have any better ideas?" Kaji inquired, raising an eyebrow. "I'm not all that popular in the city. I let Karl do as he pleased and in my blindness never actually developed relations worth anything. I would only develop relations with those Karl recommended. Karl has been in charge of the army and the guard for most of my life, and neither faction appears to listen to me. Even the faith has declared me unfit to rule. Do you have any better ideas?" Kaji challenged, for once more cynical than angry.

Yuan hung his head in shame, shaking it. "No, I don't have a better idea," he whispered, voice all but lost in the sound of the wind. "I'm just not comfortable with how much trust you're giving him, Kaji. You keep forgetting; he tried to kill you. He's leading us into the unknown, not giving us any information. I hate being blind, Kaji. I hate all the mystery and conflict, and I have no idea how going to see some Keeper of Memories can help. How much can one person really do?" Yuan glanced up, meeting Kaji's gaze, silently pleading for understanding. "We need an army. We need to start gathering forces so we can fight Karl head on."

"Where from, Yuan? Where are we going to find this army? Our people are dying. There's nothing to look forward to but death. If not because of the ancient war with the Ruel, then from the new one with the Saikin or from the ever-spreading desert. Who remains to fight?" Kaji asked, neither reprimanding nor backing down, simply stating facts as he saw them. "Is there really no escaping violence? More death?"

"Sacrifices need to be made," Yuan said. "But I have no idea if we have any to spare anymore," he admitted. "I have no idea where to look for warriors that may still be loyal to you." His lips twisted into a smile brimming with bitterness. "Assassins and Keepers of Memories I guess it is, then." A moment of silence settled over them filled with resentment and unanswered questions. "He hates me you know," Yuan commented softly, breaking the silence.

"Not anymore than you hate him," Kaji said.

"I know," Yuan admitted. "But it gets to me. Everything he does gets to me. The way he looks at me, the way he doesn't look at me, ignoring me. The manner in which he speaks to me, the fact that he doesn't speak to me. The way he hides everything. The way he looks at her, holds her, pretending everything is all right and normal when it is not, when we don't even know who we are anymore. All of it, it gets to me."

"Her?" Kaji inquired in confusion.

"The dark-haired girl, the one with the emerald eyes," Yuan explained. "Lira, I think was her name was. I heard Aniol ran from her."

Kaji raised his eyebrows, surprised at the revelation, before smiling mischievously. "So Rogue has someone special, does he?" The question was entirely rhetorical as Kaji was already planning ways to get back at Rogue for stating he needed to relieve sexual tension. He'd always believed Rogue was too much of a loner, too much of a wanderer to be attached to anyone.

"Are you even listening to me?" Yuan complained, noting the rather preoccupied expression on Kaji's face.

Kaji blinked, torn out of his contemplations for revenge. He nodded at Yuan. "Yes, I am. I'm sorry you feel that way, Yuan. Rogue is... Rogue, I guess. He does things his own way and for his own reasons. Reasons that may seem abstract and entirely incomprehensible to us, but he's a good person, Yuan. He is what he is and has done what he's done, but he really is a good person. He, like you, has stuck by me all these years. If he really wanted me dead, I can assure you, I would be, for if you think I outclass him when it comes to skill with the blade, you are sorely mistaken. I have no idea why he snuck into my room that night to kill me. I have even less of an idea as to why he did not or why he's here helping me. I didn't injure him that night, not from any skill I possess, at least. Yuan—" Kaji paused, wanting to emphasize what he was about to say. "He let me injure him."

Yuan stared at Kaji in shock. He couldn't believe that someone like Rogue would do something like that. "Let you injure him?" he whispered. "I don't understand." He frowned, baffled by the concept. He'd seen Kaji's room right after the attack, seen the amount of blood scattered about the room, and seen the lack of injury Kaji had suffered. There was a lot of blood in Kaji's room that night. Any wound Kaji had inflicted had not been shallow. "How could someone let you do that?"

"I don't know, Yuan," Kaji responded. "Like I said, Rogue has his own way of doing things, his own reasons. And as long as he stands by my side, I will not question them. Some things are better left alone, don't you think?"

Yuan held Kaji's gaze for a long moment, searching for uncertainty. Finding none he nodded turning toward Rogue once more, for once his gaze devoid of hostility, instead tinged with curiosity and contemplation as he tried to figure the assassin out. Drawing a blank, he sighed, shaking his head once more. "He still gets to me, Kaji. I still don't like going in blind," he admitted.

"I know," Kaji conceded. "But sometimes blind trust is all we really have. Especially when everything we thought we knew gets ripped out from beneath our feet." Kaji's voice was resigned, mixed with a touch of both acceptance and determination.

Yuan stared at Kaji, surprised by the wisdom in his words. It felt like he was seeing his friend for the first time, seeing him in a new light. He knew Kaji had strength, determination, and stubborn pride but had never realized how deep it all ran, how much he had kept hidden. Kaji's words showed a lot of wisdom and a lot of strength, strength of someone who had made a grave mistake and still possessed the courage to live, to try to rectify it and to hold onto hope, the courage to fight for what he believed was right in the face of all adversity. Yuan eyed Aniol, still cradled in Kaji's arms, seeming to drift to sleep as they rode through the desert, and wondered at how one silent young man could influence one as fiery and temperamental as Kaji, seeming to change the redhead with his presence alone.

# UALITY

Duality: two parts, one whole, existing side by side. The existence of one depends on the other; they are opposites that are in conflict yet in balance. They are interchangeable, giving mutually to one another in an ever-repeating pattern of exchange. True balance is defined by such duality, by such sharing, opposing forces forever in conflict yet forever keeping each other in check, weakness and strength shared.

Such duality defines the fated interaction between the Land of Silver and the Land of Gold. The two lands are so closely linked that even the smallest disruption manages to ripple through to both. So it is that the decay on one leads to the decay of the other, the two sharing pain, desolation, and death.

FLICKERS of faint orange light occasionally lit features shrouded by the depth of night. The faint smell of roasting meat wove through the air, carrying a faint touch of heat along with it, heat that was defeated by the night chill. Rogue, Kaji, Aniol, and Yuan gathered around the flames of the small campfire, shielded from the wind by an outcropping of rock. They were all wrapped up in blankets, watching the flames as they waited for their meager fares to cook. Aniol was curled up in Kaji's lap, wrapped in the same blanket, the two sharing heat with one another. The only heat Rogue and Yuan were sharing was the heat of their glares, silently challenging one another, neither willing to give, neither willing to step down.

Kaji looked between the two for a moment, gauging the level of tension before turning to Rogue and asking, "Is now a better time to ask about the Gatekeepers?"

Rogue turned to Kaji, breaking the silent staring match he'd been locked in with Yuan. He nodded, reaching for a stick. Holding the piece of wood firmly in his grasp he drew two circles in the sand, side by side but not touching. "Imagine this. This is Duiem." He pointed at one of the circles before pointing to the other. "And this is Careil." Rogue raised his hand as Kaji moved to ask a question. "Two universes, two unique existences, each existing in their own plane, each with their own rules, their own strengths and weaknesses." Rogue glanced up from the drawing in the sand, noting he was now the center of undivided attention. "Each exists on its own, is a unique entity, but at the same time they are in balance. One cannot exist without the other."

Rogue drew a few lines in the sand, lines connecting the two circles upon it. "They are connected, are meant to share their strengths and weaknesses, the weakness of Duiem counterbalanced by the strength of Careil and the weakness of Careil counterbalanced by the strength of Duiem, forever held in balance. I'm told that the strengths and weaknesses are shared by allowing energy from each world to flow into the other. In order to do this, the energy needs an open path through which to flow. These paths are referred to as 'gates' and link the two worlds to one another." Rogue drew crosses over the various lines linking the two circles. "The Gatekeepers are keys that open the paths between the two worlds, thus allowing the flow of balance between them. They watch over the gates, keep them in balance, and allow people to pass through from one world into another."

The crackle of the fire, a snap here, a pop there, and the whisper of the wind were the only sounds breaking the heavy silence that settled upon the group, all eyes upon the man curled up in Kaji's lap. Kaji and Rogue watched him as they silently contemplated the impact of Rogue's revelation on Aniol while Yuan looked on in confusion, not sure he understood any of what had been said.

Aniol was horrified to be the center of attention and longed to just sink into the ground and out of sight, suddenly feeling horribly trapped by the warm arms that had been so comforting only moments earlier. He shifted, twisting, desperate to be out of Kaji's arms and away from the eyes upon him, Rogue's words still seeming to echo through the night air. When Kaji tightened his hold, Aniol bit him, sinking his teeth into the soft flesh of Kaji's hand. Shocked by the unexpected action, Kaji released him, unable to react as Aniol leaped out of his arms and fled into the darkness.

When Kaji moved to follow, he was stopped by a hand upon his wrist. "Let him be." Rogue stated softly. "He won't go far. He'll come back. He just needs time to deal with this. There are some things you can't protect him from. This is one of them."

Kaji's shoulders slumped, and he sank back to the ground, shivering, already missing the heat of Aniol's body against his. "You mean to tell me there are two worlds, existing together?" Kaji asked, trying to get more information, desperate to distract his mind from his concern for Aniol.

Rogue released Kaji's wrist. "Basically, yes."

"Why have I never seen the other world? Never heard of it?" Kaji questioned, peering intently into the darkness where Aniol had fled.

"You have heard of it. Duiem is the Land of Gold and Careil is the Land of Silver. The reason you haven't seen it is because the Gatekeepers were killed. The gates were sealed when the Gatekeepers died." Rogue watched Kaji, ignoring Yuan as usual; Yuan, for once, was too preoccupied to notice.

Kaji tore his gaze away from the desert, turning to stare at Rogue. "I thought the Land of Silver was a myth. After meeting Aniol I thought it was a land that existed beyond the mountains of death, beyond the borders of Duiem. Even after meeting and bonding with Aniol, I still haven't seen any gates, haven't seen Careil."

"Haven't you?" Rogue challenged. "You mean to tell me you didn't see a land of water, ice, and purple mountains, ruled by the moon and by silver?" When Kaji's eyes widened, Rogue continued. "Those were visions of Careil. Aniol can be nothing but a Gatekeeper." His gaze flickered toward Yuan at the shocked gasp the blond released, turning back to Kaji to finish what he wanted to say. "Only thing is, he doesn't yet truly know how to be one."

"What about the Wardens?" Kaji whispered.

"The Wardens are meant to protect the Gatekeepers from those meaning them harm. To defend them, care for them, and ensure that the Gatekeepers don't lose themselves to the gates, thus losing their sanity and hold on reality."

"The Gatekeepers can go insane looking after the gates?" Kaji questioned in horror.

"Power comes with a price," Rogue said softly. "Great strength is needed in order to wield it."

Kaji swallowed nervously, his throat suddenly dry and thick with fear. "And how do we find Aniol's Warden?" he whispered, licking at his dry lips.

"A Gatekeeper's Warden finds the Gatekeeper. Aniol's Warden will find him when the time is right."

"But wasn't it... wasn't it the Wardens"—Kaji licked his lips again, trying to force the words past the dread in the back of his throat—"that killed the Gatekeepers? Isn't it possible that Aniol's Warden could betray him... kill him...?" Kaji paled further at the thought.

"That's just a risk that we're going to have to take," Rogue said, knowing this was a truth, a danger that Kaji had to face and accept.

"I don't want to lose him," Kaji whispered in dejection. He shivered in the silence that followed his statement, the cold wind brushing against his exposed skin echoing the deep chill he felt within. He didn't want some Warden to come and take Aniol away from him, to have any kind of link to what was his. He didn't want Aniol's sanity, his well-being to be in the hands of someone who could betray him. He didn't want Aniol to be murdered by someone who was meant to be his protector, and he didn't want anyone else taking his place at the Aniol's side.

Rogue glanced up, looking into desert, expression hidden within the shadows created by the flames. "You can come out now, Lira," he said. "I know you're there."

The whisper of bells sang as a figure stepped into the light, midnight locks one with the darkness that surrounded her. "So he's a Gatekeeper," she said softly, seating herself beside Rogue, sharing his blanket. "I was wondering why you were so fascinated with him, so adamant that you help them." She eyed Yuan and Kaji, shaking her head, brushing her hair out of her face. She pouted, turning to Rogue. "Why did you leave me behind?"

"Because I don't want you involved," Rogue retorted, raising an eyebrow in challenge. "Why did you follow?"

"Did you really think I'd remain behind?" She glared at him, unfazed by the look he was giving her.

"Yes. I did," Rogue said shortly, voice hard. "I expected you to obey my order." He frowned in displeasure and pushed her away from him, creating space between them. "And to use what little intelligence you possess. This is not the time to give in to your whims, not the time for foolish games, Lira. Go home."

"No," Lira replied heatedly, turning to stick her tongue out at Yuan, who had been glaring at her in silence from the moment she had stepped out of the shadows.

Rogue took the opportunity to catch her tongue between his fingers, watching passively as her eyes widened. "Stop that, Lira." He released her tongue. "As I've said, this isn't a game. This is far bigger than you can imagine. It's not something you should be getting involved in."

Lira crossed her arms over her chest. "Just try and stop me. If you take me home, I'll just follow. If you leave me here, I'll just follow. If you tie me up, I'll cut myself free and follow. If you get someone to restrain me, I'll get past them and follow, and if anything should happen to me, you'll have to answer to the elders."

Rogue turned away from her without another word, pointedly giving her the cold shoulder. Lira grinned in victory, sticking her tongue out at Yuan once more before jumping up and going to fetch her horse.

Later that night, just when Rogue could no longer convince Kaji to let it be, just when the tension Kaji felt reached bursting point, Aniol walked back into the camp, crawled into Kaji's lap, and curled into him, skin icy cold, lips blue, pale hair tangled by the cold wind.

Wordlessly Kaji picked up their blankets, wrapping the material around the small shivering form in his lap and around himself. Once more they shared blessed body heat. He then pulled Aniol closer, allowing the tension to leave, relief taking its place.

# REALIZATION

The Ruel were once tribe of peaceful people, people who welcomed travelers warmly into their arms, offering a shelter, a place to lay a weary head, a warm meal, and kind words. The Ruel were once a tribe that offered sanctuary, a reprieve from turmoil, from strife. They were protectors of the innocent and advocates of justice. They were always willing to help the needy, the desperate, and the weary. They were people whose counsel was sought during times of dispute, whose wisdom once ruled the Land of Gold. They were people of peace… peace long forgotten as hearts grew cold, hardened by death and conflict. The Ruel are now a tribe of war. They are warriors feared throughout the land. They are a cold race, unwelcoming of strangers, imparting upon them a kiss of steel. They are advocates of death, suspicious of all, ravaged by time, pain, and betrayal, and the sanctuary they once offered is now lost.

THE desert sands faded away to be replaced by hard stone. Swirls of various browns colored the landscape, marking patterns upon the stone, telling a tale of time, of desert winds dancing, imprinted with memories of water's existence, existence which has been long forgotten by the shifting desert sand. Kaji took in the harsh landscape, dry wood scattered here and there as a reminder of life lost. He cradled Aniol against him, their bodies shifting with the rhythm of the horse's footsteps, his mind lost in exhaustion and numbed by heat and monotony.

He'd long given up on speaking, focusing merely on getting through each heated day, looking forward to the cool night only to mourn the loss of heat when it arrived. The desert journey had been long and hard, taking every ounce of willpower each of them possessed. Muscles were weary by the end of each day, bodies ached from the long ride, and skin was rubbed raw by friction and dry from heat.

The night was not much better, chill creeping in even through their thick blankets, campfires kept small for lack of fuel. Lira shadowed Rogue in silence, ignoring the cold shoulder the assassin gave her. Yuan sulked, still not happy in Rogue's presence, and Aniol was withdrawn as usual, ignoring everyone but Kaji. Consequently, a change of scenery was more than welcome.

Kaji inspected the rocks, awed at the hidden beauty inside the patterns upon them. When Rogue halted, he reined in just behind him, confused by the sudden, unexpected halt but relieved to be stopping. His muscles longed for solid ground. "We'll camp here tonight," Rogue said, "have a decent meal, and get some decent sleep before we go any further." All but Aniol dismounted, and Rogue turned to Kaji, throwing him several empty water skins. "If you go to the right, past that dead tree and down into the ravine, you'll find a small stream of water. It's relatively safe to drink. Please go fill the skins. Yuan will collect wood, and Lira and I will set up camp."

Yuan scowled, displeased with the way Rogue was ordering everyone about. His protest was, however, silenced by a firm shake of Kaji's head. Sighing, Yuan led his horse over toward Rogue and handed the assassin the reins, making sure to avoid brushing his skin against Rogue's, wordlessly rebuffing the assassin in the same manner Rogue continued to rebuff him. Remaining silent, he glared at Rogue before turning and walking away from the circle of rock, heading toward various pieces of wood he could see lying scattered about.

Kaji shook his head in defeat. He reached up to Aniol, helped the exhausted young man down from the horse, and settled him lightly upon the ground. Smiling at him, Kaji handed him a few of the waterskins to carry. Gathering the rest, he turned and headed toward the ravine, hoping the water was fresh and cool. He was tired of heated stale water, and his mouth already watered at the thought of fresh, cool liquid upon his skin.

Aniol followed Kaji in silence, watching him move. Kaji moved with predatory grace. Aniol loved the various contradictions the defined Kaji. He loved the way Kaji moved, the strength within that body, strength tempered by gentleness. He loved the fire within Kaji's soul, the aggressive, possessive nature that sought to claim him, yet at the same time sought to shelter him. He loved the anger in Kaji's gaze, the flames, the life, the passion. He loved Kaji's gentle touch, the way Kaji seemed to unconsciously reach for him, always keeping his hands upon Aniol's skin without even seeming to realize it. Aniol loved the way the sunlight played upon Kaji's fiery hair and the way the night gave a mysterious glow to those usual eyes. He loved the heated temper and the cool command when Kaji demanded answers. He loved… Kaji.

Aniol stumbled to a halt, staring after Kaji's retreating back, mind and heart thrown into turmoil by the realization that he was already lost. He had lost himself, mind, heart, and soul to the redhead before him, to the man who demanded answers from him, who wouldn't allow him to wallow in self-pity, wouldn't allow him to deny any rights Kaji felt he had to him. He'd lost himself to Kaji, who cradled him each day, whispering to him, drawing him back from terror, from the nightmare of his visions, pulling him back to sanity and demanding that he remain there. Kaji didn't let him run, not from himself, not from emotion, and not from being driven to the edge of sanity by visions and dreams. Aniol was shocked, still trying to deal with the implications of his realization, when Kaji paused and turned to him. Aniol blinked, heart racing when Kaji reached for the waterskins he carried, taking them before twining the fingers of his left hand with Aniol's right.

He tugged, gently pulling Aniol back into motion. "Are you sure you are all right?" he asked softly, concerned by the pallor of Aniol's skin and the glazed look in his eyes.

Aniol swallowed, nodding absently as he struggled to formulate a coherent response. "I'm all right," he said softly, hoping to reassure Kaji. He was not yet ready to reveal just how vulnerable Kaji really made him.

Kaji watched him in silence for a moment, his amber gaze searching the misty blue-grey, looking for reassurance. Finally he nodded, accepting the simple response. Despite the desire to have more insight into Aniol's mind, thoughts, and feelings, Kaji was willing to give Aniol the time he was so obviously asking for. He smiled softly. "Let's go fetch the water, then, before Yuan and Rogue decide to stop giving each other the silent treatment and start killing each other instead."

Aniol returned Kaji's mischief-tinted smile with a small, shy one of his own before nodding and picking his pace up, distracting himself from his own realization by watching the landscape, noting the shifts of shadow and light, the gentle swirls of brown and the different shades merging into one another, adding mystery to a rather bleak land. He paused when a soft sound met his ear, a sound that was as familiar to him as breathing, a gentle sound he had not heard in a long time. It was the gentle whisper of water upon stone.

"Water," Aniol whispered, lips parting in relief and wonder. Eyes drifting closed as he sought to revel in the soft sound occasionally brought his way by the shifting wind. He opened his eyes again, excitement coursing through him. He was eager to see the water, to taste it and to feel it upon his flesh.

Kaji shook his head. Aniol's excitement was contagious and pulling at his own, urging him to hasten his pace. Reaching the ravine, he peered into it, gasping in awe at the sparkle of water within its depths. Kaji took a deep breath, fighting to get his excitement under control before carefully tracing a path down to the water. Forcing himself to take his time, Kaji guided them down into the ravine, step by agonizingly slow step until they were both firmly standing upon solid rock situated right beside a small stream of sparkling water.

Aniol grinned at Kaji, eyes alight with childish excitement as he hurried over to the water's edge and buried his hands into its cool soothing embrace. Cupping the water in his hands, he threw his head back and raised his hands above his head, allowing the water to trickle onto his heated skin. Sunlight reflected off the liquid as it fell, coating his skin, creating elusive diamonds that glowed in the sunlight, emphasizing Aniol's ethereal, other-worldly beauty. It was a beauty, Kaji realized, that really did belong to another world. Aniol was a child of the moon, silver-blue hair flowing about his form, skin kissed gently by dewdrops of white light.

Kaji stepped closer, he, too, burying his hands into the welcome moisture to cool his skin. Scooping some of the life-giving liquid up, he drank, soothing his throat. The moment his thirst was sated, he began to fill the empty waterskins, watching from the corner of his eye as Aniol did the same.

The sunlight still reflected off of the water upon Aniol's skin, bathing him in a rather reverent glow and tugging at the strands of fear and paranoia in Kaji's heart. Aniol seemed like a dream. Just as fleeting, just as intangible, a vision that would slip from his grasp as easily as it had appeared, never truly his.

Kaji blinked in surprise when he found himself staring straight into confused, misty eyes, Aniol's wrist clutched firmly in his left hand. He'd turned and grabbed Aniol without even realizing it, fear driving him to reach out in order to confirm Aniol was real.

The sunlight began to fade, taking with it the mystic quality it had seemed to lend Aniol, reality slipping back into place once more. On impulse, Kaji reached out and embraced Aniol, breathing in his unique scent, absorbing his heat and savoring the touch of skin upon skin before withdrawing once more. "We'd better get going," Kaji said, standing and slinging the full waterskins over his shoulder. "Before Rogue, Yuan, and Lira come searching for us."

Reaching out, he caught hold of Aniol's hand and pulled him to the ravine wall, asking him to climb ahead of him so that he may be below to catch him should he slip and fall. Kaji gave soft instructions, guiding Aniol as they climbed, smiling when he finally made it to the top, only to have the smile fade when he followed, nearly walking right into Aniol's stiff back. Steel—sharp, cold, and deadly—was pointed at their chests, surrounding them from all sides, wielded by Ruel warriors.

# RUEL

There are as many assassins' guilds as there are those for thieves, scholars, warriors, and protectors. Each has their own work ethic, their own training regiments, their own masters of shadow and steel, masters of blood and death. Yet one assassins' guild stands out, their members chosen when only seven years of age, trained with an iron hand, a secret skill imparted to children by a people hardened by war and pain, innocence stolen by initiation at fifteen. Assassins belonging to this guild are masters among masters, only two allowed to pass every fifteen years. The rest? They die.

SILVER glinted in the fading sun, its edge sharp and cold. Kaji considered drawing his own blade, hidden at his side, considered fighting for escape, but the cold expression on their captors' faces forestalled him, told him he would die before his hand even reached his blade, perhaps even taking Aniol with him. The moment one of the Ruel warriors grabbed Aniol, however, all his wisdom was forgotten, and Kaji blindly reached for his own blade, desperate to make them take their filthy hands off what was his. Cold steel at his throat froze his motion, a warm trickle of blood trailing down from a shallow cut, pooling at the hollow of his throat.

Everything was frozen in place, an instant awaiting action, awaiting that which now seemed inevitable: pain, blood, and death.

A cold voice, full of authority, broke onto the frozen silence. "Did I give you permission to place cold steel at their throats, to cut into their skin?"

One of the warriors looked up in shock, staring at someone

somewhere behind Kaji. "They are in our territory," he explained. "They are Taiyouko." He pulled Kaji's arm, raising it above the Kaji's head, allowing the fading sun to shimmer and reflect off of the red-gold encircling his wrist. "Of the royal line. Bonded." He grabbed Aniol's wrist as well, raising his bonding bracelet as well.

"Release them," the cold voice ordered, clearly expecting to be obeyed without question.

"No." The warrior blatantly rebelled against the direct order. "They must die."

"Are you questioning my authority?" the cold voice questioned, sending chills down even Kaji's spine.

"No. I'm questioning your loyalty," the warrior spat, challenge and disrespect in his tone.

There was a flurry of motion, a blur of movement that ended with cold steel pressed against the warrior's throat, a shallow cut similar to that upon Kaji's throat trickling blood. Rogue glared at the warrior, sandy hair shifting in the cool breeze, blade glinting in the fading sun. "My loyalty is never in question." Rogue drew the blade across the warrior's throat, adding a second thin cut to the one already there. "They are under my protection. Now order your men to release them. At once."

The warrior swallowed, the blade at his throat cutting in deeper with the motion as he considered his options. "Release them," he whispered, the sound barely a breath above the wind. The warrior's men released Kaji and Aniol.

"Now *you* release them," Rogue ordered, sinking the blade in a touch deeper. The warrior reluctantly released his grip upon Aniol and Kaji's wrists.

Kaji turned and headed straight for Aniol, ignoring the cold warriors still surrounding them, ignoring the cold steel still unsheathed held ever ready to be used at a moment's notice. He drew the young man close, protectively wrapping his arms around Aniol's shivering form, glaring at those who dared to lay their hands on what was his.

Rogue released the warrior, spitting at his feet before walking to Kaji and Aniol. "You should know better than to ignore my command." Rogue's words were cold and calculated. He ran an eye over the warriors in the group, noting the new faces before turning to the familiar one, their leader, Mikai. "You should know better than to attack those under my protection," Rogue snapped.

"I have the authority to drive back and kill all trespassers." Mikai retorted, ignoring the blood trailing down his throat.

"Does your authority exceed mine?" Rogue asked angrily. "Have I been declared a traitor? Stripped of my rank without a hearing? Perhaps our structure of command has changed?" When Mikai remained silent, glaring rebelliously at Rogue, Rogue nodded, his whole demeanor hard and cold. "I thought not. Go. Tell the elders that I request an audience. Tell them I shall return at sunrise with—" Rogue paused. "—honored guests."

Mikai glared at Rogue for a moment longer, challenging him with his gaze alone. When Rogue did not succumb to his attempt at intimidation, he turned to the warriors under his command and nodded, a silent message to do as they were told. Weapons were sheathed, and the warriors were soon gone, slipping into the landscape as if they were formed of a very part of it, leaving them in awkward silence.

"Rogue...." Kaji swallowed, watching the assassin carefully. "Please remove your shirt."

Rogue, not surprised by the request, silently removed his shirt, revealing tanned skin and a body firm and honed by years of training. Most telling of all, though, was a design upon his shoulder. A dark, stylized arrow accompanied by Arwen's rays was tattooed into his skin. It was the mark of Ruel, but the black design was outlined in white, clearly declaring Rogue's rank to any that saw it. Rogue was a Ruel assassin, a Ruel spy, feared by Taiyouko and Ruel alike, a fearsome warrior who was only assigned difficult and secret missions, bringing death and chaos wherever he went. One whose authority was never, under any circumstances, to be questioned. Even Kaji, knowing as little as he did about the Ruel, knew that much.

Kaji spared a moment to wonder if the warrior captain who had held them captive mere moments ago was suicidal. "When were you going to tell me?" he whispered, a tremor coursing through his body.

Rogue calmly put his shirt back on. "It's not exactly something you advertise to your enemy."

Kaji tensed at the word, realizing that Rogue was right. Technically, they *were* enemies. They were at war with one another, which explained why Rogue had broken into his room four years ago in order to kill him. What it didn't explain was why Kaji was still alive. He drew Aniol closer, shifting so he could carefully place himself between Aniol and Rogue. "Explain something to me," Kaji asked, voice wavering. He fought his fear, the anger and the betrayal he felt, trying to redefine how he saw Rogue. "Why am I still alive? Why are you helping me?"

Rogue stood still, neither approaching Kaji nor drawing away from him, watching calmly as the redhead withdrew from him. "I've told you. I want peace. You die, and any chance of the prophecy being fulfilled dies with you. Duiem dies with you and your Gatekeeper."

Kaji remained silent, suspicion clear in his stance. He was utterly confused and torn, once more questioning the people he chose to trust. Aniol touched him lightly, drawing Kaji's attention. "He doesn't mean you any harm," Aniol stated softly, knowing from the bottom of his heart that it was true, an instinct, usually hidden deep within him, beneath all his confusion, coming to the fore. "If he had, he would've done so already."

Kaji relaxed, tension and confusion draining out of him, replaced by a strange sense peace and certainty. He turned away from Aniol, seeking out Rogue. "Okay," he said softly. "I believe you." He released Aniol, took his mate's hand, and approached Rogue slowly, unable to keep the newfound wariness out of his step. "Though I don't think Yuan is going to be too happy about this when he finds out. You might want to warn him before taking us to the Ruel camp. If Yuan sees the Ruel mark, he's likely to draw his blades first and ask questions later."

Rogue nodded, waiting until Kaji was beside him before turning and leading the way back to their camp. Lira and Yuan already had a fire going when Rogue, Aniol, and Kaji arrived. Lira looked up from a pot she was throwing ingredients into. Yuan was scowling at the pot, stirring the ingredients as he had been commanded to do so or starve. "I see you found them," Lira stated, contemplating Kaji and Aniol before grinning cheekily. "Were they fully clothed?"

Aniol's eyes went wide, and Kaji groaned at the comment. He didn't need another Rogue. "Yes, we were fully clothed." He growled at the girl, dragging Aniol to the fireside and sitting down beside Yuan, taking the spoon from the scowling blond.

Lira giggled lightly. When she met Rogue's serious gaze, her laughter died in her throat.

"They know," he said softly, indicating Kaji and Aniol, "and we need to tell him." He nodded at Yuan.

"Are you sure that's a good idea?" she asked, flirtatious mirth for once absent from her tone.

The absence drew Yuan's gaze instantly to her and to the others around him. "Tell me what?" he questioned carefully, for once acknowledging both Rogue's and Lira's presence.

Kaji held his hand out to Yuan. "Your blades, please," he commanded.

"Tell me what?" Yuan demanded, panic rising, refusing to give up his weapons. He didn't like the way this conversation was going.

"That was not a request," Kaji stated coldly. "Don't make me repeat myself."

Yuan jumped at the harsh tone Kaji used, the command within it shocking him. Kaji expected total obedience. He silently handed Kaji his sword and two smaller blades, knowing he was beaten.

"All of them," Kaji snapped, placing the three blades down onto the ground, sliding them in beneath Aniol's knees and out of Yuan's reach. He held his hand out once more, expectantly, waiting. Yuan silently slid two more blades into Kaji's grasp. Kaji turned to Rogue and nodded. "He's disarmed." He contemplated for a moment. "Now you."

Rogue nodded in understanding. Walking over to Lira, he silently began to pull blades out from beneath his clothes, piling them beside her, about fifteen in total. Kaji raised a surprised eyebrow, absently wondering where Rogue managed to hide that many. When the harsh sound of steel on steel faded and last blade dropped onto the pile, Rogue stepped away from it, separating himself from his blades, placing Lira between him and the cold steel. "Rogue is Ruel," Kaji said, his arm flying out to restrain Yuan as he uttered the words.

# EETING

The Ruel are ruled by five Elders, five fathers who stand at the head of the tribe. Their word is law, unquestioned, obeyed. All report to them and stand accountable to them. So it is, always has been, and always will be, for the sharing of judgment is meant to prevent monopoly and corruption. There are five heads for five senses, each existing on their own, yet none able to govern without the other four. Of these five, there is one head, one speaker for all. There are five Elders with the right to demand answers, the right to pass judgment, and the right to question all... all but one.

YUAN lunged straight for Rogue, hands reaching for his throat. He desperately wished he'd kept at least one blade to himself. Kaji had to stand and wrap his arms around Yuan's waist to restrain him and prevent Yuan from injuring himself as a result of his own stupidity. No sane person threw themselves at Rogue. Rogue simply remained standing where he was, watching the scene with cool, detached eyes, glancing at Lira who was doing the same. "Stop it, Yuan." Kaji fought to keep the enraged man restrained, anger granting Yuan more strength than he normally possessed.

"He's Ruel!" Yuan yelled, fighting Kaji's restraint. "He's betrayed us. We're on Ruel land, aren't we?" Yuan demanded, fighting with the strength of a cornered animal with nothing left to lose.

"Yuan. Stop it!" Kaji repeated firmly. "Stop it before I'm forced to resort to desperate measures."

Yuan elbowed Kaji, ignoring the warning and the clear command he could hear in the redhead's tone. He was fuming. He felt cheated and lied to and blamed it all on Rogue. He wanted to hurt Rogue, to inflict the same pain he felt by being betrayed. Kaji abruptly released Yuan, using Yuan's forward momentum to trip the blond. Yuan fell heavily to the ground, already rolling, intending to get up so he could throw himself at Rogue when Kaji sat on him and punched him in the face, hard. Yuan blinked up at Kaji, head ringing from the force of the blow, stumped by Kaji's action. "I told you to stop it." Kaji insisted, voice low, a dangerous glint in his eye. "Now calm down and approach this rationally."

Yuan panted from exertion, staring up at Kaji in shock. "You knew? All this time you knew?" He was torn by betrayal that seemed to surround him.

Kaji shook his head. "I just found out myself," he said softly. "Though, I should've at least suspected it a long time ago. All the signs were there. I simply ignored them."

"How can you be so calm about it?" Yuan wiggled beneath Kaji, once more fighting to be released. "The Ruel are our enemy. We're going to be captured, tortured, and killed! He brought us right into enemy territory. Kaji, he betrayed us and our trust!"

"Technically the Ruel are still part of the kingdom under Taiyouko rule," Kaji pointed out. "So it's our land and Rogue hasn't betrayed us. Aniol and I were surrounded by Ruel at the stream." Kaji pointed to the shallow cut upon his throat. "They had blades at our throats and were about to kill us. Rogue stopped them and ordered them to release us."

Yuan's eyes went wide before narrowing once more in suspicion. "He ordered them to release you? He has that kind of power? Kaji, he's dangerous! I don't understand why you can't see that!"

"Has he harmed us?" Kaji asked. "Any of us? At any time during this journey? All those days where we blindly followed him through the desert, all those nights where we lay vulnerable in our tents?"

Yuan blinked at him, swallowing before shaking his head. "No," he whispered.

"No, what?" Kaji insisted wanting Yuan to say it, to admit it to him as well as himself.

"No, he hasn't."

"Then why do you insist on believing that he's going to betray us? Why won't you give him the benefit of the doubt?" Kaji asked, frowning down at Yuan in confusion.

"Because I don't trust him," Yuan retorted. "He is an assassin. He is Ruel. That's enough for me."

"That's prejudice," Kaji said sharply. "Am I to be distrusted because I'm a redhead? Or perhaps because I am a direct descendant along the Taiyouko line?"

"Of course not!" Yuan protested. "You are my king!"

"A king that's made grave mistakes," Kaji said. "A king that trusted Karl, based simply on the fact that he was my advisor, my substitute parent, my teacher, Taiyouko. All of that wasn't enough, Yuan. Not enough to trust him. What makes distrust any different? If one of our own people, my father's most trusted advisor, can betray us, why can a Ruel assassin not help us? It's our hearts and not our origins that define us."

Yuan gaped at Kaji, shocked by the dramatic change he saw in him. He glanced at Aniol, trying to figure out what it was about the young man's calm presence that could influence Kaji so much. He turned back to Kaji and the determination he could see on his face, sighing in resignation. "Okay," he conceded. "I won't attack him."

Kaji nodded. Getting up off Yuan, he brushed the dirt off his clothes and sat down beside Aniol. He watched as Yuan followed suit, dusting himself clean before sitting down next to Kaji, glaring at Rogue, who'd watched the entire scene in silence, motionless.

Rogue nodded before walking over to his blades and picking them up once more, the steel effortlessly disappearing into his clothes. He then seated himself beside Lira, watching the flames as they flickered around the pot that hung above them.

Lira broke the uncomfortable atmosphere by tossing a spoon at Yuan. "Start stirring," she ordered. "The food is going to burn if no one does anything but stare at it." Yuan instinctively caught the spoon as it was flying right at him. He blinked at Lira in surprise before wryly obeying the command.

SUNRISE filtered through the cold air, slowly heating it. The faint rays of light cast shadow on rock and dead trees forming an intricate pattern in the wild, a pattern that had been modified to house a tribe used to living with nature. Kaji stared at the wooden structures that were merged with rock, homes surrounding him, occupied by silent people now standing at their entrances, watching the procession formed by Rogue, Lira, Yuan, Aniol, and himself as they walked through the village. They were obviously unwelcome. Kaji could see shadows of drawn steel, revealed from the corner of his eye, hidden warriors, waiting for the chance to strike.

Mikai guided them through the silent village, weaving his way among structures that were so well disguised it would be difficult to think they housed any form of life. Kaji clutched Aniol's hand, silently seeking the comfort of his mate's touch, giving comfort in return. He watched as Yuan nervously fingered his blades.

They paused before a large wooden structure, the dark wood merging the dark stone that surrounded it, melding with dark shadows cast upon the ground by the rising sun. Mikai stepped to the side and Rogue walked right in, no hesitation in his step, followed by Lira, Yuan, Kaji, and Aniol, in that order. Five men were gathered inside, seated around a small fire that flickered and illuminated their grim features, watching as Rogue and his party walked in.

Lira's face lit up in joy and she ran to the man in the center, a man with dark grey hair tied firmly back, weather-worn skin, and tired eyes that had seen too much pain. She embraced him, ignoring his surprise as she kissed his cheek. "I've missed you so much, Papa," she whispered, her words echoing throughout the small room.

The man placed his hands on her shoulders and pushed her back a bit, searching her features hungrily. He'd missed his daughter. "Lira," he whispered, awe and disbelief in his tone. "My daughter." He pulled her into his embrace. "Has Rogue been treating you well?"

Lira returned his embrace before pulling away with a pout. "He keeps disappearing all the time and won't tell me where he goes. He won't let me go with him, won't let me fight, won't marry me or court me and refuses to let me play with his knives."

The Elder chuckled, lightly ruffling his girl's hair, glancing up at

Rogue with mirth in his gaze. "The usual, I see. It's great to see you, though I wish it were under better circumstances." He gave Aniol, Kaji, and Yuan a pointed look. "What brings you here, Rogue? I thought you vowed never to return? What is my daughter doing with you? Better yet, what is Taiyouko doing with you?"

"We need to see the Keeper of Memories, father," Rogue stated, giving the Elder a small respectful nod, the term he used a mere term of respect and not a literal meaning. Five Elders ruled the Ruel, five fathers to guide their children, to make decisions and to be respected.

Lira's father nodded. "He's been expecting you," he agreed. "Have you no further explanation?"

Rogue took a moment to meet each Elder's gaze directly, one at a time, before speaking. "My actions are above question by the Ruel and the Elders." He pulled rank on them, rank he had earned, paid for in blood, loneliness, and heartache, barely escaping paying with his soul.

A tense silence settled upon the room. No one had told the Elders that in centuries. No one in the assassins' guild had needed to. They remained hidden in shadow, pulling strings from behind the scenes. It was how they usually operated, manipulating those in power without the knowledge of those they manipulated. Rogue's response was daring and indicated a serious shift in time and in the slim thread of order that the Ruel still maintained amidst all the chaos. The Elders did not move, each man obviously stunned by Rogue's response and the unexpected turn of events. In all matters but for Rogue's missions, they outranked him. However, when on a mission, and in decisions regarding that mission, Rogue by far outranked them.

Lira's father nodded, glancing at the other four Elders before speaking. "So be it. You may stay here a few days, but don't expect a warm welcome for you or your friends. We have lost far too many to the Taiyouko army for there not to be animosity in the air toward the king that rules those that are killing our people. I shall order the people not to attack, but I can't promise anything. Mikai shall take you to the Keeper who awaits you."

Rogue nodded before turning and walking out of the wooden structure, followed by Yuan, Kaji, and Aniol. Mikai met them outside and once more guided them through the silent village, leading them out into the wasteland to a circle of stone and a small wooden home situated in its center.

The sun was high up in the sky by the time they arrived. Mikai gave Rogue a barely respectable nod of respect and left, leaving the four alone to face the Keeper of Memories. Faded green eyes glanced up as the door opened. Deep lines lined an old man's face, speaking of a hard life touched by grief. Although it was obvious the man was old, having lived far beyond his years, he seemed ageless, exuding an ethereal aura of one who exists out of time.

He looked at the party that entered his abode; gaze going straight to Aniol, drawn toward the light he could see around him. He bowed low, a sign of deep respect. "Welcome Gatekeeper," he whispered before glancing up again. He gave a smaller bow toward Kaji. "Welcome, Warden." After greeting Kaji, he turned to greet Rogue. His faded green eyes lit up in recognition, followed by shock and the same bow he had given Kaji. "It's been a long time, Rogue." He kept his gaze down for a moment, dealing with the shock of his revelation, which he decided to keep to himself for the moment. However, of all his reactions, the one he had regarding Yuan was the most shocking of all. He turned toward the blond and froze in place, body tense and his very breath escaping his body in a pained hiss.

# TORN APART

A Warden is meant to protect his Gatekeeper, meant to give his life for the one he serves, meant to keep his Gatekeeper sane and give him peace, reprieve from visions of things not meant to be understood. They are two halves of a whole, two forces in balance; one cannot exist without the other.

To find his Gatekeeper, a Warden is given a signal, an emotion that lets him know who he is destined to protect, to serve for the rest of his life. This emotion is strong, drawing the Warden to his Gatekeeper like a moth to flame, binding the two together.

As overpowering as this emotion is, it is not permanent. It fades with time, requiring the Gatekeeper and his Warden to replace it with feelings more true and more honest, with friendship, trust, faith, and loyalty—to replace it, perhaps, with something more.

KAJI gaped at the revelation, confused by the man's reaction to him. He couldn't believe the implication of the Keeper's greeting. He couldn't believe he was Aniol's Warden. Even more puzzling, however, was the Keeper's reaction to Yuan. Did the man know Yuan? Impossible. He couldn't know him. Yuan had never left the city, had grown up with Kaji, and by the look on Yuan's face, he was just as confused by current events as Kaji was. Even Rogue, usually cool and unruffled, was frowning in confusion, wondering about the Keeper's reactions. "Keeper?" Rogue spoke softly, using the official term of respect.

The Keeper blinked, shaken from some sort of spell and back to reality. He shifted, his features settling into his usual calm mask, untouched by time and all that it entailed, untouched by emotion and the events that had so obviously shocked him moments before. "Please forgive me. Welcome." He nodded to Yuan before turning back to Rogue. "Please have a seat, and I will see if I may assist thee. My time is short." His eyes were suddenly weary, old, and filled with pain. The things he had lived through and seen had left their scars upon him.

"Your time is short?" Rogue asked, puzzled. He glanced at Yuan in confusion. He wasn't surprised at the Keeper's discovery about Kaji, having known precisely who Kaji was from the moment the redhead had told him of the dreams and the visions he'd seen. Only a Warden linked to a Gatekeeper would be able to share the Gatekeeper's visions. As for Yuan, it just didn't make sense. What on earth could the Keeper of Memories see in the blond idiot? "Don't say that. You have yet to find an heir."

The Keeper waited for Kaji, Aniol, and Yuan to join Rogue, seating themselves on the animal skins scattered around the small room. He ignored Rogue's question. "What knowledge do you seek?" the Keeper asked, acting as if nothing out of the ordinary had happened.

Rogue was about to speak when Kaji interjected, confusion and conflict driving him to voice one of the questions fighting for dominance in his mind. "How do you know I'm Aniol's Warden?" he demanded. He was afraid of what it would mean, of what he could end up doing to Aniol, and of the betrayal it could imply. If history were anything to go by, this was not necessarily a good development.

The Keeper smiled calmly. "I see the invisible links between you, links of destiny. Can you not feel it? Did you not feel the desperate desire to protect your Gatekeeper, the burning need to be beside him all the time from the moment you met him?"

Kaji stared at the Keeper, horrified by the words and the ring of truth in them. Conflict bubbled up within his chest, threatening to overwhelm him. Was what he felt for Aniol, the unbearable desire to protect his little mate from harm, nothing more than a Warden's urge to protect his Gatekeeper? He glanced at Aniol, whose hands were trembling his lap as he fought for control over his emotions. Kaji hated the idea. Anger coursed through him. He hated being deceived in such a manner, even if it was by his own emotions. He turned back to the Keeper of Memories, features suddenly hard, tone cold. "Let me see if I understand this correctly." For once in his life, Kaji was outwardly dead calm, too torn up inside to know how to handle the grief and sudden sense of loss that poured through him. "My desire to protect Aniol? To always have him close to me? All of it is just my emotions linking me to my Gatekeeper?"

The Keeper of Memories remained silent for a long moment before nodding. "Yes. Wardens need a way to recognize their Gatekeepers and so are bonded to them in such a manner that upon meeting them, they'll have a deep burning desire to protect the Gatekeeper. If this feeling did not exist, a Warden wouldn't recognize which Gatekeeper is his. Thus a Warden is given overprotective desires, desires that can be mistaken for love," the Keeper of Memories finished pointedly, meeting Kaji's amber gaze directly, allowing his words to sink in and echo in the tension.

Turmoil was tearing Kaji apart, making him question everything that had occurred, everything he felt and believed to be true.

Aniol sensed the uncertainty and anger within Kaji. He fingered the bonding bracelet on his right arm, his own heart breaking, torn to shreds by the realization that Kaji did not love him. His worst fear had come to life. He'd given his heart, his soul—everything—to Kaji, and Kaji didn't love him. All those touches, the kisses, the protective way in which Kaji had cradled him, held him near—all of it had been nothing more than Kaji reacting to false emotions imprinted upon his mind to ensure that he protected his Gatekeeper. Gatekeeper. Aniol's lip curled in bitterness, hating that word with a newfound passion. He'd never liked it, hated what it implied, hated the expectations the word had laid upon him, and now he hated it for ripping from him the only warmth and affection he'd ever experienced, for stealing hope from him, taking it from his grasp to replace it with despair and a wound that bled more than any physical one he'd ever suffered.

Aniol stilled, gaze dropped, withdrawing completely into himself. He closed off everything around him, gaze locked onto the piece of gold around his wrist, a gold bracelet with fragile clips that seemed to signify the fragile grasp he had had on his fleeting happiness.

Aniol shifted. Suddenly standing, he raised a hand up to pull out the string that bound his hair up and away from his face. Silver-blue strands of hair fell, masking his features from all present, hiding the silent tears pouring down his face. He dropped an object into Kaji's lap before turning and walking silently out, thus releasing Kaji of any obligations he may feel bound to, bound by a misguided sense of honor and an unwarranted sense of justice. For in Kaji's lap lay a red-gold ring, inset with amber and moonstone, a thin string of silver and yellow gold upon its edge.

A long heavy silence settled upon those gathered there, raw pain throbbing in the air. Kaji clenched his fist tightly around the small bonding bracelet in his lap, knuckles going white, his own bracelet suddenly an unbearable weight upon his wrist.

Rogue and Yuan were staring at Kaji in shock. The Keeper of Memories watched him with pity in his gaze, calmly letting events play out without interference. It wasn't long before all those eyes upon him drove Kaji's emotions to a peak, pushing him to stand and leave in an attempt to escape the heavy guilt in his heart. The guilt seemed to tell him he'd done a grievous wrong, but it was a wrong he could neither see nor understand.

Kaji slipped out of the wooden abode, sinking down to the ground just outside the door, misery heavy in his heart. He rested his arms on his knees, eyeing the rather bleak landscape that echoed the bleakness within his heart, looking for pale silver-blue hair, a hint of life and a clue as to where his Gatekeeper might have gone. He didn't even look up when the door opened once more and didn't even twitch when a blond man seated himself beside him and looked at him in question.

Yuan shifted, turning away when Kaji ignored him. He obviously didn't want to talk, but Yuan cold see that this was tearing his friend apart. He longed to help but knew this was something Kaji needed to sort out by himself. His very relationship with Aniol needed redefinition. Yuan ached at the thought. He'd seen how much his friend had changed, how much wisdom he'd gained, how much softer he'd become. That couldn't all be because he was Aniol's Warden, could it?


"WHY did you do that?" Rogue asked softly, the moment Kaji and Yuan had both left.

"Do what exactly?" asked the Keeper, watching Rogue carefully.

"Why did you make Kaji question his love for Aniol? It's obvious he loves that boy. He all but worships the ground he walks on," Rogue protested.

"I know that. You know that. But does he know that?" the Keeper of Memories questioned.

"He did know that before you made him question it," Rogue pointed out. "Why didn't you tell Kaji that the emotions a Warden experiences toward his Gatekeeper, the emotions that initially draw him to his Gatekeeper, fade with time? Any emotions Kaji had that initially drew him to Aniol as his Warden are long gone."

"He didn't know he was a Warden," the Keeper explained.

"What difference does that make?" Rogue demanded.

"He needs to reconcile himself with the fact. He needs to face his responsibilities and his emotions as a Warden. Then he needs to separate them from the emotions of the lover. He needs to separate the two roles, realize the impact of each, and then integrate them once more in order to bring them back together. If he has any hope of not betraying his Gatekeeper, of truly loving him, he needs to face his fears and his confusion. He needs to define his role as a Warden and needs to admit to himself that he has fallen for his Gatekeeper."

# HANGE

Death is accompanied by life and time is accompanied by change. Existence is a cycle that repeats itself over and over again, yet never remains the same, always shifting forward. Each life added to the cycle is given choices to make, choices that can potentially shift and change the inevitable flow of existence itself. When one life ends, another begins, destined to repeat mistakes and destined to move the cycle ever forward.

Prophecy is carried by this tide and provides a slim hope that someone may make a choice that will set the river of time back on course. But it takes a lot more to heal a wound than it does to inflict it. The hope that only a few souls may be strong enough to undo the damage already done is but a small flame that fades as the generations go by until all that remains is its memory.

ROGUE stepped out of the small house, tapping Yuan on the shoulder. "The Keeper wishes to see you," he stated softly. Yuan frowned in confusion as he stood, throat suddenly thick in fear of the unknown. He remembered the Keeper's reaction to him all too well and was not really sure if he wanted to know the reason for it. What Kaji had found out was tearing him and Aniol apart. Considering the Keeper's reaction to him, how much more could the Keeper's information hurt him? He didn't want to know, yet at the same time he was drawn to the knowledge that remained hidden to him, to the knowledge that was his to own. He took a weary step back toward the door, pausing as he reached to open it, conflicted in his mind and heart, one telling him to run, the other drawing him ever closer. He opened the door and went inside, leaving Rogue with Kaji.

Rogue seated himself beside the redhead, taking in Kaji's desolate figure. "Want to talk about it?" he asked, wanting to relieve some of the strain. Yet he knew he couldn't reveal the truth to Kaji, for the Keeper of Memories was right. This was something Kaji had to reconcile on his own, for no one can know another's heart more than the person to whom the heart belongs.

"Not really," Kaji response was flat. He didn't even bother to face Rogue, eyes locked upon the bleak landscape before him. Suddenly he grimaced, running a trembling hand over his face, and contrary to his first words, began to speak. "I don't know what to think, what to feel anymore," he admitted, his voice full of strain. "I don't know who I am. Who is he? I thought I loved him. I thought that I was meant to be with him. Why else would he stumble into the bonding circle like that? And he appeared just when I was going to bond to someone else. I know he's not the one that was prophesied to be with me, that he's not of royal blood, but I thought we could overcome that. He was mine, and we make our own destiny. Don't we?"

Rogue remained silent while Kaji spoke. "Now I don't know anymore. I didn't want anyone else to have him. I didn't want to find a Warden, a protector that wasn't me. Shouldn't I be happier that I'm his Warden?" Kaji asked Rogue, desperately seeking an explanation. "But I'm not," he whispered. "I'm really not happy about it at all. I wish someone else was his Warden. I wish my emotions were my own. I wish I could love him freely without question." Kaji's words died, the last echoing across the bare stone, filled with deep pain and a eerie sense of finality.

Rogue stood holding his hand out. "Come. Let's find the Gatekeeper." He waited for Kaji to take his hand, to move and perhaps break the despairing spell of mourning they were locked in. Kaji, however, ignored him, staring blankly ahead once more, lines of misery etched into his face. The wind echoed through the crevices in the rock surrounding the Keeper's home, a mournful wail carrying the cry of grief to the heavens.

Rogue dropped his hand. He pursed his lips, suddenly angry at Kaji, angry at the Keeper for doing this to him and the Gatekeeper, angry at himself for being bound in it, for having to keep the Keeper's secret, but most of all, angry at Kaji for letting this happen—for letting Aniol slip through his fingers—and for abandoning the Gatekeeper. He turned and left, in search of a man who still required protection.

YUAN met the faded green gaze before him, eyes that seemed weary yet timeless all at once, a contradiction that didn't seem to make sense, yet, was…. He swallowed nervously, mouth suddenly dry as he stepped closer, pausing just beyond reach, waiting for the man to speak. The Keeper watched him in silence, gesturing to the furs, indicating silently that Yuan should take a seat. Yuan hesitated in uncertainty, unsure if he should take the man up on his offer. His mind screamed that he turn and flee.

Ignoring the paranoid warning in his head, Yuan took a few more steps forward, carefully seating himself before the man. He watched the Keeper carefully, wary of the moment before him, something deep within him telling him that this was going to change his life forever. He tensed when the man reached a time-worn hand toward him, touching his face. The Keeper's skin was dry and warm, and his touch was gentle as the man traced light patterns upon Yuan's skin, lips moving with silent words, words that seemed to take both an eternity and an instant to speak. "At last," the Keeper whispered, voice weary and broken, the two words the first audible ones that he'd spoken from the moment Yuan had entered the room. The first and the last.

Yuan's mouth opened in a silent cry, voice lost as his hands reached up to clutch at his forehead, staring sightlessly ahead in shock and horror. He was lost in visions of life and death, of laughter and joy, peace and pain, mourning and blood… so much blood seeping into the ground, covering everything, the very blood-soaked ground wailing in grief.

Strange words echoed through his mind, prophecy, cries for assistance, whispers of pain, desolation and tales hope lost. He saw faces, their owner's lives flashing by before him. He saw all too familiar violet eyes, framed by hair the same color as Aniol's. He saw a slim form, feet bare and clothes ragged, a thief, lying in destined arms, blood soaked as he died, life fading from brilliant his violet gaze, leaving it lifeless, glassy.

He saw gates, their keepers killed, murdered by those they trusted; saw peace turn to war; saw dancers, singers, and story weavers turn to blade. He saw desert sands and wasteland spreading. He saw water, ice, and mountains, green lands that he did not understand. He saw misty eyes and blue velvet and upon the throat of someone he did not know, he saw a familiar silver chain, a silver chain upon which hung a pale blue-white moonstone tear. He saw all this and more, scenes running rapidly through his mind, their meanings beyond his grasp at any given time but understood by a deep hidden part of him. Their order was chaotic, yet not.

Then... he saw it. A flame haired king, a Warden tied to a Gatekeeper, a Gatekeeper he loved with all his heart. It was a love the king did not recognize and his heart was torn, his mind unstable. Despite the betrayal, a small flame of hope remained, a faint flicker of light buffered by winds from all sides, barely alive, barely holding on. Destiny and fate of the world relied on one confused soul and the decisions he would make, the thread still linking him to his Gatekeeper pale, weak, fragile and breaking.

Yuan gasped trying to grab onto the thread, trying to repair it but his hand slipped through, the thread intangible, a voice echoing through his mind. "Do not interfere with free will, with destiny, watch and wait." And then there was nothing but darkness, pulling him from the burden of all that he now knew.

When Yuan awoke, the Keeper was gone, the small wooden abode already cooling with the setting sun. He stood, surprised by the soft texture of the fur beneath his hand, fascinated by it for a moment as he used its texture to distract himself from all that now filled his mind.

Unable to avoid the knowledge in his mind any longer, he stood, wearily approaching the door step by careful step, afraid of what he would see on the other side, fearing his now drastically changed perception. He discarded the blades he wore without thinking, without truly realizing he was doing so. He had no use for them anymore. He was not allowed to wield them and was no longer allowed to interfere.

He opened the door and paused, gaze instantly drawn to Kaji, only now he saw more. He saw visions of death mingled with visions of hope, swirling around with Kaji at their center. Mingled with those visions he saw Kaji's father's life play out before his very eyes, visions of things he'd been too young to know, yet he knew they were true. They spoke of a life saved and of a life given up so that hope and prophecy may live. Choices. All of it came down to choices, and the last threads of hope hung on the choices Kaji would make.

"Go find your Gatekeeper," Yuan said, drawing Kaji's attention to him. Kaji's gaze sharpened upon seeing him, immediately picking up on the changes within him. Kaji had always been sharp. He always saw things quickly. He simply didn't have the wisdom to act on what he saw or the control required to temper his hot-headed nature. But there was hope for him yet. Kaji was learning, his temperament balanced and soothed by his mate. It all made sense to Yuan now. The reason Kaji was bonded to Aniol, the way the redhead had changed, and the reason the land continued to die. It all came down to choices.

"Yuan?" Kaji whispered, unable to believe what he could see before him. Yuan was still Yuan, but he had changed. His eyes, the way he carried himself, all of it had changed in the short time he'd been in the Keeper's home.

"Go find your Gatekeeper," Yuan repeated, standing still, not about to be distracted from his purpose. Kaji swallowed at the look in Yuan's eyes and found himself standing. He nodded to the blond, swallowed his pride, and turned, heading back toward the Ruel village, leaving Yuan behind.

THE night that followed was filled with chaos, broken souls, visions, and dreams. A slim figure, pale hair shining silver in stray strands of moonlight tossed and turned, the Gatekeeper once more haunted by visions of ice, water, and death, haunted by visions of blood upon a sword, bearing the weight of the world upon his too-young shoulders, a king in every sense of the word, a child who lost his childhood too soon, a ruler of the moon. Tormented cries escaped pale lips, and an assassin reached out in order to comfort him, taking the place of the one who was meant to be there. Shocked cries escaped the assassin's lips, echoing those coming from the tormented Gatekeeper, soaring up into the night as visions were exchanged and shared once more.

Elsewhere a blond figure stared into the night, green-flecked eyes weary yet untouched by time, listening as cries of grief tore the night air apart. A flame-haired king mourned the bond he'd taken for granted, and the Ruel mourned the loss of hope. The Keeper of Memories was dead and had not chosen an heir, taking hope and knowledge of the ages past with him to the grave.

# Confusion

Keeper of Memories: Only one of Ruel blood is given the
honor to bear the name and the burden. Respected without
question, he is protected by the people he serves. He is the most
important person in the tribe, the most revered, and at the same
time the most feared. For even in a tribe of seers and prophets,
he is the one who holds the key to memory itself; he resides both
within and beyond the grips of time. He is a mystery,
misunderstood, and it is natural to fear that which you do not
understand. And so the Keeper remains respected and protected,
yet also distant, separate, and lonely.

THE next day brought chaos and confusion on all fronts. Ruel mourned
the death of their Keeper, grieving the fact that he had not chosen an heir.
He had refused all candidates presented to him over the years, and now the
Ruel feared the precious information he was a guardian of would never be
recovered. It was a loss that would cost Duiem dearly.

A blond figure deeply changed by the events of a single day returned
from the rocky wasteland he had spent the night wandering, knowing
nothing but persecution awaited him. He had to join with a people he had
hated all his life, a people that were now his.

Yuan paused beside Rogue, confused by his rather unusual ragged
appearance. In all the time he'd known Rogue, he had never seen the
assassin even remotely ruffled. Rogue never lost hold of that unemotional
mask of his, yet here he was, seated on the edge of the village, features
ragged and torn, weary from lack of sleep.

Rogue sensed his presence and glanced up at him in shock. "Yuan?"

He started before hastily correcting himself, bowing his head as he spoke. "No... Keeper," he stuttered in shock, frowning in confusion. He was unable to comprehend the person he now saw before him. Yuan had changed, greatly. Gone was the animosity he could always sense within the blond, along with the pouting and childish aura he'd always carried. It was replaced by an aura of power, of certainty, of knowledge and of deep loneliness, and all of it was out of character for the persistent, stubborn young man who followed his king to the ends of the earth.

Yuan was now beyond the reach of his displeasure, beyond the reach of Rogue's own childish actions, actions he'd taken in order to get a rise out of the blond, thus paying him back for the animosity Yuan directed at him for no valid reason at all. Yuan gave Rogue a tight, weary smile, seating himself beside the assassin. "I'm sorry, Rogue," he said in apology, his gaze lost in memories not his own. "I am sorry for knowing nothing yet judging you based on that lack of knowledge."

Rogue glanced up, shell shocked by the apology. He would have never thought to hear those words coming from Yuan's lips, and they were a testament to just how much the blond had really changed. "Keeper," Rogue stated respectfully, the word unfamiliar upon his lips, seeming almost wrong, but it was now who Yuan was.

Yuan shook his head, a flash of his old self, of frustration and animosity coursing through him, gone almost as quickly as it had appeared. "Please don't call me that, Rogue." Suddenly Yuan looked young and pained, too young for the burden he now bore, wounded by that which had been thrust upon him. "I really need a friend."

Rogue stared at Yuan in silence, even more shocked by these words than the ones that had come before. "Did you just call me a friend?" Rogue asked uncertainly.

Yuan scowled at him, speaking to Rogue with the usual animosity he'd always reserved for the assassin. "Yes, I did. Do you have a problem with that?"

Rogue raised in hands in a gesture of peace. "No, Yuan, I don't," he admitted softly. He ran a weary hand over his face. "Yuan... can I ask you something? As the... Keeper?" Yuan remained silent for a moment, calmly watching Rogue, contemplating the request before nodding. "When you look at me, as the Keeper... what do you see?" Rogue inquired hesitantly.

"You know what I see, assassin," Yuan responded calmly, watching Rogue carefully as he spoke, every inch the Keeper of Memories. He allowed his very silence to be the answer Rogue sought.

"Why two?" Rogue asked in confusion. "Why does he have two?" Overwhelmed as he was by current events, Rogue finally understood the previous Keeper's strange reaction to him. The previous Keeper had seen that Rogue, too, was a Warden.

"To restore balance and order and so that he may be protected by both Taiyouko and Ruel blood. He will lead the new order of Gatekeepers and Wardens, should the prophecy be fulfilled."

"Head of the order," Rogue whispered in realization.

Yuan nodded in confirmation. Then he suddenly changed the topic. "Can I ask you something? As a friend?" Rogue returned the silence Yuan had given him before nodding. "Will you stand by me? When I go meet with our people?"

Rogue blinked in surprise at Yuan's reference to his people, remembering the man's earlier animosity and hatred. He didn't know what to think of Yuan anymore. He didn't know how to react to the change, yet he still found himself nodding, agreeing to stand by Yuan's side when Yuan went to face the Ruel.

Yuan smiled in relief, some of the gathered tension draining out of him when Rogue agreed. "Thank you," he whispered, running a shaking hand through his hair, only just now realizing how tense and full of fear the prospect of the meeting was truly making him.

KAJI warily stepped into the dark room, afraid of what he would find. His fear was confirmed when he found Aniol seated on a bed of furs staring blankly at a wall. The Gatekeeper was emotionally blocked off from the world around him. Kaji froze in the doorway, unsure and uncertain as to what he should say or do. He could no longer relate to Aniol as a mate and had no idea where to even begin interacting with the young man as a Warden.

"Um...." Kaji licked his lips searching for something to say. "Aniol?" he prompted, settling on the simple word in a desperate bid to get Aniol to turn to him, to acknowledge him. He traced the outline of Aniol's bonding bracelet in his pocket, his own still upon his wrist. Pain crackled through him, growing in intensity when Aniol didn't bother to react to him at all. "I'm sorry," he whispered, hanging his head in shame. "I'm sorry for giving you a false impression. I really had no idea."

He glanced up to meet Aniol's blank stare, the mist in his Gatekeeper's eyes for once still, lifeless and soulless. That look, the death in that gaze, sent chills down Kaji's spine. Cold horror sank into his being with the realization of what he had done. Instinct drove him to reach out, his left hand seeking to touch Aniol, to wipe that death from his gaze and to bring back the life, even if it was only in the form of confusion. However, his motion was stilled when Aniol's hard gaze locked upon the bonding bracelet he still wore, the rejection in his eyes clear. Kaji's hand dropped back to his side, dejection and hopelessness laying claim to his soul. He licked his lips. "I'll be outside," he whispered, "in the village." And so he left the room once more, leaving behind a desolate Gatekeeper.

"I ONLY want to practice," Kaji protested, hands raised in defense, eyeing the blades that once more surrounded him, his own lying on the ground before him. He had fled Aniol's room, seeking a place to drill, intending to use physical exertion in order to vent emotion he didn't know how else to deal with. He wanted to forget the dead look in misty eyes that were once more haunting him. He'd found a clear circle of space and drawn his blade, intending to do some of his exercises, only to find himself surrounded by steel.

"What's going on here?" A familiar voice spoke from behind him, an all-too-familiar command in its tone. Rogue stepped into the circle of blades, pushing some of the steel away, pointedly glaring at the warriors who had Kaji surrounded. "The Elders have called a meeting. You're going to be late," he stated pointedly, waiting for the warriors to drop their blades. When no one moved, he raised an eyebrow, pointedly fingering one of his own blades. The warriors scattered and vanished so quickly that, if Kaji didn't know better, he would've been convinced that he'd imagined them.

Rogue turned to him, obviously angry. "What are you doing leaving your Gatekeeper's side?" he snapped. "You abandoned him when he needs you the most."

"He doesn't want to speak to me; he refuses to acknowledge me except to push me away with his very silence," Kaji protested.

"Deal with it." Rogue's response was sharp and to the point. "You created the problem, now deal with the consequences. Whether you believe he's your mate or not, regardless of whether you love him or not, he is still your Gatekeeper, and it's your duty to ensure that he is protected. It's not your duty to cause trouble and get yourself killed."

"I only wanted to practice," Kaji protested, suddenly angry as well. Rogue had no right to speak to him in that manner when he couldn't possibly understand what he was going through. It was not his place!

"You'll get practice soon enough. Stop running away from the pain you caused." Rogue grabbed Kaji's blade from the ground and handed it back to him. He then grabbed Kaji's wrist and dragged him to the center of the village where a large crowd was gathered, firmly placing him at Aniol's side.

Aniol stood on a small wooden platform to the right of a central wooden circle on which the five Elders now sat. The blanket wrapped around his shoulders made him appear small and slim, too frail to bear the burden of grief currently in his eyes. He was staring blankly at the gathered crowd, and the people were eerily silent as they waited to find out why they had been gathered together.

Rogue marched straight onto the wooden circle and bowed, giving the Elders the respect they deserved. Lira's father stood, giving Rogue a small customary nod. "Why have you requested this gathering?" He spoke clearly, loud enough for all gathered to hear.

"I have an important revelation to make," Rogue announced just as clearly.

The crowd tensed and the Elders shifted, uncomfortable with being as much in the dark about this as the crowd before them. "Then hurry up and make it." Lira's father lowered his voice, yet it still managed to carry throughout the gathered crowd, every ear on alert, every breath held as the crowd waited to hear that which Rogue wished to reveal. Rogue left the wooden circle, stepping back onto the platform he'd dragged Kaji onto.

Reaching into shadow, he pulled a tense blond figure into view, heading back toward the wooden circle.

The crowd gasped, the Elders tensed in shock, and Kaji choked when Yuan followed Rogue, an aura similar to the one he had sensed around the Keeper of Memories surrounding him. For the first time in his life, he'd actually missed Yuan's presence. He hadn't even realized Yuan was there until Rogue guided him out of the shadows behind Aniol.

"Behold. The Keeper of Memories," Rogue stated in a commanding tone, standing facing the Elders, the crowd behind him. Shocked whispers and murmurs of discontent rippled through the crowd. The Ruel were angry that the new Keeper was Yuan, a stranger of Taiyouko blood, brought to them by an assassin. They didn't understand how an inheritance, which they held most sacred, had been passed down to one not of Ruel blood. This anger was mixed with joy. The previous Keeper had not died without an heir, thus taking with him that which they held dear.

The Elders were similarly shocked, unable to comprehend what their eyes told them to be true and unable to understand why it must be so. The wheels of destiny were moving once more, and a great shift in the stream of life was imminent. That much was clear. Before anyone had a chance to react, however, a cry was taken up by one of the sentries, those left to guard the village from invasion. "To arms, to arms, we have been betrayed! The Taiyouko are here!"

# THE PRICE OF WAR

The price of war is a heavy one, characterized by death, desolation and chaos. None know the price of war more than the Ruel, a people who mastered the art. They are a people who struck out only to be pulled into a web of war filled with blood. The price of the Ruel war is beyond human comprehension, countless lives lost before they were truly given a chance to live. And that is why the Ruel became every bit as harsh and desolate as the landscape in which they reside.

In order for peace and balance to return, these hard people need to learn to trust, need to accept a stranger, and need to fight for something other than their own survival.

KAJI leapt into motion, running toward Rogue, weaving through the Ruel fighters who were all running to their stations, weapons drawn, Yuan forgotten in the chaos. He reached Rogue's side, blade already in hand, surprised that he hadn't been attacked by any of the Ruel on his way there. "Please," he panted, features strained with tension. "Protect Aniol. I'm going to fight."

"Kaji—" Rogue started, trying to dissuade him.

"Please, Rogue," Kaji pleaded. "He doesn't want me at his side right now. He doesn't trust me anymore. Please, protect him for me... until I can figure out who I am again, just until I can face Aniol and give him the answer he so desperately needs. I don't know much of anything anymore, Rogue. I don't know who I am, what I should feel, or what I should do, but I do know this: Those men out there, those men attacking the Ruel, they are here because of me. Karl sent then here. I have to fight. I can't allow the Ruel to fight an enemy they don't deserve alone."

Rogue stared at Kaji in silence for a long moment, ignoring the chaos around and taking a moment to really contemplate Kaji's words. He nodded. "Okay, but only for a little while, Kaji. Your place is at Aniol's side. That much you can't deny. As for the role you will play, decide quickly before you lose what you have forever." That said, Rogue turned and ran to Aniol, blades drawn and ready, requiring but an instant notice for use.

He spotted Aniol in the distance before him, still standing where Kaji had left him, upon the wooden platform hidden in shadow. He could almost taste the terror Aniol was experiencing, the young man's entire posture screaming it to anyone who cared to look, the emotion obviously keeping him frozen in place. Rogue growled in frustration as he began to make his way through the crowd, slipping past drawn weapons, desperate to get to Aniol's side in order to protect the Gatekeeper.

Aniol stood, clutching the blanket upon his shoulders in a death grip, fingers white with tension, eyes wide with fear and the mist within them alive once more as he watched the chaos before him unfold. A flicker of red and a flash of silver caught Aniol's eye, heading straight toward the battle and to certain death. A wounded cry escaped his lips as he shot into motion, blanket slipping off his shoulders, drifting gently to the ground in contrast to the hurried movements of Ruel fighters.

"Aniol!" Rogue reached blindly forward, trying to get to him before he vanished. Aniol moved with surprising agility and speed, disappearing into the shifting crowd before Rogue could reach him. Rogue cursed when he lost sight of him. He turned and ran toward the battle, continuing in the direction he'd seen Aniol take, desperately searching for pale silver-blue hair.


KAJI pushed his way through the crowd, ducking and dodging drawn weapons, hoping no one turned on him. All he wanted to do was fight by the Ruel's side in order to right the wrong that had so obviously been committed somewhere along the line. He wanted to find Karl, reclaim his throne, and bring back peace. That should be simple, right? Wrong. If there was one thing that Kaji had learned through all of this, it was that things were never as simple as they may initially seem.

He raised his blade, countering a strike coming from one of the Ruel. It was directed straight at him by a young man with fire in his eyes, angry at Kaji for the betrayal he represented. "Please stop," Kaji begged, doing nothing more than defending himself against the young man's blows, steel upon steel, blade sliding against blade. "I'm not with them," Kaji explained desperately, trying to dance around the crowd and keep his life at the same time. "I don't want this war anymore than you do!"

Fury suddenly drove Kaji forward, directed fully at the situation he was now in. He was angry at being misunderstood and angry at the hurt he was forced to bear. He raged against the mistakes that had brought them all to this point, mistakes made long ago that he was not responsible for. It wasn't fair that he had to deal with a war centuries old, a war he had not started but had to pay the price for. He hated Karl for stealing his throne and hated the hurt his advisor had inflicted in his name, betraying everything they stood for. But what angered him the most was the feeling of helplessness, the feeling of being carried forward by a raging river, his very strength to fight waning with each obstacle he was thrown against, lost amidst terror, anger, and confusion, losing everything, time and time again.

Kaji twisted his hand sharply, disarming the young man with that single motion. He watched the young man's blade spin and fall to the ground, his own held at the young man's throat, the tip mere millimeters from marring flesh. "I'm not the enemy," he insisted before turning and running, continuing his journey through the warriors around him, heart heavy with the realization that he was moving forward to fight his own people.


A FIELD covered in blood, sweat, tears, and corpses hindered the movement of those still living, the air thick with the clash of metal, heavy breathing, and silent cries of grief. Burning muscles begged for relief and moved by sheer will alone, repeated motion, attack and parry, kill or be killed.

There was no easy victory, no fanfare, and no war cries of celebration. There were no heroes effortlessly winning the battle. There was no glory, no time to think, no time to grieve, and no time to consider anything except for the need to survive, living just a few seconds longer in the hope that it would soon end, that each opponent would be the last man whose blood would stain the battlefield. Kaji's movements had become motion without thought, heart heavy with the knowledge that he'd killed and continued to kill those he once ruled over. There was so much blood. His hands, his clothes, all of it was stained red by it and by the sin he had no choice but to commit. He now understood Rogue's answer to a question he'd asked the assassin a few years back, asking why Rogue had become an assassin. It was necessity: kill or be killed. He never believed it could come down to this, but it had.

He raised his blade in defense, the enemy's blow ringing through his exhausted muscles, his arm barely able to support the weight of his own blade. Kaji was disheartened, no longer able to muster the rage he'd held earlier, body beaten further down with each blow he managed to deflect and each blow he himself inflicted. He no longer knew who he fought nor how long he fought before killing one man and moving onto the next. Did it even matter anymore? He continued to move, his motion blind, driven forward by sheer instinctive skill, mind long gone.

Suddenly, the resistance before him vanished. The man he fought had fallen, dead before his feet. Kaji stared at the corpses that surrounded him with dead weary eyes, his shoulders bowed by a burden too great for one as young as he to bear. His mind was no longer sharp, his senses dulled by battle, by conflict, and by grief. So he did not see a sharp blade as it cut through the air, aimed straight at his heart.

ANIOL wove his way through the crowd, past blades, spears, and arrows, desperately seeking out red hair, pausing at every shade of red he saw. His progress was often hindered by the need to throw up at the sight of all the blood and death that surrounded him, sick in body, heart, and mind. Yet, fear for Kaji's life continued to drive him forward.

He was eventually forced to seek cover, hiding in crevices behind brown stone stained red. Inching forward, he prayed that he'd remain unseen as he navigated his way through the madness that seemed to have taken over the previously desolate landscape. He sought to confirm that the one he loved still lived. It took forever, every inch forward won by sheer courage alone, fear driving him forward past the death and horror he did not wish to acknowledge. He was determined to find his heart, hoping to protect it as he himself had once been protected.

An eternity later, he spotted Kaji fighting a lone soldier. His movements were weary, seemingly dragged down by a heavy weight. Aniol's eyes went wide in terror, fear thick in his throat as he desperately clawed his way closer, keeping low, hiding among the shadows of rock. He gasped when Kaji barely avoided a blow, retaliated, and ran the man through. The soldier dropped at Kaji's feet, lifeless, the blade that was moments before threatening Kaji's life still beside him.

Aniol heaved a sigh of relief. Kaji was alive. He'd survived. He was going to be okay. That was when he saw it. A flash of silver coming from his left, a blade leaving a hand, headed straight for Kaji's heart. Aniol didn't think twice, didn't even pause to consider the repercussions of his actions, only one goal in mind: to save his heart and soul. He cried out. Leaving his hiding place he threw himself at Kaji, placing himself between the blade and Kaji's heart.

Impact.

# GATEKEEPER

## BOOK TWO

CAREIL

# $\mathcal{I}$SOLATION LAID BARE

Every coin has two sides: heads and tails. One is linked to the other, the two separate entities existing in the same space, in balance. By the same token, every tale has two sides, each colored by the unique perceptions of those who lived it. The truth? It lies in somewhere in-between, never to be truly known, for any who seek it have their own perceptions that color their judgment. Everyone exists on one or the other side of the coin... heads or tails, never existing simultaneously on both sides at once, never able to grasp knowledge from both. Gatekeepers link the two sides, merging the existence of two opposing polarities, keeping them in balance in order to exist in the same space... together.

DARK brown eyes desperately searched the battlefield, seeking a glimpse of pale moonlight hair. Rogue had promised Kaji he'd look after Aniol. He was livid that he'd let the slim form slip through his fingers, neglecting his duties as both a friend and a Warden. He cursed in frustration, throwing his daggers at anyone who dared get in his way, not even pausing to see if he killed them or not, not even retrieving his blades as he moved forward, seeking the one he was meant to protect.

Rogue spotted Kaji, covered in blood, wavering in exhaustion after killing a Taiyouko soldier. He was surrounded by corpses, dead on his feet. Rogue changed direction, now heading toward Kaji, intending to get him off the battlefield, for Kaji was obviously beyond exhaustion, drained. That weariness could get him killed. If Kaji died, all would be lost.

He'd barely even started to head in Kaji's direction when he spotted it, a flash of silver wielded by a traitorous hand, heading straight of Kaji's heart, silver steel and silver hair. He was too far away to be of assistance, to protect his Gatekeeper or do anything but watch as Aniol, the fool, threw himself at Kaji, placing himself between Kaji and deadly steel.

Pure untamed fury coursed through Rogue's veins as he turned and headed straight for the man who had thrown the blade, killing hope with that one foolish action. One man had doomed them all. Eyes glowing with rage Rogue rarely showed, he plunged his own steel into the warm body and twisted it, killing the man before he even realized Rogue was there. Screaming in rage and grief, Rogue then threw himself back into battle.

ANIOL savored the impact of the warm body before him, the heartbeat strong beneath his fingertips. He was relieved to know Kaji was alive. It was Aniol's last coherent thought just as he was consumed by white light, wiping everything from his vision. The depths of darkness followed the white light. Then black faded into white once more, only this time the color was impure, tinted by shades of yellow and marred by time.

He blinked in confusion, trying to take in his surroundings, horror coursing through him when he realized they were all too familiar. Aniol sat up from where he lay upon the cold white floor. He trembled as he stood, walking to the edge of the white room, trailing his hand along it. It was real and rough beneath his fingertips. This was no vision. He was back in the room where he'd spent most of his life, alone once more.

Aniol chocked back a sob of panic as he turned, taking in the dimensions of the familiar white room once more, taking in the bed, the lone sketchpad, and the dark brown spot that now marred the room. He approached the spot in disbelief, dark memories flooding him, memories of loneliness and emptiness and cold memories of neglect and desolation. He knelt down beside the dried blood, trailing his fingers over it.

He was surprised to find the room pretty much as he'd left it. It was just as cold, just as bleak, and just as dead. His breath caught in the back of his throat with the rush of emotion that overwhelmed him, grief and terror that threatened his sanity. His lips parted in a silent scream as the last tendrils of sanity slipped beyond his grasp. His nightmare had returned. He was alone once more with cold moisture, rough ground, and damp air surrounding him.

AMBER eyes opened in surprise, staring up at a deep blue sky, the shade of which Kaji had never seen before. The deep blue color merged with deep green. He stared at the scene in disbelief. There was so much green. Kaji never even imagined that so much green could exist in a single place. He sat up in shock, recognizing the place from the visions he'd shared with Aniol. His breath escaped him on a sharp hiss, confusion coursing through him. He couldn't even begin to imagine how this could be possible.

The last thing he remembered was being on a battlefield, among brown stone tainted red with blood and death. He'd just killed another and gotten a reprieve from the never-ending battle when a flash of silver caught his eye. Silver hair... Aniol... followed by impact.

His hands clenched beside him, cold seeping into Kaji's fingers as they did so. He glanced down, lifting his hand before his eyes, staring at the icy dirt within his grasp. He could touch it and actually hold it. He opened his hand and allowed it to trickle through his fingertips. This was no vision; it was all real.

Kaji leaped up off the ground in a rush, desperately searching his surroundings, looking for Aniol. His caught a glimpse of white tower, not all that far from where he stood, rising up into the sky, the blue color far too deep to belong to Duiem. Kaji ran towards the tower, some hidden instinct drawing him there, dread filling him with each step closer. He stumbled to a halt when his way forward was barred by a locked door. Anger coursed through him. Something told him Aniol was in there, distressed and losing his grip on reality. He didn't know how he knew this; he just did, and he refused to let anything get between him and his Gatekeeper.

Kaji raised the blade still clutched in his hand and swung, not at the lock but at the hinges, cutting through the old brittle metal with ease. He kicked the door, putting all his weight behind the blow, and was inside, running up the stairs before the door had even finished falling. He ran up the stairs as fast as his feet could carry him and arrived at a second door. This time it wasn't locked; the latch was simply in place. Kaji reached out and slid the latch open, running in as the door swung open, only to stop dead at the sight of Aniol, kneeling upon the white floor, hand resting upon the dried blood that marred the room, his face twisted in anguish.

The sound of metal clattering across the floor broke the eerie silence in the room, Kaji's blade slipping through suddenly limp fingertips just as he moved forward toward Aniol, towards his Gatekeeper and mate. Despite the conflict and uncertainty still within his heart, Kaji reached out and pulled Aniol up, wrapping his arms around slim shoulders that trembled violently in his grasp.

Kaji embraced his mate, sharing his warmth and comfort, letting Aniol know he wasn't alone. They remained like that for a long time, Aniol trembling in Kaji's arms, Kaji simply holding him in silence, giving Aniol time to calm down.

The warmth of Kaji's embrace pulled Aniol away from remembered horror, and back to sanity. He realized he was no longer alone, locked in this white room, left to despondency. Kaji was there, his warmth and the scent of his skin surrounded him. Aniol swallowed, and gathering his sanity and courage, he stepped out of Kaji's embrace, facing his nightmare with new strength.

Kaji watched, unmoving, as Aniol took careful steps towards the bed and the sketchpad that lay there. Aniol paused before the open book, brushing his fingers lightly over its surface and the image upon it before withdrawing and rubbing the black chalk residue on his fingertips, as if testing its texture and the mark it left. Seemingly satisfied, he reached out for the book. Picking it up carefully, he cradled it as if it were the most precious object in the world. He closed the book, revealing a simple sketch of the moon upon its white cover. Cradling the book, Aniol stood still, lost in thought, a vague blank look upon his face. It pained Kaji to see Aniol so lost. Just as he was about to reach out to Aniol and attempt to wipe that look away, Aniol moved, gaze sharp once more and filled with purpose.

Aniol reverently placed the sketchbook down onto the floor before lifting the slim white mattress upon the bed and crawling under it, reaching to the far right corner. His searching grasp met a cool, hard, smooth, metal surface. Gripping it, Aniol pulled it out of its hiding place, allowing the mattress to fall back down. He stood, reverently tracing his fingers over the design upon the surface of a small silver box embossed with moon and stars.

"It was a gift," Aniol whispered, answering Kaji's question before the redhead could even ask it. Kaji was shocked by the all-too-familiar design. "From the only person who ever had a kind word for me. He snuck in here when my guard wasn't looking." Aniol smiled softly in remembrance. "He gave me books to read, my sketchpad, and this." He held the box out, opening it to reveal several sticks of black chalk neatly lined up within, each stick carefully wrapped in soft cloth to protect it from breaking. "I told him it was too precious for me, too valuable, but he insisted." Aniol continued to speak, watching Kaji, gauging his reaction to the words. "This"—he closed the box, tracing the design once more—"is a royal insignia. It's the symbol of the family that rules Careil. I think my visitor was the prince. Though why he would bother to visit me, I do not know," Aniol admitted, gaze upon the box once more, lost in memories of the past.

He blinked in surprise when he realized Kaji had reached out, silently holding his hand out to him, waiting for him to take it, once more giving him the choice to trust. Glancing up from the silver box cradled in his hands, Aniol met clear amber eyes filled with sincerity. "Come," Kaji spoke softly, his words reverberating through the still air. "Why don't we leave this place and find out?"

# Vision's reality

Legends are, more often than not, colored by perception and culture and changed by time. The environment and times people live in influence perception, and so it is that the same event is often seen through different eyes. In the Land of Silver, there is no prophecy accompanying the legend of the Gatekeepers' deaths. There is no hope for redemption, only the bitter taste of betrayal. Careil never knew what truly had happened. All they knew was that the Gatekeepers had been killed, murdered by those within the Land of Gold.

Chaos followed thereafter. Ice, snow, and cold took over the land... all of it out of balance, slowly killing the earth, leaving it desolate, bare, and haunted. There were no wars following the tragedy, no outcries of rage, only death and hopelessness.

And the Gatekeepers? They were forgotten, their story fading into the mists of memory until no one even recalled their existence let alone the purpose and the hope they brought. Time changed the people abiding in the Land of Silver. They became suspicious and rash, their paranoia leading to fanatical attempts to resolve a desperate situation, the sheer hopelessness of life making them fear anything different. They feared and hated anyone who showed signs of "abnormality."

The people sought a reason for the death of Careil, a reason for the punishment inflicted upon them by a land out of control, and the easiest explanation they found was that there were demons among them, cursed with the great sin of madness and visions and dreams. And so it is that the Gatekeepers born to the Careil continue to die, killed by their own people.

THE weather was strange. It was always humid and wet and cold. There was frozen water on the ground, crunching and breaking with every step Kaji took, slippery beneath the soles of his shoes. The ground lacked grip. One would think it would be more comfortable than the deserts of Duiem, but it wasn't. Discomfort remained, now a different form, the frozen water clinging to their bodies with no place to go, chilling them to the bone.

Although wood was now available in abundance, fire remained a precious resource, the wood more often than not too wet and too rotten inside to burn. Weariness and hunger began to overtake them as they made their way through tough underbrush, fighting for every step, for only hardy plants could survive the cold that ruled Careil.

The moment daylight faded, they would huddle together in search of meager heat, fearing the unknown. Sounds of life wandered about in shadow, hunter and prey, locked in a dance of life and death. Desperation urged predators to bolder action as the land continued to die around them.

Open wounds began to fester, not for lack of care but for lack of resources. Aniol tried his best to keep the Kaji's wounds from the battle in Duiem clean and dry, using all free-flowing water they encountered, but it was a futile task. The humid air and icy cold defeated him, and a slow poison infected Kaji's blood. Wounds that were initially inconsequential gained power over life through overexposure to the elements.

Even though Kaji shivered with fever, the movement a very contradiction to the heat burning through him, he still managed to reach out in concern, brushing his fingers over every wound Aniol received from the harsh environment. He feared Aniol's wounds would follow the same path as his, slowly poisoning him, his body too weak to fight due to lack of food, warmth, and shelter.

Aniol wrapped his hand around Kaji's, moving it away from the blood seeping from a fresh cut upon his cheek. He didn't want Kaji to worry about him. He clung to the hand in his grasp, afraid to let go, the fear that Kaji would slip away from him thick in his heart. Aniol wanted to weep. Kaji's injuries appeared to be getting worse by the day, and he feared for his lover's life. He'd even gone so far as to reach for his own clothes, intending to tear the material to use as a wrap, but Kaji had stopped him, not wanting Aniol exposed to the elements. The light in Kaji's eyes was dull, the few reassuring smiles he tried to give pained and rare. Even the bright sheen to Kaji's fiery hair was gone, the strands handing limp and lifeless in his face. They were losing the battle with the harsh elements of nature and losing their will to live.

When Kaji collapsed, Aniol cried out, voice hoarse. Kneeling beside him, he released his grip on Kaji's hand, instead reaching for his face, desperately pleading for a reaction, begging Kaji to look at him, to say something, to smile. All he got was a glazed look, lit by fever and despair. Aniol shook his head, refusing to accept what he could clearly see, his heart refusing to let go. He had to go, had to leave Kaji behind, and the very idea was tearing him apart, yet he knew he couldn't carry him or drag Kaji along with him. It was the hardest decision he'd ever had to make, but he realized that if Kaji were to have any chance of survival, Aniol had to find help quickly.

Aniol untied the makeshift bag he'd made from bits of his clothing, the material holding his precious sketchbook and chalk. He placed it beside Kaji, intending to come back for it and for Kaji. Standing, he began to run, his flight wild and desperate as he forced his way through the forest. He no longer cared about the multitude of wounds the harsh environment inflicted as he fled through obstacles, no longer attempting to go around them, wood, ice, and rock tearing into his flesh, bright red blood painting his pale skin. He ran until he could run no more, and then he collapsed onto his knees. The hard, icy ground cut into his palms, the new wounds stinging for a moment before they were numb with cold.

A rhythmic sound, the clatter of hooves, caught Aniol's attention, drawing his gaze up. He sobbed in relief. Two riders mounted upon beautiful white steeds moved fluidly through the harsh environment, seemingly unhindered by the branches sticking out every which way. Aniol dragged his weary body up, biting his lip in determination, lapping at the blood upon his it when his teeth broke the skin. He stumbled toward the riders and toward salvation, crying as he walked. He reached blindly forward, too exhausted and too delirious to cry out.

The men continued to ride and talk, moving ever forward and away from Aniol's stumbling figure. Aniol whimpered in pain when it seemed they would pass him by and leave him behind, taking the last thread of hope he possessed with them. Just when it seemed that Aniol's worst fear would be realized, one of them glanced to the right and paused, his clear blue-grey gaze framed by pale silver blue hair going wide in shock.

A SMALL bandaged hand reached out to brush soft silky strands of red hair off of a pale face, carefully tracing cuts and bruises that remained uncovered. A misty gaze watched over the sleeping form, patiently waiting for amber eyes to open.

The two strangers had ridden toward Aniol the moment they'd realized he was in distress. Heading his desperate pleas they then picked him up and followed his directions to Kaji. They gathered the redhead and brought them to a warm cabin richly decorated in furs and tapestries boasting a warm fireplace in each of its three rooms. The second man with pale, white hair and pale blue eyes had then proceeded to tend to Kaji while a third, one who had met them at the cabin, tended to Aniol. The first young man, the one from Aniol's visions, had disappeared completely.

Aniol occupied the same room as Kaji, watching over the redhead as the fever raged, then faded, the herbs upon his wounds doing their work, countering the poison of infection in Kaji's blood. Kaji had slept for two days and two nights. Aniol didn't sleep at all during that time, refusing to leave Kaji's side for anything. Kaji's fever finally broke during the second night, allowing him to fall into peaceful slumber, healing sleep that would restore his energy and bring him back to Aniol.

Aniol glanced up when he heard soft footsteps intrude. Standing before him was the young man from his visions, his blue-grey gaze locked onto Aniol. "Who are you?" The boy spoke softly, yet command remained clear in his tone. He was obviously accustomed to being obeyed.

Aniol shifted, placing himself between Kaji and the boy, sensing the animosity in the boy's stance. "Aniol," he whispered in response, nervously licking his lips.

"Aniol?" The man raised an eyebrow. "Aniol who?"

Aniol swallowed, his gaze wide, mist swirling within it. He glanced down at Kaji in contemplation, wondering if he still had a right to Kaji's name, wondering if it would be all right to use it as he had no family name of his own. "Aniol Taiyouko."

The man approached Aniol then circled the bed upon which Kaji lay, gaze locked firmly upon them, arms locked behind his back. "What are you doing here in these woods?" he demanded.

Aniol shivered beneath the man's gaze. The man was angry, and that anger was directed solely at him. Aniol had absolutely no idea why, as he didn't know this boy and didn't recall meeting him, let alone doing anything to him. "We got lost."

"And where were you headed exactly?" The man raised an eyebrow, pausing beside Aniol.

"We were looking for someone," Aniol admitted, watching him. He was uncomfortable with the man's proximity to Kaji and himself. The man's hard blue-grey gaze flickered to Kaji as he leaned forward to inspect the sleeping redhead, anger still visible in his posture. Aniol sprang into motion, ducking low to place himself between the man from his visions and Kaji, wanting to protect Kaji from harm.

Aniol was so busy trying to place himself between the man he was starting to dislike and Kaji that he didn't even notice when his moonstone pendant slipped out from beneath the clothes he wore, the flame from the fireplace reflecting off the blue-white stone, tinting the silver and gold. Time froze, a mere instant of shock thick in the air, as the young man noticed the small teardrop hanging from Aniol's neck. The mere instant was over all too soon, and time rushed back in to find Aniol across the room, slammed against the wall with the man's hands around his neck. Clear blue-grey eyes burned in fury as he cut off Aniol's air.

"Where did you get this?" he demanded. Releasing one hand from around Aniol's fragile throat, he grabbed the pendant, ripping it off Aniol's neck. Aniol's fingers clawed at the hand that remained around his throat, desperate for breath, his lips turning a faint blue. His eyes bulged as he weakly tried to lash out in an attempt to free himself. The stranger watched as Aniol battled for air, pure rage burning deep within his eyes. The cold look was filled with hatred, filling the air between them with icy silence that was interrupted by the sound of steel being drawn. A blade appeared at the man's throat, threatening to break the pale skin. "I suggest you release what belongs to me," a cold voice threatened. "Release my mate or forfeit your life, for your existence matters not to me."

# Secrets

Fear and paranoia ran rampant in the Land of Silver, driving people to the edge of madness and beyond. Visions were feared as the land died around them, be they visions of the past, the future, or even visions of a desert land. White eyes marked a seer, a blind child to which the visions came, and the fear of visions was transferred to fear of those gifted with them. Those born with white eyes were believed to be demons, bringing the punishment of the gods upon the Land of Silver.

As the land continued to die, superstition began to grow and spread. The people of Careil started killing every child born with eyes marked by white, be they blind or not, and thus unknowingly began to kill their last hope. So it was that a mother with great love in her heart, wept when her child, newly born, opened his beautiful eyes and revealed that they were cursed. The white mist in her child's eyes meant that he would die. This she could not accept. Wrapping the small fragile form in a blanket, she handed her precious child to a trusted guard to protect and announced that her child had died.

KAJI'S hand trembled as he held the blade at the stranger's throat. The man had a simple choice, in his opinion. Personally, he'd prefer it if the stranger chose the latter.

Time was once more still, a mere instant seeming like an eternity, tension escalating bit by prolonged bit, but before the tension managed to reach a breaking point, a man walked in on the scene.

"Arian! Stop!" The man exclaimed, purple gaze going wide as he ran toward Arian's side. Reaching for Arian, he pulled him away from Aniol.

Aniol sank to the ground, gasping for breath, his hand reaching for his throat to gently trace the bruise already forming upon it. Kaji remained standing, blade held at Arian's throat as the newcomer knelt down beside Aniol, pulling Aniol's hand away from his throat and gently tracing the finger marks left by Arian. "I thought you were dead, Aniol." Pain-filled purple eyes met Aniol's misty ones. "They told me you were murdered and that they'd buried your body, but I never stopped searching for you."

"Mathié?" Aniol whispered, his tone pained, his throat aching with the words. He ran his eyes over Mathié's, taking in his presence while his mind tried to reconcile it with what he knew. The last time Aniol had seen Mathié was a couple of months before the attempt on his life, and after meeting and bonding to Kaji, Aniol had been convinced he'd never see Mathié again.

Mathié gathered Aniol up, wrapping the slim young man into a warm embrace. "It's all right," he said in an attempt to soothe Aniol. "I'm sorry I abandoned you. I'm sorry I let them hurt you, but could you please ask your protector to stop pointing a blade at Arian's throat? I don't think the royal guards will be too happy about it if they see, and your friend might not survive the ensuing skirmish."

Aniol frowned in confusion, wondering why Mathié would say that, but he nodded anyway, swallowing painfully. If he really thought about it, he guessed it would make sense that the guards would not want a drawn blade around their prince. "Kaji?" he rasped, looking at Kaji over Mathié's shoulder.

Kaji frowned, animosity and rage still burning in his veins, rage joined by jealousy at the familiar way in which the stranger, Mathié, interacted with Aniol. Reluctantly he lowered his blade, sheathing it once more, but he kept it in hand, ready to draw it at a moment's notice. He glared heatedly at Mathié and at Arian.

Arian sighed in relief, reaching for his throat where he could still feel the echo of the cold steel that had been pressed there. "I take you in, have your wounds seen to, and this is how you thank me?" he asked dryly.

Kaji's clenched his hand around the handle of his blade. He was itching to draw it once again. "You were strangling my mate," Kaji snapped through clenched teeth. "I don't want my life if the price for it is his."

Arian took a moment to silently assess Kaji. He tried to determine if Kaji was a threat before clearly dismissing him. "If I was going to kill him, he would already be dead," he retorted coldly.

"Arian, I would suggest you stop provoking your guests," Mathié reprimanded softly, picking Aniol up and carrying him over to the bed. Kaji was beside Aniol, gathering him towards his chest even before Mathié was done putting him down. Mathié stood, staring at Kaji, carefully watching the interaction between the redhead and Aniol. He gave a small smile of approval when Aniol relaxed into Kaji's arms and turned to face Arian. He raised an eyebrow in question. "Mind telling me why you were strangling one of your guests, Arian? Guests you decided to take in, I might add."

"I don't have to answer to you," Arian snapped in temper. "I outrank you."

Aniol jerked at Arian's words. Confusion coursed through him as he wondered how it could be possible for Arian to outrank Mathié. He was under the impression that Mathié was the heir to the throne, and as far as he knew, there was only one prince in Careil. Aniol stared at Arian, unable to comprehend what he was hearing. He was even more shocked at Mathié's next words. "I may be only a guard, but you do answer to me, my prince," he said coldly, tone filled with command. "You may outrank me, but until you come of age and assume the throne, as your guardian, you are answerable to me. You are as yet a long way from twenty-five. Now tell me why you were strangling Aniol."

Arian glared at Mathié, trying to get the man to back down with just a look. When Mathié did not, he sulked, opening the hand that clutched the teardrop moonstone pendant. "I wanted him to tell me where he got this."

Mathié glanced at the pendant. "That doesn't give you the right to strangle him," he said softly.

Arian shifted, uncomfortable with the public reprimand he was receiving. "I was angry," he admitted.

"That isn't an excuse, Arian, and you know it. As the heir to the throne, you cannot conduct yourself in such a disgraceful manner. There are options other than violence."

Arian glanced up in anger. "Other options? This is my mother's! I saw it my mother wearing it in our family portraits. . How else could he have gotten it except through theft? What respect does a mere thief deserve?"

"The right to be assumed innocent until proven guilty," Mathié retorted. "Aniol received that pendant as a gift."

"From whom?" Arian demanded to know, anger getting the better of him. "This belonged to my mother. It's one of a kind. She said so when I asked! Someone must've stolen it from her and sold it!"

"Your mother gave Aniol that pendant," Mathié said. "Now return what is rightfully his."

Arian blinked at Mathié in shock, gaping at the man. "My mother gave him this?" he asked in hurt disbelief.

"You saw a picture of it but did you ever see the actual pendant itself?" Mathié asked in response to Arian's disbelief. "Did she ever say it was missing? Did you ever see her wear it? She gave it to Aniol before you were even born. Now please, give Aniol back what is rightfully his."

"Why would she give it to him?" Arian's lip trembled in emotion. He knew his mother had loved this piece of jewelry. He had seen it in her eyes whenever she'd spoken about it. She'd told him how it had been custom made for her by his father, how it had been a precious gift and she would get a faraway look on her face when she spoke about it, as if the piece of jewelry held a secret that was dear to her. She would also get sad, as if grieving some unknown loss. When Arian saw the pendant around Aniol's neck, rage had taken over. He thought perhaps the pendant had been stolen from his mother. It would explain the look of grief he'd seen in her eyes when she spoke of it. Mathié's explanation as to how Aniol had gotten the pendant served only to confuse him and hurt him, for his mother had not given him anything that she obviously held as dear as this single piece of jewelry.

"Because she held him dear," Mathié responded softly, knowing that Arian already knew his mother wouldn't have given the pendant to just anyone.

Arian's eyes narrowed in displeasure, hating that Mathié had voiced his thoughts, thus confirming his suspicions, hurting him even more with the confirmation. He threw the moonstone pendant at Aniol before turning and stalking out in utter and complete silence.

Aniol moved forward out of Kaji's arms to grab the pendant from the air as it fell, gripping the small tear drop tightly when it was finally in his grasp. He glanced up at Mathié, his misty gaze questioning and filled with confusion.

Mathié sighed. "I'm sorry. He's gotten rather temperamental. It's only been a few months since he lost his mother."

Aniol's eyes went wide, flickering to the pendant. The mist in them came alive as he lost himself in contemplation, obviously conflicted by what he was considering. His knuckles went white with the force he used to grip the pendant, the shape of the small tear imprinting itself onto his palm. He swallowed before holding his hand out, his fist trembling violently as he did so. He released his death grip on the pendant and allowed it to fall from his fist as he kept hold of the slim, fragile chain. "I think you should give this to him. It's rightfully his," Aniol whispered, voice hoarse, thick with both the remnants of physical pain and conflicted emotion. Mathié knelt down beside Aniol, gathering the pendant up, catching it when Aniol dropped it.

Mathié grabbed hold of the pendant, snatching Aniol's wrist before he could withdraw. Turning it, he placed the pendant back into Aniol's palm, closing his fingers over it. "No. I won't give it to him and won't allow you to do so either. It's rightfully yours, not his." Mathié locked his gaze with Aniol's. "And don't let anyone tell you any differently."

Aniol blinked in surprise, glancing down at the pendant in his grasp. "But it belonged to his mother." He whispered tone laced with soft protest. "I can't keep it. Not knowing that. It wouldn't be right." Filled with conflict and shame, Aniol dropped his gaze.

Mathié reached out, placing a finger below Aniol's chin in order to tilt his face up. He leaned forward and dropped a light kiss onto Aniol's forehead. "It also belonged to your mother, my liege," he whispered as he stood and walked out, closing the door with a soft click, leaving behind two people in complete shocked silence.

# One OF ROYAL BLOOD

The thing about secrets is that they often breed in darkness, causing conflict and pain. By choosing to give her child up, to hide him, the mother subjected herself to a lifetime of questions, subjected her firstborn child to a childhood of loneliness and neglect, a guard to a lifetime of guilt, and her second born to a childhood of feeling inadequate as he reached for his mother, only to find her forever beyond his grasp, haunted by shadows he could not understand.

It's strange how damaging consequences can be even if their source is unknown. It's strange how much pain a single secret can yield and how many lives it can impact. The only thing worse than a secret is having the secret unexpectedly and accidentally revealed.

*ONE of royal blood.* The words of the prophecy, the true prophecy that had been kept from Kaji, echoed through the shocked atmosphere of the room. Those four words now held an entirely new meaning. Kaji stared at Aniol in disbelief, seeing him in a whole new light.

"My mother," Aniol whispered in shock, breaking the heavy silence in the room. He trembled, the realization that his mother had given him that which she treasured the most as she abandoned him cutting him to the core. The implications of who exactly his mother was, who he was, did not register upon Aniol's grieving mind, a mind torn by the fact that he'd been abandoned while his brother had not. He grieved the loss of a faint hope he'd never truly realized he held: the hope of someday meeting his mother, reconciling with her to belong to a family. He didn't know why it hurt so much, but it did.

The moonstone pendant slipped through his fingers to land softly upon the bed and silent tears of grief and pain poured down his cheeks. His heart was torn by betrayal and loneliness. The tears trickled down his face, along his jaw, and down onto the fabric of his clothes and the bed. Unable to bear the pain any longer, Aniol buried his face in his hands, trying to catch the wayward tears as he tried to hide his breakdown from Kaji.

Kaji reached up and brushed a few strands of hair out of Aniol's face before reaching for his right hand and gently pulling it away from his face. Aniol adjusted his left hand, covering his eyes with his palm, shamed by his tears and what he perceived could be a seemingly inconsequential reason for them—a seemingly inconsequential reason that meant the world to him.

Kaji embraced him, gently cradling Aniol in his lap. He ran his fingers over Aniol's wrist, absently tracing the scar upon it. Even though the mark had been inflicted by a malicious heart, it still represented the silent promises that bound them together. He bent forward, dropping a light kiss upon that scar, embracing it and all it meant, his heart no longer confused.

He gently rocked Aniol in his arms, waiting for the deep and silent sobs to abate. When the sheer grief and pain showed no signs of fading and Aniol continued to slip away from him, Kaji decided to take matters into his own hands. He lay down on his side, forcing Aniol down with him. He then shifted to place Aniol beside him so that they lay together, Aniol's back pressed against his chest. Satisfied that Aniol was settled safely on the bed, Kaji withdrew, turning Aniol so that the slim young man lay on his back, once more covering his face with both hands, tears escaping them, trickling down his jaw line and along his throat to pool in the hollow between his collar bones.

Kaji reached out and took hold of Aniol's hands, gently pulling them both away from his face before leaning down to drop a feather-light kiss upon each closed eyelid and catching at the tears that escaped. The liquid was salty upon his tongue. "You're mine," he whispered, following the trail the tears had left behind, first down the left cheek then the right, cradling Aniol's face between his palms. "Not my Gatekeeper." He lapped at Aniol's jaw line, catching the tears pooled there. "My mate and I promise…." Kaji moved further down, towards the hollow of Aniol's throat. "I promise to protect you, hold you dear, and keep you safe."

He caught the salty tears that had pooled in the hollow of Aniol's throat, once more moving up, seeking Aniol's pulse. Kaji realized that it didn't matter that he was Aniol's Warden. It didn't change his role as Aniol's mate, for by fulfilling his duties to Aniol as his mate he would also be fulfilling his duties as a Warden, the duties to protect the Gatekeeper, to keep him safe, sane, alive and whole. As Aniol's mate, he would do all that and more. "You are my destined mate," Kaji whispered dropping light kisses on each corner of Aniol's lips. "Promised to me by prophecy." He tried to soothe the pained breath escaping his mate. Kaji moved his hands down, trailing them over Aniol's shoulders and down his arms toward Aniol's stomach and the edge of his clothes. "Nearly stolen from me by Karl." A hard note of anger laced his tone, fury that Karl and dared to interfere with this precious union. "Nearly stolen from me by my own doubts," he whispered, sadness and regret following his previous fury.

Kaji slipped his hands beneath the hem of Aniol's shirt. He slid them up over the smooth skin he encountered there, silky warmth that begged for gentle touch trembling beneath his palms. The violent shudders of grief that shook Aniol's body calmed with each soothing touch of skin upon skin and were soon replaced by small shivers of pleasure. Ever upwards, inch by inch, Kaji rubbed his palm in soothing circles upon Aniol's skin, taking Aniol's shirt with him.

Aniol gasped when Kaji's fingers brushed over his nipple, sending electricity straight through his body and burning heat pooling in his stomach. Misty eyes opened at the violent sensation, both pleasure and pain merging together. Kaji's gentle touch mixed into the grief in Aniol's heart, slowly soothing the abandonment that consumed him.

Kaji smiled and took the opportunity to slip the thin cloth Aniol wore off, exposing the smooth white skin of Aniol's chest and stomach, skin marked by just a few healing cuts. Kaji bent his head down and kissed each and every one, running his tongue over them, finally able to taste Aniol's skin, to savor and claim. Placing his palms on Aniol's stomach, he once more rubbed his hands over it, over Aniol's chest, his slim shoulders and down his arms, reveling in the sense of freedom the motion gave him. The sheer power it gave him pulled him into a whirlpool of sensation, drowning him in a sense of possession and satisfaction as heat boiled his blood, fueling his hunger and greed for more.

He gazed down at his little mate, watching as passion darkened the blue and grey within those misty eyes, clouding them with lust, removing the grief and pain that hurt him to replace it with carnal hunger. Aniol's mouth was no longer parted with silent cries of grief; instead his lips were parted with gasps of surprise and pleasure as the sensation of Kaji's touch upon his bare skin overwhelmed him. Kaji captured Aniol's lips with his own, giving him a gentle kiss, coaxing a response from him with nips and teasing flicks of his tongue, asking Aniol to participate and give in.

A whispered sigh escaped Aniol as he returned the touch, yearning for the comfort and escape from loneliness Kaji was offering, desperately hungry for the affection he'd first truly experienced upon meeting Kaji. Arching up, he sought contact with Kaji's body, a second whimper lost in the heat and moisture of Kaji's mouth as Kaji laid claim to him, Kaji's tongue thrusting deep into Aniol's mouth.

Kaji took full advantage of the opportunity Aniol presented him, running his hands rapidly across his hips, down his thighs and his smooth legs, all the way to his ankles, efficiently pulling down soft material covering him. The softness of Aniol's skin was so much more pleasant and pleasurable than the flimsy material Aniol had worn in the heat of Duiem, the thin material no protection in Careil's chill weather.

Having efficiently discarded Aniol's clothing, Kaji set about ridding himself of his own, his own skin burning to touch Aniol's. He fumbled with his ties when Aniol arched up into him once more, the faint touch of heated naked flesh teasing him. Momentarily distracted, he sucked Aniol's tongue into his own mouth. Their kiss grew more carnal, primitive, and demanding, the very action tearing sounds of need from Aniol's throat.

Unable to bear separation any longer, Kaji threw his garments aside, slowly allowing his body to come into contact with Aniol's, savoring the sparks of fire each additional touch injected into his body, burning him with the heat of his passion. Aniol made the strangest sound, a cross between a gasp of pleasure and cry of pain when Kaji settled on his body, sliding their skin together. They were slick with sweat and the scent of lust was already heavy in the air. Aniol's toes curled with the sweet friction, the edge taken off the urgency to copulate.

Kaji released Aniol's lips and moved down, past his lover's jaw and the hollow of his throat, down to the one of pink circles upon pale flesh. He ran his tongue over the small bump, sucking and nipping at it until it rose between his lips. Aniol cried out with each bite. Kaji spent some time moving from one nipple to the other, teasing, driving Aniol mad with need and rising passion as the young man arched into him with ever-increasing force. Pleas escaped kiss-swollen lips. Replacing his lips with his fingers, he rolled Aniol's flesh between them and moved further down, lower. A sharp cry escaped Aniol when Kaji dipped his tongue into his belly button.

Aniol panted with need, his body thrashing wildly upon the sheets. He wanted more of that moist heat Kaji was teasing him with, only he didn't fully understand where or why. He was drowning in pleasure, hunger urging him to thrust up into Kaji's touch in a desperate bid to guide Kaji lower, closer to the source of all the pressure building within him. He wanted friction and release from the mad fever that seemed to have him in its grip, only he couldn't begin to fathom how he should go about getting it.

Aniol whimpered in pain when Kaji released his nipples. The flesh was still stinging, overly sensitive to Kaji's touch. He cried out in frustration when Kaji avoided the part of his body where the pressure was the most urgent, instead moving to the arch of his foot, the curve of his calf, his inner thigh; Kaji nipped and marked him with his lips as he explored Aniol's pale flesh, threatening to devour it, always hungry for more, yet still managing to avoid what Aniol most desperately wanted, that is, until….

Aniol growled deep in his throat when Kaji's tongue slid into his body and jerked toward it, wanting more of that slick heat deep within him. Kaji grabbed hold of Aniol's hips, holding him still as he licked at the entrance to Aniol's body. Claiming Aniol in the most intimate way possible, he thrust his tongue deep into Aniol's ass in carnal desire, Aniol's cries sending the fire in his blood straight to his groin. Kaji was hard and pulsing, the pressure within building to pain, yet still he held himself back, wanting to pleasure Aniol, wanting to push him to the edge of sanity and into pleasure-filled madness.

Aniol's fingers tightened in the sheets, and he panted past a throat rubbed raw by his cries of pleasure. His body arched, flexing and contracting in desperation, hungry for more of that moist heat within him. He began to keen, releasing a pained whimper from the back of his throat as his body tightened, shifting closer to his goal, still unsatisfied. His breath changed into sharp, short gasps as he approached the point of release, climax building, threatening to throw him over long before his hunger for friction was satisfied.

Just as he reached breaking point, Kaji withdrew his tongue and his touch, leaving Aniol's body burning with unsatisfied carnal desire, threatening to drive him mad. He panted deeply, his fight for air the only sound to break the silence in the room as a deep blue-grey gaze locked with burning amber, clouded by lust and hunger and burning with desire. Aniol licked his lips, swollen as a result of Kaji's kisses and his attempts to keep his cries in. The taste of Kaji was still strong upon them.

He jerked his hips seductively up, asking Kaji to continue, silently pleading for more. Kaji moved over him, his breath mingling with Aniol's, fingers intertwined in his pale strands of hair, his own red hair pooling down his shoulders. He kept his body above Aniol's, just beyond his desperate reach. "I'm on the verge of losing control," he whispered.

"Then lose it," Aniol whispered in return, reaching up to twist his fingers into Kaji's long hair, loving the sensation of the silky strands between his fingers.

Kaji growled and sat up, drawing away from Aniol. He completely missed the betrayed look expression on Aniol's face as he searched for his clothes to find a vial that had been a gift from Rogue. Vial finally in hand, he returned to his mate, and with a deep feral growl in his throat claimed Aniol's lips, this time giving Aniol no quarter as he ravaged his mouth, effectively wiping the hurt out of Aniol's gaze.

Kaji once more drew Aniol's tongue into his mouth, sucking on it, and slid his left hand down Aniol's body to the saliva-slick entrance he'd thrust his tongue into earlier. He brushed the quivering muscle before withdrawing to dip his fingers into the oil. Then, leaving no time for thought, he thrust two fingers past the wet ring, deep into Aniol's body, burying his fingers to the hilt.

Aniol ripped his lips away from Kaji's, a cry of pain escaping him. His body arched once more, this time tensing, rejecting the invasion, his passion forgotten the moment discomfort ripped through his body.

Kaji's hand stilled, fingers still buried deep within Aniol's ass. He gently licked Aniol's lips, swallowing the whimpers of pain. Kissing his mate softly, he ran his other hand down Aniol's body, over tight, sensitive nipples, his belly button, and lower, gently caressing him and watching as

Aniol relaxed into the touch, lust returning to his eyes. Keeping up his gentle touch, he began to thrust his fingers in, keeping his motion slow and controlled as he pulled them out. He twisted his fingers, scissoring them the moment Aniol relaxed.

Deeming Aniol ready for more, he moved his lips to Aniol's ear, whispering softly in warning. "I'm going to add another one."

Pleasure, heat, and fire coursed through Aniol, the third finger almost going unnoticed as he gasped at what Kaji was once more doing to his body. Kaji bruised Aniol with his hunger, marking his throat while thrusting his fingers in and out, stretching his mate. Aniol began to gasp in hunger once more, now willingly thrusting himself onto Kaji's fingers, welcoming both pleasure and the pain. He savored the friction, the invasion, somehow still seeking more, the fingers strangely no longer enough. His body was hungry for more of the sweet pain-edged pleasure with which Kaji was filling him.

Aniol's hunger fueling his own drove Kaji to withdraw his fingers, yet again pulling a whimper of loss from Aniol's swollen lips. Kaji grabbed the vial once more, spilling some of the precious oil in his haste as he covered his penis thoroughly with the lubrication. He kept his touch as light as possible lest he tip himself into release before even entering Aniol's body. Placing the vial down once more, Kaji positioned himself, meeting Aniol's gaze with his own, breath once more mingling with Aniol's.

"This is going to hurt," he whispered, the words barely past his lips as he thrust in, the single motion burying him deep into Aniol's slick, tight heat. Pleasure like nothing he'd imagined possible coursed right through him, the sudden pressure on his penis pulling a cry of pain and pleasure from him, a feral growl of possession escaping his throat along with it. Tight—it was so damned tight. Aniol's body surrounded him, pressed in on him with such sweet, moist heat, tempting him to lose control. He stilled, fighting the urge to spill himself there and then, the madness of pleasure threatening to claim him.

Aniol cried out, arching in an attempt to escape the burning pain that consumed him as his muscles stretched to accommodate something bigger than three fingers. Yet still he was hungry for more, the pain a mere inconvenience in his body's bid to seek the intangible release it was reaching for. Some instinct urged him on, knowing that the pain was somehow part of the journey.

He stilled along with Kaji, taking short quick breaths in an attempt to relax. When the pain faded, the sense of Kaji filling him began to overtake his senses. He could feel Kaji's penis throbbing deep within him, hard and hot. The contact was so intimate that he could feel every beat of Kaji's heart beating a rhythm deep in his body, the pulse echoing the throbbing of his own heartbeat. The sheer realization that Kaji was joined to him in every possible way caused the heat pooled within Aniol's stomach to burn, urging Aniol to shift his hips experimentally up, wanting Kaji deeper.

Kaji groaned, nearly coming undone when Aniol moved against him, settling Kaji deeper within his body when he'd been convinced such would not be possible. The fire ran from Kaji's body straight into his groin, demanding motion, his possessive streak demanding that no quarter be given when claiming what was rightfully his.

Kaji slowly withdrew from Aniol's body before changing direction and thrusting in, the motion aggressive and filled with hunger and lust. Aniol gasped at the friction the motion caused, lifting himself up a touch in order to give Kaji more access, pleading for more of the burning sensation the motion woke within him. Kaji took him up on his offer and began to pound into him, thrust for pleasurable thrust, losing his mind in Aniol's heat, losing himself to the passion and the rhythm of the movement, in and out, over and over again.

Aniol moved with Kaji, rocking his hips, his body adjusting to Kaji's invasion. The pain was almost completely gone, replaced by sensations of pleasure, gently rising and carrying him ever higher. Suddenly Kaji shifted his thrust, the change in angle hitting his prostate deep within him. Aniol cried out, lightning running through every cell in his body.

Suddenly, one taste was not enough; Aniol suddenly wanted more and claimed it, shifting the angle of his body so that Kaji would continue to hit that spot that sent fire through his veins. He thrust up against Kaji, returning his motion, seeking to take Kaji in deeper, with more force, to increase the sharp pleasure. Harder, deeper faster, their thrusts soon became nothing more than feral movements, each seeking their own pleasure from the other, lust driving them past the madness of desire and into the ecstasy of release.

Aniol screamed as he slipped over the edge, climax sending violent tremors through his body, causing him to tighten around Kaji. Kaji growled, giving a few last hard thrusts into Aniol's tight heat before finally losing control. Unable to hold himself back any longer, he buried himself deep into Aniol's body and followed him into climax, filling his mate with his seed, marking him with warm, sticky heat.

Kaji slumped down onto Aniol's sweat-slicked body, lazily licking at the sweat on Aniol's skin as he came down from his high, still buried within him. He reached up and turned Aniol's head, claiming his lips in a slow, lazy kiss as he held onto the last few tendrils of hazy pleasure. "Mine," he whispered softly, watching as Aniol drifted off to sleep, exhausted by his grief and the activities that had followed.

Kaji remained where he was for a moment, simply marveling at the fact that he and Aniol were now joined, awed that he had finally marked his mate and claimed him for his own. Long moments later, when remaining joined was no longer comfortable, Kaji slipped out of Aniol's body, wishing he could remain there indefinitely, always a part of him. Finding a bowl of water and cloth on a side table, Kaji cleaned them both up before pulling the blankets over them and curling around Aniol. Drawing the young man up against him, naked flesh against heated skin, Kaji lost himself in the scent of his mate and drifted off to sleep.

# DVIEM'S HEIR

Destiny is a strange thing. It defines but one goal that must be obtained but neglects to leave a set of instructions for how one is to find it. Every life that surrounds a soul burdened by great destiny has the power to influence the choices such a soul makes. This influence can often limit the choices the destined soul is able to make, thus obscuring the path towards the divine decree issued.

That is when the hand of fate needs to intervene. Fate needs to carefully influence the life of the soul touched by destiny in order to present the correct choices to be made while at the same time not interfering with the soul's right to free will.

KAJI reached out and brushed his fingers through Aniol's hair, fascinated by Aniol's sleeping form. He'd woken to find his mate fast asleep beside him. Aniol looked so innocent, even after all that had happened to him, after all the hurt and betrayal, and even after everything they'd just done. Kaji brushed a finger across the lashes, remembering the tears that had marked them. In his opinion they were a travesty. Aniol should never need to cry, should never hurt so.

Kaji sat up with a jerk, suddenly remembering the reason for the pain and tears. He crawled to the bottom of the bed, where they'd been seated when Aniol had begun to cry, and he began to sift through the folds in the bedding. Finding nothing, he gritted his teeth in frustration. His searching pattern became more frantic, more desperate, until finally he heaved a sigh of relief, looking down at the pendant he now had in his hand. The small piece of jewelry had been half hanging off the bed, caught in the folds of the sheets.

He traced his finger along the chain that had somehow managed to tangle around the moonstone tear; he was distressed to find one of the links had broken. He would have to get it repaired once more. Kaji traced a finger over the tear, wondering at the shape of the stone and the mourning it implied, seeing the pendant in a new light. Perhaps Aniol's mother had given him this specific piece of jewelry as a symbol of her mourning at having to lose him. Kaji's heart ached at the thought, wondering what the original story behind the piece could be. It was sad that the only piece of jewelry Aniol possessed would have such a tragic story attached to it.

Suddenly remembering something else he'd forgotten, Kaji scrambled back up the bed, reaching for his own scattered clothes. He rummaged around in the folds of the cloth, seeking yet again. He sighed in relief when his fingers brushed across a cold, hard surface. Gripping the object as tightly as he gripped the pendant Aniol treasured, he sat up, turning to his sleeping mate. He placed Aniol's pendant reverently down on the table beside the bed before carefully reaching out to Aniol. Lifting Aniol's right arm, Kaji placed a gentle kiss upon the jagged scar which marred it before clipping the bonding bracelet back into place where it belonged. Lost in thought, he traced the moon and sun upon it. Aniol was his, and Kaji didn't intend to let him go ever again. He would never allow the pain he'd seen in Aniol's eyes when he'd withdrawn from his mate to haunt them again.

Kaji jerked in surprise, hastily covering himself with the sheets when a knock echoed through the room. The door opened and Mathié walked in carrying a tray with steaming broth and bread upon it.

"I thought you might be hungry." Mathié explained, eyes sparkling in amusement. He walked to the table on Aniol's side of the bed and placed the tray down, smirking at the sight of Kaji's rather ruffled and very naked state. "I had no idea he could be that vocal. I struggle to get him to speak," Mathié commented lightly, glancing down at Aniol's sleeping form.

Kaji flushed, red tinting his cheeks for a moment before fading, the heat of his anger ridding him of his embarrassment. "He's mine," he hissed possessively, warning Mathié off.

Mathié raised his arms in a placating gesture. "I never said he wasn't," he agreed softly, but his tone was filled with deep sadness. "I knew that from the moment I put him down on the bed when he relaxed into your arms. I don't know who you are, but he obviously trusts you and loves you."

Kaji tensed in surprise at Mathié's words. "Loves me?" He glanced down at Aniol's sleeping form in awe. The thought hadn't occurred to him.

"Yes, he loves you," Mathié confirmed. "I can see it in his eyes when he looks at you, in his body when he allows you to touch him. I can also hear it in his voice when he speaks to you. He loves you deeply." The moment the sentimental statement was done, Mathié's gaze and voice hardened. "Whether you deserve it or not is another matter, it's not for me to judge, but know this: You'd better take care of him and treasure him. He's had more than his share of grief and pain in his life. You add to that, and I'll kill you. And if killing you is not an option, if it would hurt him more, I'll find a way to make you regret ever meeting me."

Kaji blinked up at Mathié, utterly shocked by his sheer audacity. Realizing Mathié was deadly serious, he nodded. "If I hurt him again, you won't need to make me regret it; I'll regret it with every breath I take."

Mathié's glared when Kaji used the word again, hating the implication that he'd already hurt Aniol, but decided to let it slide. He could clearly see Kaji's resolve and was willing to accept his sincerity. "Fair enough. I wanted to tell you that we'll be leaving for the palace tomorrow. I'm taking you and Aniol with us. There are some things I think Aniol needs to know and others that he needs to face and resolve. Arian probably won't be all too happy about that. He doesn't know who Aniol is yet but has to suspect something. Aniol's eye color and hair color are unique. They run only in the royal family, and Arian knows that. The fact that Aniol has the moonstone pendant would only confirm those suspicions. He will probably feel threatened by Aniol. Stay by Aniol's side and try to keep Arian in check should he approach you. If I'm not out scouting when he does choose to approach you, I'll come with him."

Kaji's amber gaze narrowed, anger coursing through him at the implications in Mathié's words. "Arian would hurt Aniol? Even though he suspects Aniol is his brother?"

"Arian is hurting right now. He's just lost a mother he worshiped, his father is dead, and he has the weight of the country upon his shoulders.

He's but a boy. He's only seen seventeen winters. He loved his mother dearly and knew there was something hurting her, keeping her distant, and now he is being forced to face the reason for it. There is bound to be animosity, anger, and jealousy there."

Kaji continued to glare but nodded in acceptance. "He'd better not try and hurt my mate."

Mathié blinked in surprise at Kaji's words, glancing at Aniol's wrist before looking for the bracelet on Kaji's. "You're bonded," he said in awe, and then he frowned in confusion. He hadn't seen the bonding bracelet upon Aniol's wrist earlier.

Mathié reached out towards Aniol's slim wrist, startled by the red gold it was made of. "Gold—" A dark premonition niggling at his senses. He turned Aniol's wrist over, looking for the bonding symbol, the symbol that merged two families and was unique to every bonded couple. Surprise shook through him when he saw it, moon and sun, made from moonstone and amber. "Duiem." He shook his head in disbelief. "It can't be." He glanced up once more, filled with incredulity as for the first time he truly saw Kaji, truly saw the man with the deep red hair and the amber eyes. "Who are you?"

The shocked words echoed through the air between them, filled with deep meaning and impact. "I am Kaji Taiyouko," Kaji responded calmly, and he watched Mathié, gauging his reactions. Mathié knew about Duiem, of that Kaji was certain. Mathié knew what he was looking at but didn't want to believe it. So Kaji continued to speak, wanting to confirm who he really was, who Aniol now was. "Fifty-seventh ruler of Duiem, mate to Aniol Taiyouko."

Mathié hissed in shock. His breath came in shallow and short bursts as he tried to deal with the revelations, what they meant, and the implications they could have. He traced the moon and sun upon the bracelet, desperately grabbing onto anything to keep from drowning in a sea of confusion. "How did you know?" Mathié asked the least significant question, the only question he was willing to deal with at the moment. "How did you know who he was?"

"I didn't. He told me he didn't know who he was, didn't know his family or his lineage, but we were bonded and I needed something for the bracelet." Kaji reached forward and brushed Mathié's hand off of Aniol's wrist, replacing it possessively with his own fingers. He reached for the pendant on the table beside him, holding it out to Mathié. "I found this. This seemed to be the only clue to his heritage that I was going to get, and since it is made of silver and moonstone, elements inherent to the land of the moon we heard about in legends, I thought that the moon would be a fitting symbol, a nice opposite to mine. I didn't know about Careil when I did it," Kaji admitted.

Heavy silence stretched between them, getting heavier with each moment that passed. Finally Mathié nodded. "Destiny is a strange thing," he whispered, watching Kaji closely, his heart conflicted and filled with confusion, shock, and hope.

"Yes, it is." Kaji agreed, thinking back to how he and Aniol had been bonded in the first place. Destiny seemed to have a hand in everything he did of late. It had brought him the pale, violet-eyed boy, Rogue, Anei, Yuan, and Aniol. All of it seemed to be fantastical, one event rolling into the next. It reminded him of a torrent of water pushing him along its chosen path, rushing headlong towards an unseen goal, purposefully heading toward something far bigger than the culmination of individual events.

# Injustice

What is it that truly defines an injustice? Circumstance? Choice? Or perhaps fate? Everything is a result of an action, a reaction to choices made. A mother abandoned her son in order to save him. She was desperate that her firstborn child, the child of her heart, might live. Yet she and the one she trusted were betrayed, driving her to grief and him to guilt.

A child innocent of the ways of the world was cursed, confined to a lifetime of loneliness and neglect until destiny took matters into its own hands. Hearts grew greedy and corrupt, fearful of what impact a single person might have on a country already in turmoil. Not even pausing to regret, the child's prison keepers, ordered the end of an innocent life, blindly ordering the death of Careil's last true hope.

KAJI rode behind Aniol, once more cradling him as they followed behind Arian. Mathié was out of sight, having ridden ahead to scout the land. One of Arian's guards rode at the fore of the party, and the other rode at the rear with two horses dedicated to supplies riding between them. The horse Kaji and Aniol rode had also been a horse for supplies but had been given to the two at Mathié's insistence. Both Aniol and Kaji were warmly dressed and heavily cloaked, Aniol all but drowning in a white cloak and Kaji in a brown one. Mathié had insisted that they wear their cloak hoods up to hide both their hair and their eyes, features that could get them killed by the people of Careil.

Kaji wondered at that but obeyed Mathié, knowing it would be wise to do so. Arian had thus far completely ignored them, not even acknowledging them when they gathered around a campfire at night. Kaji and Aniol shared their tent with both Mathié and Arian as it was the only one big enough for them all, yet the young man still managed to ignore them, speaking only to Mathié and pretending they were not there at all. It was beginning to grate on Kaji's nerves, more so when he could see the pain in Aniol's eyes, the callous way his own brother was treating him.

Kaji gripped Aniol's right hand tightly in his own, heart aching as he watched Aniol stare longingly after Arian. Deciding he'd had enough, Kaji spurred his horse on, riding up next to the prince. "Hey, Arian!" he called out, trying to get the man's attention. He gritted his teeth when Arian tensed, obviously hearing him, but the prince continued to ignore Kaji. Aniol looked up at Kaji, placing a placating hand upon Kaji's own, obviously asking Kaji to let it be, but Kaji didn't heed him. "You're being very childish. What are you afraid of? The truth? What do you hope to accomplish by ignoring us when you know very well that we're here, when you know very well who Aniol is? Are you feeling threatened by him? Because he's more fit to rule that you ever will be with an attitude like that?"

Arian turned to face Kaji, anger flashing through his blue-grey eyes, eyes that, if not for the mist in Aniol's, resembled Aniol's so much it was eerie. "I am the rightful king of Careil. Neither you nor he have the right to say otherwise."

"We have every right." Kaji retorted. "He's older than you are."

"So?" Arian questioned haughtily. "What difference does his age make? I'm the son of the King and Queen, direct descendant to the throne. Who is he but a mere thief?"

"Are you really that much in denial, that scared of what all this could mean, or are you just stupid?" Kaji said in barely restrained anger.

Arian spluttered, shocked by Kaji's words and the blunt manner in which he delivered them. He couldn't believe what this stranger had said to him. "Who are you to question your future king?" he retorted, command in his tone.

"Not one of your subjects," Kaji said coldly, the command in his tone far more persuasive, more certain and sure than the one in Arian's. "You had best realize that and realize it soon and perhaps learn a little diplomacy while you're at it. Technically speaking, you're not next in line, Aniol is!"

Arian narrowed his eyes, sheer animosity coming off of him in waves. "There's no way he is next in line. Even if we did have the same mother, there's no way he can be anything more but a bastard child, the result of an affair."

"Who happened to inherit his hair and eyes from your father's side of the family?" a soft voice interjected, Mathié reining in beside them. "Come now, Arian, you should know better than that."

"Then he's a result of an affair my father had!" Arian called out stubbornly, unable to accept what was staring him straight in the face.

"Who was gifted with your mother's precious pendant?" Mathié raised an eyebrow.

Hurt, anger, and confusion filled Arian, the one emotion chasing the next. "If he really is my elder brother, really is the firstborn son, why did I never see him? Never hear about him? Why didn't I know about him? Why was he obviously discarded? He was unwanted!" Arian demanded tone filled with pain and turmoil.

"That's not true, Arian, and it's a very cruel thing to say. It was a choice your mother had to make, a choice that tore her apart inside and killed any affection between your parents. The people of Careil are not ready to accept Aniol. The fools would sooner kill him than see him rule," Mathié stated softly, tone filled with regret and pain.

Kaji's arm tightened around Aniol's waist, pulling him closer as if to protect him from all that Mathié's words implied. Aniol tensed, shocked and hurt by them, and Arian gaped at Mathié in disbelief. "Why is that?" Kaji asked carefully voicing the question in everyone's mind, fighting to keep his tone calm.

"His eyes," Mathié said softly.

"What's wrong with his eyes?" Kaji protested, disgusted that Aniol could be killed for something he couldn't help. "They show he's a...." Kaji stopped speaking when Mathié raised his hand, gesturing for silence, cutting him off.

"The people of Careil fear white eyes and all that they imply. They kill anyone with that mark, claiming that they are demons, claiming that they are the reason Careil keeps dying, the reason for the floods, the snow storms, and the crazy weather. They don't take kindly to visions of deserts, sun, and heat when all they know is snow, water, and cold death."

"That's barbaric!" Kaji exclaimed, wincing when he remembered the war with the Ruel. If he really thought about it, how was that any better? In fact, in essence it boiled down to the same thing. He shook his head in realization, sighing deeply. "Never mind. Forget I said that," he muttered darkly.

"It's true," Mathié agreed, ignoring Kaji's retraction. "It is barbaric. All people really know anymore is fear, and fear gives rise to superstition. It's the reason Aniol's mother gave him up: to protect him from death." Mathié watched Kaji carefully as they rode.

Kaji scowled at the words, glancing down at Aniol who'd grown even more still than he usually was, withdrawing into himself with Mathié's words. "Let me see if I get this right," Kaji asked, glancing up again. "The rightful heir of the kingdom was hidden so he wouldn't be killed? Where was he hidden?"

"Not hidden. I was a prisoner in a white room," Aniol whispered, his words echoing through the air between them.

"In a white room?" Kaji questioned in sudden realization. His hand clenched. "You were locked in *that* room?" Kaji whispered in horror, sudden suspicion forcing him to continue. "Alone? That's your blood, isn't it? On the floor?" Kaji was kicking himself for not realizing this sooner. Aniol had known exactly where the silver box with the chalk had been hidden, had said it was a gift. He'd treated the room and the belongings therein as his own, a room that was locked and barred from the outside, a room he could not leave even had he wanted to. He turned towards Mathié in horror, rage flashing through his amber gaze. "She locked him away in a room? How long?"

"Kaji...." Aniol turned reaching up to the fuming redhead, trying to placate him, wanting to just let it be. "It's all right."

"It's not all right!" Kaji retorted. "How long?" he ground out between gritted teeth, demanding an answer to his question. Aniol dropped his gaze, tensing, wary of the rage he saw in it, but compelled to answer. "My whole life," he whispered hoarsely.

"His whole life?" Kaji exploded, turning to Mathié in accusation. "What kind of mother does that to her child?"

"She had no choice." Mathié responded to Kaji's anger with calm of his own, meeting the redhead's fury dead on. Arian was gaping at the two of them, glancing from Kaji to Mathié and back to Kaji once again, desperately trying to follow the turn the conversation had taken. "If she hadn't given him up, then he would've been killed. Would you have preferred that? If he were dead and in his grave?"

"No!" Kaji protested. "But locking him in a room for his whole life? How is that any better than death? I saw the room, damn it! There was nothing there!" Kaji shook in anger, clenching and unclenching his fist, not knowing what to do with the fury coursing through his veins, not knowing where or how to truly vent, seeking someone to blame for Aniol's pain. He could not accept it, would not, not even if Aniol did.

"That was my fault," Mathié admitted softly, dropping his gaze in guilt and shame. "I was supposed to get him out of the castle, supposed to disappear and raise him somewhere away from all the superstition, but I was betrayed. People I trusted to help me ambushed me and took him from me. I only found him a few years later, locked in that tower, always under strict guard. By then his mother already thought Aniol was dead. She'd given up on him, had already asked me to watch over Arian. I visited when I could. I tried to get him out, but even though they let me visit him, they wouldn't let him take him away from there, and I was no match for the three men they had guarding the tower, not alone, not without the keys. I'm surprised they let me see him to begin with. I think they were hoping I could get him to open up to them more." Mathié stared off into the distance, his back tense, waiting for the anger to rain down on him, accepting it, knowing he had failed his duty to his queen.

Kaji opened his mouth, about to yell, rage and reprimand him. He burned to accuse Mathié, to ask him why he didn't fight harder for Aniol's freedom. He was desperate to say anything to get rid of the anger he felt at the injustice of Aniol's childhood but couldn't find the words for any of it. For once in his life, words failed him completely, and Aniol glancing up at him with pleading eyes only made it worse.

"No, Kaji. Please... don't. Can't you see he's hurting?" Aniol whispered, his own eyes filled with pain, mist swirling in them. Kaji sighed in defeat, clenching his eyes closed and burying his face in the crook of Aniol's neck, taking in the scent of Aniol's hair as he forced himself to calm down.

# Journal

Gatekeepers were forgotten by the very land from which they came. Their existence faded into the mists of time, not even a legend, a whisper, or a memory kept alive in the Land of Silver. People driven mad by fear, desperation, and superstition destroyed records of their existence. They burned anything that mentioned Gatekeepers, Wardens, and Duiem, declaring the documents demon-wrought. So it was that the precious knowledge they held was lost to all common man.

WHITE light embraced him and then faded, the sensation familiar. Kaji had learned to recognize the feeling of Aniol's visions, the way in which time and space would shift uncontrollably, carrying him along. It was a similar sensation to that of actually traveling through the gate Aniol had forced them through, only it was gentler, more subtle, and possessed a dreamlike quality.

He saw desert sands, shifting, ever-changing, a wasteland dying from the heat. His breath caught when he saw them: Lira, Rogue, and Yuan tending to injuries, speaking among themselves as they worked. "I wonder if they're all right." Rogue spoke softly as he bandaged a wounded man's arm.

Yuan dipped a cloth into water, reaching out to clean blood and infection away, wiping the cloth gently over a woman's shoulder while Lira prepared more bandages. "The first memories of Aniol being here are when he came through the gate, two weeks before bonding with Kaji," Yuan stated softly. "That means he's from Careil. That's the only place they could've gone. Assuming they're not at war as the people of Duiem are, Aniol should be of some assistance, but it's only speculation."

Rogue sighed, tying off the bandage before raising a blade up into the light. He turned it, light reflecting off of the silver surface, giving the blade eerie life. "Well, at least we know they weren't hit by the blade that was thrown at them," Rogue stated softly, throwing the knife into a wooden bench in disgust. "Idiots," he muttered. "The both of them."

Kaji's protest to that statement remained unheard as he watched. "They're strongly bonded by love," Yuan said as he raised an eyebrow at Rogue's unexpected display of temper and emotion. Lately it felt like he and Rogue had exchanged roles and temperament. "You know that."

"Yeah. But it's still no excuse for idiocy," Rogue pointed out.

"It's every excuse for idiocy," Yuan said with a smile. "At least it is when it comes to Kaji. Aniol, on the other hand, is more restrained. I'm surprised he went that far."

"I only hope that Kaji stops being such a blind fool and realizes he's in love with his damned mate. He's hurting my Gatekeeper," Rogue snapped, frustrated that he'd been left behind and concerned for the safety of his friend and friend's mate, his Gatekeeper.

"There's nothing you can do about that, Rogue. You know that it's something he needs to work out for himself. The doubt was already there. My predecessor only brought it to the surface. Kaji needed to reconcile his feelings as a Warden with those as a mate."

Kaji growled deep in his throat at the words Yuan spoke. The damned bastard had deliberately made him doubt his feelings for Aniol! If the previous Keeper was not already dead, Kaji would be damned tempted to kill the man. How could he do that to him? To Aniol? That doubt had nearly torn them apart! Kaji tensed in sudden realization. He wouldn't betray Aniol. Even though he was Aniol's Warden, he could not betray his Gatekeeper because always, first and foremost, he was Aniol's mate.

But wait... had Rogue said "My Gatekeeper?" Kaji turned to the assassin, confused and torn by the implications of those words. What had Rogue meant by that?

"I know that," Rogue admitted softly. "But it was still hard to see both of them hurting so much for no reason."

"It will be better," Yuan stated softly, taking the bandage from Lira. "All in good time."

Rogue glanced up, the melancholy note in Yuan's voice drawing his attention. "So will this," he said softly in sympathy. "They will accept you eventually."

"I don't know if I want them to accept me," Yuan admitted. "Not that long ago, I would've killed any of them without a moment's regret."

"You would have regretted it," Rogue said, contradicting him. "Every life taken by force—no matter how deserving—causes regret, for when you lose that, you lose your humanity."

Yuan gave Rogue a strained, tense smile. "And I haven't? Lost it already?"

Rogue met Yuan's gaze. "No, you haven't."

Yuan shook his head, remaining silent as he continued to work, the Keeper's burden heavy upon his shoulders.

The vision faded, gently shifting and drifting away, releasing Kaji from its hold. As it left, it brought Kaji back to a reality that was not truly his own, to a land he did not understand. His heart ached as he was pulled away from those he loved, as he lost sight of the land he loved once more. Kaji shivered in the morning chill, not so much from the cold as from aftereffects of the vision he'd shared. He glanced down at Aniol's sleeping form, the young man's brow furrowed by visions he no longer shared with Kaji. They continued to torment him in his sleep, wearing down his mind and his heart.

The visions now made sense. The scattered visions of desert, ice, and people—they all suddenly made sense. They were visions of the world opposite of the one the Gatekeeper was in, visions of events that were occurring in the present, glimpses into important events as they played out.

Kaji reached out and gathered Aniol into his arms, cradling his mate in his lap as he tried to chase away the visions and dreams. Confusion ran through his mind as he tried to sort out what he'd just learned, trying to make sense of Rogue's and Yuan's words. Why had Rogue referred to Aniol as his Gatekeeper? What did Yuan and Rogue know that he did not? Had Rogue and Yuan known all along that he loved Aniol? Kaji glanced down at Aniol in surprise, shocked by the realization when by all rights he should not have been. He loved his little mate with all his heart. Loved him more than life itself. Kaji hadn't thought it possible, but it was true.

He leaned down to drop a light kiss upon Aniol's forehead, hair flowing down over his shoulders, lending the moment a quiet intimacy, an ethereal quality in the dim morning light that filtered in through the tent flap. Aniol relaxed at the gentle touch, slipping into more natural sleep, no longer plagued by visions that threatened to tear him apart with their persistence.

THERE was little to note about the rest of the journey. It was carried out in uncomfortable silence as Kaji persistently ignored Mathié, still angry at the man for failing Aniol, even though deep down he knew that there was nothing Mathié could have done. Aniol didn't deserve the pain he'd been forced to endure, didn't deserve the lack of love and the lack of affection, and Kaji couldn't accept the fact that Aniol had been failed by Mathié.

The knowledge he'd gained about Aniol's childhood cleared up many things for him. All of a sudden he knew why Aniol shied away from touch, why he always seemed so innocent, so confused by everything around him even though he so obviously possessed a razor-sharp intellect. It wasn't that Aniol was shy, or scared and withdrawn; it simply boiled down to the fact that Aniol didn't understand affection because he had been denied it all his life. It was the reason Aniol kept a distance between himself and those around him. He simply didn't know how to reach out, and Kaji bitterly blamed Mathié for allowing it to happen.

Arian had, surprisingly, gotten more pleasant, no longer blatantly ignoring their presence. He no longer gave Aniol the cold shoulder, though now it was Aniol that had withdrawn from his brother, hurt by the truth in Mathié's words.

They slipped into the city and the palace in the middle of the night, using the back entrances, Aniol and Kaji remaining hidden in their cloaks. Mathié wanted to avoid the questions Kaji's and Aniol's presence would be sure to raise. People were ready to strike out at any hint of the unknown; fear and paranoia were thick in the very air they breathed.

Kaji eyed the city with awe. The buildings were white, decorated with careful intricate swirls touched by moonlight. It truly was the city of the moon. It was tinted blue by the deep night sky, the pale moonlight giving it a mystical appearance. The very atmosphere of this world was dark and cold, run by superstition and fear as opposed to anger. It was a contradiction to everything he'd ever known, to the fiery tempers, to the war, and to the heated emotion that governed his people. Yet he realized that both worlds were just as torn, both dying a seemingly inevitable death. There was water here; there were plants, and yet this land continued to die, torn apart by that very water, by the cold and ice.

There was no balance, not in Duiem and not in Careil. It was not the lack of water that was killing Duiem, nor the lack of warmth and sunshine that was killing Careil; it was the lack of balance between the two. Suddenly Kaji realized the true impact the Gatekeepers had on the world they lived in.

Mathié led them in, stabled the horses, and took them inside. He paused beside Arian's room, pushing the curious young man in despite Arian's protests. He nodded when the two guards with them, stationed themselves at the door, and then he led Aniol and Kaji away.

He entered a dark room, carefully lighting a lamp, illuminating pearly-white walls shrouded in mystery. The thin sheets of blue translucent material that hung before them shifted, stirring trickles of dust into the air. He then walked to a fireplace. It was white, decorated in dark blue with an intricate design done in silver swirls upon it. The pattern seemed to personify serenity. Mathié pressed one of the swirls in, a latch clicking into place as he slid open a hidden drawer. Within the drawer were five leather-bound volumes tied closed with five ribbons, each one a different color: black, dark blue, sky blue, white, and purple.

Mathié carefully took the books out and handed them reverently to Aniol. "I found them by accident," he explained softly. "About six years after I lost you. They explain a lot about Duiem." He nodded to Kaji. "They speak of a land of gold and sun, ruled by a red-haired, amber-eyed king. The land is ruled by the sun, the opposite of Careil and its rule by the moon. I didn't really believe them too much until I met Kaji... until I saw that...." He pointed at Aniol's bonding bracelet, the moon and sun intertwined upon it. "There's something about balance of the two in there, sun and moon, one element complementing the other. I didn't understand it all that much, but somehow I think it will be important to you, and through you, to all of us," Mathié whispered, afraid to break the serious atmosphere that surrounded them.

Aniol blinked up at him in surprise, unsure what he should think of all this. He glanced down at the leather volumes in his hands. Their pages were worn by age. These books had obviously been kept hidden for a long time. He trailed his fingers over the volumes reverently, awed at the thought of the information and insight they promised.

Kaji watched his mate in silence, he, too, curious as to the revelations and secrets those five volumes might reveal. He watched as Aniol opened one of the books, running his fingers gently over the pages, taking in their texture, their reality, as if afraid the books would disintegrate in his hands as he touched them. Mathié reached for the books once more, pulling out one of the volumes in Aniol's hands, the one tied with a dark blue ribbon with a silver edge. "This one is a Gatekeeper's journal," he said, drawing both Aniol's and Kaji's attention to the book he held.

# KNOW WHO YOU ARE

The people of Careil rejected all forms of mystical knowledge. They did not wish to acknowledge the existence of Gatekeepers and clung to superstition instead. Those who did not want to be blinded were overwhelmed by the sheer number of those who did not wish to see, and so hope and reason were swept away. In all the chaos, rage, and destruction, one boy, a prince of the land, still held onto hope. He still believed in the Gatekeepers. Desperate to stop the destruction of all the records that was sweeping Careil, he had a secret compartment crafted in his room. Then saving what he could, he hid five books, each bound in a different color, holding knowledge he desperately wanted to keep alive.

Sealing both the fireplace and the compartment, he prayed that one day, when the time was right, it would be found. To ensure the safety of the precious documents he had hidden, he declared that fire never burn in his room again as symbol of mourning for all that Careil had lost. This symbol of mourning managed to remain intact throughout the generations that followed, the precious books kept protected from harm, waiting for the day they would be found.

ANIOL traced the blue, silver-edged ribbon, afraid to open the book, afraid of what it might contain and what that information might mean to him. Mathié had left after revealing the books, leaving Aniol and Kaji alone in the dimly lit room as the pale light chased away the darkness of early morning. Kaji had taken the other books, leaving the journal with Aniol.

Kaji skimmed through the information they contained, surprised to find that although it was rather scattered, some of the information was reasonably accurate. The first book, the one bound in white ribbon, contained snippets of Duiem's history, events that were overshadowed by the betrayal of the Gatekeepers and Duiem's subsequent downfall. These events included natural disasters and development history, as well as outlines of treaties and agreements that were formed both within Duiem itself and between Duiem and Careil. Inside, Kaji also found a sketch of Duiem's royal insignia, the sun that was upon the bonding bracelets he and Aniol wore. That would explain how Mathié had known about Duiem and had known who Kaji was.

A second book, the one bound in sky blue, gave more detailed information about the treaties with Duiem from Careil's perspective, listing Careil's responsibilities to Duiem and various clauses as to what would be done should Duiem not meet Careil's expectations. Kaji found this book particularly interesting, as it detailed trade and military agreements as well as cooperative efforts to share resources and assist in disaster management between the two worlds. He wondered where Duiem's copies of these agreements were, wanting to know what the agreements were from Duiem's perspective.

The book bound in purple ribbon was simply a list of bondings that had occurred in the royal line of Careil, the ones that linked Duiem's royal line with Careil's carefully marked. It seemed that every couple of generations or so Careil and Duiem would re-establish a link to one another through bonding. The recorded bondings between Duiem and Careil were never the direct line, though, making Kaji wonder if his to Aniol was the first, and if so, it made him question why this was.

The book bound in black was another journal, a Warden's journal. Kaji glanced up at Aniol, noticing that the young man still had not untied the ribbon to open the book it bound. He placed the Warden's journal down and moved closer to Aniol so that they were seated beside one another, knees touching. Reaching into Aniol's lap, he untied the ribbon, watching as the dark cloth pooled into Aniol's lap. He glanced up and met Aniol's misty eyes, noting the confusion swirling in their depths. Ignoring the uncertainty he could sense radiating off of Aniol, he opened the book in Aniol's lap, glancing down at the text scribbled on the inside of the cover. It was a dedication and a plea for remembrance.

*I am hiding these books in the hopes that someday they are found,*
*And in the hopes that Duiem may once more be remembered,*
*I pray that the Gatekeepers may one day return,*
*And that these books may perhaps give a Gatekeeper hope,*
*Knowledge, and insight into that which has been forgotten.*

*Gatekeeper... know who you are!*
*Marked by misty-white gaze,*
*Seeing visions of desert sands,*
*Doomed to death by foolish people,*
*Last hope for the land.*

Aniol blinked in surprise, the words in the book seeming to echo all the pain and confusion he'd experienced during his life. He glanced up and met Kaji's gaze. Kaji reached out and took Aniol's hand in his, gripping it tightly, offering Aniol comfort and support. He then reached over for the book he had discarded and held it out to Aniol.

"This is a Warden's journal," he stated softly. "I think these two journals are perhaps a pair."

Aniol nodded before glancing back down to the journal he held in his lap. He turned the page and entered the life of another.

ANIOL closed the book with a frown. He'd read it from cover to cover. The book held a lot of information, yet he understood very little of it. The Gatekeeper who had written it spoke of his training, spoke of the gates and how to open them, and spoke of those who had guided his ability and helped him to understand it, but the narrative had been vague, describing concepts that were better experienced than explained. Aniol understood the theory the book had tried to explain but had difficulty visualizing it and correlating it with the conflicting experiences he'd had.

The book held vital information, but that knowledge was influenced by the perception of the Gatekeeper who had written it. The Gatekeeper had spoken about his relationship with his Warden and how the link had felt, yet it was nothing like what Aniol felt for Kaji. The emotion behind it was different, so it didn't really help him understand what a Warden really was.

Aniol was beginning to suspect that there wasn't a true standard definition for the relationship between a Gatekeeper and his Warden. He suspected that it was like any other relationship: it was meant to be defined by the two who participated in it, with the difference that the Warden was initially drawn to his Gatekeeper, initially given feelings that urged him to protect his Gatekeeper. Both the Warden and the Gatekeeper still had free will and could still choose how the relationship between them was defined, which would explain why it was different between him and Kaji.

Aniol eyed Kaji as he continued to read. He loved Kaji and didn't think of him as his Warden. Kaji was and always would be, first and foremost, his mate. Aniol put the book down before crawling over to said mate. Ducking his head beneath the stray strands of Kaji's red hair, he leaned up and kissed him, suddenly wanting Kaji to know how much he loved him, how much he needed him.

Kaji blinked, surprised when his vision of the yellow pages in his lap was obstructed by pale hair, then misty eyes and pale skin as Aniol looked up and kissed him. Sheer shock and surprise kept him unresponsive as Aniol's lips moved gently over his own, the kiss shy but desperate. Kaji couldn't believe it. Aniol had actually taken the initiative, had come to him, and was seeking touch. He dropped the book he'd been reading and gathered Aniol into his lap, carefully returning the embrace, keeping the kiss soft, light, and filled with affection.

When they finally broke contact, Kaji brushed Aniol's hair back, awed by the emotion he could see on Aniol's face. Kaji could now see that Mathié had been right. Aniol loved him, and Kaji suspected that the kiss was Aniol's way of trying to tell him as much. Aniol never was one for words.

Kaji smiled, trying to soothe the touch of confusion and uncertainly he could sense in Aniol and trying to banish the fear of rejection he could see in his lover's eyes. "I love you too," he whispered in reassurance, watching as Aniol relaxed in relief. Leaning forward, he dropped a kiss onto the young man's forehead, the corner of his eye, his nose, and finally his mouth, claiming Aniol's lips in a soul-searching kiss.

Aniol's heart soared with Kaji's response, tears gathering in the corner of his eyes. Kaji loved him. Kaji treasured him. Kaji saw him as more than a Gatekeeper; he saw Aniol as his mate. Aniol clutched the bonding bracelet on his wrist as he fought back the tears of relief. He'd been happy to see the bracelet back on his wrist, happy that Kaji had put it back, but he'd remained uncertain as to what it really meant. He was afraid to trust something that had already been taken away from him once; he'd been confused by what Kaji had meant by it. The four simple words whispered by Kaji wiped that uncertainty and fear clean away, leaving relief and happiness in his heart, bubbling warmth that threatened overwhelm him. It was a feeling Aniol was unaccustomed to, but it was also a feeling he wanted to keep.

A soft knock on the door interrupted the moment and caused them to draw away from one another. Aniol remained in Kaji's lap, breathing softly.

"You really should eat some breakfast," Mathié said, stepping in. He ignored the position the two were in. "Looks like neither of you received any sleep, and some food will do you good. I had a room prepared for you but it looks like you spent all night reading." Mathié confirmed his suspicions by glancing at the books that lay scattered about the floor, some open, others not. All were unbound.

Aniol glanced at Kaji, silently asking if he thought it was okay. When Kaji nodded, he slipped out of Kaji's lap and stood, waiting for the redhead to join him before he followed Mathié out. Mathié led them through the passages towards the breakfast room.

Aniol followed Mathié around the corner, freezing in place when he saw who occupied it. Sitting at the head of the table was Arian, and on his right was a rather plump man with balding silver hair and rather colorless pale grey eyes. The man was reaching over the table to hand Arian something, obviously trying to placate the young man who was glaring heatedly at him. Fear, panic, and dread surged through Aniol's veins as he realized who the man with Arian was. The moment of recognition brought his nightmares forth and drove him to flee. Whimpering in the back of his throat, he turned and ran away, back toward the room they had just left.

# OLD CRUELTY

A Gatekeeper was locked away in a cold, white room, denied affection, communication, friendship, love, and touch. He was forced to grow up in a desolate emotional desert that slowly killed his soul and left him unable to understand the true meaning of affection. So it was that the Gatekeeper was exposed to a form of cruelty that did not involve physical pain.

KAJI turned, about to follow after his mate, wondering what had made him react in such a manner, but he was forestalled by Mathié's arm blocking his way. Mathié shook his head, glancing back into the room pointedly, a gesture that was all too soon followed by a smooth voice, a tone Kaji was all too familiar with. It was the tone Karl had used on him many a time. "Mathié! Is this the interesting guest you were telling me about? The guest you invited me over to breakfast to see?" The rather plump man who had been seated beside Arian walked around Kaji, eyeing him. "My, my...." He clicked his tongue, the sound echoing in the back of his throat. "He really is interesting. Where's he from? Are you sure he isn't a demon, with those fiery eyes and that red hair?"

Kaji's skin crawled, a sudden premonition of ill intent striking him full in the face. Suddenly he knew what it was Aniol had fled from. Aniol knew this man, knew him and feared him. He'd looked extremely ill the moment he'd seen him, as if he would fall over at a moment's notice, and Mathié, Kaji suspected, had brought them here to test a theory. Kaji glanced at Mathié in silent anger. Why did the man Aniol trusted so insist on hurting him?

Mathié shook his head, placing a finger to his lips, glancing at the man who was still circling Kaji, eyeing him as a vulture would its prey. "No, Laithe, he's not a demon. You should know that. His eyes are clear." Mathié pushed Kaji gently into the room.

Kaji fumed, rage bubbling just barely below the surface of his skin.

Mathié positioned himself on Kaji's right, forcing Laithe to settle for his left. Leaning up, he whispered softly into Kaji's ear. "Work with me here. I'm trying to find out if he's the one that held Aniol captive all his life. I think he thought Aniol was a seer and was hoping to use that ability to overthrow the crown."

Kaji gritted his teeth, trying to keep himself from exploding. He realized that the information Mathié was trying to get was important, but the fact that Mathié was hurting Aniol to it really grated on Kaji's nerves. Laithe reminded him far too much of Karl, except Laithe had far less finesse. As far as Kaji was concerned, Laithe was barely worth the air his lungs were stealing. "You upset him," Kaji whispered in return, his displeasure clear.

"Who's upset?" Laithe asked, reaching out to touch Kaji's arm.

Kaji was just about to give Laithe a really rude response, intending to tell him that it was none of his business and that he should keep his damned hands to himself, when Mathié interrupted him. "Kaji's brother is upset that he had to stay home while Kaji here got to come to the palace," Mathié explained smoothly.

Laithe raised his eyebrows at that. "Oh? Did he also inherit your strange coloring?" he asked, turning his washed-out gaze onto Kaji once more. "If he did, you really must let me meet him. I do like rare and strange features upon a person."

Laithe's words chilled Kaji to the core, dousing his anger and cooling it to frozen rage. Kaji's heart was weighed down by dread, the implications in those words sending his mind into turmoil. He didn't even want to contemplate what this man may have done to Aniol because of his misty eyes. It was strange that the feature that marked Aniol as the last hope for salvation also marked him as a target for grief, exacting a heavy price simply for bearing it. The price for atonement, restoration of balance, and peace was Aniol's pain. It was a bitter realization that Kaji found very difficult to bear.

"No, unfortunately not," Mathié replied. "If he too had such unusual features, I would've brought him along. I know that this is something of great interest to you as you're currently researching the abilities anyone marked with strange features inherits. That's why I brought Kaji here, after all. So that the two of you could talk." Mathié subtly pushed Kaji toward the breakfast table.

Mathié slid out a chair and rather pointedly guided Kaji into it as he continued to speak. "So I guess I shall leave the two of you to it then. I must apologize for taking Arian, though. Something has come up that requires his urgent attention." Grabbing a napkin, Mathié unfolded it and placed it onto Kaji's lap in a single, fluid motion, using the action to hide the fact that he was whispering in Kaji's ear. "Please forgive me. I'll give you a better explanation later. I will go check on Aniol." He got up once more and headed straight for Arian. "Your highness. An urgent matter has come up and requires your attention."

"But—" Arian began, about to remind Mathié of the promise he'd made.

"It should take but a moment of your time to assess, your highness." Mathié gave Arian a pointed look. It was a look the young man knew rather well.

Arian, knowing better than to disobey, scowled at Mathié but sullenly did as he was being asked. Dropping his napkin onto the table, he stood, head raised haughtily as he turned away from Mathié. "Fine, lead the way then," he replied, clear command in his tone, giving the impression that it was he and not Mathié who was in charge.

Kaji knew better. He'd seen the exchange between Mathié and Arian. Laithe, however, had missed it. He was too preoccupied with trying to get Kaji's attention to bother watching them. That said and done, Arian and Mathié walked out, leaving Kaji alone with the piranha.

Kaji's hid his deep-seated frustration and smiled at Laithe, his expression barely cordial. He couldn't bear the thought of remaining civil to the man whose presence he abhorred as much as if not more than Karl's. He clenched his hands beneath the table, ignoring the food laid out before him while Laithe ate eagerly, throwing questions at Kaji between bites.

KAJI'S eye twitched when Laithe tossed yet another inquiry at him, seeking to discover any abilities beyond the norm he might possess. So far he'd been asked if he ever felt strange, if anything strange had ever happened around him or to him, if he'd ever felt any strange power within him, if he believed in the power of dreams, and if he believed that the future could be foreseen or changed if the outcome was known beforehand. All of which he'd responded to using vague negative responses.

"Ever had a vision? Any vision," Laithe asked, grey gaze eagerly locked upon Kaji as he stuffed more food into his mouth.

"Can't say that I have," Kaji said, keeping the response non-committal. He most certainly was not about to tell the man about Aniol and the visions he'd shared with his mate. He hated the direction all of Laithe's questions took, hated how they all seemed to confirm Mathié's suspicions. Laithe was far too interested in seers and visions of the future for his curiosity to be innocent in nature.

Kaji was beginning to suspect that Mathié was right. Laithe was probably the man who had kidnapped Aniol and held him captive in that small white room. He also suspected that the reason Aniol hadn't been killed was because this man somehow knew that the white in Aniol's eyes marked a supernatural ability for visions. What Laithe had obviously *not* realized was that Aniol's visions were not of the future. They were of Duiem, because Aniol was a Gatekeeper, not a Seer. When Laithe had realized the visions Aniol had were not of the future, he had then decided to dispose of Aniol. That would explain the blood in the white room. Kaji gritted his teeth, threatening to grind them down to nothing at the thought, his hatred toward the man rising tenfold.

"Really?" Laithe raised his eyebrows in surprise. "No visions of the future? No strange dreams? Not even visions of a future filled with sun and dry sand?"

Kaji bit back a growl of rage, chilled by the last words, a seal, a confirmation of his suspicions. This *had* to be the man who had held Aniol captive. If not directly, then he knew the person who had. He'd said nothing about Duiem, about the sun and desert sand to Laithe, yet Laithe seemed to know about Aniol's visions. The only way this man could know of such visions was through Aniol, seeing as the records of Duiem and

Gatekeepers had been burned, the five ribbon-bound volumes the only records to survive.

The five books had remained hidden until Mathié had found them and passed them onto Aniol. Those volumes would have given Laithe considerably more information than the man currently seemed to have. They would've prevented him from mistaking Aniol's visions as visions of the future and would've explained exactly who and what Aniol was; consequently, it was highly unlikely Laithe had ever seen them.

"No," Kaji snapped, his response short and abrupt. "I have not had strange things happening to me and have had no strange visions. I know nothing about a future filled with sun and sand! Now if you'll excuse me, I, too, have some urgent matters to attend to." He stood and gave Laithe a rather stiff bow.

Swallowing the growl and rage that was gathering in his throat and demanding release, he turned and stalked out, heading straight to the room he and Aniol had spent the night reading in. He raised a hand and was just about to knock when Aniol's soft voice interrupted him, the softly spoken words increasing the chill already within him. "They tried to kill me."

# RECOLLECTION

Perception and knowledge influence the manner in which everything is experienced and remembered. Those who betrayed the Gatekeepers perceived their action as a defensive blow meant to prevent the people of Careil from obtaining more power than those in Duiem. They remembered the betrayal and the turmoil that followed and so they also remembered the Gatekeepers.

Careil, on the other hand, was unaware of the Gatekeepers' deaths. The gates between Careil and Duiem closed, and Careil began to die, for no apparent reason. The slow death of Careil twisted perception, driving the people to believing they were being punished for some unknown wrong they had committed. They began to reject anyone they perceived as different, blaming the punishment their land was receiving on those who could still see the sun that they longed would return to warm their frozen land. So it was that within Careil, the memories of Gatekeepers were driven into obscurity.

ARIAN was surprised when Mathié led him through the palace to a section no longer in use. He absently wondered what Mathié was up to but was not about to ask, as he was doing his utmost to ignore him. He wanted Mathié to know he was displeased with him. Unfortunately, Mathié seemed to be immune to anything Arian could throw at him. This really grated on Arian's nerves, and he had no idea what to do about it.

He blinked in surprise when Mathié abruptly stopped walking. Jerking to a halt beside Mathié, Arian frowned in confusion at the door they were standing before. It was an old room. It used to belong to a prince a long time ago, but it had been sealed off after his death. Barely anyone ever came here anymore. He wondered why Mathié had brought him here. He watched curiously as Mathié pushed the door open. He was surprised by the ease with which it opened.

Dim light filtered through the doorway, illuminating a pale figure seated in a corner of the room, arms wrapped around his knees. It was Aniol. Arian stepped forward toward his brother, the action instinctive, brought on by a desire to understand what he saw.

"You two need to talk," Mathié stated softly from behind him before closing the door with a soft click.

An uncomfortable silence filled the atmosphere, hanging thick between the two. Aniol ignored his presence, and Arian stood still, staring at his brother in shock. Aniol looked broken, hurt, and haunted, and for some reason this bothered him. His concern found release in aggression. Arian raised his nose haughtily into the air before speaking. "Still ignoring me, I see. Think you're that high and mighty even though no one even knows you exist? Am I not good enough to be your brother?" His tone dripped sarcasm.

Arian gasped in shock when Aniol glanced up at him in surprise, genuinely seeming to notice Arian's presence for the first time. The expression that marred his brother's face was filled with terror, the intensity of which Arian had not expected to encounter, let alone have to deal with. Aniol's eyes were wide, more white than anything else. The mist within them seemed to have a life of its own, taking over Aniol's gaze, taking him to another time and place.

"No," Aniol whispered. "It's not you. It's me that is not good enough."

Aniol's words sent guilt sharply through him. Arian swallowed past a lump that had suddenly formed in his throat, and took a few steps toward Aniol. Bending down, he noticed his brother's frame. He'd always believed himself to be small and slim of stature, but he was nothing like Aniol. He was taller than his brother and had a bigger build. If Mathié hadn't told him that Aniol was older, he would've been convinced that he himself was the older brother. "Are you all right?" Arian asked, concerned. He was unable to explain why he felt that way, but the why didn't really matter. Suddenly he wanted to reach out to the brother he'd so blatantly rejected. Even so, he still wanted to kick himself. It was a stupid question.

He could see Aniol wasn't all right, but he had no idea what else to do.

Aniol remained silent for a moment, his gaze resting upon Arian, He was looking for something. Seeming to have found what he sought, he shook his head, silently telling Arian that he wasn't all right.

It was in that moment that Arian was granted Aniol's trust. He received an honest answer from Aniol, one that allowed him to reach out even further. Arian swallowed once again, shocked. He hadn't expected Aniol to be honest with him. He'd actually expected Aniol to shun him, to push him away, and so it took him a moment to gather himself together once again. He sat down beside Aniol before asking carefully, "Want to talk about it?"

"Not really." Aniol's hands clenched in his garments.

Arian scowled, completely at a loss as how to proceed, now that Aniol had told him he didn't want to talk about it. Suddenly deciding that there were other things he and his brother needed to work through, he cleared his throat, uncomfortable with what he was going to say. "I'm sorry for the way I treated you when I first met you." His voice was gruff, and he continued when Aniol looked at him in obvious confusion. "For strangling you... for breaking the pendant... and uh... for ignoring you and saying all those things." Arian turned bright red in humiliation. He was unaccustomed to having to apologize. Usually Mathié was the only one who ever questioned his actions, and he'd learned to ignore him a long time ago.

"It's all right," Aniol said softly. He'd long ago forgiven his brother for that. Arian was, after all, the only family he had left.

Arian licked his dry lips. "I didn't know... about you. No one ever told me I had a brother." He dropped his gaze, guilt thick in his throat. "I had no idea you had been taken, locked up like that...."

Aniol shook his head, watching as Arian berated himself. He wanted to reach out and soothe Arian's concern but was loathe to touch him. He was wary to touch anyone except Kaji, and Kaji's was the only touch that did not scare him. He frowned in consternation, rapidly twisting the cloth he clutched. "It's not your fault." He wanted to wipe the guilt off of Arian's face. He wanted Arian to stop blaming himself on his account.

Arian glanced up at Aniol, catching the look of desperation upon his face. He could see Aniol was waging war against emotion he had no hope of understanding. Arian bit his lip, mind racing, trying to figure out what to say or do to make things better. Settling on the idea of offering physical comfort, he reached out, only to stop when Aniol flinched away. Silence settled between them once more, every second stretching out uncomfortably, threatening to reach a breaking point.

Arian broke it, unable to allow the silence to continue any longer. "How did you get away?" he asked. "Mathié said he couldn't get you out. How did you get out?"

Aniol tensed, dropping his own gaze as Arian's questions brought unwanted memories back to the fore. He considered his words for a moment before speaking softly. "Someone else got me out. I don't know who. I never really saw them clearly."

"Someone rescued you?" Arian asked, extremely interested and eager to have his curiosity, macabre as it may seem in the circumstances, appeased. He hadn't even known he had a brother, and now wanted to know everything about him. He wanted to know how he'd gotten free, how Aniol had ended up where he found him, and why Mathié could've possibly thought that Aniol was dead. The snippets of conversation between Aniol, Kaji, and Mathié that he'd managed to overhear didn't make all that much sense to him. He wanted to puzzle them out, to fit them together in the order in which they belonged. His brother was a mystery to him, and he wanted to figure it out.

"Not really," Aniol said, his voice filled with pain.

"Not really? Then what did they do?" Arian couldn't help but ask, dread filling him. Aniol's expression told him the response wasn't going to be a good one, but Arian wanted to hear it nonetheless.

"They tried to kill me." Aniol paused, allowing an awkward silence to settle for but a moment before continuing. "Someone came into the room and hit me. All I remember is a moment of pain followed by darkness. They took me somewhere... towards water... chained me, and then they threw me in. I tried to fight, but they were too strong for me." Aniol buried his face in trembling hands, trying to get a hold of his emotions. That was when warm arms embraced him, their touch familiar and welcome. Kaji was there.

Kaji pulled Aniol close. He glared at Arian, taking his anger out on the young man even though he knew that Arian probably had little to do with Aniol's current state. He knew Aniol needed to talk about the things that had happened to him, needed to face them and deal with them, but it still tore him up inside to see his mate so distressed. Kaji twisted a strand of Aniol's hair around his fingers, glancing away from Arian to look down at Aniol, who was shaking in his arms. He waited patiently for the tremors to subside, sharing his silence and concern with Arian before asking, "What happened after that?" He, too, was curious, wanting to know more about his bondmate. He wanted to know how Aniol had come to him, how he'd survived all that had been done to him.

"I don't really know," Aniol admitted softly. "I passed out, and when next I came to, I was lying on stone, staring up at a pale blue sky, lit by bright sun. I didn't know sunshine could be that bright or that hot. It was so hot that the shackles were burning my skin." Aniol winced in remembrance. "I was thirsty."

Kaji remained silent, simply running his fingers through Aniol's hair, giving him time to continue. Aniol pulled away from Kaji, turned in his lap, and pulled a face when he met Kaji's concerned amber gaze head on. "That's when the men found me. They took me through the desert." His sentences were short, abrupt, and pained as he forced himself to speak. "They had to take the chains off. The chains were too heavy for the sand. They didn't have a key but still managed to take them off." Aniol frowned in confusion as he tried to understand how that could be possible. He realized he didn't actually remember the chains coming off. Shaking himself out of his momentary contemplation, he forced himself to continue, his voice thick. They only reason Aniol continued was because he knew he needed to tell Kaji the truth, for both their sakes. "They put a collar around my neck. Then they tied me up to the end of a rope. They made me walk behind their beasts each day. I thought I was going to die. I was so thirsty, so hot, so cold, and so tired...." Aniol paused for a moment, letting his words sink in. He knew Kaji understood what he was talking about. Kaji knew what a journey through the desert entailed, as he'd lived through it at Aniol's side the second time Aniol had been forced to endure it.

"Then we got to the city. There were so many people. So much noise. They kept touching me, pushing into me." Aniol's face was filled with disgust at the memories of the invasive touch, touch that had threatened to drive him mad. "They said they were taking me to the slave market… that they would sell me. They said they'd get good money for me because—" Aniol nearly choked on his words, "—because my coloring was so rare."

Kaji tensed, the hand that had still been playing with Aniol's hair momentarily freezing in place. "I'm sorry," he whispered, drawing Aniol back into his arms.

"The young man we met in the sewers, the one with hair like mine, cut me free," Aniol mumbled into Kaji's neck. "I ran. My captor chased after me but I ran and then fell—" He swallowed before finishing on a whisper, relieved to have the story done with. He was already tired of trying to make himself understood, unaccustomed to speaking so much at once. "I fell onto you."

# Cold Heart

A single man driven by pride and ambition stole a child meant to die in the hopes of furthering his lot in life. He then proceeded to demand that the child supply him with visions of the future, hoping this knowledge would assist him in overthrowing the throne. The child, however, could not meet his demands. These demands grew more heated as the child matured; the man's actions more violent with each obscure answer he received. Finally, when he realized that he would not receive what he sought from the child, he cold-heartedly ordered the child killed and hired men to do the work for him. The child had become a liability instead of the asset the man originally hoped for.

SILENCE hung heavy in the air, filled with shock and horrified understanding. Neither Kaji nor Arian knew what to say. Kaji still wondered about all that Aniol had not spoken about, about his childhood, the days he spent in that horrible white room, and most of all about the man he'd fled from—Laithe. Kaji swallowed, trying to gather up the courage to ask. He didn't want to hurt Aniol, not when he could see that he was already hurting, but he felt that he needed to know. The questions and unconfirmed suspicions were driving him mad. Finally gathering the required courage, he asked, "What about Laithe?"

"What about me?" A chill coursed through Kaji's and Aniol's veins, the cold voice all too familiar, undesired and hated. Aniol tensed, the mist in his eyes roiling, mirroring the storm of emotion that boiled in his blood, fear, horror, and denial demanding recognition.

Kaji pulled Aniol against his chest, burying Aniol's face against his shoulder, hiding it from Laithe, trying to hide Aniol's identity for as long as he could, hoping Laithe would leave. But he knew it was in vain. Laithe was too much in the habit of getting into other's business to simply let this slide.

Laithe frowned. Something about Aniol bugged him, pulling at his memory. That hair, that exact shade of hair ran only in one family, and technically Arian was supposed to be the only one that still bore it. His breath escaped him as shock rocked him, causing him to pale. "Aniol—" He choked on the word. "You're supposed to be dead!"

Pure unrestrained fury tempered by cold hatred filtered through Kaji's blood, and he snarled, a pure animalistic sound of rage, the kind of rage that bordered on madness, unrestrained and uncontrolled. He moved to throw himself at Laithe in a bid to tear his throat out when a cold hand settled upon his cheek.

"Please," Aniol whispered, his lips white and trembling. "Please don't." Aniol could feel Kaji's rage, could read the emotion in the way Kaji held himself. "You're hurting yourself." Aniol's voice was filled with pain, fear, and concern. He was terrified of what Laithe finding him would mean, but what scared him more was the anger and hatred in Kaji's eyes. It would probably drive the redhead to do something that would hurt him later, something that he would regret.

Kaji searched Aniol's misty gaze and found concern and fear there. Aniol didn't want him to hurt the man who had so obviously hurt him. Kaji couldn't understand it, but he loved Aniol and was willing to concede for his sake. His desire for blood was washed away and replaced a sense of calm that allowed him to realize that his heart ached to share the pain Aniol had suffered. Kaji drew Aniol back into his arms and faced Laithe with resolution and determination instead of hatred. "If you ever lay hands on him again, hurt him again, or even look at him wrong, I will make sure to see justice done."

Laithe swallowed hard, suddenly fearing what the redhead could do to him. "There's nothing you can do to me," he retorted. "You have no proof. You also have no power here."

"He may not, but I do," Arian said. "What did you do to my brother?" he demanded, his voice suddenly cold.

"My liege?" Laithe seemed to just realize that Arian was there. "Is that what they've told you? These impostors? That's not your brother. They are but after your throne. I have been trying to stop them from succeeding. I overheard them planning your death, and that one"—he pointed at Aniol—"even went as far as dyeing his hair so that he could impersonate you! It's an outrage!"

A moment of silence hung in the air. "That's not true," Aniol whispered, breaking the silence. He turned and faced Laithe head on. "It's the other way around," he said, his words barely over a whisper but echoing through the room, ensuring that all present heard them. "You kept me locked up. You kept coming to me, kept asking if you were going to be successful, if the poison or the assassin was going to succeed in killing the king and queen. You were very upset when the queen survived. That was the first day that you beat me." Aniol swallowed, forcing himself to face the malicious rage he could see bubbling just below the surface in Laithe's eyes. "You told me I was useless. You told me my visions were useless and that you were sorry you'd let me live." Aniol swallowed; his throat was thick. "I nearly died that night, you know. If Mathié had not come, had not forced the guard to let him in, I would have died that night."

"You should have died that night." Laithe said viciously, anger ridding him of his common sense, causing him to forget in whose presence he was uttering the incriminating words.

Aniol tensed, suddenly filled with uncharacteristic anger. He'd never allowed himself the right to the emotion before, but Kaji had made him realize that that his life was worth something to at least somebody. "No," he replied, causing Laithe's jaw to drop in shock. Aniol had never in his life contradicted him. "I did not deserve to die," Aniol continued. "I didn't deserve what you did to me. I didn't understand what you wanted from me. I didn't understand why you asked me if I had had visions regarding the royal house, regarding the moon and stars. I couldn't understand why you were always demanding visions of the future, why you wanted them from me when all I could see was desert sand. I didn't know why you kept asking me if I'd seen a silver-blue haired young man in my dreams, if I had perhaps seen him die."

Arian gasped in shock. Suddenly he knew all too well what Laithe had done to his brother, and worse, he knew why he had done it. He went cold, realizing that this man was responsible for the deaths of his parents—for the death of his beloved mother. Pain and betrayal stole his breath, each gasp a battle, each one more difficult than the one before.

"That's a lie!" Laithe exclaimed, suddenly realizing how incriminating the situation was becoming. He turned to Arian, whose face was bloodless, his lips pale as he fought for breath, and continued to speak, pleading with Arian lest his admission get him killed. "All of it is a lie. There's no proof! How can you believe an impostor, a demon claiming to be your brother, over me? Look at his eyes; they are white! He should be dead! I would not associate with a demon like that!"

Arian didn't believe Laithe's words. Deep in his heart he knew that Aniol spoke the truth. Aniol was his brother. Of that he was certain. Mathié wouldn't have said so if it wasn't true. Mathié wasn't stupid, and Aniol had his mother's pendant. What more proof did he need? What really hurt Arian was that this man, one of the noble court, a man he had dined with, socialized with, and trusted, had from the sounds of things plotted to kill him and had succeeded in killing his parents. Laithe had killed his mother. He continued to gasp, hyperventilating.

Aniol gasped, crawled out of Kaji's lap, and rushed to his brother's side, wrapping his arms around Arian in concern without even thinking, without realizing that he was instigating contact.

Meanwhile, Kaji snarled and threw himself at Laithe, angry that the man had dared to call his mate a demon. His forward momentum was, however, once again halted, this time by Mathié, who rushed into the room followed by three others. Mathié held a blade at Laithe's throat, but he was looking at Arian in concern, watching as Aniol desperately fought to get his brother to breathe properly. "I'm sure I can handle it from here, Kaji," Mathié said, meeting his gaze before glancing at Arian once more. He kept his blade at Laithe's throat. The other three men remained in the doorway, watching the situation unfold. "Get the damned healer!' Mathié ordered in frustration, watching as Arian continued his battle to breathe. One of the three men turned and ran, seeking a healer.

"Calm down," Aniol urged softly, holding his brother's face in his hands. "It's all right," he whispered, his voice soft and musical. "It's over. Mathié will handle it. It's all right. Just breathe." Aniol took slow breaths in illustration, keeping Arian's attention. "Slowly. In... out.... In... out. It's going to be okay." He kept it up, forcing Arian to copy him until Arian's breathing began to ease and color returned to his lips. Aniol heaved a sigh of relief and burrowed into Arian's arms.

Mathié, too, breathed a sigh of relief, smiling at Arian and the puzzled expression on his face. He was obviously confused by having Aniol in his arms. "Try not to kill Arian," he whispered to Kaji, who was eyeing Arian with jealousy. Mathié then winked at Arian before leading Laithe out the room, followed by the other two men.

# OTHER SIDE

Every tale has at least two sides colored by perception; every tale is marked by circumstance and understanding. Careil and Duiem are two sides of the same tragic tale. Gatekeepers are a forgotten memory in one world, a legend in the other, but they exist in neither world.

Consequently, neither land truly understands them, their impact, or their purpose. And so each land needs to learn, needs to start anew in order to merge perception and understanding, working together in the pursuit of truth.

"YOU can't just kill him," Kaji said, watching Arian pace back and forth, anger and distress written all over his features. Kaji, Aniol, and Arian were in Arian's bedroom. The healer had rushed into the room to look Arian over, but by then Arian had recovered most of his color, his distress replaced by anger. Regardless of the improvement, the healer had insisted Arian lie down and rest, take time to recover from his panic attack, and much to Arian's distress, he had overridden all the young man's protests.

Arian had pleaded with Aniol to come with him, desperately wanting to speak with his brother. He wanted more information, wanted to get his facts straight, and he wanted the only family he still had near. Aniol, unable to deny his newfound brother anything, had agreed. And so they found themselves in Arian's room, where the young man was doing anything but resting.

"As much as I agree with your sentiment, it would be dangerous to have him killed without a trial. You could risk your throne. It would be more diplomatic to let the court deal with this," Kaji said. "Revenge is not worth your throne or the price your country will have to pay if you should be dethroned. Think of all the chaos that would follow a disruption in power."

Arian blinked, turning to Kaji in surprise. He hadn't expected to receive advice of such nature from the redhead. It seemed as if Kaji knew exactly what he was talking about, making Arian wonder exactly who he was. Come to think of it, he didn't even know what Kaji's relation to his brother was. They were close, that much was clear, but Arian began to wonder exactly how close. "Can I ask you a random, unrelated question?" he asked, watching Kaji.

Kaji's amber gaze widened just a touch at the unexpected change in topic, the movement imperceptible to anyone but Aniol. "Sure," he replied warily, uncertain as to what Aniol's brother could possibly wish to ask him.

"Who are you?" Arian asked. He leaned against the wall by the window to his room, resting his weight on his hands to keep himself from fidgeting.

Kaji raised his eyebrows in surprise at the question. "Kaji Taiyouko."

"That doesn't really tell me who you are," Arian said. "All that tells me is your name. I want to know who you are. Why do you know so much about politics? Where are you from?"

Kaji glanced at Aniol, who'd gone still against him. Both Kaji and Aniol were seated on Arian's bed, watching him. Aniol was kneeling, leaning against Kaji, the fingers of his right hand intertwined with the fingers of Kaji's left, their clasped hands hidden from Arian's sight. "You wouldn't believe me if I told you," Kaji said.

"Try me," Arian challenged. "How much more unbelievable can it be than Aniol's existence?" He pulled a face, giving Aniol a look of apology. "I don't mean anything bad by that," he explained, hoping Aniol wouldn't take insult. It wasn't a nice thing to say, but it was the truth. He had been rather shocked to find out he had a brother, and what's more, a brother who was older than him and, technically speaking, should inherit the throne of Careil.

Aniol gave Arian a small smile, shaking his head to indicate that he hadn't taken offense. He understood his brother's confusion. He himself had gone through similar emotions since being kidnapped and nearly killed. "It's all right," he said softly.

"You would be surprised," Kaji said, exchanging another glance with Aniol. "I myself found it difficult to believe Aniol's existence when I found out who he is." Kaji squeezed Aniol's hand in reassurance as he spoke. "And *we* still believe in Gatekeepers. Careil has forgotten their existence. This makes it very difficult to explain."

"Who Aniol is?" Arian's gaze flickered to his brother in confusion. His first instinct was to believe that Kaji was referring to finding out that Aniol was the firstborn of their royal line, but something told him that wasn't it. "Gatekeepers?"

"It's a long story," Kaji said.

"Why don't we start with my first question then? Who are you?" Arian prompted, dread filling him. He'd just been overwhelmed with information, information he wished had been broken to him differently, and it seemed it was only the tip of the iceberg. Just who exactly were these two individuals who had invaded his life, turning it upside down? And what was the significance of everything that was currently happening? For if there was one thing that he did know, it was that this was bigger than he was.

Kaji remained silent for a moment, considering his words. He turned to Aniol, and at his mate's nod, he turned back to Arian and began to speak. "I am Kaji Taiyouko, firstborn of the Taiyouko line and heir to Duiem's throne. Well, technically speaking, I'm the current ruler, except that it would appear I have been dethroned."

"Dethroned?" Arian gaped at Kaji, confusion running through him. He didn't know what he'd expected but knew it hadn't been this. He'd never even heard of Duiem and had not the slightest idea where it was.

Kaji gave Arian a bitter smile. "Yes, dethroned. It would seem that I've been declared unfit to rule."

"Why?" Arian questioned, uncertain whether he believed Kaji. He couldn't understand how it could be possible. As far as he knew, the entire kingdom, everything in Careil was ruled by him. He'd been under the impression that Careil covered the whole planet. He wasn't aware of any other kingdoms, yet at the same time he couldn't imagine why Kaji would possibly lie. Kaji's words couldn't ring more true. It explained the way the he spoke and the way he carried himself. It also explained the authority that seemed to be ingrained into him, Kaji continually using it as if it were the very air he breathed. Arian had picked up on that authority rather quickly after meeting Kaji and sometimes felt the urge to obey the other man himself.

"Someone I trusted betrayed me," Kaji stated, for once the bitterness he'd always felt when talking about this absent. Meeting Arian had taught him one thing. He was only human and as such susceptible to making mistakes. That didn't make him incompetent or define him as a failure. What he had to do now was correct his mistake. Kaji accepted it and knew that Arian had to come to the same realization.

Arian blinked, Kaji's words all too familiar. They brought to mind his own bad experience, the consequences of Laithe's deception still to be truly seen or understood. He swallowed the bitterness that welled up within him. He had no desire to dwell upon it as there were more pressing matters at hand. "Where is Duiem?"

"On the other side of the gate," Kaji kept his response short and simple, fully aware of the fact that he was being cryptic. He could see the next question forming on Arian's lips and was ready for it.

"Other side of the gate? What gate?" Arian frowned in confusion.

Kaji was about to launch into the explanation he'd ordered in his mind when he was forestalled by a light touch. He glanced down to see Aniol's hand resting on his arm.

"Duiem is another world," Aniol explained. "It's difficult to believe. As far as I understand it, there are two worlds that exist together: Careil and Duiem. Careil is cold more often than not. It's full of water and is dying because of floods. Duiem is a desert planet, dry and dying because of lack of water. The gate Kaji is speaking about links Careil to Duiem and vice versa, only it's closed. Only Gatekeepers...." Aniol paused, before correcting himself. "Only I can sense it and open it. When I nearly drowned, I must've opened a gate and gone to Duiem. That's how I survived," Aniol said in sudden realization.

Arian blinked in confusion. All of this seemed like a fairy tale, meant to stimulate children's imagination. If it was not a story, then perhaps it was the delusion of a madman. But a deep sense told Arian that neither

Aniol nor Kaji, and certainly not both of them, were mad. "Let's see if I understand this correctly," Arian started carefully. "You're a Gatekeeper?" he asked, the word unfamiliar upon his tongue. When Aniol nodded, he continued. "And you went to another world?" Another nod. "A world ruled by Kaji?" When Aniol nodded again, Arian raised a hand to his forehead and rubbed at the dull headache that threatened as he tried to understand all of this. "Um," he floundered, looking for something else to ask.

"Give me a minute," Aniol said as he rose. "I'm going to fetch something that might help." He shook his head when Kaji moved to follow him, mouthing, "Stay. I'll be all right." That said, he slipped out of the room.

Arian frowned, confused by his brother's departure and the strange silence that seemed to follow it. He turned back to Kaji who was watching him closely. "Another world, huh?" Arian pulled a face before suddenly changing the subject. "I'm sorry to hear you've been dethroned."

"It's all right," Kaji replied, a bit of respect for Arian growing in him. Even if he seemed a little confused, Arian was taking this far better than he would have under the same circumstances, and that in and of itself demanded his respect.

"Can I ask you another, perhaps more personal question?" Arian asked awkwardly, afraid to anger Kaji, seeing as they were finally on relatively decent speaking terms.

"I can't promise that I'll answer, but sure," Kaji teased lightly with a smile, trying to get Arian to relax a little.

Arian returned the smile half-heartedly, still tense and confused. "Who are you to my brother?"

Kaji's smile brightened. "He's my precious mate," he said, raising his arm with the bonding bracelet upon it.

Arian stared, astounded by the familiar moon and a bright amber sun. "Really?" he exclaimed in surprise. "You're my brother-in-law?"

Kaji nodded. "Yes, and Aniol is my heart."

Arian remained silent, taking in Kaji's words and the emphasis he put on them. Aniol was really lucky. He had someone who held him dear, someone who loved him wholeheartedly. Arian experienced a moment of jealousy, a moment of longing for the same.

Slipping back into the room, Aniol paused at the strange silence that dominated the atmosphere. He glanced from Kaji, toward Arian, and back to Kaji once more, trying to figure it out. Seeing no animosity, he relaxed and walked up to Arian. Aniol gave him a shy smile before silently holding out five ribbon-bound volumes.

# Addiction

Hope for redemption is such a slim thread to clasp. The destiny of two worlds lies upon the shoulders of but a few, yet many breaths are held in anticipation of the choices that will be made, choices that shall shape destiny and shift the scale towards life or death.

ANIOL curled deeper into Kaji's side and buried his face into Kaji's neck, savoring the warmth and the comfort he found there as he drifted between waking and sleep. Kaji reached for Aniol's hair and absently began to play with the strands, twisting the pale tresses around his fingers, releasing them and then repeating the entire process. Kaji's mind raced, filtering through all he'd learned.

It had been a hectic morning filled with drama, pain, and shock. It had hit Kaji hard, but had hit Aniol and Arian even harder. It was definitely a morning he didn't wish to repeat. They were now in a room that had been assigned to them. The room was decorated in deep purples interspersed by touches of white, reminding Kaji a little of a midnight sky touched by moonlight. Aniol's pale form upon the deep purple sheets only served to reaffirm the illusion, giving the entire room a dreamlike quality.

They'd left Arian shortly after giving him the books to read, wanting to give him a little privacy to deal with everything that he'd learned. They'd then tracked down Mathié, and, exhausted by the night they'd spent reading, asked if they might get a room to rest in. Mathié, still distracted by Laithe, had nodded and simply led them to the room they were now in. They had collapsed upon the bed, Aniol had curled into Kaji's side, and both had fallen into blissful, dreamless sleep.

Kaji had woken a little while ago. He was surprised to find Aniol still curled up beside him. Remaining where he was, he then proceeded to watch his little mate sleep, a rather content smile upon his lips. Aniol looked so innocent and for once, at peace with himself. He watched as Aniol drifted through the various stages of sleep, drifting toward wakefulness. All the while he played with Aniol's hair, waiting patiently to be acknowledged.

Misty eyes peered up at him, awake but still filled with sleep. Aniol looked utterly adorable like that, so innocent, so pure, a touch baffled and very relaxed... absolutely perfect for.... Kaji bent down to drop light kisses upon Aniol's eyelids, wanting to capture the moment. Drifting down, he sought Aniol's lips, languidly invading Aniol's mouth with his tongue, exploring it, tasting it, and savoring his flavor. It took but a moment for Aniol to respond, a soft whimper—a sound wholly Aniol—escaping his lips.

Kaji smiled, swallowing the sound as he set about ravishing Aniol, teasing the cavern of Aniol's mouth with his tongue, brushing then withdrawing, daring Aniol to respond, urging Aniol to take over the embrace, and teasing him with promise of more. He loved how vocal Aniol was when they kissed, when they touched, and when they did all those naughty things that kept invading his mind every time he lay watching his mate. It was such a contrast to Aniol's usual quiet, withdrawn demeanor. Kaji wouldn't have believed it if he hadn't heard it for himself: the whimpers, the gasps, and the screams of pleasure.

Kaji withdrew from Aniol, and the action dragged a whine of protest from his mate. Hmm... definitely vocal. He licked his lips, eyes sparkling in amusement at the sight of Aniol, looking up at him out of cloudy eyes, marked with a touch of lust. His lips were parted as he panted softly. There was faint moisture upon them, the only evidence of the kiss they had just shared.

He trailed his hand down Aniol's side, touching him lightly through his clothes. His gaze was locked upon Aniol's eyes. He enjoyed the subtle shift in color he could see in them and loved the way those eyes darkened with each touch, blue and grey deepening while the mist within them cleared. He couldn't get enough of Aniol, his velvety soft skin, his lips, his silky strands of hair, his rare smile, and most of all, the sounds he made when lost in passion. The vocal expression of pleasure was such beautiful contrast to everything that seemed to define Aniol.

That single time of free rein upon Aniol's body had gotten him addicted. Instead of appeasing his hunger, it had made him hungry for more. And so he decided to draw those sounds out once more, aiming to claim his mate again. This goal in mind, he teased Aniol with gentle touch, giving him just a taste of what Kaji knew his Aniol wanted, giving himself a taste of what he hungered for.

Lust bloomed within him at the gasp of pleasure that escaped Aniol's lips as his fingers brushed over Aniol's nipples. They were still sensitive to his touch, even through all that cloth. He bent down, intending to mark Aniol, only to pause when Aniol interrupted him.

"Someone is knocking," Aniol whispered, his breath still a touch too fast.

Kaji frowned when he realized that someone indeed was. He hadn't initially registered the sound, having other more interesting things on his mind. Blood rushed to his head, staying there for but a moment before rushing back down to other, more interesting areas of his body, sending the heat of lust through his veins. "Ignore it?" Kaji whispered the question, licking at his lips. He still wanted to take this further, his body demanding he claim what he'd merely sampled and then been denied for the days of travel that had followed.

Aniol watched Kaji's tongue, licking his own lips in echo. His breath quickened and his eyes darkened with lust once more. He nodded mutely, willing to agree to anything that would draw this moment out. Suddenly a little too hot, Aniol shifted; his body reacted in remembrance, hungering for the pleasure promised in Kaji's gaze, demanding that Kaji do more than brush his fingertips across Aniol's skin. Aniol raised his head, moving toward Kaji's mouth, intending to claim Kaji's lips in a hungry kiss. He reached out, now knowing exactly what he wanted and what his body desired.

"Aniol?"

Aniol's forward movement was halted by the uncertain question. It was Arian. His tone was filled with question and confusion, his voice wavering with the last syllable.

Kaji noticed the subtle change in Aniol, noticed the concern that flickered through that misty blue-grey gaze and realized that Aniol would be unable to ignore his newfound brother. Releasing a deep growl of frustration, the sound rumbling though his body, Kaji turned away from Aniol and slipped out of bed highly disgruntled. He grabbed a pillow and held it in front of himself as he made his way over to the door, the sound of his footsteps muffled by the deep blue carpet.

Aniol sat up. A faint flush colored his cheeks, and his body ached in protest of the interruption. He hastily pulled the sheets up over his lap, closed his eyes, and forced himself to take deep breaths in order to get his wayward body under control.

Kaji opened the door and growled low at Arian, glaring at the young man heatedly before turning and marching back to the bed. He sat down beside Aniol, the pillow now in his lap.

Arian blinked, shocked by Kaji's greeting, and remained by the door, suddenly unsure of himself. He had no idea what he'd done to warrant such a reaction.

"Well, come on in," Kaji sighed in defeat. Arian jumped at Kaji's tone and hastily stepped into the room. Closing the door, he dropped his gaze in fear. He was ashamed to admit it, but Kaji really scared him. Kaji heaved a sigh of frustration and rubbed his forehead, trying to remind himself not to lose his temper. He took a moment to calm himself down before speaking to Arian again. "It's all right," he soothed, his tone much calmer. "I'm just being moody. Is there anything we can help you with?"

Arian glanced up, eyeing Kaji for a moment. When he saw no rage on Kaji's features, he stepped closer, walking over to the bed and sitting down in front of Aniol. He watched in confusion as his brother blushed, shifting slightly away from him. He remained still, waiting until Aniol settled once more before holding the five books out to Aniol.

"Thank you. They are a little confusing, but I think I get the general idea. This one"—he pointed to the volume with the sky blue ribbon—"seems to be very important to Careil... to me. If we ever see Duiem again that is. That one," he said, pointing to the book wrapped in black ribbon, "is a little strange, but nowhere near as strange as that one." He pointed to the one with the dark blue ribbon. "Can you really do that?"

Aniol blinked, staring down at the books in his hands, running his fingers over the Gatekeeper's journal as he contemplated his answer. "I don't really know," Aniol said. "I barely understand the concept of gates, let along how they work," he admitted, lost in thought. "I think it's what I did... when I drowned, when I saved Kaji... only I'm not sure. Both times were different. They felt different, and somehow I don't think it's supposed to feel different every time."

"But you've been to Duiem?" Arian inquired.

Aniol glanced at Kaji before turning back to Arian. "Yes."

"And to travel between Duiem and Careil you would need a gate, right?" Arian was trying to clarify his understanding in any way that he could.

"As far as I understand it, yes," Aniol said, watching Arian, wondering where his brother was going with this.

Kaji, too, was confused by Arian's line of questioning. He reached out and took Aniol's hand, absently playing with it, seeking the comfort of the shared touch.

"And to open a gate you need a Gatekeeper," Arian continued. "You are a Gatekeeper."

Aniol nodded. "Yes." He'd told Arian as much earlier, but it seemed that Arian was only now beginning to understand what that could mean.

Arian shifted, turning away from Aniol. He looked out the window, suddenly uncomfortable with Aniol's rather direct stare. "If that book is to be believed, Gatekeepers have something to do with balance between the worlds," Arian said. "The Gatekeeper that wrote it spoke of balance of forces and of keeping the worlds alive by balancing what travels between them. I think that the reason that Careil started to die is because the Gatekeepers disappeared. And it keeps dying because the Gatekeepers keep getting killed. I assume Duiem is also in chaos?" Arian turned to Kaji as he asked the question, already knowing the answer but seeking confirmation.

Kaji nodded, truly respecting Arian, amazed that the young man had managed to draw the correct conclusions, digging through to the heart of the matter in such a short span of time. He suddenly realized that Arian, when the young man came into his own, would make a formidable king, a brilliant ally, and a fearsome enemy. "Yes, Duiem, too, is in chaos," he confirmed.

# SHIFTING THE SCALE

Life and death: there is such a fragile balance between the two. Every choice that is made has the power to tip the scale of existence toward one or the other. Most people don't stop to think and consider what the consequences of their actions may be and rush through life, blindly making choices, choices that may end up destroying them.

Others spend their whole lives constantly worrying about consequences and fear the risk too much to truly ever live, spending their whole lives in obscurity, never reaching out for happiness and never claiming their lives for their own.

Then there are those who see all too well the impact of the choices made, who reach out with understanding in order to make a difference. There are those who fight to control the fragile balance, those who sacrifice their own life and happiness to pay the price to shift the scale and restore life once more.

"YES, Duiem is also in chaos," Kaji confirmed.

Arian nodded at the confirmation, having expected nothing less. He held Kaji's gaze, determination in his own. "I'm sick of watching my country die. I'm sick of the suspicion, the hidden whispers of accusation, and the blame everyone places on one another. I'm tired of living in fear, hearing of death, watching the weather wreak havoc upon the land, and watching my people wreak havoc upon one another. A Gatekeeper lives. There is hope." He glanced at Aniol before turning to Kaji once again. "We need a peace treaty. We need to work together to restore that balance that the Gatekeeper who wrote that journal speaks about. We need to save Careil and Duiem."

Kaji smiled at Arian, a little surprised by the young man's determination but more than pleased with it. He would need the peace treaty Arian had suggested and needed Arian's co-operation. If the gates were to open, thus allowing Duiem and Careil to exist together once again, a war between the two worlds was the last thing he wanted. Both Careil and Duiem had too much to lose. "Do you have the authority to negotiate such?" Kaji asked. "The way I understand it, you're as yet underage and have yet to assume the throne."

"I'm the legal heir." Arian's gaze flickered to Aniol, apology in his eyes.

Aniol nodded in understanding, knowing that the current situation was not Arian's fault. He accepted it as such. He had no need for the throne of Careil, didn't even intend to fight for it. His place was by Kaji's side, in Duiem, not in Careil. Duiem was the place he'd learned about affection and the place in which he'd learned to trust, to open up, and to be himself. He'd discovered love there, and as such it was more his home than the land he'd spent most of his life in.

Arian turned back to Kaji and continued to speak. "Even if I'm yet underage, I still run my country. Mathié is my guardian and insists that I know what's going on. He insists that I actively make decisions regarding Careil. He checks them, guides me, and signs along side me. I do not think he would protest to a peace treaty. I doubt he would protest to my attempts to bring peace and balance back to Careil."

Kaji watched Arian, and his respect for the young man—no, the king—before him grew in leaps and bounds. "Then you are very fortunate," he said. "I wasn't so fortunate. It's my guardian who betrayed me. Are you willing to set up a peace treaty with me, even though I've been dethroned? Even though, technically, I do not have that kind authority right now?"

Arian grinned at Kaji, leaning forward to look him straight in the eye. "You'll get your throne back. Even if I have to kill the man that betrayed you myself. Of that you have my word. And considering your temper, stubbornness, and the fire with which you protect my brother, I somehow get the feeling you won't need me to go that far."

A moment of silence filled the room, Arian and Kaji each assessing the other, weighing the determination and the strength that each possessed.

Kaji nodded in acceptance. "So be it."

Arian moved back away from Kaji, relaxing suddenly, revealing just how tense and uncertain he'd been and revealing just how great a leap of faith he'd taken. "We need to figure out how to open the gate. That way you can go back to Duiem and assess the situation. I'll deal with my own court." Arian's gaze went hard. "Fish out all those that seek to betray me."

Kaji nodded in agreement. "Only one question: how do we figure out how to open the gate?"

Aniol blinked when both Arian and Kaji turned to him, obviously expecting his input, probably hoping he knew the answer. He clenched his hands in the sheets. "I don't really understand any of it," he said softly. He traced his finger over the book. "It didn't feel the same. None of it did." He frowned as his mind raced, contemplating the contents of the Gatekeeper's journal before glancing up to meet Arian's gaze and asking, "Does the sanctuary of air and water still exist?"

"Sanctuary of air and water?" Arian asked slowly, for a moment confused by what Aniol could possibly be referring to. Suddenly his features cleared in realization. "You mean the place where the Gatekeeper who wrote that journal learned to be a Gatekeeper?" When Aniol nodded, Arian shook his head. "I don't actually know. It's not very likely, considering that I've just learned what a Gatekeeper is myself."

"It was in the mountains," Aniol said, watching his brother. "Far away from civilization. It was run by a small group of people. The Ruel in Duiem survived, maybe there's still something there. It's possible, right?" Aniol was desperate. He wanted to understand his ability and needed to be able to control it. He was longing to be able to help.

Arian nodded. "I guess it would be possible. People fear the mountains because of the water, ice, and rock that keep coming down, bringing death. No one goes there. They're considered to be cursed, so I guess it could be possible." Arian considered his next words for a moment before glancing down at the journal in Aniol's lap. "Okay, we go to the mountains and search for the sanctuary of air and water, then." He smiled sardonically. "After all, what do we have to lose?"

Kaji shook his head returning the rather dry smile Arian was giving them. "Our lives."

"Those are already forfeit if we do nothing," Arian said.

"I know," Kaji said. "I just wanted to point out the risks. Random question: Do you have any idea where in the mountain range we would begin to look?"

"Not really," Arian admitted, exchanging a glance with Aniol. "The diary does give a few clues, though. The Gatekeeper speaks about the position of the stars. Now all we need to do is figure out more or less when that diary was written and how much those stars have moved since. That way we can plot the current position of what the Gatekeeper was referring to and trace it back historically to its relative position all those years ago."

Kaji gaped, overwhelmed. "Could you repeat that?" he asked in shock.

Aniol reached over and closed Kaji's jaw with a finger, rather amused by the expression on Kaji's face. "He wants to identify the star constellations the Gatekeeper speaks about in his diary and use astronomy to track down that Gatekeepers' location when he wrote this diary," Aniol explained. "You need to figure out when the diary is written because stars don't stay still. They move."

"Oh." Kaji glanced at Aniol, surprised that his mate, who technically hadn't been schooled, could understand that and explain it so well.

"I've read a lot of books, " Aniol said, sensing Kaji's unspoken question.

Kaji nodded turning back to Arian. "Okay… how do we do that?"

"We ask for help from an astronomer," Arian declared. He turned to Aniol, reaching out for the Gatekeeper's diary. "Is it all right if I borrow that?"

Aniol clutched the diary, suddenly fearing that the book would be lost if given to another. He stared at Arian with wide, desperate eyes, afraid to voice his doubt. Arian picked up on it, though. Considering what had just happened, it wasn't surprising that Aniol would be afraid to entrust the book to anyone. If truth be told, Arian was surprised that his brother had trusted *him* with that knowledge. "Don't worry. I won't give anyone the book. I only wish to copy the relevant pages."

Aniol relaxed and handed the book over to Arian. Arian picked it up and stood to leave. "Thank you," he said, thanking both men for more than just the book. He gave Aniol a shy smile that reminded Kaji a lot of Aniol's smile before turning and slipping out of the room, leaving them alone in the silence of the room once again.

Aniol blinked, a little surprised at Arian's rather abrupt departure. He remained still for a moment, lost in thought, silently contemplating Arian's smile, his brother's words, and everything that had been discussed and decided. Well into his thoughts, he suddenly realized Kaji was still touching him, absently playing with his wrist, his fingers, and the palm of his hand. The touch was light, gentle, a mere soft brush of comforting warmth upon his skin, but to Aniol's overly sensitive body, it was also rather arousing.

He glanced at Kaji, noting the frown upon Kaji's forehead, a little frown that indicated that the redhead was deep in thought, lost in the turmoil of his own mind and completely unaware of what he was doing to Aniol. Aniol caught his breath, pleasant warmth pooling in his stomach at the turn of thought his own mind had taken, the desire rising rather quickly to the surface.

He gently withdrew his hand from Kaji's, drawing his mate's gaze to him in confused surprise. Gathering the books in his lap, he then proceeded to carefully place them upon the bedside table, careful to ensure no harm would come to them. He dropped his hands back into his lap and turned to meet Kaji's puzzled eyes. Aniol remained silent, watching Kaji for a moment before moving. He slipped out of the sheets and crawled over to Kaji, fascinated by the confusion in his amber eyes. He crawled into Kaji's lap and settled there. Wrapping his arms around Kaji's neck, Aniol then gave him a hungry, pleading look, his warm breath brushing Kaji's lips. Suddenly unsure of himself, Aniol paused, consternation upon his face. He licked his dry lips, trying to gather the courage to ask for what he wanted. Seeing as he'd already come this far, he forced himself to continue, whispering, a slight waver of uncertainty in his tone. "Can we continue?"

Kaji blinked in shock, nearly pinching himself in his disbelief. "Continue?" He nearly kicked himself at his own rather incoherent response, still stunned by Aniol's uncharacteristic daring. Still trying to catch up, he completely forgot to control his mouth. This certainly did not helping him maintain the image of cool control that he wished to maintain.

Aniol hummed in the back of his throat, rocking his body against

Kaji's, a faint pink tint coloring his cheeks when the movement shifted his lower body just a touch closer to Kaji's. "Please," Aniol whispered, rasping as his breath quickened as a direct result of the friction he'd instigated. He sent Kaji a hopeful glance, the expression a touch ridiculous when seen through his flush of embarrassment. "Can we?"

# DESIRE

Lust, desire, love. Such feelings have never in the history of Careil and Duiem been known to exist between a Gatekeeper and his Warden. A Warden is drawn to his Gatekeeper by a desire to protect a particular stranger. This desire then fades and is meant to be replaced by respect, friendship, duty and a mutual desire to protect their two worlds. A Gatekeeper and his Warden are not meant to fall in love. It is a boundary that existed between the two, a boundary that seemed to be taboo to cross, for what right did a Warden have to fall in love with his Gatekeeper?

What right did a Gatekeeper have to love anyone at all? Love could distract him from the fragile balance of his duties. It was always thought that it was better that way, that it was the only way to truly keep balance, a great design that was meant to work and uphold peace. But even the greatest designs can have their flaws....

KAJI moaned as their bodies connected. It was he who was supposed to be driving Aniol over the edge, not the other way around. Deciding to turn the tables, Kaji reached for Aniol's face and leaned forward to capture Aniol's lips in a searching kiss.

Aniol hummed in pleasure, reveling in the pleasure Kaji pulled from him. Aniol couldn't get enough of the feeling, the taste, and the wonderful sensation that Kaji's tongue brushing his sent through his body. He titled his head up a fraction of an inch, subtly deepening the kiss, submitting to Kaji's dominion.

Misty eyes drifted closed in pleasure as Aniol focused on the heat of Kaji's mouth, his lips and the invading tongue lapping at his own, sucking, nipping, and exploring. Sweet, blessed, damp heat, originating at his mouth flowed through his body, pooling in his groin.

Kaji's passion extracted an eager, hungry response from his body, pulling a sigh from his throat and a demanding shift from his body. Aniol's hands drifted from Kaji's neck to his shoulders, clinging to his clothes. Using Kaji's shoulders as support, Aniol raised himself a little to rub against Kaji again. His previous embarrassment was forgotten as a new heat colored his skin, slowly covering it with a thin sheen of salty dampness.

Kaji moaned in frustration. Aniol's movements threatened to drive him over the edge with their innocent sensuality, something Aniol was completely unaware of, making it that much more deadly. He grabbed hold of Aniol's hips, holding his mate in place, keeping Aniol from rubbing himself against him while Kaji continued to ravage his mouth.

Aniol whimpered. Tearing his lips away from Kaji's, he wrapped his legs around Kaji's waist, trying to bring their bodies into closer contact, frustrated by the way Kaji held him back. He opened misty eyes dark with lust and jerked his hips, trying to overpower the hold Kaji had on him. "Please…." A pained, pleading whine escaping him.

Kaji shook his head, moving forward to drop kisses along Aniol's throat, nipping at the salty skin hungrily. Aniol threw his head back with a hiss, pleasure mixing with faint pain. He arched toward Kaji's body and drew another frustrated growl from the redhead.

Kaji had had enough. Aniol was driving him mad, threatening to make him spill himself right there and then, fully clothed and with nothing more but a touch of friction instigated by his twisting hips. Growling deep in his throat, he slid his arms up from Aniol's hips, panting when Aniol took the opportunity to buck up against him, increasing the delicious friction that threatened to make him lose control before he accomplished what he wanted. Gritting his teeth in restraint, ragged breath hissing out as he fought for control, Kaji gently pried Aniol's hands off his shoulders. Returning his grip to Aniol's hips, he tried to push him off his lap, hampered by Aniol's legs, which were still wrapped around his waist.

Kaji glanced up to see hurt upon Aniol's face. Aniol was utterly confused by Kaji's action. "Work with me here," Kaji whispered, voice ragged, sweat gathering on his face with the effort of his restraint.

Aniol bit his lip, dropped his gaze in guilt, and unwrapped his legs, allowing himself to slip off of Kaji's lap. Shame coursed through him with the realization that Kaji didn't seem to want him. Aniol fought back tears of disappointment as he thought about how wanton he'd been, wishing he could take his foolish behavior back. Before the tears had a chance to fall, however, his self recrimination turned into a gasp of surprise.

Kaji turned him and pulling him back into his lap so that Aniol's back was pressed against his chest. Kaji then slid his hand into Aniol's clothes, rapidly pulling Aniol's shirt up and off. That accomplished, he slid his hands back down Aniol's chest, eliciting a sharp cry from his mate when his palms brushed over Aniol's nipples, a fleeting touch as his palms passed over the pert skin on their way down, slipping over Aniol's shivering stomach and into the band of his pants, trailing over heated skin on their way to their destination.

Kaji gripped Aniol's hip, his free hand seeking out Aniol's heat. Wrapping around Aniol's penis, Kaji slid his hand gently down, eliciting a cry of surprise and ecstasy from Aniol. When Aniol's hips bucked into his hand, Kaji smiled, a feral glow of satisfaction in his amber gaze. This was much better. He was back in control and had Aniol where he wanted him.

He brushed his fingers over the moisture gathering at the tip of Aniol's penis, surprised by the shiver of pleasure that rippled across Aniol's body. Burying his face in the crook of Aniol's neck Kaji took a deep breath, allowing Aniol's scent to wash over him before nipping and lapping at the sensitive skin there, timing his mouth with the pumping hand that continued to tease Aniol. He kept his touch soft, teasing, brushing up and down over Aniol's throbbing heat, each drawn-out motion urging more of those sweet whimpers from Aniol's parted lips.

Kaji's hand kept his hips in place, and so Aniol resorted to arching his back out from Kaji's chest, his hands clenched in the cloth of Kaji's pants, head resting upon Kaji's shoulder and exposing his throat to Kaji's hungry mouth. Liquid heat filled him, rushing to his groin. His skin was on fire, burning with Kaji's every touch, and it drove Aniol's lust even higher. Every cell in his body demanded more, reaching for release as he rushed along with a painful crest of desire that threatened to wash his sanity into the torrid waters of burning passion.

Aniol cried out in frustration when the heat within him reached fever pitch. He thrust erratically into Kaji's grip—he wanted Kaji to stop teasing him—but Kaji released his penis and slid his hand further down Aniol's thigh to slowly pull Aniol's pants down to his slim ankles. Aniol lifted his feet, allowing Kaji to slip the clothing entirely off, still thrusting into empty air.

Kaji's hand trailed back up Aniol's leg, brushing his lover's inner thigh. He paused, taking a moment to tease his mate just a little more before gripping Aniol's penis firmly. Kaji moved his hand roughly down over Aniol's thick, hard heat, finally giving Aniol the friction he so desperately wanted.

Aniol cried out at the resulting wave of pleasure, bucking once more into Kaji's hand. He was surprised to find that he could freely do so. Kaji's right hand was no longer on his hip. Instead it was trailing up his body to pinch his nipples, sending multiple sensory signals of passion clamoring through him. Aniol arched, thrust, and thrashed, pleasure driving his fevered body toward the height of ecstasy, Aniol's body moved with the rhythm of Kaji's hand, increasing the pace with each thrust, seeking release until no rhythm remained, only wild thrashing and hard friction. "Kaji...." Aniol whimpered, his breath escaping his lips in short hard gasps. "It's... it's... coming."

Kaji bit into Aniol's skin at the words. Tightening his grip around Aniol's penis, he pulled his hand, violently down, throwing Aniol over the edge, a loud hoarse cry of ecstasy escaping his mate's throat.

Aniol was finally sated. Comfort and pleasant relaxed warmth replaced desperation, pain, and hunger. Aniol relaxed, slumping back in Kaji's arms, pleasantly satisfied. He hummed sleepily when Kaji continued to touch him. Obviously picking up on the sated relaxation, he traced lazy patterns upon Aniol's skin.

Kaji continued to drop hungry kisses upon Aniol's throat, now moving down to his shoulder blade. Running fingers along Aniol's thigh, he moved his touch over the hip bone and round to the back.

Aniol murmured in sleepy protest when Kaji pushed a single finger into his relaxed body, the feeling strange now that he'd come down from his passion-filled high. He shifted, a soft whine of protest escaping him as he tried to figure out if he wanted to push himself onto the exploring finger or pull off of it. It felt strange and uncomfortable, but at the same time he remembered what had happened the last time Kaji had stuck his fingers there.

Kaji nipped at Aniol's skin. Ignoring the whine of protest, he pushed a second finger into Aniol's ass, taking advantage of the Aniol's relaxed state.

Aniol murmured in protest when the feeling of discomfort increased, yet he didn't draw away. Although uncomfortable, it also felt good, especially when Kaji moved his fingers gently in and out, rubbing Aniol inside. Aniol's whimpers of protest gradually changed to murmurs of pleasure, the friction of Kaji's fingers inside of him slowly sending heat back into his groin, the feeling of discomfort fading with each thrust. Aniol wiggled, shifting and changing the angle of Kaji's fingers within him in an attempt to ease the discomfort and maximize the pleasure. A light flush heated his skin once more, and he released but the slightest hiss when Kaji added a third finger.

Aniol gripped Kaji's knees, lifted himself, and then allowed himself to drop down once more, timing his movements to the thrust of Kaji's fingers, the motion slow and sensual. Occasionally he'd twist his hips as he continued to test the various angles of entry. Each thrust sent heat through him, and it slowly gathered in his groin. It was a familiar sensation, milder than it had been before Kaji had sent him over the edge. Aniol shifted once more, thrusting slowly back down only to gasp, eyes flying open, lethargy forgotten, as electricity sparked through him, making him instantly hard once more when he'd been convinced that such was not possible.

Each thrust now brushed against his prostate, causing him to ache all over again. Throbbing hunger beat a new rhythm in his blood, and his body demanded more. He wanted Kaji's throbbing penis buried deep within him, invading him, pounding into him over and over again. Kaji's fingers were suddenly not enough, not thick enough, not hard enough, and not long enough to touch him as deeply as he desired. Aniol whimpered, his body thrusting violently up and down upon Kaji's fingers as he tried to get them deeper into his body.

Kaji grabbed Aniol's hips with his other hand once more, trying to calm Aniol's sudden desperate movements. He continued to thrust his fingers slowly in and out of Aniol's puckered entrance, controlling the tempo, deliberately watching the lust rise out of control in Aniol once more. He wanted to bring his mate to completion one more time before burying himself into the silky heat that was now damp with sweat and Aniol's seed that had marked Kaji's fingers. "Just one more time," Kaji kept telling himself, and then he could have that body beneath him once again, writhing in pleasure, crying and gasping out his name for any to hear.

Aniol, however, was having none of it. Snarling in frustration, Aniol tore himself from Kaji's grasp, lifted himself off of Kaji's fingers, and turned to face Kaji once more. Unable to bear it any longer, tired of the teasing, Aniol reached for Kaji's pants, pulling them down and impaling himself upon Kaji's hard penis before the redhead even had time to register what was going on. Aniol hissed in pain, tears gathering at the corners of his eyes.

Kaji, groaned, Aniol's unexpected tight heat nearly causing him to spill his seed. He stared at his mate in shock, reaching out with trembling hands to brush the tears away. He struggled to keep from pounding relentlessly into Aniol now that he was finally buried in that silken heat. "Aniol?" he rasped, breath ragged.

Aniol swallowed, eyes clenched tightly shut. He shifted, adjusting the penis buried deep in his ass. It hurt, but the pain was edged with such sweet torture. Aniol wrapped his legs around Kaji's waist once more before lifting himself and then allowing himself to drop back down onto Kaji's length, savoring the friction of that hardness against the walls of his most intimate space.

For Kaji, that was the last straw. Losing the last vestiges of control, Kaji grabbed Aniol's hips and supported Aniol's slim body as he began to thrust long and deep, invading the sweet tight heat offered to him. He pounded against Aniol's flesh over and over again as he sought to make Aniol his once more.

Aniol gasped, clutching Kaji's shoulders as the redhead pounded into him, each thrust brushing against that spot deep inside him, the spot that threatened to drive him mad with pleasure. Each thrust sent electricity coursing through his body and heat straight to his groin, making him painfully hard.

Aniol keened in the back of his throat, about to lose control of himself once more, about to spill, only to have release denied him. Aniol's eyes shot open when Kaji's fingers wrapped around the base of his penis, effectively blocking his release. The pressure continued to build with each continued thrust into his body, harder, faster, in and out at a frenzied pace. When Aniol looked, Kaji's eyes glowed with a feral heat, filled with lust, hunger, and possessiveness. Aniol whimpered, digging his nails into Kaji's skin when Kaji continued to deny him his release, pounding into him like an animal in heat, body jerking out of control.

Suddenly Kaji leaned forward, claimed Aniol's mouth with his, and came into Aniol's body with warm sticky heat. Kaji released his hold on Aniol's penis, thrust sporadically and pumped his seed into Aniol's tight heat, marking him. He swallowed Aniol's scream of release when his thrusts finally sent his mate over the edge as well, the walls of Aniol's tight ass clamping down upon his still-hard length, milking it, Aniol's own seed marking their chests with the force of his release.

# White Tears

Careil is the Land of Silver, the land of the moon where the sky cries white tears filled with grief, weeping for forgotten memories and the death of hope. Each white tear is a manifestation of sorrow and mourning, an unnoticed cry, ignored by those that live there. The white tears drift slowly down, ever increasing, covering the land with a frozen blanket. The meaning behind the silent increase of sorrow has long been forgotten as the land continues to slowly die.

Blind eyes no longer see, no longer realize the true significance of the deteriorating weather, convinced that it must be simply an uncontrollable force, merely existing for the sake of existence itself. Hearts heavy with grief refuse to see that the land grieves along with them. They bitterly blame the land and the elements beyond their control for all their sorrow, only wounding the land further with their ignorance. White tears are mourning and loss. White tears float down slowly from the sky.

KAJI glanced up at the grey sky in surprise, blinking in shock when the sky began to cry, white, cold tears drifting down to land upon his hair and skin. Releasing his reins, he held his hand out, trying to catch the sky's tears. He stared at the white flakes on his hand in wonder and disbelief. It seemed that the legends were true. The sky really could weep tears of white.

Aniol, as usual, in front of Kaji as they sat astride the horse, glanced down at Kaji's hand before looking up at him, baffled by Kaji's action. He blinked in surprise when he noticed the expression of wonder on Kaji's face, the redhead's lips slightly agape as he stared at his hand. Aniol turned back to Kaji's hand, trying to figure out what it was that had surprised Kaji so. Finding nothing to explain the strange reaction, he frowned in puzzlement. "Kaji?" he inquired gently, wanting to know if his mate was all right.

Kaji blinked, staring at Aniol for a moment before glancing back up at the sky, watching the slow drift of those white tears. "The sky is crying white tears," Kaji whispered in surprise. "Gentle, white, cold tears."

Aniol frowned in puzzlement, mind racing before realization struck. Kaji was from Duiem, from a land of desert sands, a land that was dying of thirst and heat. It was unlikely that he would know what was happening. He reached out to poke the white flakes that had settled in Kaji's cupped hand. "It's snow," he explained. "Frozen water."

"Frozen water?" Kaji questioned glancing back down at the snowflakes gathered in his hand. He moved his hand to his mouth and lapped at the flakes, surprised when the ice melted in his mouth, the cold solid matter quickly dissolving into cool liquid that trickled pleasantly down his throat. It was the strangest sensation, as if shifted and changed in the heat of his mouth. "So it is." Kaji confirmed, voice filled with awe. "That might explain why the legends refer to it as white tears, then."

"Legends?" Aniol inquired, wondering where Kaji's mind was drifting to.

"Yes, the legends that we have about a Land of Silver where the sky cries white tears. The legends about Careil and the Gatekeepers," Kaji explained, meeting Aniol's puzzled gaze.

"They really speak of white tears?" Aniol asked, contemplating the comparison, glancing up at the sky he watched the snowflakes drift slowly down, each one seeming to dance lightly in the air. A deep feeling of melancholy settled upon him as he lost himself in memory. He'd spent many days watching the snow from the lonely white room he'd been locked in, many days shivering from cold while he watched the land die, the sky weeping as it did so. The comparison made more sense that it had a right to, he realized.

"What are you thinking about?" Kaji asked, watching his mate withdraw into himself, the mist coloring his beautiful blue-grey eyes white.

"I think it's a very appropriate comparison," Aniol whispered, reaching out to catch a snowflake. "It's sad and lonely and feels like the sky is releasing slow, forgotten tears of grief."

Kaji wrapped his arm around Aniol's waist, giving in to his instinct to offer him comfort. He sensed that Aniol was referring to more than just the falling snow. "I'm sorry."

Aniol blinked in surprise, watching Kaji for a moment as he contemplated his words and the possible reason for them before nodding in acceptance. "It's all right. It's over now," Aniol said, confirming Kaji's suspicions.

Kaji nodded in agreement and dropped a light kiss onto the top of Aniol's head. "Yes, it is," he whispered.

Aniol smiled, the motion a small soft tilt to his lips. He dropped his hand back down to the horse's mane and contemplated the new meaning snow now had for him. Now he would always think of it as white tears, its very existence now binding him to Kaji in shared memory of discovery. He closed his eyes and allowed his head to drop back, resting against the warmth of Kaji's chest. "Perhaps this time they are tears of joy," he said.

"Tears of joy?" Kaji asked softly. He, too, was caught in the moment and didn't want to break the rather strange melancholy that had settled upon them, sorrow and longing strangely mixed with acceptance, hope, and quiet happiness.

"Yes." Aniol's breath misted upon the chill air. "Tears of joy and happiness."

"Why joy?" Kaji asked, moving his hand from around Aniol's waist to absently run his fingers through the pale silver-blue strands of Aniol's hair.

"Because someone remembers," Aniol responded, taking the moment to contemplate the environment around him. He could feel life, hidden beneath all the death. It was a subtle flow of energy in the back of his mind that he'd just discovered.

"Remembers?" Kaji's voice dropped low in reverence, the words barely a breath upon the chill air before him.

"Yes...." Aniol remained silent for a moment before finishing his thought. "Someone remembers the reason for its grief, and so it's happy. It's reaching out once more. Hope and life is awake again," he whispered, unaware of the abstract nature of his explanation. All of it suddenly make perfect sense to him. The land was reaching for a newly discovered thread of hope: Him.

Kaji dropped his hand, wrapping it around Aniol's waist once more, holding him close in silence. Aniol was currently lost to him, lost in the recesses of his own mind, seeing things Kaji couldn't even begin to understand, but Kaji was unconcerned. If the small smile on Aniol's lips was anything to go by, his mate was not in any immediate danger of being overwhelmed or losing himself.

The procession stopped. Kaji halted his horse beside Arian, Mathié, and Eunae, the astronomer Arian had gone to for help. She was a spunky woman with a charming smile and an innocent dancer's grace. Long black hair fell down her back, a rather unusual color for someone in Careil. Her eyes were a deep clear blue, almost as deep and mysterious as the stars she loved so much.

She glanced up from the map she was scrutinizing and took a moment to eye the lay of the land before them. Eunae scanned the horizon, the land, and the grooves and ridges before settling upon a group of stone structures in the distance, a smile of satisfaction upon her lips. She pointed at the stone structures. "It looks like we found it."

Kaji followed her finger, his breath catching in the back of his throat at the sight of the rather beautiful intricate stone structures. They were painted in shades of blue and white, blending elegantly into the landscape and sky. Excitement bubbled up within him. They'd found it. With only the stars and an old Gatekeeper's journal as a guide, they had actually found it. He couldn't believe it. He'd been convinced that there was no possible way they could find such an obscure place and even more convinced that if they did, they would never know it. He'd fully expected nothing to remain. Yet here they were, looking at what could only be the sanctuary of air and water.

Aniol was staring at the buildings in wonder, a strange nervous excitement in his blood. He was eager to go see what he could discover but at the same time feared it. He feared possible disappointment and the knowledge he might gain. No matter what happened, it was going to change him, that much at least was clear. The mist in Aniol's eyes moved, gathering, causing the blue-grey in his eyes to pale as his anxiety rose. Suddenly he wasn't all that sure that he wanted to go through with this.

There was just too much uncertainty before him, and it was making him as taut as a drawn bowstring.

Kaji, picking up on the tension in Aniol's body, slid the hand he had at Aniol's waist under his shirt, gently brushing his fingers over Aniol's stomach and around his belly button, trying to soothe him. He hoped he could get Aniol to relax before he hurt himself with all that rising tension. "It'll be okay," he whispered softly, the words for Aniol alone. "No matter what happens, I won't leave you."

Aniol searched Kaji's features in uncertainty. Seeing nothing but sincerity, he nodded and allowed himself to relax. He let go of his own anxiety, relying on Kaji for support. Even though he was still nervous, he felt better once more.

Kaji turned to the rest of their party, raising an eyebrow when he realized that somehow he and Aniol had become the center of attention. Arian ginned at him and gave him thumbs-up, glancing down at the hand he had in Aniol's shirt. Mathié and Eunae were a touch more discreet, merely exchanging glances with one another before turning back to face their destination. Kaji narrowed his eyes at Arian, silently warning the young man off. He slid his hand till it was resting flat upon Aniol's stomach in an incredibly possessive gesture. Aniol blinked up at him in surprise, confused by Kaji's action. Kaji smirked at him before sliding his hand suggestively down, stopping when Aniol glared at him heatedly. He dropped a light kiss into Aniol's hair, meaning it to be a gentle, soothing gesture. Then he turned back to Arian. "Shall we get going then?"

Arian nodded, his grin fading to a simple, rather sad smile. "Yes, I guess we should. It would be better to get there while it's still light." He flicked his reins, urging his horse into motion once more. He was glad his brother had Kaji with him.

The rest of the journey to the buildings passed in silence, each person lost in their own introspection, trying to figure out what they would find once they arrived at the sanctuary of air and water. As they moved closer, they realized that the tint of pale blue upon the land was not shadow upon snow. Instead, it was water. The sanctuary was built on the edge of a large lake. The lake was strange and had a supernatural quality about it. The water was still and clear, yet, for some reason it was unfrozen, even thought the temperature was rather chilled at this height.

Their pace slowed when they approached the buildings; they were surprised to find a woman standing at the entrance to what was now obvious to be a small village. She was wrapped in a pale pink shawl, and she watched them approach, waiting for them. She glanced up at them, looking straight at Aniol with clear pale blue eyes framed by pale violet stands of hair. "It has been a long time," she said softly, yet her voice carried clearly through the chill air. "Gatekeeper."

# Sanctuary

## OF AIR AND WATER

The sanctuary of air and water is a forgotten place, lost within the mists of time and memory. Those who reside there are keepers of knowledge and of hope; they watch over the Gatekeeper's training ground, the center of flow and balance.

The sanctuary is inhabited by people of peace. They are set apart to fulfill a given purpose: to hold dear the memories of that which sustains life. Air and water are opposed to Duiem's earth and fire, and together the four elements sustain a fifth: life. For to live, one needs balance.

The sanctuary is where the main gate between Careil and Duiem is located. This gate provides the primary channel through which balance is upheld, and it is the epicenter of all power between the two lands.. With power comes responsibility, and so the keepers are required to test strength of mind before truly handing down the knowledge they possess, before initiating a Gatekeeper. For the channel, the pathway taken by the elements, is the Gatekeeper's mind, body, and soul. A surge of that power courses through the Gatekeeper's veins through dreams and through breath. This power can drive a weak mind mad. And so it is that only the truly strong receive the knowledge of their powers and access to their inheritance.

ANIOL blinked, rather disconcerted that yet another person seemed to have been waiting for him and was unsurprised by his presence. He shifted, suddenly uncomfortable, and he glanced up at Kaji, seeking support. Kaji wove the fingers of his right hand with Aniol's, squeezing gently. The entire party was still and silent, waiting for some signal as to what was expected of them now that they had arrived.

The woman bowed low. "We've been expecting you and your party." Her gaze moved over the gathered individuals, giving each one present a small bow. "If you would follow me, we've prepared quarters and a meal for you." She turned and headed into village, obviously expecting them to follow.

Mathié and Kaji exchanged glances before moving, the click of their horses' hooves echoing loudly in the strange silence. The cobblestone street that ran through the center of the village was empty and deserted. The stone buildings surrounding them were just as silent.

Kaji was astounded when they arrived at what was obviously the center of town, which was unexpectedly filled with people, life, and laughter. He reined his horse in to stare in shock, Arian and Eunae stopping behind him and Mathié before him. Children ran around the center circle, playing games as teased each other and giggled with glee. Older people wandered from stall to stall, exchanging greetings and trading goods, all in an amiable mood.

Kaji tensed at a light tug upon his pants and glanced sharply down, searching for the possible threat, only to meet deep violet eyes framed by pale silver hair. A little girl was staring up at him out of wide curious eyes, a slight pout to her rosy lips. "Hello," she said, staring innocently up at him with awe. "I'm Midrea. You're new. We never have new people here." She wrinkled her nose. "'cept babies. Who are you?"

Kaji glanced at Aniol, seeking help. He was completely out of his element, surprised to find life here to begin with, let alone so much of it. Aniol simply returned Kaji's stare, just as confused by current events. Kaji sighed and bent down to speak to the little girl. "I'm Kaji."

"Oh, where are you from?" she asked.

Kaji swallowed, wondering what he should give in response. "Duiem," he replied, deciding that honesty would be easiest. He doubted this little girl would know where it was and braced himself for her next question, only to blink in surprise at her reply. "Oh. The desert world. Mommy says it's hot there. Not cold like here. I asked her if I could go see, and she said no. Mommy said we can't go there because the gate is closed. I want to go see the sand." She pouted.

Kaji blinked at her, looking to Mathié with question in his gaze. Mathié shrugged in response. "I didn't know that there was anyone still living in the mountains," Mathié confessed. "It's been taboo to come here for so long that no one really ever tries anymore."

Kaji nodded, glancing back down at the little girl, only to find the woman in the pink shawl had picked the little girl up. She'd obviously realized they were no longer following her and had returned to see what the holdup was about. "Midrea." She shook her head in exasperation. "Don't bother our honored guests."

"But Mommy." The little girl pouted, tugging on the pink shawl with her small hands. "He's from Duiem." She pointed at Kaji. "I want to go see the sand. Is the gate open?"

The woman looked up at Kaji before turning to Aniol in surprise. "You opened a gate," she said in wonder, making Aniol the center of attention once more.

Aniol shifted, uncomfortable with her scrutiny. He sighed in relief when she nodded and turned to a rather large man who stood beside her, smiling warmly in greeting. "This is Jidian, my husband. You'll be staying at our place. It's a little small, but we should be able to accommodate all of you. If you don't mind sharing rooms that is." She glanced back up at them in question.

Kaji eyed the little girl and her mother in speculation, wondering what else they knew about his land and about the gates and about the Gatekeepers. He nodded in acceptance. "We're grateful, milady," he replied, somehow sensing that this woman demanded respect.

Several others had now noticed their presence, and they all gathered around the mounted party. Some whispered among themselves while others called out cheerful greetings. Aniol shifted, pressing himself into Kaji's chest, uncomfortable with the crowd that had formed around them. Kaji embraced Aniol, lending his mate some comfort. The woman in the pink shawl noticed, eyeing Aniol for a moment before turning to the crowd and ordering them to return to what they'd been doing, commanding them to give their honored guests some space. The crowd reluctantly backed away.

The woman turned back to them, speaking directly to Kaji. She realized that she needed to go through Kaji to get to Aniol. She bowed her head to him. "Warden. Forgive me my ignorance. I am Adelicia, Careil's Keeper." She glanced up at him, staring straight into his eyes. "The knowledge of the Gatekeepers and their art has been passed down to me by my predecessor. Our sole purpose is to instruct Gatekeepers who come here seeking our guidance and the knowledge we possess. I am a little surprised he—" She paused to bow to Aniol in respect, before turning back to Kaji and continuing to speak, explaining her position to the one she now realized was the Gatekeeper's protector. "—managed to open a gate, but it is a testament to his true power."

Aniol gulped and pressed himself further into Kaji's embrace. He didn't care whether he had power. In fact, he feared it more than anything. Aniol felt bitterness course through him as he allowed himself to truly contemplate the power Adelicia spoke of and the price it had thus far forced him to pay. It had stolen his family, his childhood, and any sense of normalcy he might have had. It had led to nightmares, loneliness, attempted murder, torture, and pain, and all for what? So that he could help people who wanted him dead? Who condemned him and labeled him a demon? What was the point of helping people who hated him? Aniol fought back a sob as the true impact of everything hit him, a rushing wave of realization that tore at his soul and threatened to break him.

Kaji glanced down in sudden concern, feeling the sob rack Aniol's small frame. Panic and confusion filled him; he didn't understand what had set his mate off so suddenly. He rubbed Aniol's stomach, trying to calm the sobs to no avail.

Aniol folded in on himself, curling up into a fetal position as best as he could while still mounted upon the horse, the silent sobbing becoming violent and uncharacteristically vocal.

Arian reached out towards Aniol, wanting to comfort his brother, but he dropped his hand when he realized that Aniol was out of his reach. The deep pain in Aniol's terrible sobs caused his own heart to ache as well, even though he didn't understand the reason for the rather sudden tears.

Kaji looked desperately around, noting the attention they were drawing. Everyone was staring at them, all drawing unknown conclusions. He suddenly wanted to be out of public view. He longed to find out what had set Aniol off but didn't think his mate would be willing to talk in such a public place.

Adelicia, understanding Kaji's desperation, turned and led them out of the center of town and to her home, stopping before a rather nice and surprisingly spacious stone structure. Reining in, Kaji slid off the horse, wincing at the forlorn whimper his action drew from Aniol's lips. He reached up and pulled Aniol down into his arms before striding into the home, ignoring the horse as well as their packs upon it.

Adelicia took him to a room decorated in white and silver with a touch of pink and closed the door softly after Kaji walked right in, heading straight for the bed. Kaji dropped down onto the bed, Aniol still cradled in his arms, and desperately ran his fingers through Aniol's hair. He murmured nonsensical words of comfort, gently rocking Aniol's trembling body as he himself fought back the panic that threatened to overwhelm him. He couldn't afford to let the panic win, couldn't afford to break, because he needed to remain strong for Aniol.

Aniol's violent sobs calmed slowly, fading to a few sniffs followed by silence. Kaji clenched his eyes closed for a moment, taking the time to fight down the tremors that threatened him before glancing down at Aniol. Aniol's eyes had gone dark, the blue in them completely wiping out the traces of grey.

He watched as life returned to those eyes, the turmoil that had colored them a moment before calming to acceptance. He remained still and allowed the silence to embrace them as a small pale hand reaching out to cup his cheek, the touch of Aniol's fingers soft upon his skin, gently tracing the lines of concern upon Kaji's face.

"Being a Gatekeeper will save you as well," Aniol whispered, his voice filled with wonder. It was such a strange emotion to follow all the tears of grief. "Not only those that hate me, but you as well." Aniol's tone was full of love and happiness. Leaning forward, he gently brushed his lips against Kaji's, asking for entrance, asking for and offering comfort and acceptance.

#  RENEWED FLOW

Flow is a complex dance of elements that runs through the gates, exchanging strength between Careil and Duiem. It is a two-way dance that demands balance. There is power in that flow, sheer overwhelming energy just waiting to be tapped, to be manipulated, to be consumed, and to be controlled.

Gatekeepers are required to control the flow of energy, to keep it in balance, to tame its wild spirit and the destructive energy within. It takes a strong mind and a strong will to tell the very elements what to do and where to flow. It takes iron control and needle-like precision to control the raging, fluctuating river of energy.

ADELICIA came to fetch Aniol just before sunrise, reaching out to wake him. Unfortunately for her, he was curled into Kaji's side, and the motion disturbed Kaji as well. He woke in an instant and was holding a dagger to her throat before he even registered what had disturbed him. Upon realizing that it was Adelicia, he lowered the blade, giving Aniol a concerned glance. Aniol hadn't told him the reason for the tears he'd shed, but Kaji suspected it had something to do with what Adelicia had said.

She requested that Aniol follow her, and when Kaji moved to accompany them, she shook her head and said that she needed to see Aniol in private. Kaji bristled, ready to start an argument. He was just about to start protesting when Aniol placed a placating hand upon his arm, softly telling him that he would be all right. After a moment of silence, Kaji conceded, watching with narrowed amber gaze as Aniol and Adelicia left.

Adelicia led Aniol through the quiet stone village toward the silvery, still water beside it. She halted at its edge. Aniol paused beside her, wondering why he'd been brought to the waterside. "There isn't any more time," Adelicia said, pointing at the water.

Aniol frowned in confusion, staring at the still water. Pale moonlight reflected off its surface, giving it a silvery white glow. He glanced back at Adelicia in question, silently waiting for her to continue.

"The land is dying, the water is tainted, and the gate is on the verge of being destroyed." She turned back to Aniol, her face filled with sorrow. "I'm sorry," she whispered, grabbing Aniol's face between her cold hands.

The moment Adelicia's hands touched his skin, Aniol felt a subtle click in the back of his mind. It felt as if a small latch had been released, suddenly releasing the force that had been building behind it. His mouth dropped open in a silent scream of pain as power crashed through him, waves of crackling energy, all of it out of control, burning his flesh with heat the one moment and tearing it apart with cold the next. Opposing elements waged war in his blood, mind, and soul. The sheer force of it overwhelmed him, raging out of his control. Each wave was a contradiction, a flow of force that both his mind and body were unprepared for.

He was surrounded by too much changing color, and his very environment possessed no definition of form as he stared before him. His eyes were completely white, covered in mist, no longer seeing the world before him, lost in sight unique to him.

His senses were overloaded with extremes: dry and wet, cold and hot, all of it flowing and rippling over his nerves. The power was a raging river swirling within him, seeking escape through the fragile channel it had found, rushing toward equilibrium with a force that threatened to tear Aniol apart. Just when it seemed he would go mad with the sheer force of it all, he saw it: a blinding revelation hidden deep in the back of his mind. He needed an anchor to stem the raging force.

THE moment Aniol and Adelicia left, Kaji began to pace. He couldn't shake the dark premonition that had taken hold of him. A sense deep inside that told him something was about to go wrong. What was even worse, he knew that Aniol was going to be affected by it. He didn't think that Adelicia meant Aniol any harm, but something was off, a dark heavy sense in the air that told him he should be at Aniol's side and not here pacing back and forth in the damned bedroom. Only he had no idea where Adelicia had taken Aniol.

Kaji glanced up when soft footsteps paused at the doorway. Adelicia's husband, Jidian, stood there, just shy of entering the room, watching Kaji with a frown of concern. "Can I perhaps be of assistance?" he asked.

Kaji spared him a glance, growling at him in frustration. "I want to know what's going on," he demanded, command clear in his tone, expecting to be obeyed without question. Anger burned in his amber gaze, fear and concern driving him to be a little more aggressive that he should be.

Jidian jumped at Kaji's tone, watching him fume for a moment before stepping into the room and seating himself upon the recently vacated bed, sheets still rumpled and warm from the bodies that had lain there. "We've been waiting centuries for Gatekeepers to return," Jidian explained, his tone calm, a sharp contrast to the panic and aggression in Kaji's voice. "This place exists to train Gatekeepers. They are taught by our Keeper, in this case... Adelicia. The rest of us are meant to protect her. Without her, a Gatekeeper cannot truly receive access to their power. They are unable to get past the mind block that exists to keep them sane."

Kaji ceased his pacing, taking in the information he was being given. "Mind block?" he asked, already suspecting what it might refer to but wanting to make certain.

Jidian nodded. "As far as I understand it, a Gatekeeper is born with a mind block. It is only released when the Gatekeeper has been fully trained, and even then, only if the Gatekeeper is able to control the forces that flow through the gates. It prevents them from having full access to their power until they are ready to handle it."

"And if a Gatekeeper is unable to control those forces?" Kaji questioned on a whisper.

"If a Gatekeeper completes the training and fails the mind test, the mind block is not removed and the Gatekeeper is sent home, to perhaps live a normal life."

"What happens if a Gatekeeper's mind block is removed and it turns out he *can't* control those forces?" Kaji asked, his own question sending a chill of dread down his spine.

"The Gatekeeper dies," Jidian stated simply.

*The Gatekeeper dies.* Those three simple words echoed through the air, hanging between Jidian and Kaji, dark words filled with dark meaning and premonition. Kaji shivered at the impact of those three words. He'd actually expected that response but had hoped against it. "How is a Gatekeeper trained?" he whispered, wanting to know if a Gatekeeper was ever truly prepared for such responsibility. He wanted reassurance that Aniol would be safe and would be prepared for what he was expected to do.

"I don't know how a Gatekeeper is trained. That's always been kept secret between the Gatekeeper and the Keeper, but I do know it's rather rough." Jidian paused. He knew what Kaji wanted to know and took a moment to find a way to tell him the truth, knowing full well that Kaji wasn't going to like what he heard. "The problem with the training, though. is it takes a long time, months, sometimes even years...." Jidian's words died out, their very implication thick in the air between them. Kaji dreaded what Jidian was implying and so did not respond, simply waiting for the confirmation that would shatter his world. "Time we no longer have," Jidian admitted reluctantly.

Kaji's breath escaped his lips with a hiss, the blood rushing from his face when his premonition suddenly found a source. "Please tell me I'm mistaken," he pleaded, skin pale. "Please tell me you're not implying what I think you are."

"Adelicia no longer has the time in which to train your little Gatekeeper," Jidian whispered in confirmation, wincing at the sudden anger in Kaji's amber gaze. "I'm sorry."

Kaji snarled in rage, his fear and panic rising at an incredible rate. It slipped beyond his control and drove him into desperate action. He turned and raced out of the bedroom. Throwing the front door open, he ran into the early morning light. He headed straight to the water, somehow sensing that Aniol would be there. His Gatekeeper needed him.

Kaji's gasped when he finally emerged from a rather surprising maze of pathways just in time to see his mate framed by the rising sun. Yet, it was not wonder that took his breath away; it was outright horror and disbelief. Aniol was standing at the lakeside, face twisted in agony, eyes pure white. He was covered in blood—his own blood—running from his nose and his ears, the red liquid trickling down and marring his pale skin.

Kaji picked up pace, running as fast as his feet would carry him, his blood pounding in his ears. His every heartbeat echoed through him, beating a rhythm of life he feared Aniol might no longer have. He literally threw himself at Aniol, wrapping his arms around his mate's slim form in desperation, trying to hold on to him, desperate to hold him.

To anchor him.

ICY chill ran through him, causing his entire body to shake unnaturally. Even though Rogue was surrounded by desert heat and blazing sun, he was cold. Rogue's teeth chattered and his lips turned blue. He gasped, wrapping his arms around himself protectively, skin tingling as cool energy continued to soak through him.

He glanced down in shock, staring at the water pooling at his feet, water literally trickling up from the dry sand, sand that had not seen moisture in centuries. He rubbed at his arms, trying to warm himself, trying to rid himself of the all encompassing chill, but it continued to flow through him. It rushed through his body, down from his head and into the ground, flowing in one direction, heading straight toward the puddle at his feet.

KAJI blinked as heat rushed through his body. His blood boiled, burning with the heat of desert sand. The heat flowed through him, into the ground, melting the ice upon which he stood, turning the ground to mud. The flow of heated energy used him to anchor itself to the ground, using him to escape from Aniol's body.

Aniol's temperature returned to normal, the blood flow slowing as his body found relief. The mist in Aniol's eyes began to fade, slowly clearing as reality returned to him once more, the current pain in his body but a fraction of the searing pain that had been threatening to tear him apart while the opposing elements had waged their war within him. Aniol had but one lucid moment in which to realize that he was once more cradled in Kaji's arms before darkness claimed him.

# RESTORATION

Restoration: Such a beautiful word, filled with such deep
meaning and so much hope. The very process is a
reestablishment of that which should be, that which was lost,
stolen, damaged, and torn apart. Each step leads to recovery and
healing, slowly removing wounds and scars as it reaches out for
the original unaltered state, for that balance which existed before
the chaos began.

A Gatekeeper is key to restoration. A Gatekeeper's very
existence is a gentle flow, a soft touch of healing as opposed to a
wild river of destruction. A Gatekeeper is able to clean the chaos,
slowly recovering the balance of that which was originally
created to exist in harmony.

Restoration is a heavy burden to bear, for the control
required to repair damage is far greater than that required to
maintain balance. It is a heavy burden that requires precision and
fine control, the very weight of it heavy upon a mind required to
stem the energy from raging forcefully into balance. Though still
out of balance, the shift needs to be slow and controlled, for if
the energy be allowed to move freely, if it remains unanchored,
the rush to equilibrium will be as harmful as the loss of balance
in the first place.

ANIOL'S body hung all but lifeless in Kaji's grasp. Blood stained Aniol's
clothes and skin, and Kaji's hands. The heat continued to flow through
Kaji's body, but now with less force. It became a subtle flow, tingling
upon his skin, the energy merely using him as an anchor to guide it into
the land of ice. Kaji gathered Aniol close, lifting him up into his arms. He

was relieved that Aniol still breathed.

Kaji choked when his rage bubbled up into his throat, temporarily stemming the flow of angry words he wished to release. Fighting his own emotion, Kaji forced his anger down far enough so he could speak. "How could you?" Kaji demanded, forcing trickles of fury out. "How could you release the block without training him?" Kaji was now screaming at the top of his voice, face tinted red with pure, unadulterated anger. "He trusted you!"

Adelicia remained silent. Kaji's anger flowed all around her and filled her with regret. But she knew there had been no other way. They didn't have the time to train Aniol properly. Aniol had already opened the gate before, had slipped through it, and so it had been safer to have him rely on his instincts than to give him incomplete training and then remove the block upon his mind.

Kaji fumed when he received no response from Adelicia. Glancing back down at Aniol, he noted his pale skin with concern. Deciding that taking care of his mate was more important than raging at Adelicia, Kaji turned and walked away without another word.

He barely managed to make it to the doorway when he was accosted by a worried crowd. Arian, Mathié, and even Eunae were all waiting for him. They'd heard the door slam when Kaji ran out and had rushed out to see what the commotion was all about. Arian gasped in horror at the sight of his brother covered in blood. He reached out without thinking but flinched away when Kaji glared at him.

"I need warm water and a cloth. Now." Kaji demanded as he pushed past the concerned people. He headed straight for the bedroom and placed Aniol down upon the bed, not caring about staining the white sheets. He glanced up in relief when Arian slipped in, carrying a bowl of warm water.

Arian handed Kaji a soft cloth and placed the bowl carefully down beside him before dipping a second cloth into the warm water and wringing it. Arian shifted and gently began to wash the blood away, silently supporting Kaji. He completely ignored Kaji's glare of displeasure, filled with jealousy that was for a moment directed at him.

Kaji resigned himself to Arian's assistance. He continued to clean the blood off Aniol's skin and winced when he revealed marks upon the pale flesh. Some appeared to be burns; others appeared to be the result of frostbite. The injuries were in conflict with one other and must have been caused by the unknown force that had taken over Aniol.

Long moments and several fresh bowls of warm water later, Aniol was finally clean. Leaning forward, Kaji allowed his forehead to rest against Arian's. He stared into Arian's eyes, heart aching with how much they reminded him of Aniol. "Thank you," he whispered tiredly, these first words breaking the tense silence between them. Drawing back, he turned and tucked Aniol into bed, his hand brushing over the soft silk night clothes they'd changed Aniol into.

Aniol remained asleep for four days. Each of these was filled with weary silence. Everyone was cautious around Kaji, moving as if they were walking on eggshells. They were all afraid of the temper they could see simmering just below the surface, tempered only by concern. Kaji ignored Adelicia completely, refusing to acknowledge her presence for fear of harming her. Adelicia nonetheless continued to be their hostess, ensuring they had enough to eat, a place to sleep, and plenty of herbs for Aniol's skin, which healed quickly and remarkably well with barely a mark remaining upon it. The tension in the house continued to build beneath the calm surface, concern driving everyone mad. Tempers were short, patience was nonexistent, and worry was ever present. Each moment Aniol slept was filled with fear that he would never wake.

Kaji refused to leave Aniol's side. He refused to eat and even refused to even sleep. He simply ran his fingers through Aniol's pale hair, whispering soft words of reassurance, every so often asking Aniol to come back him. All the while, the tingling flow continued to run through him, a consistent force he grew so accustomed to that he no longer even realized it was there. It had become as natural as breathing to him.

Outside the weather continued to grow slowly warmer. The ice had completely melted, and plants were gaining new life. The lake sparkled with life, no longer stained by the dark mark Adelicia had pointed out to Aniol just before aggressively releasing the lock upon his mind. Even the air itself had warmed considerably, allowing a rather peaceful atmosphere to settle upon the stone village. The warm weather was moving from the village out into the mountains and further into Careil, bringing with it the pleasant scent and sound of early spring, a season Careil had not truly seen in centuries. The peaceful, happy atmosphere was a great contrast to the despair and despondency that surrounded the little Gatekeeper who had opened the central gate, anchoring the flow of energy in each land to keep it from tearing him apart.

Kaji eventually passed out from sheer exhaustion, his body giving in and submitting to restless sleep that held little peace, only to wake suddenly when Aniol's slim form moved beneath the hand that rested upon Aniol's chest, a slight shift of one seeking a more comfortable position. He sat up, cupped Aniol's face and stared at his pale features, filled with desperate hope when a small groan escaped those pale lips. Relief filled him at the sound. Life was returning to Aniol's body.

"Aniol?" Kaji whispered desperately.

Soft footsteps paused by the doorway before stepping uncertainly in. "Is he awake?" a soft voice filled with hope asked. Kaji glanced up, surprised to hear Arian speak. He shook his head in denial, features haggard and drawn, too distressed to even try to answer aloud. He glanced at the object in Arian's hands, a tiny green plant with a small pure white tip, cradled within a small brown pot. It was a flower, the first fragile flower to bloom in Careil in centuries. It represented hope and new life, paid for in blood.

Arian shifted uncertainly for a moment before stepping further in, holding the fragile plant out. "I thought he might like this," he whispered hoarsely, fighting his own distress.

Kaji nodded, dropping his gaze back down to Aniol when he felt the young man shift once more, a small sign of life that had been missing for so long. "Aniol?" he whispered again, his voice filled with pain, wanting nothing more than to see that familiar mist.

Arian walked to the bedside and placed the small potted plant down beside Aniol. He had carefully removed it from the earth, planting it in a little pot in the hopes of showing Aniol the life that was returning to Careil. His eyes widened when Kaji gasped, and his gaze flickered to Aniol, afraid that Aniol had died.

Blue-grey eyes were watching Kaji, gaze tinted with pale white mist, still heavy with sleep and confusion. A sob escaped Kaji's lips, all his pent-up emotions suddenly seeking escape when Aniol opened his eyes. He bent down and aggressively claimed Aniol's lips in relief, wanting to confirm that his mate still lived. He thrust his tongue into the warm cavern of Aniol's mouth, tears pouring down his face, flowing freely out of control. Kaji dominated the kiss, reveling in the heat and the taste, most of all reveling in the timid reaction he was receiving from Aniol. A timid reaction that grew wilder as Aniol thrust his tongue against Kaji's in response to the desperation behind Kaji's aggressive claiming.

Arian blushed and dropped his gaze when Kaji hungrily attacked Aniol's mouth. The action drew a soft mewl of pleasure from Aniol, who was equally oblivious. Arian reached out and adjusted the little pot upon the table, giving his hands something to do while he stilled his thumping heart, a heart that was jumping with joy at the realization that his brother was awake. Happiness and excitement hummed through his veins, making Arian long to throw himself at his brother. Unfortunately, that desire was unobtainable for now as Kaji was momentarily claiming all of Aniol's attention for himself. Knowing his time would come, Arian slipped out of the room, gently closing the door as he departed, ensuring that his brother and Kaji received needed privacy.

# KAELA

A gate is an entry point that balances two worlds that coexist, sharing the flow of energy between them. A single heartbeat creates the rhythm required to keep the flow of life. The cool energy that sustains Careil is an extreme contrast to the warm flow that sustains Duiem, yet the two need one another in order to survive. Too much cold leads to chill, and too much heat leads to fever, and both can ultimately lead to death. So it is that the two pools of energy must be kept in careful balance, maintaining just the right temperature and just the right flow as each passes through the central gate, a gate that controls the very heartbeat of Careil and Duiem, a gate that controls Kaela: the pathway.

There exist several gates, several points of entry and several points of flow, but all of these are linked to only one central gate, only one heartbeat, and this is to be controlled by the head Gatekeeper. It is a key point, a vital point that defines life itself, and thus it requires extra care. Thus it is that the Keepers of Careil and Duiem gather there with their protectors to ensure that no harm comes to the heart of Kaela, the central path of flow and the key to life and death.

Great power flows through Kaela: torrents of energy rush towards harmony, balance and flow, keeping Careil and Duiem alive, beating in sync, two parts of a great whole. The two worlds are two sides if a single coin, opposite, yet one. Such great power needs an anchor to keep it from rushing in too quickly, to keep it from becoming a destructive force. So it is that the head Gatekeeper has two Wardens, one each for Careil and Duiem. One each to keep the flow anchored and under control.

KAJI withdrew when the door clicked shut, taking in the life he could now see in Aniol. Aniol's pale skin was now flushed with color, color that had been lacking for far too long. He smiled down at Aniol in relief and wiped away the tears that poured down his own face. It was a rather useless action as those tears were soon replaced by more. The moisture trailed down his cheeks, gathered at his chin, and then dropped onto Aniol's skin. They were tiny drops of salty moisture filled with deep meaning and deeper emotion.

Kaji choked back a vocal sob. He didn't want to break down like this, but he couldn't help himself. Four days of anxiety just begged for release and poured out of him in the only way it knew how. Before he knew it, he was sobbing, tears pouring down his face faster than he could wipe them away.

Aniol sat up, frowning at Kaji in confusion. His own heart ached, and he desperately wanted to reach out, to brush away the falling tears. Aniol bit his lip in hesitation, afraid he would do something wrong. Kaji's sobs echoed through him, and unable to bear it any longer, he timidly reached out to gently embrace his mate.

Kaji grabbed a hold of Aniol as one would a lifeline, drawing him closer and into his lap as he vigorously returned the embrace, taking a moment to savor the fact that his mate was once more with him. His tears dried up to be replaced by happiness and contentment.


THE next morning Aniol, Kaji, Adelicia, Mathié, and Arian walked to the water in order to see what more Aniol could learn about the main gate linking Careil and Duiem. Aniol's eyes widened as they approached the lake. He stared at the shimmering circle that hung suspended in midair in utter disbelief. It twisted and moved with a life of its own. Vibrant colors merged and danced across the deep blue sky, shades of red, orange, and yellow entwining with blue, purple and white, embraced in a lovers' dance. His breath hitched at the sheer wonder and beauty of it.

Kaji glanced to the side at the sound and noted the awe upon Aniol's face. He followed Aniol's gaze forward, and, seeing nothing, frowned in confusion. "What do you see?"

"Light," Aniol whispered. "Vibrant colored light, dancing in the sky." He pointed up at the sky situated just above the water of the lake that now sparkled with renewed life.

Kaji tilted his head to the side, squinting as he, too, tried to see what Aniol saw. Sadly, he failed. A sudden thought occurred to him when he remembered the visions he'd shared with Aniol. He placed his hand on Aniol's arm. Closing his own eyes, he focused on trying to see through Aniol's eyes instead of his own. A gasp of wonder similar to that released by Aniol escaped his lips when the darkness before his eyelids faded, replaced by the vision Aniol had just described. It was absolutely beautiful. Breathtakingly so. It was a single shared moment of awe between them.

Kaji's eyes snapped open, and the vision faded away. He staring at Aniol in surprise. He hadn't really expected it to work, but now that it had, he was beginning to understand exactly how intimate the link between a Gatekeeper and his Warden could really be. He smiled when Aniol turned to him, his misty gaze filled with gentle, confused query. Leaning forward, Kaji dropped a light kiss upon Aniol's nose in response, whispering softly. "I love you." He reached for Aniol's hand and twined their fingers together as they followed Adelicia to the water's edge.

Kaji still couldn't believe how much the landscape had changed since they'd first arrived. The ground was now covered with bright green patches, plants breaking through it, finally allowed to bloom in the rather pleasant warmth that now hung over the village. The ice was now completely gone, its only reminder an occasional cool breeze the ruffled their hair. Excitement was thick in the air as people explored the changing environment around them. They were filled with wonder at things they'd never seen before. Little children played at the water's edge and reached out to touch the small threads of new life in astonishment.

Aniol blinked in surprise when a little boy no older than five ran into him, falling down to the ground at the impact. Releasing Kaji's hand, Aniol bent down to help him up but froze in mid-motion when the boy looked up at him, bright violet eyes filled with white mist. The boy pouted up at him, bottom lip trembling as he fought back tears. Spurred into motion by the tears that threatened to fall, Aniol reached the rest of the way forward and lifted the little boy up into his arms.

"I'm sorry," he stated softly, the musical quality of his voice seeming to fascinate the little boy who was just noticed the mist in Aniol's own eyes. Suddenly he smiled and pointing at Aniol's eyes, spoke.

"Gai'keepa." Wriggling out of Aniol's arms, he giggled lightly and then dashed away, resuming the unknown game he'd been playing.

Aniol looked up to meet Kaji's equally shocked gaze, both of them surprised by the unexpected sight of another Gatekeeper, a little Gatekeeper who still needed to grow up in order to come into his powers, but most surprisingly of all, a Gatekeeper who had not been killed. Kaji reached down, gripped Aniol's hand once more, and pulled his mate up. Sending him a little smile, he softly whispered a single word: "Hope."

Aniol winced, remembering what being a Gatekeeper had thus far cost him before nodding in agreement. He realized that the little boy's life was probably going to be very different from his own. as he himself was the boy's hope for a better future in the same way that Kaji was his. He squeezed Kaji's hand tightly before following after Adelicia once more, pausing beside her, at the water's side.

"You should be able to open a gate right here. Once open, it will allow us to travel between Careil and Duiem. Technically, the gate is already open," she explained. "There's already energy flowing between Careil and Duiem. All you need to do is make it tangible so that you and whoever may wish to go with you may step through."

Aniol nodded, still a little puzzled but wary to voice his questions. He gave an inner sigh of relief when Kaji voiced his question for him, the redhead trying to find out if this too would risk his mate's life. "How is he supposed to do that? Is it dangerous? Can it kill him?"

Adelicia shook his head, watching Kaji for a moment before speaking. "The gate is already open, and the forces are already anchored. That is the most dangerous part of opening the gate, especially when there's no balance or when the balance is as messed up as it currently is. It's dangerous because the forces use the open gate to try and restore balance. But once the forces are anchored, they are in the Gatekeeper's control, and he can command them. To make the gate tangible, all the Gatekeeper is required to do is to picture the gate and reach out to the forces at his disposal, creating the picture he sees. The picture exists within the very force that flows through the gate. In essence, all a Gatekeeper needs to do is reach out for it."

Aniol took a deep breath when Adelicia fell silent. He was, once again, the center of attention as everyone waited for him to open the gate. He glanced at Kaji as he thought about what he was about to do. They would finally be able to go home, for Duiem was now truly his home. Careil, with the exception of Mathié and Arian, was a place filled with bitter memories and loss.

Kaji gave him a small smile and nodded in acceptance. He planned to keep a close eye on Aniol. He fully intended to force him to stop at the first sign of pain or danger.

It was all the reassurance Aniol needed. He allowed his eyes to drift closed, and he took a few moments to calm himself before reaching out to the energy he could feel. The energy had become a part of him and shifted in response his very willpower. He smiled when a picture began to form in his mind. Adelicia had been correct. The picture he saw was a deep memory embedded in the very breath of the land and the flow of life that sustained it. He manipulated the picture, shifting it and drawing upon it to clarify it in his mind. He reaching out to it until he sensed the dry desert heat that was now thick with moisture, changed by the open gate. He reached out for the fire and earth, each of those two elements defining the very core of Duiem, and drew them to the water and air which represented Careil. Bringing the two together, he set them side by side, balancing the one beside the other, forming an entryway. A gate.

Aniol carefully opened his eyes, focusing slowly to meet the shocked stares of four people. They'd all believed he could, but somewhere in the back of their minds each had doubted the true possibility of it, having never seen it before. Turning away from Kaji, Arian, Mathié, and Adelicia, Aniol turned to the small, shimmering gate that floated in the air just before the water's edge, obscuring the view of the water with a view of Duiem, a view through which he met a fifth and sixth shocked expression. Yuan and Rogue stood on the other side, staring at him with jaws agape, water containers hanging forgotten in their grasp.

# IDENTITY

Both the royal families of Careil and Duiem can be identified by their features, features specific to their bloodline, as in all things, always opposite.

Predominantly, dark features identify those of Duiem and light features identify those of Careil. People of Duiem can usually be noted by brown and green in their gaze, their eyes flecked with amber symbolizing fire, earth, and day. Their hair tends to be varying shades of red, brown, and dirty blond.

Those born of Careil bear blue and violet eyes, and sometimes gray. Their hair comes in various shades of blue, violet, silver, and white, and on rare occasions, their hair is black. The coloring possessed by the people of Careil symbolizes water, air, and night.

The royal bloodlines each possess specific characteristics uniquely theirs. Duiem's heir possesses a pure amber gaze, burning with fire from within, hair a bright shade of red never seen on any other, representing the sun. Careil's heir bears blue-grey gaze and pale silver-blue hair, representing pale moonlight.

ADELICIA was the first to recover. Smiling at Yuan and Rogue through the gate, she gave Yuan a small bow of respect in acknowledgment of his status before turning to Aniol once more. "You need to close the tangible part of the gate once you've stepped through it," she instructed. "At least until the war in Duiem is settled. We cannot risk Kaela to war."

"Kaela?" Aniol inquired, wondering what Adelicia was going on about. Adelicia pointed to the gate shimmering in the air before them. Bending down, she caught a little boy who tried to run through it. He giggled in glee, clutching a small pale purple flower in his fist. "The pathway," Adelicia explained. "It is the name of the central gate that you have just opened."

"How do you know there is a war in Duiem?" Kaji demanded suddenly. "I don't recall telling you such."

Adelicia nodding at Rogue, who was visibly armed. "The Ruel, a people of peace, are geared for war. Also…." She waved at the gate. "The gate remembers. The energy released by the Gatekeeper tells me of a war centuries old between a people of peace and Duiem." She stared at him pointedly.

Kaji scowled at her but did not argue further. Instead he turned to Aniol. "You ready?" he asked softly, suddenly eager to go home. He'd missed Duiem, and only now that he was faced with the sight of it did he realize how much. True, he couldn't hear anything from the other side, but simply seeing it, simply knowing it was only a few steps away, made him long for it. Aniol nodded and took a wary step forward, his fingers tightly holding onto Kaji's.

"I'm going with you."

Aniol blinked and jerked to a halt, rather surprised by the unexpected words. He turned to stare at Arian, shocked that his brother had uttered them.

"Arian, no!" Mathié protested. "You're needed here."

Arian turned to Mathié, shaking his head. "No, Mathié. I'm not. You have full power to rule until I come of age. I know you've been ensuring that I make the decisions, but technically, until I come of age, you don't need me to rule. As my guardian you have full authority over the land, at least for the next four years or so. You've done a good job so far, working against prejudices that have become ingrained in our people. You opened trading once more and have worked to ensure that our people feel they belong to Careil. You let them know the crown cares about their predicaments. You even uncovered the truth about my parents' deaths, and for that I am eternally in your debt. But right now my place is at my brother's side, in Duiem, helping with the war and renewing treaties long forgotten."

"You come of age at twenty-one?" Kaji whispered in Aniol's ear. In order to be considered a full grown adult, one needed to be twenty-five in Duiem. When Aniol simply shrugged in response, Kaji turned his focus back to Arian, contemplating the young man before him. He guessed it made sense, if Careil's youth was as level-headed and sharp as Arian was. Those of Duiem tended to lean more on heated emotion, and that could get dangerously out if hand if not tempered by the wisdom of age.

"Then I'm coming with you," Mathié said.

Arian shook his head in denial. "You know you cannot. You are needed here, Mathié."

"I swore to your mother that I would protect you. I swore I would allow no harm to come to you. I failed your mother when it came to Aniol. I cannot fail again when it comes to you," Mathié pleaded with Arian. He knew Arian had made up his mind and also knew that he had a valid point. It proved that Arian was growing up and was now making decisions that were to Careil's benefit; however, Mathié didn't have to like it. He couldn't accept the fact that he might fail his queen again.

"It needs to be done," Arian said. "Balance needs to be restored, and I need to be a part of that, even if it is but a small part. You've trained me well." Arian smiled at Mathié, trying to soothe his concern, the concern of a parent who was worried about his child growing up. "I'm sure they will protect me. They need me as much as I need them," Arian pointed out, noting the small smile upon Kaji's lips.

Mathié nodded in reluctant acceptance before turning to Kaji to issue a demand. "You'd better take care of him, my liege. That young man is my life."

Kaji nodded in understanding. "I will. There's been enough bloodshed already."

Mathié nodded before turning back to Arian. "And you'd better come back soon, and in one piece, mind you. I'm too old to be sitting at your sickbed worrying about you."

"Will do," Arian agreed. Throwing his arms around Mathié, he embraced the man who had become a father to him, a man who had unknowingly carried the weight of two worlds upon his shoulders, bearing it with grace and dignity and coping by dealing with one thing at a time. Arian withdrew from Mathié and walked over to Aniol's side. Taking the hand that was still free into his own, he gripped it tightly, rather nervous at the prospect of leaving Careil.

Aniol glanced up at Arian, surprised by his unexpected behavior, but he allowed it, knowing his brother needed the contact. He was strangely unbothered by it. In fact, he was rather pleased that his brother was reaching out to him for comfort. He was happy that Arian, family he never knew he had, was coming with him to face what awaited them in Duiem. Taking a deep breath Aniol stepped forward once more, taking Kaji and Arian with him as they stepped through the gate.

The opening faded the moment they reached the other side, Aniol willing it to close.

Rogue gaped at Aniol and Arian, pointing from the one to the other. "There are two of them," he stated in disbelief, shocked by how much Arian resembled Aniol. He'd never heard Aniol mention any family. Kaji had even implied that Aniol didn't even know who his family was and that it had nothing to do with memory loss. Yet now he found himself staring at a young man who possessed an uncanny resemblance to the little Gatekeeper, a stranger who resembled Aniol so much that they could be nothing other than family.

Kaji smiled at Rogue and stepped forward to embrace the assassin before moving onto Yuan. "I missed you so," Kaji declared, laughing happily. He was excited to see his two closest friends once more. He truly had missed them. Deeply. He stepped back and grinned stupidly at Rogue, eyes sparkling in mischief. He had information that Rogue wanted, information that was going to shock him, and Kaji was enjoying the feeling of power it was giving him. "What will you pay me?" Kaji retorted in response to Rogue's unspoken request for more information regarding Arian.

Rogue gaped at Kaji, affronted and insulted by Kaji's challenge. How dare the redhead demand compensation for a little information after everything Rogue had done for him? Was he not sacrificing enough to help Kaji get his throne back? To stop the war and restore peace once more? Rogue was about to give Kaji a sharp response when he noticed the humor in Kaji's eyes and realized the grin was one of pure mischief and not malice or cockiness. Suddenly returning the grin, he leaned forward to ruffle Kaji's hair. "Why, you brat! You almost had me there. Come now, spill it. I know you want to."

Kaji continued to grin, pointedly turning to Yuan first. "Yuan." Kaji bowed to Yuan before turning to Rogue and doing the same. "Rogue. I would like you to meet Arian. Arian—" Suddenly he frowned. His grin faded completely and he turned to Arian, embarrassed. "You know, I never did ask you for your family name."

"Chandra," Arian said, smiling when he realized what the reason for Kaji's embarrassment was. He had been in Careil for quite some time, and in all that time had never asked for Arian's family name. He had introduced Aniol using his own family name instead.

"Chandra," Kaji repeated, turning to Aniol. "Your name was Aniol Chandra." His tone was filled with awe. Another mystery that formed part of Aniol's life had just been solved. Suddenly he decided it had never really been all that important. He knew exactly who Aniol was. "I like Aniol Taiyouko better," he declared.

"So they *are* family!" Rogue exclaimed, drawing Kaji's attention back to him.

Kaji grinned again, once more enthralled by his little game with Rogue. "Yes, they are related. Arian is Aniol's younger brother, and that's not all." Kaji paused, waiting for the tension to build a touch. Just as Rogue's curiosity was about to peak, he dealt the vital information. "Arian is the king of Careil. He's as yet too young to rule, and his guardian Mathié is currently acting as regent, but that won't be the status quo for much longer." His eyes sparked in triumph at the look of utter shock and disbelief on Rogue's face. It wasn't often that one got Rogue to react to anything, and Kaji was loving every minute of it.

Yuan, on the other hand, remained impassive. He was not surprised. Fate was a fickle mistress, and the visions he'd inherited made that fact more than apparent to him.

Rogue's breath escaped him with a hiss, realization hitting him broadside in the face. "One of royal blood," he whispered softly, realizing that somehow everything was falling into place. He held his breath for a moment while he contemplated this and its impact. Perhaps, finally, the prophecy may be fulfilled.

The humor faded from Kaji's face, and he nodded in agreement. He knew Rogue was referring to the prophecy, one which he was more intimately acquainted with than Kaji ever had or ever would be. "One of royal blood," Kaji confirmed drawing Aniol closer before continuing softly, "but even if he had not been, I would still refuse to let him go. He's mine."

Rogue nodded, seeing Aniol in a new light. He glanced between Arian and Aniol, contemplating what he'd just learned. He bowed before Arian, the movement both a greeting and a show of respect. As he moved up once more, however, he froze, meeting Arian's gaze head-on for the first time. His breath escaped his lips once more when he realized the true depth of the blue-grey gaze, revealing a color that was usually masked by mist in Aniol's eyes.

# Assassination

Sometimes even the best intentions are not enough to avoid the true darkness that exists in the world. Sometimes all the morals in the world cannot prevent an inevitable choice that may need to be made, a sacrifice to prevent further sacrifice.

It is easy to judge when you have never been faced with a desperate situation, when you have never been faced with having to choose the lesser of two evils, when both outcomes are undesirable. It is easy to judge when you stand on the sidelines, never truly understanding that which truly drives desperation.

ROGUE was the first to break the stare, and he shook himself out of his reverie. He turned to Aniol and contemplated him for a moment before speaking. "You opened the gate a few days ago. Didn't you? And you somehow used me to do it." Rogue pointed at the land that surrounded them. The wasteland had changed since they'd left it. No longer was it merely dry hard sand. There was now a small stream of water at their feet, growing by the minute. Scattered through the wasteland were other emerging signs of life, a few blades of grass, bright green in contrast to the dull murky brown of the earth.

"Duiem is coming back to life," Rogue stated softly before pointing up at the sky. The sky was no longer pale and harsh. Instead it was now filled with darkening clouds, originating at the gate Aniol had opened. "And the sky is going dark in the day. Change is dawning."

Aniol looked up at the sky and smiled at the sight. He knew exactly what those clouds were. Their very color promised a storm, the first storm Duiem had seen in centuries. He reached up for the sky, laughing softly in happiness. "Duiem is going to get rain," he whispered in awe, realizing exactly how monumental that very concept truly was. The documents he'd helped Kaji sort had told him water was scarce, and those clouds promised both a new life and hope.

"We are?" Kaji whispered, tone filled with as much awe as Aniol's. He, too, glanced up at the sky, awed by the sight. The clouds looked similar to those in Careil, like those that had cried the white tears. "So it seems." The moment seemed to require respect, stillness and contemplation, and so the group remained silent for a moment, each lost in the impact of the news.

Suddenly Kaji broke the rather reverent atmosphere with a loud exclamation of joy. Picking Aniol up, he spun him around in glee. "We're getting rain!" Kaji called out at the top of his voice, giddy with joy.

SEVERAL minutes later they gathered in a small wooden abode. Rogue was shuffling papers around, preparing to explain what had been going on since Kaji and Aniol left Duiem. Kaji had calmed down and accepted the fact that they had to get back to more serious matters and had willingly followed Rogue to what the assassin now dubbed the war room.

"There were a lot of injuries from the surprise attack but surprisingly few casualties," Rogue explained, pausing to meet Kaji's gaze directly. "Yuan and I have been helping to treat the wounded. We have negotiated with my people and with the exception of a few, they are willing to fight by your side."

"Really?" Kaji asked, shocked by Rogue's words. He couldn't believe the Ruel, people who had been at war with his kingdom for centuries, would be willing to fight on his side. "How did you manage to convince any of them to do that?"

Rogue remained silent for a moment, allowing the question to hang in the air before responding. "I'm not the only one tired of war, Kaji. I told them that you wanted to bring peace. We told them that you are bonded to a Gatekeeper, and that the prophecy is finally being fulfilled. Furthermore, you fought at their side when Karl's army attacked us. My people saw that. They respect that. They respect the fact that you were willing to risk your life to save people you are technically at war with. Out of everything they've learned, your courage is what truly won them over."

Kaji stared at Rogue in shock, shaking his head in disbelief. "Was Karl there?" he asked.

"No." Rogue shook his head. "Unfortunately Karl did not accompany them, but then I doubt he would take such a risk. He'll probably send more men out to fight for him and never leave the palace. It's what any man with a decent self-preservation instinct would do. The only logical way to get to him is to go to him."

Kaji sighed, running a weary hand through his own red hair. "Is there no way to avoid this war?" he asked tiredly. "Those are my people."

"I know," Rogue said. "I really don't see an alternative, though. Karl has sent more people out. He's become rather active since dethroning you, and he has immobilized several contingents of troops toward both the Saikin and us. He's telling everyone that you're dead and hanging anyone that questions his right to the throne, claiming that your father entrusted it to him. Things really can't continue like this."

Kaji nodded, hope and energy draining right out of him. He sank into one of the seats around the table, looking at the people gathered there. When they'd walked in, the room had been occupied by three Ruel warriors. They had slipped out in order to give Kaji, Yuan, Rogue, Aniol, and Arian some privacy. With the exception of Rogue, they were all now seated, waiting for Rogue to continue. "So what's the plan?" Kaji asked, glancing at all the pages scattered across the rough wooden table.

Rogue flipped the map he had spread out so that Kaji could read it. Aniol and Arian both leaned forward to get a better look at it. "We take the war to him," Rogue declared. "We can't run anymore. It looks like he's planning to surround us, and we can't allow that. We have one advantage on Karl's men. We know the terrain. We go around as many groups of soldiers as we can and through those we cannot, back to the city, to the palace and to Karl. We need to get you reinstated as head of state."

"But it was the church that declared me unfit to rule," Kaji pointed out. "How are we going to reinstate me without the support of the church?"

Rogue nodded in agreement. "You raise an interesting point. I wondered about that. You were dethroned rather quickly. Far too quickly for my liking, so I had the faith investigated. Seems there's discontent with the current head, who seems to bear a grudge against you for not bonding with his daughter. I think it was a bid for power on his part. It would appear that most of the followers of the faith were against the bonding in the first place. They firmly believed that prophecy would not demand that such an important tradition be broken. They were convinced there had to be a mistake, because the faith and crown are forbidden to become one. They have to remain separate to ensure balance. It's so ingrained into their belief that most doubted the prophecy, believing that prophecy would not allow for such heresy to occur. Seems they were right." Rogue nodded at Aniol. "They were overruled by the head, which, I find to be rather interesting. I hear his daughter ran away with a stable boy."

"Serves him right." Kaji said, thinking back to how the man had allowed Aniol to be tortured. "Say," Kaji began, a sudden thought occurring to him. "Now that we're on the topic of women, how is Lira?"

Rogue pulled a face, resisting the urge to run his hands through his hair in frustration. "She ran off. She said something about proving herself to me and then disappeared. I'm rather concerned about her, and her father sent some men after her, but we can't afford to drop everything and look for her. Not at this rather critical time. I will never understand women."

"She ran away? Why?" Kaji frowned. "I thought she worshiped the ground you walked on. She was like your shadow."

Rogue shrugged, suddenly looking a touch guilty. "We exchanged words."

Kaji narrowed his eyes in suspicion. "What kind of words?" he asked carefully, wondering what Rogue and Lira may have possibly argued about.

"I told her that I would never marry her," Rogue stated bluntly.

Kaji raised his eyebrows. "I take it she didn't take that too well."

"No, she didn't, though I can't understand why. I've refused her before." Rogue sighed, sinking down into the last unoccupied seat.

"Maybe she's tired of waiting and hoping," Aniol said, breaking into the conversation. He met both Kaji's and Rogue's surprised stares with his own, filled with calm and knowledge. "You may have refused her before, but she has probably been waiting and hoping you would change your mind," Aniol explained, the words spoken from experience. "Hope is a difficult thing to let go of. Maybe she's tired of waiting and hoping. Maybe she is desperate, trying the only thing she can think of to keep her herself from facing the truth that has been staring at her for a long time. It is a truth she does not want to see, a truth that may break her if she acknowledges it."

Rogue and Kaji considered his words, seeing the possible truth in them. Yuan and Arian watched Aniol, both aware that Aniol spoke from bitter experience.

Sensing the tension, Arian reached forward and turned the map that Rogue had placed before Kaji, drawing everyone's attention back to the conversation at hand. "You might want to shift your focus this way a little." Arian pointed at a spot on the map. "If I were attempting to invade this area"—he pointed at a red mark—"where I assume we currently are, I would aim for here, here, and here." His fingers moved across the map. "This...." He pointed at a rather rocky route. "This is a difficult route and rather risky to bring an army through. So I doubt that any troops are going to be sent there. It doesn't appear to hold any advantages for a skirmish for either side."

Arian glanced up, realizing everyone was looking at him. Aniol appeared surprised, Yuan knowing and Kaji contemplative. Rogue, on the other hand, seemed amused. Arian met Rogue's amused stare dead on, challenge sparkling in his own, daring the assassin to tell him what was so funny about his idea. He pointedly continued, practically glaring daggers at Rogue as he did so. "I say you send some people through there, people capable of sneaking into the city and getting to Karl. If he's as sneaky as you make out, I doubt head-on confrontation is going to work. Even if it does, it's going to be costly. That pretty much leaves assassination." Arian and Rogue were deadlocked, each measuring the other up, challenging the other silently, neither stepping down.

Kaji didn't like it, but Arian really did have a point. If they wanted to avoid unnecessary death, they needed to get to Karl as soon as possible. They needed to kill the war at its source. As much as Kaji loathed the idea of killing Karl and even more so the thought of resorting to assassination, he really didn't see a viable alternative that allowed him to save lives. If done correctly, one life, Karl's, may be the price to pay in order to save many. It truly was the lesser of two evils, and who better to do it than a professional assassin, or more specifically, Rogue? The most surprising fact, though, was that Arian had somehow picked up on that little piece of information without being told.

# CHECKMATE

Determination is the sheer will to achieve a goal no matter what may stand in the way. It means ignoring or overcoming obstacles that may block the route, refusing to give in and refusing to give up, reaching out for that which is desired.

It is this quality that is sought by prophecy, requiring one to go against the norm as well as against the flow of destiny. It requires one to change the flow of destiny to suit one's own needs. So it is that prophecy waits, seeking the right person, the right fire, and the iron will with which to overcome all that may stand in the way.

ROGUE weighed Arian's words before nodding in acceptance. "That's pretty much the most viable option I can see as well." He glanced at Kaji. "The problem is that Kaji is generally very much against assassination." Rogue watched the redhead, silently gauging his reaction, wondering what Kaji was going to say. He was thankful the suggestion had not come from him.

Yuan remained silent. He wanted to side with Kaji but knew that he was no longer allowed to take sides. It was a restriction he was finding extremely difficult to conform to when it concerned his friends. Even so, despite the fact that he agreed with Kaji's general standpoint on assassination, he realized that Arian and Rogue did have a valid point. Assassination did appear to be the most viable option, the only solution left open to them that would allow them to save lives. There had already been more than enough death in Duiem. The knowledge he now possessed showed him that Duiem could afford little more. If they could avoid further death, then they should. So it was that he remained silent, watching the situation play out.

Kaji shifted in his seat when both Rogue and Arian stared at him and glanced at Yuan, surprised by his silence. Aniol was watching him, his misty gaze filled with question, sadness, and resignation. It was that moment and that look that told Kaji exactly what Aniol thought the best action would be. Sighing in defeat, he ran a hand through his hair. "I guess we give it a try, then," he said, turning back to Rogue and Arian. It sickened him that he would agree to resort to such measures, but he knew it was for the best, for the good of his people.

Arian nodded, relieved to have Kaji agree with him. He turned back to face Rogue and watched the assassin for a moment, gauging him before speaking, thus taking a chance on a suspicion he had. "I guess you'll be going, then." He paused a moment before continuing, barely giving Rogue a chance to register shock, assuming Rogue's agreement. "I'm going with you."

"Like hell," Rogue snapped, still fighting to hide his shock. For the life of him he couldn't figure out how Arian had known he was an assassin. He eyed Arian, taking in his deceptively frail appearance. It was deceptive because his pale complexion hid lean strength, strength Rogue was beginning to see from the way Arian moved and handled himself. "There's no way I'm taking a brat with me."

Arian returned Rogue's glare with one of his own. "You can't stop me," he said coldly, tone filled with command. He held the assassin's stare, trying to dominate Rogue with his very presence alone. "I want to go with you, and I will go with you."

"Want to try me, brat?" Rogue said, bristling. He hated the way Arian was challenging him, more than a touch affronted by his audacity. There was no way he was going to allow himself to be dictated to by a brat and one that was so much younger than him to boot. This was his territory, his domain, and he didn't need some cocky, arrogant child slowing him down on what was going to be a rather sensitive undertaking.

"Do you want to endanger political relations between Careil and Duiem? Because if you do, I can rather quickly arrange that," Arian retorted. He was not above blackmail when it came to getting what he wanted. Mathié had taught him well. True, this was something Mathié had tried to teach him *not* to do, but occasionally it served him well nonetheless.

Rogue narrowed his eyes in animosity, well and truly cornered. He didn't want to endanger Duiem any further. He wanted the chaos to stop, wanted balance and healing, and Arian was using that desire against him. He realized that it was not an empty threat, that Arian as the heir to Careil's throne did have that kind of power. He really could deliver on his threat simply by refusing to ally with Duiem once the gate was permanently opened once more. He glanced at Kaji, wondering what Kaji thought of the situation, only to see that the redhead was smirking. "You don't have a problem with this?" Rogue challenged, affronted that Kaji seemed to be deriving some form of amusement from this.

"No, of course not." Kaji quickly composed himself to hide his amusement at Rogue's predicament, suddenly every inch a king in charge. It really was a rarity to see Rogue outwitted, and rather interesting to see that it was being done by a seventeen-year-old boy, not yet old enough to rule let alone challenge the assassin. "Because I'm going as well."

"No!" Rogue exclaimed, frustration apparent in his demeanor. He couldn't take Arian, Kaji, and Aniol with him, for where Kaji went, Aniol went. It was too risky. The mission would be dangerous enough without having additional people tagging along.

"Remember what he said," Kaji indicated Arian. "I wouldn't want to endanger political relations between Careil and Duiem before I'm even able to establish them. I promised that I would protect him, and seeing as he's determined to go along, I'm going as well." Kaji focused a gaze was filled with determination on Rogue. "I need to return to my city, Rogue." Kaji knew he had to go. It was his duty. He couldn't abandon his people. "I need to correct my mistake. This is my responsibility, and there's no way I'm allowing you to go there alone."

"We just spent weeks getting away from the city," Rogue said angrily. "There's no way I'm taking you back there. I didn't lead you through the desert only to take you back and have you die!"

"Be that as it may, I will not stand on the sidelines while others fight my war. If death awaits me, then so be it," Kaji said.

"You just fled your city! It's sheer foolishness!" Rogue was fuming, desperately fighting his temper and his fear of losing the strong, fiery, stubborn king he knew they would need to rebuild what had been lost.

"And I intend to go back." Kaji slammed his palm down onto the table, standing to loom over Rogue's seated form. "I'm not a coward, Rogue. I refuse to run away from a problem I created." He spoke calmly, radiating authority and determination. "I will not hide and let others fight the war without me."

"And how exactly do you presume to assist me?" Rogue challenged, tone low and heated, not in the least intimidated by Kaji's outburst. "You're not an assassin," he pointed out calmly, absently playing with a blade that appeared from nowhere.

"Even an assassin may need a distraction to get back into the city," Kaji pointed out just as softly, every bit as calm and collected as Rogue. He knew heated temper was not going to win him this one. "I can assure you, there's no way Karl is going to leave himself unguarded, and he's not stupid. He will be waiting for someone to enter the city, waiting for someone to try exactly what we're trying. He won't let you slip back in without a fight."

"I could always use the same route we used to escape." Rogue raised an eyebrow, silently daring Kaji to break his logic.

Kaji held his stance, a small smile on his lips. "I assume that by now Karl knows we are no longer in the city, right?" He knew that even if entering and exiting the city was impossible, Rogue's information channels would still remain open. There were several ways and means in which to pass on information without using an actual messenger. Rogue had taught Kaji that.

Rogue contemplated the question and the turn the conversation seemed to have taken. He was suspicious but could find no reason not to respond honestly. "Yes, he knows," Rogue confirmed. "You were seen both in the desert and here when his men fought us, and Karl has received reports thereof. That's why he's sending more men here."

"Then he knows we managed to slip out of the city somehow. He's not stupid. He would have the sewers searched, and even if he has yet to find the exit we used, all the entrances back into the city are well-documented. He will be expecting someone to try and sneak back in, not out, and he will probably shift his focus to the sewer entrances in the city."

Rogue stared at Kaji in silence, slowly taking in what had just occurred. He was shocked by the change in the redhead. A couple of months ago, Kaji would've never been so devious and wouldn't have dared to challenge Rogue so. He glanced at Aniol, realizing that the Gatekeeper had greatly impacted Kaji's life and changed him. Balanced him. Kaji was not stupid, not by any means. His weakness was that he usually allowed his emotions rule him, reacting before thinking about it, but it seemed that was becoming a thing of the past. Kaji's sharp intellect was coming out with the relative calming of his temper.

Kaji nodded in satisfaction when Rogue remained silent, all protest gone. Dropping back down into his seat, he smiled calmly, taking control of that which should have been in his control in the first place. "Then it is decided. We leave tomorrow at sunrise."

"What about the Ruel? Who is going to lead the Ruel?" Rogue questioned, trying one last desperate tactic to keep Kaji where he would be relatively safe. He didn't want Kaji exposed to any greater risks than absolutely necessary, didn't want to risk Kaji's life if he could help it but was beginning to realize that the decision lay with Kaji himself. Kaji's life was his own to risk, and as much as he wanted to, Rogue had no right to deprive him of the right to do so.

"The Ruel can take care of themselves," Kaji responded, nodding to the doorway, knowing that the Ruel warriors who had vacated the room upon their entry were still standing there, more than likely listening. They would have been fools not to. He smiled when sounds of shifting confirmed his suspicions. "They were doing it long before we arrived and shall continue to do so long after we are gone."

Rogue remained silent, truly defeated. He'd run out of arguments. He sighed, sheathed his blade once more and resigning himself to the fact that he was going to have to continue to worry about the rather brash redhead and the two pale-haired individuals who now accompanied him. "Meet me here at sunrise. Don't be late, or I'll leave you behind."

Arian grinned, overjoyed. Kaji remained a touch more composed, taking a moment to savor his victory, surprised at how far he'd managed to get without losing his temper.

"I knew you were an assassin," Arian declared, proud of himself and his accomplishments. This was the first time that he'd been involved in anything like this without Mathié's guidance.

Rogue was roughly pulled back to a question he still burned to have answered. He itched to know what it was about him that gave away the fact that he was an assassin to a brat of a boy. Rogue raised a questioning eyebrow at Arian, hoping the young man's intuition would carry him further, hoping Arian would realize what was asking and would give him the information he sought, because for some reason—pride, perhaps—he could not bring himself to actually ask.

Arian noted the questioning gaze and grinned when he realized that Rogue wanted to know how he had known. Impulsively he stuck his tongue out at Rogue, and revealing his more childish side, remained pointedly silent, his posture daring Rogue to do something about it.

Checkmate.

# Final confrontation

Love. What is its true meaning? What is its true purpose? What is one willing to give up for the one they love, their heart, their soul, their other half?

A tale speaks of a king who was meant to die but was gifted with life through the sacrifice of another. The reason for this was prophecy itself, for prophecy requires that the decedents of the Taiyouko line atone for their sins. Should they fail, should the line die, hope and Duiem would die with them.

So it was that a king with flaming eyes and flaming hair, targeted by death, was saved by one willing to sacrifice so that the one he loved may live, so that hope for redemption may remain. A Duiem king foolishly wandered the streets in search of his soulmate. An assassin hid in shadow, aiming to kill the Taiyouko line, aiming to destroy hope and bring about the promised chaos, and released an arrow upon the vulnerable king.

A ruffian in torn clothes, feet bare, with eyes haunted by all that he had seen, destined to be scorned and ignored, placed himself between the king and the cold steel, thus placing himself between his destined bondmate and death. So it was that he paid the price for the king, taking his place. His pale silver-blue hair drifted across his face as he fell, the life in his deep violet gaze fading, dying out till nothing but death and darkness remained. His name was Kiev.

THE journey back through the desert was not as bad as it had been the first two times Aniol had made it. Dark clouds gathered in the sky, heavy with unshed tears, thus cooling the air considerably during the day. Nights were not as cold because this time they were better prepared for them, all sharing a Ruel tent. Aniol cuddled up against Kaji, Arian against Aniol, and Rogue against Arian. The first night that they spent like that was awkward for Arian. He didn't know what to make of being pressed against Rogue, but neither Kaji nor Rogue would let him sleep on the outside, and Kaji point-blank refused to be separated from Aniol. Arian finally relented. He ignored Rogue's smirks during the days that followed.

And so it was that the journey proceeded, leading Kaji, Aniol and Rogue back to where it all began, only this time they were on the outside trying to look in.

Kaji clutched Aniol's hand in a death grip, high-strung emotion rolling off of him in waves. Aniol glanced at him, noting the tightness around Kaji's features in concern. Kaji looked nervous. Glancing away, Aniol returned his attention to the city before them, to Kaji's beloved home. The buildings were colored by various shades of orange, red, and purple as they slowly faded into shadow along with the setting sun. He didn't like what they were about to do. The very idea tied his stomach up in knots, but he knew it was inevitable. Death was inevitable. He tightened his grip around Kaji's in reassurance, trying to offer Kaji his silent support. Aniol wanted him to know that regardless of what may happen, he would remain by Kaji's side.

Rogue had already scoped out the city, seeking a way in without endangering Kaji, Arian, and Aniol. Unfortunately he found Kaji had been right. Karl really did have all the entrances back into the city carefully watched. So it was that Rogue had resigned himself to their original plan. He had attempted to contact Anei in order to request that the thief help them with the distraction they'd planned but had been unable to get in touch of the head of the thieves' guild. This worried him considerably and placed him very much on edge. How bad did the situation in the city have to be for him to be unable to contact the head of the thieves' guild?

Out of sheer desperation and rather obvious lack of resources, Rogue had agreed to Kaji's rather simple plan. It was dangerous, but then again, it was no less dangerous than any of the other possible options still open to them. He just hoped that Kaji and Arian could hold their own, because two people rushing in against the numbers Karl was sure to have was nothing short of suicidal. Rogue made Kaji promise to keep it short, promise to flee before the guards managed to open the door and come after him.

Rogue only needed a few moments of distraction to scale the wall and slip over it into the city. Thereafter the night would keep him alive, as he hoped it would do for Kaji and Arian. Aniol had been ordered to remain hidden, as he had no battle experience whatsoever.

Kaji was armed with Ruel blades and a Ruel bow, as was Arian. Both handled the weapons like professionals. Rogue expected as much from Kaji. After all, he had ensured that he receive decent weapons training. As for Arian, seeing the boy handle the weapons with expert grace had relieved Rogue. At least the boy had some form of weapons training and was not going into this completely unprepared. Arian's death would hit them just as hard as Kaji's, and Rogue hoped that neither would occur, for the impact of it would be devastating, just as devastating as Aniol's death would be. In actual fact, Rogue would have preferred it if neither of them ever saw battle, but he was unable to win against both Kaji and Arian.

Kaji exchanged glances with Arian, noting how his silhouette grew dark in the fading light. The chosen time of attack was dusk, so the shadows of the city wall would help obscure them while the fading light would still illuminate those who stood upon the wall to look out at the desert.

"Now," he whispered, running out of their hiding place brandishing the bow. Arian followed, holding his own. Both fired arrows at the wall in rapid succession, and so the battle began.

AN OUTCRY spread through the city as guards were struck down one at a time, dark blood obscured by shadow, appearing black in the fading sun. A flurry of activity followed the outcry of attack, figures moving toward the entrance to the city where two lone, foolish men had chosen to attack. This left an opening in the guard that had been set inside the city, small and obscure but more than enough to allow a professional assassin in. Ghosting past those too preoccupied to see, Rogue slipped into shadow and made his way to the palace with one goal in mind.

The initial chaos at the city gate was quickly followed by chaos in the city. Shadows in the night took the opportunity presented to them and stirred the city into rebellion, fighting against the one who had kept them out of business since Karl's rise to power. Residents in the city watched the uprising, initially surprised by the breakout of small skirmishes that quickly escalated to battle. However, it wasn't long before they, too, rose to join in, tired of being suppressed by Karl's men, fear and discontent finally reaching a breaking point. Suddenly there was outright war within the city, and Karl's guards were overwhelmed by rebellion.

Rogue spared a moment to pause and smile at the uprising. It was fascinating to see residents brought to war by a few thieves who had taken advantage of the distraction presented to them by Kaji and Aniol. It looked like they were receiving Anei's help after all. The head of the thieves' guild was not one to sit around doing nothing when opportunity presented itself.

Initially Rogue had intended to wait till late into the night before attempting to assassinate Karl, but he suddenly changed his plans, fear and anxiety thick in his heart. A distraction was all well and good, but this one was quickly getting out of control, and Rogue desperately hoped that Karl had yet to realize what was going on. If the advisor were to realize that his own city was rising up against him, he would be sure to tighten security in his immediate vicinity, and they could not afford to let him live to continue to wage war within Duiem. Spurring himself back into action, he took full advantage of the chaos and ran straight to the palace. Every step of the way, he prayed, to every god he'd ever had the inclination to believe in that they all would make it through this alive.

Rogue slipped into the palace with ease, using one of the many routes he'd established over the years. He headed straight for the advisor's rather luxurious quarters, slipping past all the guards on duty. It wasn't all that hard when one knew how. People have an amazing tendency to forget to look up once in a while. It would seem that the guards were, as of yet, still unaware of the fighting going on in the city, and this was working to his advantage.

Actually slipping into Karl's rooms was ridiculously easy, easier even than getting into Kaji's, for the redhead was at least aware of Rogue's nightly forays into the palace. Karl, on the other hand, seemed to be naïvely oblivious to the idea of being attacked from within and had focused most of the guards around the perimeter of the palace and the city, thus neglecting to properly protect himself. Perhaps it was due to lack of resources as opposed to lack of strategic thinking. Either way, it was a perfect setup for an assassin.

Rogue crept toward Karl's bed, noting the rather still silence in the room and the figure sprawled upon it. Rogue was rather baffled by the fact that Karl appeared to be sleeping. At this early hour? When the sun had barely finished setting? It didn't make any sense. It made a whole lot more sense when Rogue stepped closer. Karl was only half sprawled upon the bed, feet still on the ground. His eyes were open wide, staring blankly up at the ceiling while he lay in a pool of his own blood. He was already dead.

Sheets of paper splattered in blood surrounded his lifeless body, clearly telling a story. Karl had been seated upon his bed, reading some papers when he'd been killed.

Rogue glanced up and turned to a corner of the room, a corner darker than the rest, and watched as Anei walked out, absently playing with a blood-covered blade. The thief smiled at Rogue, bowing low in greeting. "Fancy meeting you here, Rogue," he commented dryly.

Rogue glanced at the door to Karl's room, fearing the guard stationed there may have heard Anei.

Anei gave Karl a dirty look before turning back to Rogue, speaking further, providing the explanation he knew Rogue desired. "I wanted to see the pain on his face as he died. He tried to take what's mine, and no one steals from a thief."

Rogue stared at Anei in disbelief, unable to believe that the thief had killed. "You are not an assassin," he pointed out.

Anei gave Rogue a small smile, wiping the blood off of his blade onto the sheets on which Karl still lay. "Thief, assassin." He shrugged. "What's the difference? Both live in the shadows of night, both take that which does not belong to them: gold, life. Both are stealing." Anei watched Rogue for a moment before elaborating. "He took Lira. I wanted to watch him die. Besides, he was bad for business," Anei added as an afterthought. That said, the thief walked out the front door, right past the guard, a guard that fell into step beside him. That was when Rogue realized that most of the palace guards looked familiar.

KAJI and Arian were struggling to get away from the city walls as archers fired at them with their every attempt to escape. Kaji had run out of arrows and was desperately trying to do what he'd promised Rogue he would do. Arian was in a similar position, but he had resorted to throwing blades with grace and precision that could rival Rogue's, grace and precision far beyond Kaji's. It would seem that strategy was not the only training Arian had received from his mentors. As soon as possible, Kaji would need to do something to make up for the lack of training he'd received— assuming he lived long enough.

Steel continued to rain down upon him from all around, Arian's blades and the rebellion in the city the only things that were keeping them alive. Most of the guards' attention had thankfully shifted away from them moments before they ran out of arrows, shifting toward the city and the civilians who were becoming more of a threat than the two intruders at the city entrance. Even so, two stubborn archers refused to give up in their attempts to kill Kaji and Arian, enraged by what had been done to their comrades.

Kaji turned and prepared to make a run for it. The longer he remained where he was, the less likely it would be that he would survive. Keeping an eye on the archer who aimed for him, he prepared himself to run, keeping in mind he would need to dodge the steel that was sure to come his way. He neglected to see that a third archer had joined his two comrades, aiming straight for Kaji's heart, calmly waiting for the opportunity to strike. Kaji ran and skid to a halt, abruptly changing direction when the archer he was watching loosed an arrow. The third archer smiled when the redhead did exactly what he'd been expecting. Releasing his own arrow, he watched as it sailed through the air straight toward his target and buried itself deep into a small body that had thrown itself directly into the arrow's path at the last moment.

The archer lowered his bow at a cry, an order to cease battle that rippled through the city, messengers crying out Karl's death, leaving Karl's guards without reason to fight. Karl had lost and no longer needed the protection he had demanded, no longer needed the loyalty of his men, men who were beginning to realize they stood no chance against the city that had chosen to rebel, and so the archer lowered his bow in surrender, surrender that came a moment too late.

Kaji turned, looking back when he heard the impact of steel upon flesh. It was a sound he could mistake for no other. Aniol didn't make a sound as he fell, blood trailing from his pale lips and rushing from the wound in his chest. Kaji's life flashed before his very eyes, horror and grief crashing through him as he turned and ran back to Aniol, disregarding the fact that he was putting himself back into danger, not caring that he may die. He collapsed beside Aniol and pulled him into his lap. Nothing but a soft gurgle escaped Aniol's lips, speech lost to blood. Kaji watched in horror, heart shattering into tiny pieces as the light faded from those misty eyes, beautiful misty eyes he had so fallen in love with.

Karl was dead. The gate was opened, and the powers anchored. Duiem and Careil no longer died with each moment, and the healing had begun. Somewhere far away a child played beside the clear waters that held Kaela. White mist lived within his violet gaze, marking him as the next Gatekeeper. But that didn't seem to matter because Kaji's little Gatekeeper, his heart and mate, breathed his last breath lying in his lover's arms.

Storm clouds broke over Duiem and rain fell upon dry earth, the land weeping in grief.

# Finished

Loss. Sometimes we have to lose in order to see that with which we were blessed, in order to understand the true value of life. Such loss can define the very course of our existence, our hopes, and our dreams.

Sometimes, all we need is but a single moment, a miracle to find that which we lost, that which we would be willing to reach beyond the realms of life and into the realms of death for. Such miracles are rare and reach beyond the very limits of prophecy itself. It is such moments that define hope, love, and eternity.

KAJI stared at Aniol in disbelief, unable to cry or grieve. He couldn't believe that his mate was gone. Warm rain fell upon his skin, soaking him in minutes, the sky shedding tears where he had none to share. He felt hollow and empty inside, emotionally every bit as dead as the body that lay in his arms. Trickles of water trailed across his skin and across his cheeks, falling down upon Aniol's soaked form. He hated how still and lifeless Aniol was, his body still deceptively warm.

Deep cold trailed over Kaji's skin, sinking into his bones, a chill he almost mistook as originating from his own body. It took him a moment to realize that the cold was originating from the region of his shoulder and not his shattered, aching, empty heart. Kaji glanced up, his own empty amber gaze meeting a violet one, filled with sadness and grief. The violet eyes were framed by pale silver-blue hair, hair so much like Aniol's. Before him stood the boy who had helped him before.

"He's not gone yet," Kiev said. He knelt beside Kaji, withdrawing his cold touch. A coherent corner of Kaji's mind, the one not immersed in grief, wondered why Kiev's touch was cold. He remembered that the last time the young man had touched him, his touch had been just as cold and just as light, almost intangible. Kiev inclined his head toward the arrow in Aniol's chest. "Take it out," he commanded softly.

Kaji gaped at him, hope and horror coursing through him at the pale young man's words. Aniol was no longer breathing. Such an act as the boy described would be futile as it was obvious he was dead, but Kaji couldn't completely kill the hope in his heart, the tiny thread that reached for something he couldn't make himself believe in.

Kiev glanced up meeting Kaji's gaze with his own clear violet one. "Trust me," he said softly, desperate pleading in his gaze. "We're running out of time, and I'm incapable of touching it. See?" Kiev reached for the arrow. The object slipped right through his hand. "I cannot pull it out of his body. I no longer have the energy for such things. My time here is nearly done."

Kaji stared at him in shock, a touch of fear threatening him. Kiev's hand had faded as it slipped through the object, becoming intangible, a mere whisper of illusion. He jumped when Kiev reached out to him, speaking desperately. "Now, Kaji, please… before you *do* lose him."

Kaji's hands trembled violently as he pushed the arrow further in, knowing that to minimize the damage he needed to push the arrow out the other side. It would do more harm if pulled out the way it had gone in. The barbs on its head would tear organs and skin apart. Kaji nearly sobbed in panic, horrified by what he was doing, hating the fact that he was hurting his mate even further even though he knew that Aniol was no longer there. Snapping the end of the arrow off, he slipped the weapon from Aniol's body, his own hands covered in Aniol's blood. Done, he glanced up at Kiev once more, desperate question in his gaze. What remained of the weapon slipped out of his hands, and rain washed the blood off of it, cleansing it.

Kiev reached out to Kaji's hand, trailing a finger over his skin when he didn't pull away. "Did you feel the energy moving through you when he opened the gate?" He watched Kaji closely. "Do you still feel it, coursing through your veins? It means he's still here, that the gate is still open. Use it to heal him," Kiev urged, hands trailing along the route the energy took through Kaji's body, adding a flow of chill to the now familiar heat, clearly marking the route and direction the energy was taking.

Kaji gasped when he realized that the chill was merging with the energy that ran in his blood, pinpointing it for him and drawing a map he could use in his mind. He was about to ask how, about to plead, beg, and demand that Kiev show him, when suddenly he knew. A dull picture formed in the back of his mind, and Kiev withdrew.

Kaji grabbed onto the picture, snatching the energy within his grasp. He was surprised at the ease with which the flow seemed to obey his mind's command. He redirected the flow, changed it, and shifted it toward Aniol. He clung to all the elements within his grasp, drawing on those naturally within Duiem and those slipping into Duiem from Careil. The gentle merger of wind and water came from the falling rain and the earth and fire came from the ground upon which Aniol lay and from within his own body. These elements were already present in Aniol's body, only they seemed to be fading.

Kaji used the energy in his own body to understand and manipulate the energy in Aniol's. He glanced up in surprise when new energy joined his own, wind and water coming from a source other than the gentle rain. Rogue stood behind him, silently resting his hand upon Kaji's shoulder. He instinctively seemed to know what Kaji was trying to do and directed the energy he possessed into Kaji. The four elements flowed and danced, weaving a new pattern, and through fragile balance created a fifth element, a faint glow that grew with the careful manipulation of energy, gentle formation of life.

The wound in Aniol's chest began to close, skin knitting itself together as Kaji and Rogue watched, incredulous. They were unable to believe what they saw, yet at the same time they put more effort into the careful manipulation of balance, both straining with the control the effort required. A faint touch of color appeared on Aniol's skin, a gentle flush of pink, of life, and last but not least, breath. There was a gasp as oxygen once again renewed its flow. Aniol's chest rose high at the intake of breath and fell with its expulsion before settling into rhythm. The energy slipped out of Kaji's and Rogue's control, returning to its natural state, flowing away as if it had never even been restrained to begin with.

Kaji all but sobbed. Drawing Aniol fully into his lap, he clutched him tightly, rain washing away the tears that ran down his cheeks.

Then he blinked, feeling a cold touch upon his forehead, and looked up to meet Kiev's violet eyes, gratitude shining clearly in them. Kiev had kissed him upon the forehead and was now leaning down to kiss Aniol upon the cheek; it was a gentle touch, real yet at the same time intangible.

"Thank you," Kiev whispered, happiness drawing out the ethereal beauty he possessed, the same ethereal beauty possessed by Aniol.

Kaji watched as Kiev glanced up and to the side, a gentle smile gracing his lips as he looked at something just beyond Kaji's sight. Seeing the love and affection in that expression, Kaji turned to look and gasped when he realized what it was that Kiev was looking at, or more specifically who it was that Kiev was smiling at. Standing beside him was a ghostly figure, a king with flaming hair and burning eyes, who smiled down at Kiev with love in his gaze. "I've finally found you," the king whispered, gently drawing Kiev into his embrace.

Amber eyes met Kaji's own, the exact same shade shared by the two. The ghostly king remained still, holding his little thief close to his heart in an embrace that would last the rest of eternity, for he had finally found him after decades of waiting and searching. "I'm sorry," the ghostly king whispered to Kaji before adding to the gratitude Kiev had already shown. "Thank you. I love you, Son."

"I love you, too, Father," Kaji whispered, tears flowing freely down his face as the ghost of his father vanished. His father had finally found his destined mate, the young man who had given up his own life to save his, just as Aniol had done for Kaji.

It was finished.

# EPILOGUE

ANIOL squeaked in surprise, his hand flying to his mouth in embarrassment. The sound was just as unexpected to him as it was to Kaji. A deep chuckle rumbled through his body, originating in Kaji's chest and passing into Aniol's, traveling through intimate touch. Aniol was currently cradled in Kaji's arms, rather surprised at finding himself there. Kaji had waltzed into the room, plucked the book Aniol had been reading out of his hands, and tossed it to the side as he had scooped Aniol's slim form up, thus leading to that rather ungraceful squeak and the resulting humor.

The war was over, both the one with the Ruel and the Saikin. Kiyou Jai, the head of the Taiyou order, the man who had had Kaji declared unfit to rule, disappeared in the chaos that followed Karl's death. Kiyou Zerei, his replacement, had been more than happy to reinstate Kaji after deep apologies from the clan on behalf of their wayward brother. The moment Kaji was reinstated he called for peace. He demanded that the troops return and that the people work together in order to atone for the damage a foolish war had wrought upon the land. The moment those words left his lips, work and diplomacy began to roll in.

Perhaps the most surprising development was the one concerning Anei, who had rather gracefully refused the huge reward Kaji had attempted to give him. Instead, he invited Kaji and Aniol to his wedding. He was to wed Lira. She had fled to the city, running away from Rogue, and there she had met and quickly fallen in love with Anei.

Rogue moved to Careil. He followed Arian back, his spirit of adventure driving him. Although puzzled by the realization that he no longer wished to stay at Aniol's side as a protector, Rogue had left without regret. Aniol already had a Warden by his side, one who loved him more than life itself. His desire to leave Duiem made sense the moment he stepped into Careil. The energy, using Kaji and him as anchors, swapped polarities, fire and earth moving to Rogue and wind and water to Kaji. His presence in Careil consequently balanced out Kaji's presence in Duiem, thus balancing the flow of energy more effectively now that they were no longer on the same plane. Having a new world to explore was an added bonus.

Rogue went as Arian's bodyguard with benefits. His benefits boiled down to being able to spy on Careil's underground network. He was also given permission to stick his nose into Arian's business, which he took full advantage of. Arian gave as good as he got and became quite the handful. What puzzled the assassin the most was the boy's ability to disappear without a trace. The fact that he remained unaware of Arian's skill with the blade did not help solve this mystery. Kaji remained pointedly silent about that fact. It was nice to have a secret Rogue was, as yet, not privy to.

Kaji had been kept incredibly busy, actually running his own kingdom for a change. It was both stressful and time-consuming. He was swamped with diplomatic issues he'd never had to deal with before. So it was that he'd had little time to spend with his mate. But he was finally making headway. He was slowly discovering who he could trust and could now begin to delegate some of his workload into the hands of these individuals. This left him with a little free time which he fully intended to use constructively. He intended to spend every minute rediscovering his bond with his mate.

Aniol blinked in surprise when Kaji suddenly set him down. His cheeks turned bright pink when the redhead promptly stripped him without so much as a by your leave. Reaching up, Kaji pulled out the clip that now bound Aniol's hair. The pale strands fell gracefully down, tickling the bare skin of Aniol's back as they did so. Aniol's hair had barely stopped moving when it was once more whipped into motion, flowing behind Aniol as he stumbled after Kaji.

The huge bath in Kaji's bathroom was filled to the brim, a combination of oils carefully mixed in. The heady scent of them was divine and rushed to Aniol's head, making him dizzy. It was only when Kaji pulled Aniol right in that Aniol realized his lover, too, was naked.

Kaji dragged Aniol to the place where they'd first bathed together. Seating himself on the bench mounted into the wall, he pulled Aniol into his lap. The moment Aniol was firmly settled, he reached for a beaker and proceeded to pour water over Aniol's head, soaking the hair through. He ran his fingers through the silky strands and then began to wash it, gently massaging Aniol's scalp. He smiled when a groan of pleasure escaped Aniol's parted lips, enjoying the sweet sounds only he was privy to.

Aniol's eyes drifted closed, his body melting into Kaji's embrace. The soft touch of Kaji's fingers upon his scalp sent pleasant warmth through his body, a gentle caress that was making him sleepy. Water ran through his hair, down his neck, over his shoulders, and down his back as Kaji rinsed the sweet-smelling soap out of his hair, taking special care to do it properly before moving on.

Aniol's eyes opened wide, a gasp of surprise escaping his already parted lips when Kaji's hands drifted lower, rubbing soap into his skin. Heat burned through him at Kaji's touch, wicked fingers finding all his sensitive spots, deliberately lingering at each for a moment before moving on as he made his intentions abundantly clear. Aniol whimpered when Kaji's fingers drifted past his thighs. They brushed his skin, just short of touching his rapidly hardening penis, and moved the bar of soap slowly down Aniol's thigh to his right knee and down his calf.

Kaji moved his mate's limbs, settling Aniol astride his thighs, facing away from him. He smirked at the bright red flush that colored Aniol's skin, cheekily nipping at the sensitive skin on Aniol's shoulder as he dropped the soap and shoved his finger straight into Aniol's ass, no longer even pretending to wash him.

Aniol gasped at the sudden invasion. The warm water from the bath drifted into him as Kaji gave a few thrusts with his finger, rapidly adding a second, scissoring his fingers as he thrust, preparing Aniol for him. Aniol panted softly, lifting himself and thrusting himself back down onto Kaji's slick fingers, suddenly hungry for more. It felt strange, Kaji's slick fingers thrusting into him followed by the invasion of warm oily water to be followed by Kaji's slick fingers again. It was such a sweet contradiction, hard burning heat, gentle soft warmth followed by hard burning heat. The sensation was driving him crazy and making him growl deep in his throat as he pushed against Kaji's hand, silently pleading for more.

Kaji obliged. He finally added a third finger, drawing a groan of pleasure from Aniol when he filled him further, but it was still not enough. It couldn't be enough. Aniol wanted Kaji to fill him to overflowing, wanted Kaji to claim him fully and dominate him with violent thrusts, invading his body entirely. Aniol lifted himself, using Kaji's knees as support, and thrust harder, taking Kaji's finger's deeper. He desperately sought that evasive pleasure within himself, wanting Kaji to thrust harder, deeper, at a different angle, fill him more.

Aniol released a desperate keen, a sound crossed with a whimper and sob, all but begging for release when Kaji slid his fingers from his body. The slick warm water, rushed into his stretched ass, lubricating it with the oil mixed therein, but it wasn't enough, the soft liquid too intangible to give him what he really wanted.

Aniol screamed when Kaji thrust violently in, finally giving him what he sought. He could feel Kaji's penis deep in his body, splitting him apart and filling him as it moved in and hit his prostate, and to his embarrassment, pulling a rather sudden orgasm from him. Violent shudders of release shook his body, pleasure setting his nerves ablaze. Sensation overwhelmed him, his every nerve suddenly magnified one hundredfold. He could feel the warm water and slick oil and Kaji's hands caressing his skin, but most overwhelming was the feel of Kaji's penis throbbing deep within him, filling him to overflowing, still hard and blazing hot.

Then Kaji began to move in short rapid thrusts, barely leaving Aniol's body before thrusting back in, again and again, the movement jerky, desperate and hungry. As their slick heated skin slapped, Aniol gasped, the shudders of release slowly changing back into desperate need as Kaji drew lust from him once more.

Kaji's slick fingers wrapped around his penis and mimicked the thrust of Kaji's penis within him, sending electricity through Aniol's body, crackling across his already sensitized nerves, making him hard and hungry all over again. Heat mixed with the scent of musk and sex upon the air, overpowering the sweet scent of the oils within the bath water. Burning sensation and the friction of Kaji's thrusts filled him, over and over again, faster, harder, and deeper till the pounding of flesh upon flesh consumed him.

Growling deep in his throat, Kaji bit down onto Aniol's shoulder. Release overtook him, causing him to jerk out of control, still thrusting in and out of Aniol's eager body as he pumped his seed into his mate's heat.

Hot, sticky liquid filled Aniol as Kaji came within him, emphasizing yet another form of heat. It amazed him how many different types of heat a single act could generate, the burning heat of hunger and lust, the hard, throbbing heat of Kaji's length within his body, the stinging burn as his body split to accommodate the invasion, the gentle heat of the water that surrounded them, and the sticky heat of Kaji's seed filling him.

Aniol continued to sink Kaji's twitching penis deep into his body, desperately seeking his own release, wanting to join Kaji in the sixth type of heat that this single act could generate, the heat of bliss. He reached for his own penis, seeking to bring himself to completion, only to have Kaji slap his hand away. Gripping Aniol's penis tightly in his fist, he violently thrust over it, the rhythm matching that of his own ragged thrusts into Aniol's body. Aniol screamed again, his own release washing over him with the force of a tidal wave. Aniol's body clamped down upon Kaji, draining the last of the seed from him.

Drifting down from the euphoria he'd just experienced, Aniol lay completely lax within Kaji's arms. Kaji was still buried within him. He was happy and sated. This was true bliss and well worth all the pain he'd suffered to obtain it. When he moved, Kaji's penis slipped from his body, only he didn't get any farther than that. His movement was restricted by the tightening of Kaji's arms.

"Where do you think you're going?" Kaji asked, his amber eyes glowing possessively.

"To get a towel," Aniol said, baffled by Kaji's action.

"We're not done yet." Kaji's voice rumbled through his chest, the vibration carrying over to Aniol's lips. "We have a honeymoon to make up for." Not giving Aniol time to respond, Kaji aggressively claimed his lips and set about seducing him once more.

RAYNE AUSTER always had a passion for writing. However, growing up, she didn't have the patience to finish what she started. Most of her projects died before even seeing the light of day. While studying for a master's degree in computer science, she decided to post what she wrote online. That is when she discovered the joy of sharing the stories in her head. Unable to bear the thought of leaving her readers hanging, she finished her first piece of fiction. The satisfaction of actually completing a story quickly led to further inspiration, and she hasn't looked back since.

Visit Rayne's web site at https://sites.google.com/site/rayneauster/.

You can contact Rayne at rayne.auster@gmail.com.

Also by RAYNE AUSTER

http://www.dreamspinnerpress.com

Lightning Source UK Ltd.
Milton Keynes UK
UKOW05f1806051216
289229UK00002B/499/P